Unzipped

Lori Foster

Janelle Denison

Crystal Green

Unzipped

HARLEQUIN®

TORONTO • NEW YORK • LONDON
AMSTERDAM • PARIS • SYDNEY • HAMBURG
STOCKHOLM • ATHENS • TOKYO • MILAN • MADRID
PRAGUE • WARSAW • BUDAPEST • AUCKLAND

ISBN 0-373-83678-3

UNZIPPED

Copyright © 2005 by Harlequin Books S.A.

The publisher acknowledges the copyright holders
of the individual works as follows:

TANTALIZING
Copyright © 1999 by Lori Foster

HIS EVERY FANTASY
Copyright © 2003 by Janelle Denison

PLAYMATES
Copyright © 2004 by Chris Marie Green

This edition published by arrangement with Harlequin Books S.A.

® and TM are trademarks of the publisher. Trademarks indicated with
® are registered in the United States Patent and Trademark Office, the
Canadian Trade Marks Office and in other countries.

www.eHarlequin.com

Printed in U.S.A.

CONTENTS

TANTALIZING
Lori Foster

To Bonnie Tucker:
funny, caring, a very special friend—
you're all these things, Bonnie. Your Sunday
long-distance calls are a tonic that keeps me smiling
for hours. I look forward to them, just as I do to
each of your hilarious, loving books. Thank you.

Chapter One

TUGGING AT THE HEM of her miniskirt, Josie Jackson came the rest of the way into the noisy room. Seeing to the end of the bar was almost impossible in the near darkness with blue-gray smoke clouding everything. But she finally spied a man, his back to her, sitting on the end bar stool, just where he was supposed to be.

Brazen, she told herself, trying to get into the part she needed to play. *Daring, sexy, confident.* She'd scare the poor man to death and he wouldn't be able to leave quick enough.

Josie had chosen the busy, singles meeting place, hoping that would end it right there. But he'd surprised her by agreeing with her choice. At least, her sister claimed he'd agreed. But her sister had also said he was "perfect" for her, which almost guaranteed Josie wouldn't like him. Susan had described him as responsible. Mature. *Settled.*

Josie was so tired of her sister setting up blind dates, and she was even more fed up with the type of man her sister assumed she needed: stuffy, too proper and too concerned with appearances. Men who didn't want anything to do with romance or excitement. All they wanted was to find someone like them so they could marry and get on with their boring lives.

She was twenty-five now and had spent most of her life working toward her goals, pleasing her sister with her dedication. Well, she'd reached those goals, so it was time for other things. Past time. She deserved to have some fun. Bob Morrison may be interested in a nice little house in a nice little neighborhood with a nice little family, but Josie Jackson had other plans, and if the location for this meeting hadn't put him off, one look at her would.

She sauntered toward him. There was a low whistle behind her, and she felt heat pulse in her cheeks. The next thing she felt—a bold hand patting her bottom—almost caused her to run back out again. Instead she managed to glare at the offender and stay upright on her three-inch heels. No small feat, given that she normally wore sturdy, rubber-soled shoes. She *could* do this, she told herself, she could...

All thought became suspended as the man turned to face her.

Good heavens. Her breath caught somewhere in the region of her throat and refused to budge any farther. She stared. *Well. He certainly doesn't look stuffy, Josie girl, not in those nice snug jeans and that black polo shirt. This can't be the right man.* For once, he seemed too...right, too masculine and attractive and sexy. Definitely sexy. Fate wouldn't be so cruel as to actually send her a gorgeous, stuffy man. Would it?

She forced herself to take another halting step forward, hampered by the tight miniskirt, the ridiculously high heels and her own reservations. "Bob? Bob Morrison?"

His dark eyes were almost black, as was the shiny, straight hair that hung over his brow, unkempt, but still very appealing. His gaze went from a slow, enthralled perusal of her mostly bared legs to her midriff where he paused, looking her over from chest to belly, his look almost tactile in its intensity, then he reached her face. He drew in a long breath, apparently feeling as stunned as she did. She waited for him to speak, to do or say something that would prove her assumptions had been correct, that he wasn't what she wanted in a man, that he was another typical offering from Susan who was supposed to further domesticate her life.

But then he stood, towering over her, six feet of gorgeous, throbbing male, and he smiled. That smile could be lethal, she thought as it sent shivers deep into her belly. The man exuded charm and warmth, and there was absolutely nothing stuffy or uptight about him. In fact, she felt like Jell-O on the inside. Nothing stuffy about that.

He held out his hand—a large hand that engulfed her own and seemed to brand her with his strength and heat. With the type of voice that inspired fantasies, he said, "I'm...Bob. It's very nice to meet you, Josie."

HE WASN'T USUALLY a liar.

Nick Harris took in the exquisite female before him and forgave himself. Lying was necessary, even imperative, given the fact he was faced with the most gorgeous, sexy woman imaginable—so close, and yet, not for him. He'd tell a hundred lies if it would keep her from walking out. Bob wouldn't appreciate being impersonated, of course, but then, Bob hadn't wanted anything to do with her. He'd been more taken with her sister, that rigid woman who had conspired the entire meeting. What Bob saw in Susan Jackson was beyond Nick, but now he could only be glad. Bob's preferences in women had Nick sitting here on a Saturday night, prepared to make excuses for his friend and partner.

Thank God he'd agreed to do it. If he hadn't, he might have missed her, and she was well worth the football tickets he'd wasted. She was well worth giving up *all* sports.

She looked surprised, as surprised as he felt, her green eyes wide, her soft mouth slightly open. Her full lips were painted a shiny red, and he could see her pink tongue just behind her teeth. Damn, the things he'd like to do with that tongue....

Belatedly his manners kicked in. "Would you like to sit down?" Normally he was known as a gentleman, as a reasonable man, sane and intelligent and given to bouts of outstanding charm. But he felt as though he'd just been pole-axed. And it only got worse as she flipped her long silky red hair over her shoulder, shrugged, then lifted her shapely bottom onto the bar stool next to his. That bottom held his spellbound attention for a few moments, before he could finally pull his gaze away. Her very short black skirt, hiked up as it was, revealed slender thighs. She crossed her legs, swinging one high-heel-clad foot. He swallowed, heard himself do it and told himself to get a grip. He couldn't let her see how she'd affected him.

"Can I get you something to drink?"

She hesitated, and he could almost see her considering, but then she shook her head. Those sexy green eyes of hers slanted his way, teasing, flirting, causing his muscles to twitch. "There's a lot of things I do, but drinking isn't one of them."

It took him a second to recover from that look and the outrageous words she'd spoken. He hoped to hell he'd interpreted them right. "Oh? Religious reasons? Diet?"

Her lips curved and her long lashes lowered. "I just like to have control at all times. I want to know exactly what I'm doing, how I'm doing it and who I'm doing it with. Alcohol tends to muddle things."

As she spoke, a pink flush spread from her cheeks to her throat to the top of her chest, where the scooped neckline of her blouse showed just a hint of cleavage. Light freckles were sprinkled there, like tiny decorations, making him wonder where other freckles might be. He'd heard things about redheads, but he'd always discounted them as fantasy, nothing more. Now he had to reassess. This redhead seemed to exude sensuality with her every breath. And he was getting hotter than a chili pepper just looking at her.

He'd have to wrest control from her, despite her just-stated preferences, if he wanted to survive. Never had he let a woman get the upper hand in any situation, not since he'd been a teenager and his stepmother had taken over his life. He didn't intend to let this little woman, no matter how appealing she was, call the shots. Not even if those shots might be to his liking.

She'd temporarily thrown him, but now he was getting used to looking at her, to breathing her musky scent and hearing her throaty, quiet voice. And she kept peeking looks at him, as if she were shy, which couldn't be, not looking the way she looked. Or maybe she was feeling just as attracted as he was. That should work to his advantage. At least he'd know he wasn't drowning alone.

He ordered two colas, then slowly, giving her time to withdraw, he slid his palm under hers where it rested on the bar. Her eyes widened again, but she didn't pull away. Her hand was slender, frail. Her fingers felt cold, and he wondered if it was from being outside, or from nervousness. But there didn't seem to be a nervous bone in her luscious little body.

"You're not exactly what I expected." With Bob's usual tastes in women, he'd thought to find a conservative, righteous prude, someone who resembled the sister, Susan. That woman could freeze a man with a look—and she'd tried doing just that to him when she'd first come to him and Bob for an advertising campaign. The woman had taken an instant dislike to him, something about spotting a womanizer right off, so he'd left her to Bob. And when the date had been engineered, he'd expected to find a woman just as cold, just as plain and judgmental. He'd expected mousy brown hair and flat hazel eyes. A quiet, circumspect demeanor.

But Josie Jackson was nothing at all like her sister. It was a damn good thing Bob hadn't come. He might have had a heart attack while running away.

The thought inspired a grin.

"It makes you smile to get the unexpected?"

She sounded almost baffled, and he chuckled. "This time, yes. But then, you're a very pleasant surprise."

Small white teeth closed over her bottom lip. He wanted them to close over his lip. He wanted them to close over his—

"You're not what I expected, either. Usually my sister lines me up with these overly serious, stuffy, three-piece-suit types. They're always concerned about responsibilities, their businesses, appearances." Her eyes met his, daring him, teasing him. "You wouldn't be like that, now would you?"

He stifled a laugh. She thought she was taunting him, he could tell. But at the moment, responsibilities and business were the farthest thing from his mind, and he hoped like hell she wouldn't expect him to worry about appearances. He never had.

Bob would, but he wasn't Bob.

"No one has ever accused me of being stuffy." That was true enough, since Bob usually lamented his lack of gravity. Come to think of it, maybe it was his casual attitude that had made the sister dislike him so much. Not that he cared. Formality had been his stepmother's strong suit, so he naturally abhorred it. He believed in keeping the business sound, but he didn't think it had to rule his life. Evidently Josie agreed, though she looked shocked by his answer. Interesting.

Not willing to wait another minute to hold her, he stood and pulled her to her feet. "Let's dance."

She balked, her legs stiffening, her expression almost comical. She tried to free her hand, but he held tight, determined.

"What's the matter? You don't dance, either?"

"Either?"

"Like the drinking." He rubbed his thumb over her palm, trying to soothe her. He didn't want her bolting now, but if he didn't get her in his arms soon, he was going to explode. He'd never been hit this hard before, but damned if he didn't like it.

"I dance," she said, then looked down at her feet. "But not usually in heels like these."

He, too, looked at her feet. Sexy little feet, arched in three-inch heels. Tugging her closer he said, "I won't let you stumble." His voice dropped. "Promise."

As he led them onto the dance floor her throat worked, but she didn't deny him. It was crowded with gyrating dancers, bumping into each other. He used that as an excuse to mesh their bodies together, feeling her from thigh to chest, holding her securely with one arm wrapped around her slender waist, his hand splayed wide on her back. She felt like heaven, warm and soft, and incredibly he felt the beginnings of an erection. His thighs tightened, his pulse slowed.

Even in her heels, she was only a little bit of a thing. His chin rested easily on the top of her head, and he felt the silkiness of all that hair floating around her shoulders, curling around her breasts. Wondering what it might feel like on his naked chest, his belly, made him clench his teeth against rising need. It was almost laughable the reaction she caused in him. But it was like his own private fantasy had come to life before his eyes. From her long lashes to her freckles to her shapely legs, he couldn't imagine a woman more finely put together than her. Or with a sexier voice, or a more appealing blush.

The blush was what really did it, with its hint of innocence mixed with hot carnal sexuality. *Damn.*

His hand pressed at the small of her back and he urged her just a bit closer. Her small, plump breasts pressed into his ribs, her slender thighs rubbed his. She sighed, the sound barely reaching him through the loud music. But the softening of her body couldn't be missed.

His lips touched her ear and he inhaled her scent. "That's it. Just relax. I've got you."

And he intended to keep her. At least for now.

He wondered how he could get around Bob and her sister. There was no doubt Susan Jackson wouldn't appreciate him being with Josie. She'd been very open about her immediate dislike and distrust. They'd spoken for a mere fifteen minutes, him using all his charm to soften her, before Susan had made her opinion of him known. Of course, maybe he had poured the charm on just a bit thick, but then prickly, overopinionated, pushy women like Susan Jackson irritated him. They reminded him of his stepmother, who had been the bossiest woman of all.

At what point should he tell Josie who he really was? Bob

had claimed she would be crushed by his inability to meet her, that she was a wallflower of sorts who counted on her sister to set up her social calendar due to a shy nature and a demanding career. But the woman moving so gently against him, neither of them paying any attention to the beat of the music, in no way resembled a wallflower or a driven, career-minded lady.

There was the possibility Bob might want to reset the date once he realized what he was missing, despite his ridiculous requirements for a woman and his initial interest in Susan. But of course, Nick wouldn't allow that now. Circumstances had decreed that he meet Josie first. And finders keepers, as the saying went. Bob could damn well concentrate on the contrary Susan for his future wife. Why Bob was so determined to court a wearisome little housewife-type anyway didn't make sense to Nick. Especially not when there were women like this one still available.

Putting one foot between hers, he managed to insinuate his thigh close to her body. She jerked, startled, then made a soft sound of acceptance. He felt her incredible heat, the teasing friction on his leg as they both moved, and he shuddered with the sensations. With a little dip and a slow turn, he had her practically straddling his thigh. She gasped, her breasts rose and fell and her hands tightened on his chest, knotting his shirt. Such a volatile reaction, he thought, feeling his own heartbeat quicken.

"I'm glad I came tonight." The words were deep and husky with his arousal, but he wanted her to know, to understand how grateful he felt to Bob for bailing out. Things were going to get complicated, of that he was certain, but he didn't want her to misunderstand his motives.

The smile she offered up to him made his gut tighten. "Do you know, I thought you'd be horrified by this place."

He looked around, not really enjoying the busy singles' bar, but not exactly horrified, either. Located on the riverbank, with a restaurant downstairs and the dance floor and bar upstairs, it was a popular meeting place. "Why?"

They had to shout to be heard, so he began moving them toward the corner, away from the other dancers and out of the chaos. He wanted to talk to her, to know everything about her, to understand the contrast of her incredible looks and her shy smiles. He wanted to taste her, deep and long.

"From what my sister told me about you, I gathered you were a bit...sedate."

Bob was sedate. Hell, Bob was almost dead, he was so sedate. *He was Bob.* Cautiously he asked, "What else did your sister say about...me?"

"That you were dependable."

They reached the edge of the floor, and he snorted. "Dependable? Makes me sound like a hound."

Her soft laugh made him change his mind about the corner and lead her to a balcony door instead. It was chilly enough in early September, with the damp breeze off the river, to deter other dancers from taking in the night air. As they stepped out, he released her and she wrapped her arms around herself for warmth.

Below the balcony, car lights flashed as traffic filled the parking lot and navigated the narrow roads around the bar. Boat horns echoed in the distance, and a few people loitered by the entrance door, waiting either to come in or go out. Their voices were muted, drowned out by the music. He turned to face Josie, seeing her eyes shine in the darkness, that red hair of hers being lightly teased by the wind. He reached out and caught a long curl, rubbing it between his fingers.

"Are you disappointed that I'm not dependable?"

"You're not?"

"No." He owed her some honesty, and his outlook on life was something he never kept from a woman, any woman. Not even one that he wanted as badly as he did this one. "I'm safe. Trustworthy. You don't have to be afraid of me." She grinned and he tugged on her hair until she stepped closer, then he released her and looked over her head at the night sky. "I'm a nice guy. I'm secure. But I'm not the type of man you want to depend on, Josie."

She lifted a hand to brush her hair from her cheek and studied him. "Are you fun?"

The epitome of temptation, she stood there looking up at him, her eyes huge in the darkness, her body so close only an inch separated them. He touched her cheek and felt her softness, the subtle warmth of her skin. "Do you want me to be fun?"

She stepped away, moving across the balcony and bracing her hands on the railing. Eyes closed, she leaned out, arching her back and letting the wind toss her hair. Turning her face up to the moon, she said, "Yes. I think I deserve to have fun. I want to do things I haven't done and see things I haven't seen. I want to put work aside and enjoy life for a change."

Looking at her, at the way her stance had tautened her bottom in the snug skirt, her legs braced with the high heels putting her nearly on tiptoe, her hair reaching down her back... He couldn't resist. He stepped up to her until his legs bracketed hers, his groin pressing into her smooth buttocks. She would feel his erection, but he didn't care.

With a soft push, he acknowledged her shock, her surprise and her interest.

Leaning down, he kissed the side of her neck, her ear. He spoke in a soft, intimate whisper. "I can show you lots of ways to enjoy yourself, Josie."

There was a split second when he thought she'd draw away, and already his body grieved. But then she leaned her head back to his chest and tipped it to the side to give his mouth better advantage. He tasted the sweet heat of her skin, his tongue touching her, leaving damp kisses behind that made her shiver. He flattened one hand on her abdomen and his fingers caressed her. His heartbeat drummed, the pleasure twisting, escalating.

"Yes."

The word was caught in a moan, and Nick closed his eyes, not sure he'd heard it. "Josie?"

Turning in the tight circle of his arms, the railing at her back keeping her from putting any space between them, she flickered a nervous, uncertain smile and said again, "Yes. Show me."

Excitement mushroomed. Already his body throbbed with sexual heat. Slowly he leaned down, keeping her caught in his gaze, letting the anticipation build. He heard Josie drawing in choppy breaths and knew she was as turned on as he. His mouth touched the softness of hers and she made a small sound of acceptance, her hands curling over his shoulders.

Her lip gloss tasted of cherries, and he licked it off, slowly, savoring her every breath, her sighs. She tried to kiss him, but he sucked her bottom lip into his mouth, nibbling, until her lips were lusciously full from his administrations, begging for his kiss.

Her tongue touched his and he covered her mouth, unable to resist a moment more. She was so hot, so sweet.

And it took him about thirty seconds of incredible kissing to figure out she was damn innocent, too.

She didn't return his kisses, or his touches. She only accepted them, clinging to him, a sense of wonder and expectation swirling around her. He led, but although she was willing, she didn't quite follow. In fact, it seemed almost as if she didn't know how.

With a groan, he pulled back, dragging his gaze over her body, so sexy, revealed in the short tight skirt and low-cut blouse, her hair wild and free, her smile shy but inviting. *Inviting what?* His heart threatened to punch through his ribs, and he silently cursed in intense frustration.

Josie Jackson was a little fraud. Despite all the packaging, despite the seductive words and gestures, she was probably more suited to Bob. But that idea made Nick half-sick with anger and he swore to himself Bob would never touch her. He wouldn't allow it.

He knew women, had been studying them since he'd first become a teenager. He knew the good in them, the gentleness and pleasure they could offer. And because of the feminine members of his family, his stepmother and his mother, he knew the bad, the ways they could manipulate and connive.

This little sweetheart was up to something. But then, no one had ever accused Nick Harris of turning down a challenge—especially not one this tantalizing. Mustering a grin, he let his fingers fan her cheek, her temple. "We both know what we want, honey, so why don't we get out of here and go someplace quiet?"

He waited for her to refuse, to call him on his outrageous bluff. Then she'd explain, and he could explain, too, and they could start over, taking the time to get to know each other. And for a second there, she looked like she would refuse.

Instead, she knocked him off balance by nodding agreement, and whispering quietly, shyly, "You can lead the way."

Oh yeah. He'd lead the way all right. Right into insanity. He wasn't in the habit of rushing women into bed, certainly not only minutes after meeting them. He wasn't an idiot. But all the same, he took her proffered hand and started back toward the exit. Excitement rushed through his body with every step.

Excitement and the sure knowledge that he was about to make a huge tactical mistake, one he'd likely live to regret, but he was helpless to stop himself.

Chapter Two

"DID YOU DRIVE?"

"No, I, ah, took a cab." Because her car was as sensible and plain as she was, and would have given her away. Her plan wouldn't have worked, she would have lost this opportunity. She closed her eyes on the thought.

"I'll drive, then."

"Okay." Josie could hardly speak for the lump of excitement in her throat. She'd started out acting a part, and now she was going to get to live it. With this gorgeous, sexy man...*her sister had found?* Incredible. Maybe Susan was finally starting to understand her better. She'd have to thank her... No, she wouldn't. She still didn't want people meddling in her life and setting up blind dates. It was past time she put an end to that high-handed habit. Besides, if her sister knew how incredible Bob Morrison was turning out to be, she wouldn't want Josie to see him anymore. She certainly wouldn't approve of them slipping off together to do...all the wonderful things she'd never dared to dream about.

Josie wasn't even certain *she* approved of herself. Things like this just didn't happen to her. Men didn't notice her, and she'd always accepted that. But now everything felt so right, so instinctive. She'd never considered herself impulsive, but then, she'd never had the attention of a man like Bob. And it wasn't just his sexy looks. It was his smile, a tilting of that sensual mouth that made her feel special, and the fact that since they'd first met, he hadn't taken his eyes off her. He held her gently, and she'd felt a trembling in his hands that proved he was affected by the madness too. When he spoke, his voice was deep and husky, his words persuasive, telling how much he wanted her.

She had only to look at him and her stomach took a free fall, as if she'd just jumped from a plane and didn't care where she landed. All her life she'd been cautious and circumspect, first pleasing her parents, and after their deaths, trying to please her sister. Susan took Josie's failures personally, so Josie had made certain to always succeed. She made Susan proud with her respectability and propriety, her overachiever attitude. And she had found a measure of happiness in the structured stability of that role.

But now she had a chance to taste the wild side, to sow some wild oats and experience life. And it was so exciting, being spontaneous for a change. Nature summoned, sending all her hormones into overdrive, making her hot and shaky and anxious. For once, she was going to let nature have its way.

"Don't you even want to know where I'm taking you?"

Josie paused, stung by his apparent irritation. From one second to the next, he'd gotten quiet and surly. When he turned to look at her, she saw that his dark thick brows were low over his eyes, his mouth a thin line. So far, that mouth had done nothing but smile at her and give her the most incredible, melting kisses imaginable, but now he was angry. She took a cautious step back. "What's wrong?"

He held her gaze, then with a growl of disgust, raked a hand through his midnight hair, leaving it disheveled. "Nothing. I'm sorry." He reached his hand toward her, palm up, and waited.

Josie bit her lip, uncertain, but the feelings, so many different feelings, were still curling inside her, demanding attention. It felt new and wonderful wanting a man like this, knowing he wanted her, too. After the blow of losing her parents, she'd drawn into herself and let Susan, with her natural confidence and poise, take over her life, direct it. And as the big sister, Susan was determined to give Josie every advantage, to protect her. She'd helped Josie through high school and then college, giving up her own education so Josie could have the best. She'd helped Josie start a career, and now, evidently, her goal was to help Josie get married to a suitable man.

If it hadn't been for Susan, Josie would have been alone in the world. The knowledge of what she owed her sister was never far from her mind. But she didn't want to settle down with some stuffy businessman. She wanted all the same things other women wanted—romance and excitement and fun—only, she was a little late in recognizing those desires.

He'd said he was a safe man, trustworthy. And she had to believe it was true, because Susan never would have set her up with a man who couldn't be trusted. Susan's standards were high, nearly impossible to reach, so he had to be a very reliable sort, despite his comments to the contrary. She smiled and put her hand in his.

His fingers, warm and firm, curled around her own, then he lifted her hand to his mouth, his gaze still holding hers, and kissed her knuckles. Just that small touch made her tummy lurch and places below it tighten. His tongue touched her skin, soft and damp, dipping briefly between her middle and ring finger and she felt the touch sizzle from her navel downward. She almost groaned.

The look he gave her now was knowing and confident, hot with his own excitement. "Come on."

Josie licked her dry lips. "You haven't told me yet where we're going."

"Someplace quiet. Someplace private. I want you all to myself, Josie."

Prudence made her pause again. He wanted control of the situation, but this was her night, the only fantasy she was ever likely to indulge in. "I'd like to know, exactly, where we're going."

He looked down at her, then his large hands framed her face. He seemed almost relieved by her questions, like he'd been waiting for them, expecting reluctance. "Scared?"

"Should I be?" She wasn't, not really, but that didn't mean she held no reservations at all. She'd led her life on the safe side, never even imagining that such a turmoil of sizzling emotion existed. It would take a lot to make her turn away now, especially since Bob was the first man who'd ever tempted her to be so daring. The ruse she'd started was over. Now she was only doing as she pleased, being led along by her feminine instincts. And enjoying every second.

His thumb touched the side of her mouth, moved over her bottom lip and then ran beneath her chin, making her shudder, her breath catch. He tipped her face up, arching her neck and moving her closer to his tall strong body at the same time. "Open your mouth for me, Josie."

She did, parting her lips on a breath. His mouth brushed over hers, light, sweet, his tongue just touching the edge of her teeth, coasting on the inside of her bottom lip. "Don't ever be afraid of me."

"I won't." She clutched at his shirt, wishing he'd do that thing with his leg again, pressing it against her in such a tempting way. "I'm not."

He smiled, his look tender. "Not afraid, but I can feel you shaking."

Quaking was more like it. Her legs didn't feel steady, her heartbeat rocked her body and little spasms kept her stomach fluttering. His mouth came down again, his teeth catching gently on her bottom lip, nipping, distracting. Josie closed her eyes, wanting him to continue. He couldn't know that this was all new to her, so she confessed, "I'm not afraid. I'm excited."

"By me."

Two simple words, so filled with wonder—and with confidence. "Yes. I...I want you." Saying it made her skin feel even hotter, and she tried to duck her head, knowing she blushed. But he wouldn't let her hide. Catching and holding her gaze, he gave her an intense study, as if trying to figure her out. Josie wondered how much more obvious she could be.

The wind blew, damp and cool, and it ruffled his thick, straight hair. When she shivered, he broke his stare to gather her close, holding her to his warm chest and wrapping his arms tight around her. Being held by this man was a singular experience. She'd never imagined that anything could feel so *safe*. Or that she needed—wanted—to feel that way.

"You might not be afraid, Josie, but I am."

That startled her and she pushed back from him again. "You're not making any sense, Bob." He flinched and she took another step back, separating their bodies completely. Frowning with possibilities, with hurt and embarrassment, she whispered, "If you don't want me, just say so."

That got her hauled back up against him, his mouth covering hers and treating her to a heated kiss the likes of which she hadn't known existed. His tongue stroked; he sucked, bit, consumed. It made her toes curl in her shoes, made her nipples tighten painfully. She gasped into his open mouth and pressed her pelvis closer. The thick, full bulge of his erection met her belly, making a mockery of her notion that he might not want her.

As if he knew how her body reacted, she felt his thigh there again, giving pressure just where she needed it. One palm gripped her hip, keeping her from retreating, and his other slowly covered her breast, caressing, dragging over her nipple then gently stroking with the edge of his thumb. He made soothing sounds when she jerked in reaction. She couldn't bear it, the feelings were so wildly intense. She moaned and clutched at him.

"Damn." His head dropped back on his shoulders, his eyes closed while his throat worked. He kept Josie pinned close and his nostrils flared on a deeply indrawn breath. "Let's get out of here before I lose my head completely."

He showed no more hesitation, moving at a near run, making Josie hobble in her high heels trying to keep up with him.

He led her to a shiny black truck and opened the door. But the minute she started to step up into the thing, she realized she had a definite problem. "Uh, Bob…"

He made a sour face that quickly disappeared. "Hmm?"

"I, ah, I can't get into your truck."

Reaching out, he tucked her hair behind her ear, cupped his hand over her shoulder, caressing, soothing. "I've told you I won't hurt you, Josie. You can trust me."

A nervous giggle escaped her and she was mortified. She never giggled. "It isn't that. It's, well, my skirt is too tight."

His gaze dropped, then stayed there on the top of her thighs. She saw his broad shoulders lift with a heavy breath. "Looks…good to me. Not too tight." He swallowed, then added, "Perfect, in fact. You're perfect."

Perfect. Josie knew then, there was no changing her mind. No man had ever told her she looked perfect. No man had ever given her much attention at all. Of course, she'd never given them much attention, either, or dressed this way before. She'd only done it now to discourage Bob from liking her, thinking him to be another prig, a suit with an image to protect and a family-oriented goal in mind. But seeing as he *did* like her like this, she vowed to be more flashy every day, because she liked it, too. It made her feel feminine and attractive and… She still couldn't manage to get into the dumb truck.

"Bob, I can't step up. And your seat's too high for me to reach."

He blinked, his gaze still lingering southward, then he chuckled. "I see what you mean. Allow me." He picked her up, swinging her high against his chest with no sign of effort. He hesitated to set her down inside.

"Bob?"

He groaned. "Don't... Never mind. I think I like holding you. You don't weigh much more than a feather." He pulled her close enough to nuzzle her throat, her ear, to kiss her mouth long and deep before reluctantly putting her down on the seat and closing the door.

When he climbed behind the wheel, Josie decided to be daring again. "So you like small women?"

"I never did before."

Leaving her to wonder what he meant by that, he started the truck and drove from the lot. "I was thinking, why don't we go to your place? We could drink some coffee and...talk."

Uh-oh. Josie shook her head. There was no way she could take him to her condo where her functional life-style and boring personality were in evidence everywhere. In her furniture, her pictures, her CDs and books. Nursing magazines and pamphlets were on her tables. Nostalgic photos of her deceased parents, along with photos of her and Susan together, decorated her mantel. He'd see her with her hair braided, her turtlenecks and serious, self-conscious mien.

That wasn't the woman he wanted, and she couldn't bear it if he backed out on her now.

"I don't think that's a good idea."

He glanced at her curiously as he wove through the traffic. "Why not?"

Why not? Why not? "Um, my neighbor, in the condo complex, was planning a big party and I bowed out. If she sees me, she might be hurt, or insist I come to the party after all." It was only a partial lie. Most of the condo owners were nice, quiet, elderly people, living on retirement and Social Security. They were her friends, the only people she felt totally comfortable with. They loved her and appreciated whatever she did for them, no matter how insignificant. For them, she didn't have to measure up, she could just be herself.

Until recently, there had never been parties at the condo. Now, with Josie's encouragement, Mrs. Wiley was known for entertaining—but hers certainly weren't the type of parties Josie would be comfortable taking Bob to. Mrs. Wiley could be affectionately referred to as a "modern" grandma.

Bob nodded his understanding, his brow drawn in thought.

She squirmed, then suggested, "Why don't we go to your place instead?"

"No." He shook his head, shooting her a quick look. "Not a good idea."

"Why?"

"I, um... You know, I hesitate to suggest this, because I don't want to insult you."

"Suggest what?" Her curiosity was piqued. And she couldn't imagine any suggestion on his part being an insult, not when they both knew what it was they wanted, what they planned.

"My father has a small houseboat docked on the river, not too far from here. It's peaceful there. And quiet. Just like home, only smaller. And floating."

How romantic, and how sweet that he feared insulting her. "I think it sounds like heaven, but...I thought Susan told me both your parents were dead."

"My..." He turned his face away, his hands fisting on the steering wheel.

"Bob?"

Now he groaned. When he did finally look at her, he appeared harassed. "They are. Gone that is. Deceased. But they left me the boat and I guess I...still think of it as theirs?"

He'd ended it on a question, as if he weren't certain, which didn't make any sense. Unless he was still dealing with the loss of them. She herself knew how rough it could be. It had taken her months to get over the shock of her parents being gone, and by the time she realized how selfish she was being, Susan had just naturally taken control, cushioning Josie from any other blows. Even though Susan was older, it had still been a horrendous thing for her to deal with on her own.

It was obvious Bob had a difficult time talking about it. Josie sympathized. "My parents died when I was fifteen. Susan took on the responsibility of being my guardian. It hurts sometimes to remember, doesn't it?"

His gaze seemed unreadable. "Does it hurt you?"

"Yes. I still miss them so much, even though it's been ten years. And...I feel guilty when I think of everything Susan gave up for me. We have no other relatives, and because she was nineteen, she was considered an adult and given legal custody." It wasn't as simple as all that, but Josie didn't want to go into how hard Susan had fought for her, the extent of what she'd given up.

He reached for her hand. "I doubt Susan would have had it any other way. She seems... determined in everything she does."

"You're right about that. She's a very strong person." Josie smiled, then decided to change the subject. "Tell me about the boat."

His fingers tightened. "No. Talking about taking you there makes it damn difficult to drive safely."

He never seemed to say the expected thing. "Why?"

"Because I wish we were already there." He glanced at her, his look hot and expectant. "I want to be alone with you, honey. I want to touch you and not stop touching. I want—"

She gasped, then mumbled quickly, "Maybe we shouldn't talk about it." She fanned herself with a trembling hand and heard him chuckle.

After a minute or two had passed in strained silence, he said, "Okay. I think I've come up with some innocuous conversation."

Relieved because the silence was giving her much too much time to contemplate what would come, Josie grinned. "Go ahead."

"Tell me about where you work."

"All right. But I assumed Susan had already told you everything. I don't want to bore you with details. I know she can go on and on with her bragging. Not that there's really any reason to brag. But she does act overly proud of me. As I said, she rightfully takes credit for getting me through college and giving me a good head start."

His mouth opened twice, without him actually saying anything. He shrugged. "I'd rather hear it from you."

She supposed he just wanted words flowing to distract him from what they were about to do. She knew it would help her. She'd never felt so much anticipation and yet, she suffered a few misgivings, too. Spontaneous affairs weren't exactly her forte. The fear of disappointing him, and herself, made her stomach jumpy. So far, they'd been moving at Mach speed. What would happen if she faltered, if her inexperience showed? She couldn't even contemplate the idea. The fact of her nonexistent love life was too humiliating for words.

"I do home-nursing care. I started out working for an agency, but I hated the impersonal way they functioned. I always got close to the people I worked with, and they became friends, but as soon as they were released from care, I wasn't supposed to see them ever again. So I decided to start my own business. Susan already knew, through the experience of starting her flower shop, how to go about setting things up, and she helped a lot. It took me a while to get everything going, but now I'm doing pretty well."

"You like your work?"

"Yes. So far it's been the only thing I've been really good at, and it gives me comfort."

She knew her mistake instantly when Bob frowned at her. "What exactly does that mean?"

"It means," she said, measuring her words carefully, "that I'm trying to make changes in my life. I'm twenty-five years old, and I've reached most of my business goals. So I've set some personal goals for myself. Things I want to see happen before I'm too old to enjoy them."

He gulped. "Twenty-five?"

"Does that surprise you? I mean, I know Susan must have told you all about me, what I do, my supposed interests, my normal appearance."

He rubbed one hand over his face, as if in exasperation. Shifting in his seat, he cast a quick glance at her. "Uh, yeah. She did." His voice dropped. "But you're even more attractive than I thought you'd be. And you seem more...mature than twenty-five."

"Thank you." Josie wondered if much of her maturity came from spending all her free time with the elderly. They were so caring and giving, offering her a unique perspective on life.

"You mentioned personal goals. Tell me about them."

He sounded so genuinely interested, she hated to distract him. But it wouldn't do for him to learn *he* was a personal goal. If he discovered the reserved life she'd lived, how sheltered her sister had kept her, would he decide against taking her to the boat? She wasn't willing to run the risk.

"Everyone has personal goals. Don't you? I think I remember Susan saying something about you trying to double your company assets within the next five years. Now that's a goal."

He mumbled something she couldn't hear.

"Excuse me?"

"Nothing."

Turning down a narrow gravel drive that headed toward one of the piers, he slowed the car and gave more attention to his driving. But he kept glancing her way, and finally he said, "It's my partner who's actually into building up the company. I'm satisfied with where we are for now. We're doing well, and to expand at the rate he wants, we'd have to start putting in tons of overtime. That or take on another partner. I don't want to do either. Work isn't the only thing in my life. I want to have time for my grandfather. I want to see other people and pursue other interests. Work is important, but it isn't everything."

Marveling at the sentiments that mirrored her own, she said, "I can't believe this. My sister mentioned your partner, but she said only that he was arrogant and she didn't like him. She said his only goal seemed to be joking his way through life. In fact, I think she refused to work with him, didn't she?"

Even in the darkness, she could tell he flushed, the color climbing up his neck and staining his cheekbones. "Yeah, well, she took an instant dislike to…Nick. I couldn't quite figure out why—"

"Susan claims he tried to schmooze her, to charm her. She can pick out a womanizer a mile away, and she said that Nick is the type who draws women like flies with his *false charm*."

With a rude snort, he glared at her. "That's not true. And besides, Nick is very discreet."

"He's evidently not discreet enough. Susan is very liberated and doesn't like being treated any differently than a man. From what she said, I assume your partner is a bit of a chauvinist. 'Pushy and condescending' is how she described him."

He muttered a short curse. "Yeah, well, Nick doesn't particularly like pushy women, either, and your sister is pushy!"

Josie didn't deny it; she even laughed. "True enough. I consider it part of her charm."

A skeptical look replaced his frown. "If you say so. Anyway, it was easier for her to work with…me."

Josie laughed. "Susan said you had the best advertising agency in town. And she showed me the ads you worked up for the flower shop. They're terrific. She's gotten a lot of feedback on them already." Josie patted his arm. "Susan claims you're the brains of the agency, while this Nick person only adds a bit of talent. But I'd say you're pretty talented, too. And not at all what I expected."

"Oh?" He sounded distracted, almost strangled.

"I'm beginning to think finding me dates is Susan's only hobby, and I would have wagered on you being another guy like the last one."

That got his attention. "What was wrong with the last one?"

"Nothing, if you like men who only talk about themselves, their prospects for the future, the impeccability of their motives. He laid out his agenda within the first hour of our meeting. He actually told me that if I suited him, after about a month of dating, he'd sleep with me to make certain we were compatible, then we could set a wedding date. Of course, he'd require that I sign a prenuptial agreement since he worked for his father, and there could be no possibility of me tinkering with the family business." She laughed again, shrugging her shoulders in wonder. "Where Susan finds so many marriage-minded men is beyond me."

After muttering something she couldn't hear, he turned to her. "I hope you walked out on him at that point."

"Of course I did. And then I had to listen to a lecture from Susan because I didn't give him a chance. She claimed he was only nervous, since it was our first date and all."

He grunted, the sound filled with contempt. "Sounds to me like he's a pompous ass." He tilted his head, studying her for a moment. "You know, it strikes me that your sister doesn't know you very well."

Josie didn't know herself, or at least, the self she was tonight, so she couldn't really argue. "No. Susan still sees me as a shy, self-conscious fifteen-year-old, crying over the death of our parents. Afraid and clingy. She put her own life on hold to make certain my life didn't change too much. She's always treated me like I was some poor princess, just waiting for the handsome prince to show up and take me to a mortgage-free castle. Now she thinks of it as her duty to get me married and settled. She's only trying to see things through to what she considers a natural conclusion to the job she took on the day our parents died. It's like the last chapter in my book, and until she's gotten through it, I'm afraid she won't stop worrying about me long enough to concentrate on her own story."

"You're hardly in danger of becoming an old maid. Twenty-five is damn young."

"I know it, but Susan is very old-fashioned, and very protective. Convincing her to let up isn't going to be easy."

"You're pretty tolerant with her, aren't you? In fact, you're not at all like she claimed you to be."

"I can imagine exactly how Susan described me." Josie couldn't quite stifle her grin, or take the teasing note out of her words. "Probably as the female version of you."

He shifted uneasily as he pulled the car into an empty space right behind a long dock where a dozen large boats were tied. He turned the truck off and leaned toward her, his gaze again drifting over her from head to toe, lingering on her crossed legs before coming up to catch her gaze. "We're here."

She gulped. Her stomach suddenly gave a sick little flip of anxiety, when she realized that she didn't have a single idea what she should do next, or what was expected of her.

"Josie." His palm cradled her cheek, his fingers curling around her neck. "I want you to know, I'm not in the habit of doing this."

"This?" The breathless quality of her voice should have embarrassed her, but she was too nervous and anxious to be embarrassed.

"I'm thirty-two years old, honey. Not exactly a kid anymore. I know the risks involved in casual sex, and I'm usually more cautious. But you've thrown me for a loop and... hell, I'm not even sure what I'm doing. I just know I want to be with you, alone and naked. I want to be inside you and I want to hear you tell me how much you want me, too."

Her words emerged on a breathless whisper. "I do."

He held her face between both hands, keeping her still while he looked into her eyes, studying her, his gaze intense and probing. "I can't remember ever wanting a woman as much as I want you." He kissed her briefly, but it was enough to close her eyes and steal her breath. "This can't be a one-night stand." He seemed surprised that he'd said that, but he added, "Promise me."

She nodded. She'd have promised anything at that point.

"Tell me you won't hate me for this."

That got her eyes open. "I don't understand."

His forehead touched hers. "I'm afraid I'm going to regret this, because you're going to regret it."

Her hand touched his jaw and when he looked at her, she smiled. "Impossible." She'd never been so sure of anything in her life.

He hesitated a second more, then opened his door with a burst of energy and jogged around to her side of the truck. She'd already opened her own door, but he was there before she could slide off her seat. It seemed a long way down, hampered by her skirt, so she was grateful for his help. But he didn't just take her hand. He lifted her out and didn't set her down, carrying her instead.

He didn't have far to walk. The boat he headed for was only partially illuminated by a string of white lights overhead, draped from pole to pole along the length of the pier. His footsteps sounded hollow on the wooden planks as he strode forward. Holding her with one arm, he dug in his pocket for a key and fumbled with the lock on the hatch, then managed the entrance without once bumping her head. She barely had a chance to see the upper deck, where she glimpsed a hot tub, before he began navigating a short, narrow flight of stairs. When they reached the bottom, he paused, then kissed her again, his arms tightening and his breath coming fast.

He lowered her to her feet by small degrees, letting her body rub against his, making her more aware than ever of his strength, his size, his arousal. It was so dark inside, Josie couldn't see much, but she didn't need to. He led her to a low berth and together they sank to the edge of the mattress. When he lifted his mouth, it was to utter only one request.

"For tonight," he said, "please, call me anything but Bob."

Chapter Three

HE'D LOST HIS MIND. That could be the only explanation for making such a ridiculous comment. Not that he'd take it back. If she called him Bob one more time, he'd expire of disgust—that or shout out the truth and ruin everything.

But now she'd gone still, and he could feel a volatile mixture of dazed confusion and hot need emanating from her. Damn it all, why did things have to be so confused, especially with this woman?

"I don't understand."

The soft glow of her eyes was barely visible in the dark interior of the boat as she waited for him to explain. But no explanation presented itself to his lust-muddled mind, so he did the only thing he could think of to distract her. He kissed her again, and kept on kissing her.

Night sounds swelled around them; the clacking of the boat against the pier, the quiet rush of waves rolling to the shore, a deep foghorn. Her lips, soft and full, parted for his tongue. He tasted her—her excitement, her sweetness, her need. She pulled his tongue deeper, suckling him, and he groaned.

What this woman did to him couldn't bear close scrutiny. He didn't believe in love at first sight; he wasn't sure love existed at all. Certainly, *he'd* never seen it. But something, some emotion he wasn't at all familiar with, swore she was the right woman, the woman he needed as much as wanted. Her scent made him drunk with lust, her touch—innocent and searching and curious—made him hungrier than he'd known he could be. She presented a curious, fascinating mix of seductive sexuality and quiet shyness. She spoke openly and from her heart—leaving herself blushing and totally vulnerable.

Lord, he wanted her.

Working his way down her throat, he teased, in no hurry to reach a speedy end, wanting to go on tasting her and enjoying her for the whole night.

If she'd allow that.

He listened to her sighs and measured her response, the way she urged him. He wanted this to be special for her, too. If later she hated him for his deception, he needed to be able to remind her of how incredible the feelings had been. It might be his only shot at countering her anger, of getting a second chance. It might be the only hold he'd have on her. So it had to be as powerful for her as it was for him. And with that thought in mind, he rested his palm just below her breast. Her heartbeat drummed in frantic rhythm and he realized she was holding her breath suspended while she waited.

With his mouth he nuzzled aside her blouse and tasted the swell of her breast, then moved lower, drawing nearer and nearer to her straining nipple. His progress was deliberately, agonizingly slow.

Using only the edge of his hand, he plumped her flesh, pushing her breast up for his mouth, for his lips and tongue and teeth. He kissed each pale freckle, touched them with his tongue. Josie squirmed, urging him to hurry, but he knew the anticipation would only build until they were both raw with need.

"Please..." she begged, and the broken rasp of her voice made him shudder.

"Shhh. There's no hurry," he whispered, and to appease

her just a bit, his thumb came up to tease her stiffened nipple through her bra, plying it, rolling it with the gentlest of touches. Her back arched and her fingers twisted in his hair. He winced, both with the sting of her enthusiasm and his own answering excitement. The tip of his tongue dipped low, moving along the very edge of her lace bra, close to her nipple, but not quite touching.

"*Bob.*"

"No!" He lifted his head, kissing her again, hard and quick. "Shush, Josie. You can moan for me, curse me or beg me. But otherwise, no talking."

"But..."

Through the thin fabric of her blouse and lace bra, he caught her nipple between his fingers and pinched lightly, feeling her tremble and jerk and pant. Her response was incredible, as hot as his own, and it had never been this way before. He tugged, his mouth again on her throat, lightly sucking her skin against his teeth, giving her a dual assault. She cried out, and the interior of the small cabin filled with the begging words he wanted to hear.

"Oh, please..."

It was a simple thing to ease her backward on the berth until she was stretched out before him. Knowing she lay there, his, waiting and wanting him, was enough to make him come close to embarrassing himself. The possessiveness was absurd, but undeniable, even after such a short acquaintance. Looking at her, his hunger was completely understandable. His erection strained against his jeans, full and hot and heavy, pulsing with his every heartbeat.

His fingers stroked over her cheek. "Be still just a moment."

He fumbled behind him, looking for the small lantern they used for fishing. He wanted to see her, but he didn't want harsh light intruding on their intimacy or maybe bringing on a shyness she hadn't exhibited so far. As he lit the lamp and turned the flame down low, the soft glow spread out around the cabin, not reaching the corners, but illuminating her body in select places—the rise of a breast, the roundness of a thigh, a high cheekbone and the gentle slant of a narrow nose. Those wide, needy eyes. Nick dragged in another deep breath to steady himself, but it didn't help.

Never had he seen a woman looking more excited, or more inviting. Her hands lay open beside her head, palms up, her slender fingers curled. She watched him, her eyes heavy and sensual and filled with anticipation. One leg was bent at the knee which had forced her skirt high—high enough that he could just see the pale sheen of satiny panties.

Nick stood, then jerked his shirt over his head. His gaze never left her, and as she looked him over, taking in every inch of his chest, he smiled. Her eyes lingered on places, so hot he could almost feel their touch, and her body moved, small moves, hungry moves. Impatient moves.

Guilt over his lies filled him, but he knew he'd do the same again. He'd do whatever was necessary to get to this moment, to have Josie Jackson—such a surprise—watching him in just that way, waiting for him.

Susan Jackson could think whatever she wanted, as long as Josie accepted him.

The shoes came off next, then his socks. He unsnapped his jeans and eased his zipper down just enough to give some relief. His eyes closed as he felt his erection loosened from the tight restraint. He took a moment to gather his control.

"What about your pants?"

The throatiness of her voice, the rise and fall of her breasts, proved how impatient she was becoming.

Lowering himself to sit on the edge of the cot again, he smiled and touched the tip of her upturned nose. He wanted to gather her close and just hold her; he wanted to be inside her right this second, driving toward a blinding release. The conflicting emotions wreaked havoc with his libido and made his hands tremble.

"Fair's fair. You have some catching up to do."

He leaned down, bracing himself with an elbow beside her

head while his free hand began undoing the tiny buttons of her blouse. He kissed her again, soft teasing kisses that he knew made her want more. But he wouldn't give her his tongue, just skimming her lips and nipping with his teeth while she strained toward him. When she reached for him, he caught her wrists and pinned them above her head. "Relax, Josie."

A strangled sound escaped her. "Relax? Right now?"

His chuckle was pure male gratification. "You said you wanted some fun, some excitement. Will you trust me?"

"To do what?" Rather than sounding suspicious or concerned, she sounded breathless with anticipation.

Her blouse lay open and he pulled it from her skirt to spread it wide, exposing her lace bra, which did nothing to hide her erect little nipples. He couldn't pull his gaze away from them. "To give you as much pleasure as you can possibly stand." As he spoke, he carefully closed his teeth around one tight, sensitive tip, biting very gently, then tugging enough to make her back arch high and her breath come out in a strained cry.

"You have sensitive breasts." He shuddered in his own response.

"Please..."

Licking until her bra was damp over both nipples, making them painfully tight, knowing how badly she needed him, he showed her just how much pleasure she could expect and the extent of his patience in such things. He loved giving pleasure to a woman, loved being the one in complete control, but never before had it been so important. This time wasn't just to make being together enjoyable, but to tie her to him, to make her need him and what he could do for her. *Only him.* He had to build a craving in her—a craving that only he could satisfy.

He had to believe this explosive chemistry was as new for her as it was for him. Knowing women as well as he did, her inexperience was plain. She hadn't touched him other than to desperately clutch his shoulders or his neck when she needed an anchor. And her surprise had, several times now, showed itself when he'd petted her in a particularly pleasurable place. Thinking of all the places he intended to touch her tested his control.

He caught her shoulder and turned her onto her stomach. Lifting her head, she peered at him over her shoulder, but he only grinned and began sliding down the zipper that ran the length of her skirt. The skirt was still tight, hugging her rounded bottom and distracting him enough that he stopped to knead that firm flesh, filling his hands with her and hearing her soft groan. He bent and kissed the back of her knee through her nylons. She squirmed again, her body moving in sexy little turns against the berth.

His mouth inched higher, bringing forth a moan. She buried her face in a pillow, her hands fisting on either side of the pillowcase.

She'd worn stockings, fastened with a narrow garter belt. *He loved stockings.*

Such a little flirt, he thought, forcing away all other musings because he didn't want to get trapped in his own emotional notions. Using two fingers, he unhooked a stocking and moved it aside so he could taste soft, hot flesh. Her thighs were firm, silky smooth, now opening slightly as he nuzzled against her.

"Bob..."

He gripped her skirt and yanked it down. She squeaked, and buried her head deeper into the pillow. The silky panties slid over her skin as he caressed her rounded buttocks, then between, his fingers dipping low, feeling her dampness, the unbelievable heat, her excitement. His heartbeat thundered and he retreated, afraid he'd lose himself in the knowledge she was ready. *For him.*

He kissed her nape, down her spine. The bra unlatched and he pulled her arms free, then turned her again.

Even in the darkness he could see her crimson cheeks, and

the way she held the bra secure against her breasts gave him pause. Josie wouldn't know how to use her body to get her way. She had no notion of the power women tried to wield over men; everything she felt was sincere. His hands shook.

In no way did he want to rush her, or coerce her into doing anything she didn't want. Her body might be ready for him, but emotionally she was still dealing with the unseemly rush of their attraction.

Stretching out beside her, he pulled her into his arms and simply held her, stroking her hair and back. He wanted to give her time to understand what was happening, to accept it. She needed to know he would never force her into anything, that she could call a halt at any time—even though it might kill him.

So he held her, passively, patiently. But he couldn't control the pounding of his heart beneath her cheek, or his uneven breaths, or the tightness of his straining muscles as his whole body rebelled against the delay.

"What…what's wrong?"

He sighed. For whatever reason, she had planned this. There was no other explanation for the way she'd come on to him, her verbal innuendoes, her willingness to come to the boat with him. But she was also very unsure of herself—amazing considering her natural sensuality and her allure, how completely she responded to his every touch.

He took her small hand and flattened it on his chest, holding it there. "Josie, are you certain you want to do this?"

She reared up, staring at him with something close to horror. "Don't you?"

The laugh emerged without his permission. Her innocence delighted him. "Honey, I think I'd give up breathing to stay in this boat for a week, loving you day and night—and twice in the afternoons." He touched her face, tracing her brows and the delicate line of her jaw. "But I don't want you to do anything that bothers you. There's no hurry, you know. If you'd rather…"

She frowned and said with some acerbity, "I'd rather you not torture me by stopping now." Then, after a second of lip-biting, she released the bra and it fell to the bed.

Nick halted in midbreath. Damn, but she had pretty breasts. Full and soft and white. He didn't move, but he forced his gaze from her luscious breasts to her face. "What do you want, Josie?"

"I want…" Pink spread from her cheeks to her breasts, and he half expected her to shy away once more. Instead she said, "I want you to kiss me again."

Very softly, in a mere whisper, he asked, "Where?"

Her nipples were pointed, pink, tempting him. Already he could almost taste them on his tongue. When her hand lifted, hovered, then touched exactly where he wanted his mouth to be, he groaned. "Come here."

He stayed perfectly still, leaving it to her to make the next move—a small salve to his conscience for being so manipulative. But he did open his mouth, his gaze on her breast, and with a small sound of excitement she leaned over him.

Her nipple brushed his lips, and he lifted a hand to guide her, to keep her close while he enclosed her in the heat of his mouth and suckled softly. Her arms trembled as she balanced above him, and her harsh breathing, interspersed with moans, made his jeans much too tight and confining. He felt ready to burst. Her pelvis bumped the side of his hip, then again, more deliberately, pressing and lingering. She pushed her heat against him, trying to find some relief, and he groaned.

His patience, his control, were severely strained by the taste of her and her generous reaction to him. Only the sure knowledge that this had to be perfect, that she had to believe they were magic together, kept him from losing control.

He slid both hands into her panties and dragged them down her legs while he switched to give equal attention to her other breast. With slow, unintrusive movements, he stripped her, never interrupting his ministrations to her body.

When she was finally naked, he shifted to put her beneath him, then shucked off his jeans. Holding her gaze, he led her hand to his erection and guided her fingers around him, silently instructing her to hold him—hard. She whimpered and he cupped his hand over her mound, only stroking her, tangling his fingers in her tight curls, his explorations soft and soothing.

Her movements were clumsy, but so damn exciting, he couldn't bear it. Especially with her expression so dazed, so dreamy, locked to his, letting him feel everything she felt, letting him touch her in ways no other man ever had. It added unbearably to the physical excitement.

He couldn't take it. Her scent filled him and he pressed his face into her throat, his mouth open, her skin hot. She reluctantly released him when he moved down in the bed, trailing damp kisses over her breasts, her ribs and abdomen, her slightly rounded, sexy little belly. Then to where his fingers teased over hot, damp feminine flesh.

"No!"

"*Yes.*" Never had he wanted anything as much as he wanted to know all of her. Her scent, powder fresh and woman tangy, was a mixture guaranteed to make him crazed. He kissed her, holding her thighs wide and groaning with the excitement of it, with the taste of her. She was deliciously wet, softly swelled, and he groaned again, his tongue delving deep, his open mouth pressed hard against her. Her hips shot upward and she cried out. Pressing one hand to her belly, he held her still and continued. With each thrust and lick of his tongue, she shuddered and wept, begged and cursed. Knowing his control to be at an end, he closed his mouth around her tiny bud and suckled sweetly, his tongue rasping, and two fingers gently pushed deep inside her.

He felt the contractions build, and he reveled in it, using every ounce of his experience to see that her orgasm was full and explosive. He'd never heard a woman cry so hard, or be so natural about her response, without reserve, without pretense, raw and intense and so very real. It fired his own imminent climax, and he pressed his erection hard into the berth's mattress as he rode along on her pleasure. When she quieted, spent and limp, her legs still sprawled open to prod his excitement, he had only seconds to locate a condom from his discarded jeans and enter her before he knew he'd be lost.

His thrust was deep and strong, and froze him. With a small, weak cry, her body stiffened in shock, and he stared at her, not sure he wanted to believe the unbelievable. She was twenty-five. She was gorgeous and sexy and so responsive, she could make a man nuts. His pulse went wild. "Josie?"

Her body shuddered and he felt the movement all through him, making him squeeze his eyes shut tight.

She took several deep breaths before saying, "I—I'm okay."

He pressed his forehead to hers, straining for control, trying to keep his hips perfectly still, his tone soft and calm. "You're a virgin?"

"I...was. Yes."

But not anymore. Now she was his. His heart thundered with the implications, ringing in his ears, making his blood surge with primitive satisfaction. But his brain couldn't decipher a damn thing, couldn't even begin to sort through it all. Discussions would have to wait until later; his body took over without his mind's consent.

Very slowly, measuring the depth of his stroke against the smallness of her body, he thrust, his lower body pulling tight as he pushed into her. Josie arched again and groaned around her tears.

His second slow thrust had her crying out—in startled pleasure. A third, and she wrapped around him and continued to hold him tight while he growled out his release, pressing himself deep inside her, becoming a part of her, making her a part of him. When finally he collapsed over her, she squeezed his neck and kissed his ear, his temple. Her breath was gentle against his heated skin. He shuddered with a fresh wash of unfamiliar, unsettling sensation, something entirely too close to tenderness.

After several minutes had passed and they could both breathe again, she stirred and whispered against his ear, "You are the most incredible man I've ever met."

The wonder was there in her tone, nearing awe. He started to smile, wanting to echo her words, wanting to kiss her again, to start all over. She was special, and she needed to know that, needed to know that somehow they'd been destined to meet, destined to be here, locked together in just this way, with him a part of her. He was thirty-two years old, and in his entire lifetime, never had a woman made him feel this way, hungry and tender and touched to his very soul by her presence. It should have scared him, but it didn't. Not yet.

She'd given him a precious gift, not just her virginity, which was a rare thing indeed, but her honesty, her openness. She went against everything he believed, every truism he'd ever taught himself over the years through endless empty relationships. Holding her left him…content. What he felt was somehow special; he knew that instinctively. He needed to make her understand it, too.

But then she smoothed her hand over his hair and kissed his shoulder, and added in a shy whisper, "Thank you, Bob," and he felt reality smack him hard in the head.

Damn, maybe the time for explaining had finally come, because he didn't think he could bear one second more of hearing her call him by another man's name, not after what they'd shared, not after he'd concluded they were meant for this night—and many more nights like it. And what better way to ensure she listen to him, that she give him a chance to reason with her, than to keep her just like this, warm and soft and spent beneath him.

He leaned up and saw her small smile, the glow in her eyes, the flush of her cheeks. The need to kiss her soft lips was intense, but he held back, knowing his responsibility now. "Josie—"

She lifted her hips, causing an instant, unbelievable reaction. He should have been near death, should have been limp as a lily in the rain, but it took only one small suggestive squirm from her and he was back to the point of oblivion, of not caring about anything but her small body and the way she held him. Her hands, having been idle before, now dug into his buttocks, keeping him a part of her, urging him deeper, and she smiled. "Do you think we could...start all over? I'm afraid I might have missed a few things the first time around."

Her frank, innocent way of speaking made his head spin. "Oh?" He winced at his own croaking tone and the weakening of his resolve. "Like what?"

She seemed to touch him everywhere, her fingers dragging through his chest hair and gliding innocently over his nipples, sliding downward to explore his hips and thighs. "This time, I want you to tell me where to touch you. And where to kiss you. And where to suck—"

Her words broke off as he devoured her mouth, and he thought, *Tomorrow. I'll confess all tomorrow.*

But for tonight he would drown her and himself in pleasure. And with her moving beneath him, urging him on, it seemed like the very best of plans.

JOSIE KNEW THE SUN was coming up by the way the light began to slant in though the slatted shutters. It might become a beautiful fall day, but she wouldn't mind spending it inside this very cabin, with this very man, doing exactly what they'd done throughout most of the night.

Poor Bob. He slept like the dead, but no wonder, considering the energy he'd expended all night. The bed they rested on was very narrow, and not all that comfortable. Of course, out of necessity, she'd spent most of the night resting on him, her head on his shoulder, her breasts against his wide hairy chest, one thigh over his lower abdomen. The man was so sexy, she could spend all night, and the whole day, just looking at him, trying, without much success, to get used to him.

How long this fantasy could last was her only troubling thought. She wasn't the woman he'd made love to repeatedly last night, the woman who threw caution to the wind and lived for the moment.

She was a sensible woman, with a responsibility to her job, to those who relied on her—to her sister. She led a quiet life in a quiet condo, had an understated wardrobe and tidy hair. Her car, a small brown compact, was paid for and got good gas mileage. She had a sound retirement plan at the local bank. Other than last night, she'd never been in a nightclub. She bought Girl Scout cookies religiously, and kept emergency money in an apple-shaped cookie jar at home. Most of her social life was spent in the nonthreatening company of people over the age of sixty-five.

The wild woman who'd indulged in the outrageous night of sex would have to confess sooner or later to being a complete and utter fraud.

Her palm drifted over his chest, feeling the crisp dark hair, the swell of muscle and the hardness of bone. *Let it be later,* she silently pleaded, not wanting it to end, not wanting to own up to her own deceptions. Knowing she should let him sleep, but unable to help herself, she pressed her cheek against his throat and breathed his delicious, musky, warm-male scent. It turned her muscles into mush and twirled in her belly. Possessiveness filled her, and she wanted to scream, *He's mine.*

Instead, she pushed reality away and continued to explore his undeniably perfect body.

Heat seemed to be a part of him, incredible heat that seeped into her wherever she touched him, heat that moved over her skin when he looked at her or spoke to her in that sexy deep voice. She hadn't needed a blanket last night, not with him beneath her, giving off warmth and securing her in his arms. She inhaled again, and marveled at the scent of him. His skin was delicious, musky and inviting, stretched tight over muscle and bone, covered in sexy places with dark, swirling hair.

His nipples, brown and flat and small, hid beneath that hair. And his stomach, bisected by a thin line that grew thicker and surrounded his penis with a perfect framework, drew her fingers again and again. She'd never really looked at a man before; she'd never been this close to a naked man.

She could have looked at Bob forever.

Curiosity drove her to bend over his body, examining that male part of him in some depth. Thick and long and rock hard when he was excited, but now merely resting in that dark nest of hair, it looked almost vulnerable.

Her chuckle woke him and he stirred. To her fascination, it took only a split second before he changed, before he grew erect, filling and thrusting up before her very eyes.

Her gaze shot to his face and was caught by the intensity, by the seriousness of his stare.

"I died and went to heaven last night, right?"

His voice was thick with sleep, his midnight black hair mussed, his jaws shadowed by beard stubble. He was a gorgeous male, and she suddenly wondered how awful she might look after a night of debauchery.

He lifted a hand to her cheek and his fingertips touched her everywhere—her nose, her lips, her lashes and brows. In that same, sleep-roughened voice, he whispered, "You have to be an angel. No woman could look this beautiful first thing in the morning."

Josie blushed. She wasn't used to hearing such outrageous compliments, or seeing such interest in a man's eyes. His fingers sifted through her hair, feeling it, dragging it over her shoulders, then over his chest. He lifted a curl to his face and inhaled, smoothed it over his cheek.

"Come here."

Ah, she knew what that husky tone meant now. She'd heard it many times last night. She'd be dozing, enjoying the feel of him beneath her, when suddenly his lips would be busy again, touching and tasting whatever part of her skin he could reach. His large, wonderfully sensitive hands would start to explore, innocently at first, then with a purpose.

He'd roused her several times in just that way throughout the long night. And each time she'd look at him, he'd say those words. *Come here.*

She wanted to hear him say them every morning, for the rest of her life.

Still holding a lock of her hair, he tugged her down until her lips met his, until he could steal her breath with a kiss so sweet, it brought tears to her eyes. He shifted, prodded and urged her body until she was arranged to his satisfaction—directly on top of him.

"Mmm. You're the nicest blanket I've ever been covered by." His large, rough hands held her buttocks, pressing her firmly against him. His stubbled cheek rubbed her soft cheek, giving her shivers. "And you smell good enough to be breakfast." His voice was thick with suggestion as he nuzzled the smooth skin beneath her chin.

Thoughts of the things he'd done to her, the shocking way she'd responded, made heat rush to her cheeks with the mixed meanings of his words. The bold things he said, and the way he said them, made her body pulse with excitement.

She kissed the bridge of his nose and wondered how to begin, how to start a confession that well might put an end to the most wonderful experiences she'd ever imagined. She had no doubt he'd tell her not to worry, that it wouldn't matter. At first. But when he got to know her, when she was forced to revert back to Josie Jackson, home-care nurse, community-conscious neighbor and responsible sister, he'd lose interest. She couldn't be two people, no matter how she wished it. And the woman he'd made love to all night would cease to exist because despite the isolation of it, she loved her job and cared about the people she tended.

She opened her mouth to explain, to try to find the words to rationalize what she'd done, the insane way she'd behaved. But he forestalled her with his questing fingers, tracing the space where her thigh met her buttocks, then gently pushing between. She should have been shocked, and hours ago she would have been. But no more, not after the pleasure he'd shown her. She trusted him to do anything he wished, knowing she'd enjoy it. And she did.

If the sound of quickened breathing was any indication, he liked touching her as much as she liked being touched.

With his free hand at her nape, he brought her mouth to his again so that words were impossible anyway. And unwanted.

When again she lay over him, so exhausted and replete she could barely get her mind to function, much less her limbs, he said, "We need to talk, honey."

True enough. They hadn't had too many words between them last night. She pressed a kiss to his heart and lifted her head until she could see him. His expression was worried. And serious. Very serious.

She started to wonder if he'd already realized she was a fraud, when she was distracted by the loud hollow thumping of footsteps on the pier. Bob turned his head, his brows now knit in a frown. A voice broke the early-morning stillness and they both jumped.

"Nick!" Pounding on the wooden door accompanied the shouting. "Damn it, Nick, are you in there?"

Josie stared at Bob, dumbfounded. In a whisper, she asked, "Does Nick use your parents' boat, too?"

With a wry grimace, he said, "All the time. But he never brings women here. Remember that, okay?" He lifted her aside. "Stay still, honey. And be real quiet. I'll be right back."

She was treated to the profile of his muscled backside and long thighs while he stepped into his jeans, zipping them, but not doing up the button. He looked sexy and virile and too appealing for a sane woman's mind. When he turned back to her, his gaze drifted over the length of her body. He grabbed up the sheet and reluctantly covered her. More pounding on the door.

"I know you have to be in there, Nick!"

"It looks like our magical time is up, sweetheart." His sigh was grievous, but he pressed a quick kiss to her lips. "Promise me you won't move."

"I promise."

"*Nick!*"

He closed his eyes briefly before shouting back, "Hold your horses, will you?"

He was out of the cabin, the hatch shut firmly behind him, before Josie could form a second thought.

Chapter Four

AS SOON AS NICK stuck his head out the door, Bob pounced. "I've been hunting all over for you." He looked harried and unkempt, very unlike Bob who prided himself on his immaculate appearance. Nick had a premonition of dread.

"Shh. Keep it down, all right?" He took Bob by the arm and led him down the pier toward the parking lot. He kept walking until he was certain he'd put enough space between Bob's booming, irritated voice and the boat. He didn't want Josie to overhear their conversation. A cool damp breeze off the river washed over his naked chest and he shuddered. "Now tell me what's wrong."

Bob stared at him, disbelieving for a moment. Then his expression cleared and he barked, "*What's wrong?* What do you mean, 'what's wrong?' I want to know what you did with Josie Jackson!"

It was a fact that Bob, even though he was a grown man, was much too naive to actually be given the full truth. Besides, what he'd done with Josie was no one's business but his own. This time Nick didn't mind lying in the least. "I haven't done anything with her."

Without seeming to hear, Bob paced away and back again. "Susan's almost hysterical. She's been phoning her sister all night, and finally she called me this morning to see how our damn date went. She thought *I'd* done something with her! I didn't know what to say."

Though the morning sun glared into his eyes, Nick decided it was way too early to have to deal with this, especially since all he wanted to do was get back to Josie. The image of her waiting for him in bed made his muscles tighten in response. "What exactly did you tell her?"

Bob's face turned bright red. The wind whipped at his light brown hair, making it stand on end, and he hastily tried to smooth it back into its precise style before stammering a reply. "—I told her business caused me to cancel at the last minute."

"Damn it, Bob—"

"I couldn't think of a better lie! And I couldn't just come out and tell Susan she's the one I'd rather be seeing, that I canceled because of her."

"Why not?" When Bob had first suggested Nick break the news to Josie for him, and why, he hadn't been overly receptive to the idea. He'd imagined Josie would be a lot like Susan, and he hadn't wanted another confrontation with an irrational female. Susan had disliked him on the spot; he remembered being a little condescending to her, just as Josie had related, but he'd had provocation first. The woman was rigid, snobbish and demanding. Not at all like Josie.

Bob had hit it off with Susan right from the start. To Nick, it was obvious they were kindred spirits, the way they formed such an instant bond. So he'd tried not to be too judgmental, and he'd done his best not to cross her path again.

But his largesse was limited. He hadn't wanted to do her any favors by meeting her wallflower sister.

Thank God he'd changed his mind.

"I've told you a dozen times, Bob, Susan will likely be flattered by your interest. You should give her the benefit of the doubt."

Susan's like or dislike of him no longer mattered to Nick, though her disparaging him to Josie had been tough to accept. Nevertheless, the desire to defend himself had been overshadowed by the need to keep Josie's trust.

And after last night, he considered any insult he'd suffered more than worth the reward. He owed Susan, so maybe he'd give her Bob.

"Ha! I'll be lucky if she ever speaks to me again. She was outraged that I would cancel on her sister." Bob rubbed both hands over his face. "I told her Josie had mentioned spending some time alone, and suggested she maybe wasn't up to talking right now. Susan decided Josie was depressed because I cancelled the date, and that made her even angrier."

Nick's grin lurked, but he hid it well. Poor Bob. "Josie wasn't depressed."

"Obviously not. But I never dreamed you'd bring her here and keep her all night."

"What makes you think she's here?"

Bob clutched his heart and staggered. "Oh, Lord, she is, isn't she? If she's not with you, then where would she be? Susan will never forgive me, I'll never forgive myself, I—"

Nick grabbed Bob and shook him. "Will you calm down? Of course she's here. And she's fine." More than fine; Josie Jackson was feminine perfection personified. He thought of how she'd looked when she'd promised not to move, and he wanted to push Bob off the pier.

He hastily cleared his throat and fought for patience. "The thing now is to get Susan interested in you."

Bob was already shaking his head, which again disrupted his hair. "She's convinced I'm perfect for her little sister. She won't stop until she pushes us together."

"Trust me." Nick kept his voice low and serious, determined to make a point Bob wouldn't forget. "You and the little sister will *never* happen."

Bob blinked at what had sounded vaguely like a threat. "Well, I *know* that." He waved a hand toward the boat and added, "The fact that she's here, after meeting you just last night, proves she's isn't right for me—"

He gasped as Nick stepped closer and loomed over him. "Careful, Bob. What you're saying sounds damn close to an insult."

"No, not at all." He took a hasty step back, shaking his head and looking somewhat baffled. After a moment, he smoothed his hands over the vest of his three-piece suit and straightened his tie. "I only meant...well..." He looked defensive, and confused. "You're acting awfully strange about this whole thing, Nick. Damn if you're not."

Nick made a sound of disgust. Behaving like a barbarian had never been his style, and he certainly didn't go around intimidating other men. Especially not his friends.

And he usually didn't feel this possessive of a woman. This was going to take a little getting used to.

He clapped Bob on the shoulder and steered him toward his car. "Forget it." When they reached the edge of the gravel drive, Nick stopped. He was barefoot after all, and in no hurry to shred his feet. Not when he had much more pressing issues to attend to. "Now my advice to you is this. Give Josie a little time to call her sister. I'll let her use my cell phone. Then go see Susan. She'll want someone to talk to, to confide in. She's been worried all night, and you can play the understanding, sensitive male. Pamper her. Try to let her know how you feel. Ease her into the idea. But don't tell her Josie was with me."

Bob had been nodding his head in that serious, thoughtful way of his, right up until Nick presented him with his last edict. Then he looked appalled. "You want me to lie to her?"

"You've already lied to her."

"When?"

Nick shook his head at Bob's affronted expression. "You allowed her to believe you did her ad campaign when I'm the one who did it."

"She wouldn't have worked with us if she'd known you were doing it. She doesn't like you much, Nick."

Bob acted as though he were divulging some great secret.

"You also lied to her when you told her why you didn't meet with Josie. What's one more lie?"

"But last night she was so upset, I just drew a blank. I didn't mean to lie. Now it would be deliberate."

Nick's patience waned. "Do you want Susan or not?"

"She's a fine woman," Bob claimed with nauseating conviction. "Dedicated, intelligent, ambitious, with a good head for business."

Nick made a face. "Yes, remarkable qualities that could seduce any man." She sounded like any number of other women he knew. Driven and determined. "She'll take over your life, you know."

Frowning at Nick's cynicism, Bob protested, "No, if I'm lucky, she'll share my life. And that's what I want."

"It's your life. Just don't say I didn't warn you."

"Damn it, Nick—"

"Okay then." Bob wasn't an unattractive man, Nick thought, trying to see him through a woman's eyes. He was built well enough, if not overly tall. He wasn't prone to weight problems and he didn't drink to excess or smoke. He still had all his hair, and at thirty-six, he might be overly solemn, but he wasn't haggard. He was tidy and clean.

Susan would be lucky to have him. "I've got a deal for you."

Eyeing him narrowly, Bob moved back to put some space between them. "What sort of deal?"

"Will you quit acting like I'm the devil incarnate?" They'd often been at odds with each other, both personally and professionally, due to the differences in their life-styles and outlooks on things. But in business and out, they managed to balance each other, to deal amicably together. They were friends, despite their differences, or maybe because of them, and for the most part they trusted each other. "I want to help you."

"How?"

"I can get Susan for you, if that's what you want." Nick didn't quite understand the attraction, but he'd always lived by the rule To Each His Own. If Bob wanted Susan, then so be it. Maybe Bob could keep her so busy she wouldn't be able to find the time to make insulting remarks about him to Josie.

"I can find out from Josie exactly what Susan likes and dislikes, what her fantasies are—"

"Susan wouldn't have fantasies!"

The bright blue morning sky offered no assistance, no matter how long Nick stared upward. When he returned his gaze to Bob, he caught his anxious frown. He felt like a parent reciting the lesson of the birds and the bees. "All women have fantasies, Bob. Remember that. It's a fact that'll come in handy someday. And it'd be to your advantage to learn what Susan's might be. I'll help. Within a month, you'll have her begging for your attention." And he and Josie would have had the time together without interference.

There was no doubt of Bob's interest. He couldn't hide his hopeful expression as he shifted his feet and tugged at his tie. "Okay. What do I have to do?"

"Just keep quiet about Josie for the time being. You know Susan doesn't exactly think of me as a sterling specimen of manhood. If she knows I'm interested in her sister, she'll go ballistic. She'll do whatever she can to interfere. I get the feeling Susan has a lot of influence on Josie." Or at least, she had in the past. For twenty-five years Josie had remained a virgin—the last ten under Susan's watchful eye. But last night, she had decided to change all that—with *him;* it still boggled his mind.

A sense of primitive male satisfaction swelled within him, along with something else, something gentler. He assumed it was some new strain of lust.

After glancing back at the boat, he decided he'd spent enough time with Bob. "Go home. Give Josie about an hour to contact Susan." An hour wouldn't be near long enough, but he'd have to make do. He could be inventive. And he had a feeling Josie would appreciate his creativity. "After that, go over to her house."

"I can't just drop in."

"Trust me, okay?" He gave Bob a small nudge toward his car. "Tell her you were concerned about her. She'll love it."

Bob peered at his watch. "She's probably at the flower shop now. I suppose I can drop in there."

"Great idea." Nick gave him another small push to keep him moving. "Let me know how it goes, okay? But later. Call me later."

Bob left, mumbling under his breath and thinking out loud, an annoying habit he had, but one that Nick had no problem ignoring this morning. He heard Bob drive away, but still he stood there staring down the dock. Confession time had come, much as he might wish it otherwise. With mixed feelings he started toward the boat. Josie would understand; she had to. He hadn't had near enough time with her yet.

His relationships, by choice, never lasted more than a few months, but he was already anticipating that time with her— and maybe a bit more. He wouldn't let her cut that time short. But first he had to find a way to get through to Josie, to gain control of his farce and make her understand the necessity of his deception. As he neared the boat, he went over many possibilities in his mind.

Unfortunately, none of them sounded all that brilliant.

JOSIE HEARD HIS FOOTSTEPS first and froze. Her heartbeat accelerated and she tried to finish fastening her garter, but her fingers didn't seem to want to work. Stupid undergarment. Why had she chosen such a frivolous thing in the first place? At the time, she certainly hadn't suspected that anyone would ever know what she wore beneath her suggestive clothes. But it had felt so wickedly sinful to indulge herself anyway. And she'd felt sexy from the inside out. Maybe that had in part given her the courage to do as she pleased last night.

She would never regret it, but last night was over, and she

wanted to be dressed when Bob returned. At first, she'd sat there waiting, just as he'd asked her to. But after a few moments she'd gotten self-conscious. She'd read about the awkward "morning after," and though she'd never experienced one herself, she knew being dressed would put her in a less vulnerable position. And she needed every advantage if she was to make her grand confession this morning.

Then suddenly he was there, standing in the small companionway, his hands braced over his head on the frame, looking at her.

He was such a gorgeous man, and for long moments she simply stared. His jeans, still unbuttoned, rode low on his lean hips and his bare feet were casually braced apart, strong and sturdy. She could see the muscles in his thighs, the tightness of his abdomen.

His dark hair, mussed from sleep and now wind tossed, hung over one side of his forehead, stopping just above his slightly narrowed, intense dark eyes. He wasn't musclebound, but toned, with an athletic build. Curly hair spread over his chest from nipple to nipple, not overly thick, but so enticing.

Not quite as enticing as the dark, glossy hair trailing from his navel southward, dipping into his jeans. She knew where that sexy trail of hair led, and how his penis nested inside it. Josie had intimate knowledge of his body now, and she blushed, both with pleasure and uncertainty.

"You moved."

The whispered words caused her to jump, and her gaze shot back to his face, not quite comprehending.

"You promised you'd stay put, naked in my bed."

He sounded accusing and she managed a shaky smile. Though she wasn't exactly what one would call *dressed*, with only her stockings, bra and panties on, she still felt obliged to apologize. "I'm sorry. You were gone so long...." Her voice trailed off as he gazed over her body. Feeling too exposed in only her underthings, she shifted nervously. "Bob?"

She saw him swallow, saw his shoulders tighten and knew he must be gripping the door frame hard. "You have a very sexy belly."

"Oh." She looked down stupidly, but to her, her belly seemed like any other. She cleared her throat. "Is everything okay, then?"

He hummed a noncommittal reply.

"Should I take that as a 'yes'?"

"What? Oh, yeah, everything's fine. Just a misunderstanding. Forget about it." He stepped into the room and knelt before her, and everything inside her shifted and moved in melting excitement.

He lifted her hands from her thigh, where she'd been fumbling with the garter. Wrapping his long fingers around her wrists like manacles, he caged them on the berth, one on each side of her hips. "I'm not sure last night was real, Josie. I've been standing outside, trying to think of what to say, of where we go from here. But to tell you the truth, I don't want to go anywhere. I want to halt time and stay right here alone with you. To hell with the world and work and other people."

She started to speak, to tell him even though it was Saturday and she wanted nothing more than to stay with him, she had a few patients she needed to check on. But he leaned forward, releasing her hands so he could cradle her hips. He kissed her navel and her mind went blank. Hot sensation spread through her belly as his tongue stroked, dipped. She wound her fingers into his silky hair and held on.

"Did you find the head okay?"

"Hmm?" It took a moment for the whispered question to penetrate, hummed as it was against her skin. The head? Then she remembered that was the nautical term for the toilet. "Yes, yes thank you."

"Are you hungry?" He rolled one stocking expertly down her leg while pressing hot kisses to the inside of her knee. "There's some food in the galley, I think. And coffee."

Each whispered word was punctuated with a small damp kiss, over her ribs, her hip bones, between. No, she didn't want food.

Gasping, she tried to speak, to tell him, but only managed a moan.

"Josie, are you sore?" He kissed her open mouth, gently forcing her back until she lay flat on the berth with her legs draped over the edge. He knelt on the floor between her widespread thighs, his hard belly flush against her mound, his chest flattening her breasts. His fingers trailed over her skin from knee to pelvis and back again, taunting her, making her skin burn with new sensitivity.

"I'm...fine."

Cupping her face to get her full attention, he said, "How is it you were a virgin, sweetheart?"

She didn't want to talk about that now. She wasn't sure she ever wanted to talk about it. She tried to shake her head but he held her still.

"Josie?"

Sighing, she considered the quickest, easiest explanation to give. A confession might be appropriate, but she didn't want it to intrude right now, to possibly halt the moment, which seemed an extension of the night, so therefore still magical. It was all so precious to her, and she wanted to keep it close, to protect it.

"I started college young, when I was barely seventeen." She drew a shuddering breath, speech difficult with him so close. "I've always been something of an overachiever, which always made Susan proud. But because I was young, and she had to be mother as well as sister, she naturally kept an extraclose eye on me. Not that it was necessary. My studies were so time-consuming, I didn't have room for much socializing anyway. We had clinicals at seven o'clock most mornings, plus the regular classwork. It took all my concentration to get my BSN."

"And since college?"

She shrugged. "I spent two years working in a hospital, then two years gaining home health-care experience so I could open my own business. There were so many federal and state licenses to get, so much red tape, again I had little time for anything else. Now I work with the elderly. The…opportunity to meet young single men just isn't there. So, bottom line, I've been so wrapped up in getting Home and Heart started, I haven't had time for dates. And with my job, the dates can't find me anyway. That is, if they're even looking."

"They're looking, all right. Trust me."

She gave him a smile, which seemed to fascinate him. With gentle fingers he touched and smoothed over her lips, the edge of her teeth. He kissed her—feather light, teasing. She had to struggle to follow their conversation. "Maybe I'm the one who didn't know where to look, then."

He didn't smile. "But you found me last night?"

No way would she admit her guise had actually been to discourage and repel him, not after the very satisfying outcome. She feigned a nonchalant shrug. "Susan is always attempting to fix me up with dates. Most of the guys are total duds, at least for what I want out of life." She smoothed her hands down his back. "But you were perfect."

"I'm so glad I was the one." He pressed his face into her neck and gave her a careful hug. "And I still can't imagine how a woman as sexy as you remained a virgin for so long."

Trying to laugh it off, she said, "I'm discriminating, so it was easy."

He licked the smile off her lips. "I want to make love to you again, Josie. I want to be inside you and hear you make those sexy little sounds, feel your nails on my back."

For the longest moment, words failed her. Finally she managed, "Me, too."

He shook his head. "I need to talk to you first."

Josie felt dread at the serious tone of his voice. His brows were lowered, and he looked regretful, almost sad. A slow panic started to build, making her stomach churn and her chest tighten. She tried to sound casual as she made her next suggestion. "Why don't we save the talking for later?"

Using his words against him, she dragged her nails slowly, gently, down his spine, holding his gaze, seeing the darkening of lust on his face. She slipped her hands inside his jeans and felt his firm, smooth buttocks.

"Josie…"

It sounded like a warning, which thrilled her. "Do you really want to see me again?"

"Damn right."

Slowly his hips began the pressing rhythm she'd grown accustomed to last night. Even through his jeans, she felt the heat of it, the excitement.

She could hardly believe he was still so very interested—it simply wasn't the reaction from men that she was used to. She wasn't about to give up such an opportunity. "How about Sunday? We could get together to talk then. Right now, I'm not at all sure I can listen." She had some morning calls to make, but the rest of her day would be free, and tomorrow was soon enough for confessions, soon enough to see her fantasy end.

With his lips against her ear, he whispered, "Just give me a time."

"Noon."

"I think I can manage to wait until then." He raised up to look at her. One hand cupped her cheek, the other cupped her breast, plying it gently. She drew in a long shuddering breath and his fingers stroked her nipple while he watched her face, judging her reaction. "But remember, Josie." He pinched her lightly and she moaned. "It's your idea to wait to talk until then. Promise me."

Struggling to follow his logic and his conversation, she said, "I promise."

He kissed her then, and they both knew she hadn't a clue as to what she'd just promised. They also knew, at the moment, it didn't matter.

"MAYBE YOU SHOULD call your sister."

Nick gazed at Josie from across the cab of the truck. She looked sleepy and sated, and he wanted to turn around and take her back to the boat. Damn, he'd never met a woman who affected him so strongly. But he had promised Bob.

He reached down and picked up the receiver in his truck, then handed it to her. "Here. Why don't you call her now?"

"A car phone?"

"Hey, we're a growing company. We have to stay up-to-date."

She smiled, that beautiful killer smile that showed all her innocence and her repressed sensuality. *All for him.* He couldn't remember ever sleeping with a virgin before. Even his first time had been with an older, experienced girl. Somehow Josie didn't epitomize the squeamish, whimpering image of a virgin he'd always carried in his mind. He eyed the mini-skirt and high heels she wore, and grinned. No, she was far from any woman he'd ever known, but she was exactly what he might have visualized in an ideal fantasy.

Before she could use the phone, he took her wrist. "I've been thinking."

She politely waited for him to continue, and he cleared his throat, praying for coherent words to come through. "Last night took me by surprise, Josie."

"Me, too."

Damn, that soft, husky tone of hers. He felt his body stir and cursed himself for being ruled by his libido. It was brains he needed now, and a little old reliable charm.

"What we've done, I know it's out of the norm for you, but I want you to know it wasn't exactly the typical conclusion to one of my dates, either. I'm not in the habit of having sex with women I barely know."

He peered at her, trying to judge her reaction to his words, but her eyes were downcast, her hands gripping the phone in her lap.

"You're beautiful, Josie. I want to see you and make love to you again, but other people might not understand."

Her head snapped up. "Susan said you were conservative, but... You're dumping me because of what other people would think?"

The truck almost swerved off the road. "No! That's not what I'm saying at all. I just don't want us to...share what we've done. I don't want the world and its narrow-minded views to intrude."

She frowned, apparently thinking it over. "You want to keep our relationship a secret?"

Damn, why couldn't he have said it so simply? He couldn't recall ever stammering over his words this way. "Would you mind? At least for a little while?"

A shy grin tilted the corners of her mouth. "No. Actually I was wondering what in the world I was going to tell Susan. She wanted us to hit it off, but I'm certain this wasn't exactly what she had in mind."

He tipped his head in agreement. Susan would want to cut his heart out, he had no doubt. "You're probably right."

"I'm not ashamed that we were together, but she'd never understand or approve."

He stiffened, already anticipating Susan's interference. "Do you need her approval?"

"No, of course not. But it's important to me because *she's* important to me. If she knew where I was last night, she'd be upset. She would never judge me harshly, but she'd worry endlessly and I'd never hear the end of it. I'd like to avoid that."

He'd like to avoid it, too. At least until he got everything straightened out.

Cautious now, he made a necessary suggestion. "You could tell her we didn't hit it off, and that you canceled. From what you told me, that shouldn't surprise her. And then she wouldn't ask you tons of questions that you'd feel awkward answering."

Laughing, she punched in her sister's number. "No, she won't be surprised. It's what I usually do. But I can't outright lie to her. That wouldn't be right."

Before he could say anything more, Susan had answered, and even Nick could hear her frantic voice booming over the line. He kept one eye on the road, and one eye on Josie. He half expected his cover to be blown at any moment. Then Josie would look at him with those big green eyes. She'd detest him and his damn deception and she'd forget her promise to let him explain on Sunday.

But Josie grinned and her look was conspiratorial as she explained to Susan that she'd had a change of plans last night—an understatement if there ever was one—but that she was perfectly fine.

"I've asked you to stop worrying about me, Susan. Please. I'm a big girl now. If I choose to stay out late, or to unplug my phone, that's my own business. You can't panic every time I don't answer one of your calls."

Nick reached across the seat and took her hand. She hadn't lied, but she'd hinted at an untruth, and he suddenly felt terrible for putting her in such a position. As Susan claimed, he was a reprobate; lying came naturally to him. But they were never lies that hurt anyone, and he'd never lie to his grandfather, the only close family he had. Yet he'd forced Josie into a corner. He'd find a way to make it up to her, all of it.

"I'll pick up something for lunch and come over to the shop after I finish my rounds today. We can chat." There was a moment of silence, then Josie winced. "Susan, I'm sorry. Really. I didn't mean to make you worry. No, I'm sure he really is a terrific man." She grinned at Nick. "I suppose I can think about giving him another chance, but let's talk about that later, okay? Yes, Susan, I'll honestly think about it. I have to go now. No, I really do. I'll be by later. Love you, too."

She hung up and then began giggling.

"What's so funny?"

"She came to the automatic conclusion that I stood you

up. You should have heard her. She sounds half in love with you herself. You're intelligent and conscientious and you have a good mind for business. Strong praise coming from Susan."

Nick remembered his promise to Bob. Given the way the two of them echoed their appreciation of each other, it shouldn't be hard to fix them up together. It might not even take the entire month he'd allotted to the project. "Is that what Susan likes? I mean, are those the qualities most important to her?"

"Yes, but in some ways, she's a fraud. Susan pretends to be all seriousness, but she's a sucker for a box of chocolates or a mushy card. I think deep down, she's hoping for someone to rescue her from herself."

He slowed the truck and glanced at her as Josie directed him at a turn. "What do you mean?"

"She rents every mushy movie in the video store. She'd never admit it, but I've found romance novels by the dozen hidden in her house, under couch cushions and her bed pillows. Of course, I've never said anything to her. It would embarrass her to no end. But I think she'd really like some guy to come along and share a little of her load. She's had to shoulder so much responsibility at such a young age."

Intrigued, Nick wondered if he could ever get Bob to sweep into Susan's life. Already, he was forming plans in his mind. Maybe this would be even easier than he'd thought. "So you think Susan would be impressed with a man who treated her gently? That wasn't the impression I got. If I remember correctly, I—that is, *Nick* tried to show her some old-fashioned courtesy and she bristled up like a porcupine."

"You'd have to understand Susan and all she's struggled for. She was only nineteen when our parents died, just starting college herself. The authorities wanted to take me away from her, to put me with someone more established, more mature. She had to fight to keep me with her. It made her angry, the inequality between men and women, and it wasn't just because she was young, but because she was female. I think she went overboard trying to prove her independence and her worth, but I can understand her feelings. She likes to be treated with respect, and she hates to be patronized."

The image of Josie as a frightened little girl whose parents had died, and whose sister had to struggle to keep her, disturbed him. Neither her life nor Susan's had been easy, and his appreciation for Susan grew. He decided to urge Bob to start wooing her now, to send her a small gift. She deserved it.

They stopped for a red light and he turned slightly toward Josie. Pushing sad thoughts from his mind, he lifted her hand to his mouth and kissed her knuckles. "What about you?" He wouldn't mind sweeping this woman off her feet for a romantic weekend. The idea held a lot of appeal. "Do you read romances?"

Josie shook her head and her red hair fell forward, curling over her breast. Deliberately he stroked the long tress, letting the back of his hand brush her nipple.

She sucked in a breath and blurted, "No."

"No?"

"No, I don't read romances. Horror stories are more my speed." She spoke quickly, her voice rasping from the feel of his hands on her body again. He liked it. He liked her easy response and her eagerness.

Now wasn't the time, though, so he removed his hand and pulled away with the flow of the traffic. "Horror stories?"

"Mmm-hmm. The more gruesome, the better. I have all the classics—*Frankenstein, Werewolf, Dracula*. And all the modern authors, like King and Koontz. I'm something of a collector."

Her small, earnest face beamed at him, guileless, sweet, as she described her interest in the macabre. Somehow the images wouldn't mesh. "Horror?"

She laughed at his blatant disbelief. "It fascinates me, the way the human mind can twist ideas and stories, that ordinary men and women can write such frightening things. It's incredibly entertaining. I'll be appalled and frightened the whole time I'm reading, ready to jump at every little sound. And when I get to the end, I just have to laugh at myself. I mean, the ideas are so unbelievable, really. But still, I wish I had that kind of talent. Wouldn't it be wonderful to write a book like one of King's and have it made into a movie?"

He couldn't stop the wide grin on his face. "You're something else, you know that?"

Again she ducked her head, hid her face. "I'm sorry. I've been going on and on."

"And I've enjoyed every minute."

It wasn't long before Josie directed him into her condo complex. The ride hadn't taken nearly as much time as he'd wished for. He started to get out, but she stopped him.

"If we're going to keep things a secret, my neighbors probably shouldn't see you. You know how gossip spreads."

Anxiety darkened her eyes and he wondered at it. He looked past her at the large complex, wondering which condo she owned. "They'll see me tomorrow when I pick you up."

"I was thinking I could just meet you somewhere."

He wanted to say no. He wanted to insist on seeing her home, to try to gain some insight into why she'd suddenly decided to cut loose, to throw her caution to the wind. He wanted to know all her secrets.

But he had secrets of his own to keep, at least for the time being, so he couldn't very well push her without taking the chance of exposing himself.

He considered his options. The boat was out; they'd never get around to talking if he took her there again. And he still couldn't let her in his house until he'd given her a full explanation. Then it struck him.

"There's a monster movie marathon at that little theater down the street from my office. Right next door to it is a small café. Meet me there. We can grab a sandwich and talk, then take in a few movies." He hadn't exactly planned to have his confession in an open forum, but perhaps it would be better in the long run. Josie didn't strike him as the type to cause a public scene, so she'd be more likely to stay put and hear him out if there were curious spectators about. At least he hoped she would.

Her face had lit up with his first words. "I read about that marathon. I had promised myself I'd find the time to go, even if I had to go alone."

His heart twisted in a wholly unfamiliar way and he pulled her forward for a brief, warm kiss. His lips still against hers, he spoke softly. "Now neither of us has to go alone."

Unexpectedly she threw her arms around him. He held her tight, wondering at her apparent distress. He was the one with the damn secrets; he had a feeling everything would explode if he let her out of his sight.

"Tomorrow," she said, swallowing hard. "Tomorrow I have to explain a few things to you."

That was his line. He kissed her again, first on her rounded chin, then her slender nose, her arched eyebrows. "Then we'll both explain a few things. It all went so fast, I guess we're both still off-kilter. But I swear, it will be all right, Josie. Do you believe me?"

"I want to. But tomorrow seems a long way off."

"Much too long."

She stared at him a moment, then opened her door. "I have to go. I have the feeling that if I don't I'll attack you right here in your truck for all the world to witness." She laughed as she slid off the seat, but he couldn't find a speck of humor, not with his body reacting so strongly to her words.

Before closing the door, she turned to face him and her cheeks pinkened. She looked shy again, and much too appealing. "Last night was the most wonderful night of my life."

He smiled.

"Thank you, Bob."

She slammed the door and hurried up the walkway, hobbling just a bit in her high heels.

His forehead hit the steering wheel with a solid thwack. The most perfect woman he'd ever met, sweet and sexy and open and *real*. She made him smile, she made him hot. She intrigued him with this little game she played, looking the vamp while being the virgin. She was every man's private fantasy, not just his own.

And damn it, she thought he was Bob.

Could life get any more complicated?

Chapter Five

"TELL ME THE TRUTH! Did you cancel or did he?"

Josie opened her mouth, but Susan cut her off. "If he canceled, I'll give him a piece of my mind. That's what he first told me, you know. That he was the one who'd backed out. But I found that so hard to believe. I mean, he's so conscientious and he did promise me."

"I canceled."

Susan's frown was fierce. "I don't suppose I'll ever know the full truth, will I? You're both telling such different stories. But never mind that."

She sat across from Josie and stared her in the eye. Josie almost winced. She knew that sign of determination when she saw it.

"You have to give him a chance, Josie. He's different from the rest. He's...wonderful."

Josie stared at the limp lettuce in her salad. She didn't have an appetite, hadn't had one all day. All she could do was think of Bob and miss him and wonder what he was doing right now, what he'd say tomorrow when he learned she wasn't the woman he thought her to be. She wasn't exciting and sexy and adventurous. She was dull and respectable; all the things she claimed to disdain.

She could just imagine what a man like Bob would think of her. She wanted to change things; she wanted to go places, be daring and fulfill every fantasy she could conceive. She'd been such a coward, living a narrow life while sinking everything she was, everything she wanted to be, into her business. She'd escaped the grief of losing her parents, of being a burden to her sister, despite Susan's disclaimers. She'd escaped any risks of being hurt—and any chance of enjoying life. But she wanted to change that, now.

Last night had been an excellent start.

But her sister wouldn't think so. "I don't need your help picking my dates, Susan."

"What dates? You never go out!"

The outfit she'd worn for Bob was the only one like it she owned, and she'd bought it to repel him, not attract him. What would he think of that? What would he think when he saw her in her standard comfortable wardrobe, meant for visiting the elderly and running errands?

She needed to find some middle ground—somewhere between the woman she was and the woman he thought her to be. And she only had until noon tomorrow to do it.

"Are you listening to me?"

Josie pulled her thoughts away from the monumental task she'd set for herself and smiled at her sister. "Yes, Susan, I'm listening. You think Bob is wonderful." Privately she agreed. More than wonderful. Incredible and sexy and... She sighed. Such a very perfect man—who thought she was a different woman.

"I do. Think he's wonderful, that is. And you would too if you'd just stop being so stubborn. He's perfect for you, Josie."

Amen to that. Now if only she could make it come true.

"And handsome—not that it matters in the long run what a man looks like. It's his integrity and responsible attitude that are important. But he really is an attractive male. Proud, intelligent. Courteous. And a brilliant businessman. He did such a fabulous job on my ads. Business has been pouring in."

Something in Susan's tone cut through Josie's distraction.

She shoved her salad aside and contemplated her sister's expression. Susan had leaned forward on the counter, her own take-out lunch forgotten. She had both hands propped beneath her chin and a starry look in her hazel eyes.

That look was the one normally reserved for expansion plans for the flower shop, or matchmaking. Josie drew a deep, thoughtful breath. The heady scent of flowers and greenery filled her nostrils. The air inside the shop was, by necessity, damp and rich, heavy. As an adolescent, Josie had always loved the shop. It had been a one-room business back then, catering mostly to locals, but with Susan's hard work and patience, it had grown considerably over the years. This was a special place, where Josie had always felt free to confide in her sister. Many serious talks had occurred at this exact counter.

This time, however, Susan seemed to be the one in need of a chat.

She sighed a long drawn-out sigh, and Josie felt a moment's worry at the wistful sound. "What are you thinking?"

Susan jumped. Normally her thoughts would be on a new business scheme to implement in the shop, a moneymaker of some sort. Or a way to get Josie's life headed in the direction Susan deemed appropriate. Not this time. "I was thinking of how apologetic Bob was for how things turned out. *He* was sorry for making me worry so much."

Josie was startled. "You talked with him?"

"Of course I did! Haven't you listened to anything I've told you? Bob stopped by earlier and apologized for causing me concern. He admitted he should have called me himself last night, to explain about the change in plans. He's promised me it won't happen again. Now, when do you think the two of you can reschedule?"

Josie narrowed her eyes, her thoughts suspended. Bob had been here, talking to Susan? Why would he ask her not to say anything, but then risk calling on Susan himself? It didn't make any sense. "He told you he would reschedule?"

"Yes. We, um, talked for quite some time as a matter of fact. You know, he has big plans for the advertising agency. Someday he'll be a very prosperous man, a name to be recognized. You wouldn't have to continue working if things went well between the two of you."

Josie couldn't help but grind her teeth. Bob had told her he wasn't all that interested in expanding the company. Had he lied, or had Susan misunderstood? She felt buried in confusion and conflicting emotions. "I like my work, Susan, and I'm not ever going to give it up."

"Josie, you know how proud I am of you. I think it's incredible all that you've accomplished. And I love you for all your hard work and dedication." Susan patted her hand. "But it's a terrible job for a young single woman. You never have an entire weekend free, and I can't remember the last time you took a vacation. It's no wonder you never meet any nice men."

"Like Bob?" Josie whispered.

"Exactly!" Susan looked flushed again, and she averted her gaze. "We discussed the problem of your work, how you can't keep any regular hours, and Bob suggested that he wouldn't mind if his wife had a job like my own, running her own shop, meeting new people. A nice nine-to-five job where you'd be home in the evening to share dinner with him, and be there on the weekends to spend time with the kids. Maybe he could help you hire someone, so you wouldn't have the full load yourself...."

Susan's words trailed off as Josie jerked to her feet, hitting the fronds of a large fern with her elbow and almost smacking the top of her head on a hanging philodendron. She cursed, surprising both herself and Susan.

How dare Bob discuss her life with her sister? He had no right to make plans for her behind her back, or to even think of trying to rearrange her life.

She felt as though Bob had betrayed her, and it hurt. Damn it, it hurt much more than it should have. It took two deep breaths to calm herself enough to speak. "Susan, I appreciate your concern, you know that. But you're meddling in my life and you just can't do it anymore. I'm a grown woman. I *like* what I do, and it's important to me. I'm not giving up my work for anyone, *Bob* included."

"Well." Susan looked subdued, but just for a moment. "We were only thinking of the future, wondering how you're going to fit a family into that hectic schedule of yours."

Josie growled, appalled at Bob's arrogance. Just because she'd slept with him, he thought he had the right to start rearranging her life? "Family! I've barely gotten started on the dating."

"Not for lack of trying on my part!"

"Susan." She said it as a warning, long and drawn out. Having her sister fuss over her was one thing; she loved Susan, so she could tolerate the intrusion. But Josie couldn't have Susan discussing her, planning her life, with every man she deemed marriage material.

"All right. I can take a hint." Susan made a face, acting much aggrieved. "But I hope you'll agree it's worth your time to pursue this association."

"Relationship. Time spent between a man and woman, outside of business, is called a relationship, not an association."

Susan waved a dismissive hand. "The point is, you need to compromise a little, Josie, if you ever hope to marry a man as perfect as Bob. He has his life all planned out, down to the last detail. All his business expansions, the house he'll build, even the names he'd like to give his children. Believe me, he's worth your efforts."

Josie straightened her shoulders and stared at Susan, shocked. Realization slowly dawned. For the first time in memory, Susan seemed genuinely attracted to a man. And not just attracted, but totally enthralled. Maybe even *in love*. Josie swallowed, trying to sort through her own muddled feelings to see the situation clearly.

"Did you ever stop to think, Susan, that Bob might be worth *your* effort?"

Blinking owlishly, as if she'd never heard anything so preposterous, Susan stood and began clearing away their half-eaten salads. "Don't be ridiculous."

"Why not?" Josie summoned the necessary words past the lump in her throat. "It seems to me you admire him a great deal. Admit it, you want him for yourself." She wouldn't think of Bob, of what they'd shared last night. She couldn't.

Josie drew a deep breath. "Since I...don't want him, there's no reason for you to deny yourself." She went to Susan and took her hands. "I love you, Susan, you know that. But you have the most irritating habit in the world of thinking I deserve the very best of everything—even if it's something you want for yourself. You've been doing it since the day Mom and Dad died, putting my needs before your own. You sold the house, then used all the money for me to go to college while you dropped out. You bought me a car when I graduated, when you had to take the bus."

Susan looked away, embarrassed, but Josie only continued in her praise. Susan deserved it—and much more. "You've been the very best of sisters. I can't tell you how much I appreciate all you've done for me, for being there when I didn't have anyone else, for being my best friend and my mother as well as my big sister." Josie swallowed back her tears, and ignored the wrenching heartache.

She squeezed Susan's hands, her gaze unwavering. "You don't have to do it anymore. I can take care of myself now. If you're attracted to a man, to..." She swallowed, then forced the words out. "If you're attracted to Bob, let him know. You deserve to give it your best shot."

Before Susan could respond, the bell over the door jingled and a man walked in carrying a fancy wrapped package. "For Miss Susan Jackson?"

Susan stepped forward, eyes wide, one had splayed over her chest. "For me? Oh my goodness, who's it from?"

Josie tipped the delivery man and then peered over Susan's shoulder while she fumbled with her package.

"It's chocolates!" Susan peered at the box, holding it at arm's length. "I can't imagine who it's from."

Josie had a sick feeling she knew exactly who had sent the extravagant gift. Her knees felt watery and she perched on a stool. "Read the card."

Looking like a toddler on Christmas Day, Susan tore the small envelope open with trembling fingers. She read the card silently, her lips moving. When she turned to Josie, she bit her lip in indecision.

"Well?" Josie urged.

"It says…" Susan cleared her throat, and her cheeks turned pink. "It says, 'With all my regard, Bob.'"

How…prosaic. Josie would have thought Bob could do better than *that*.

Susan halted, her smile frozen. "It doesn't mean anything, Josie."

Very gently Josie said, "Of course it does."

"No. He knew I was worried about you last night and this is his way of showing me he understands."

"I think it's his way of showing you he's as interested as you are."

"No! Don't be silly. He's simply a very considerate, kind man. He's always thinking of others, even that disreputable partner of his, Nick something-or-other. Now there's a man who can't be trusted! I could tell just by looking at him, he's entirely too used to getting his own way. But Bob is different. He's scrupulous and…"

While Susan droned on and on, trying to convince Josie while simultaneously pulling open the silver ribbon on the box, Josie did her best to keep her smile in place. Her stomach cramped and her temples pounded. She'd made such a colossal fool of herself, and possibly damaged something very precious to her sister. The problem now was how to fix things.

Susan went in the back room to put the chocolates in the refrigerator and Josie did the only thing she could think of to do. She grabbed up one of the little blank cards in the rotating stand by the cash register and filled it out. It would be easier to write the words than to face Bob and say them out loud. In fact, if she had her way, it'd be a long, long time before she had to lay eyes on him again.

She added Bob's name to the outside and attached the card to a basket of dieffenbachia and English ivy, spiked with colorful tigridias. The plants were supposed to help filter the air of chemicals, and right now, she thought the air needed a little cleaning. She stuck a large bow wrapped with a wire into the middle of the thing along with the yellow address copy from an order form. She shoved it up next to the other plants due to be sent out in the next half hour.

After dusting off her hands in a show of finality, she reseated herself. She didn't really feel any better for having made the break clean, but at least it was over. If her conscience wasn't clear, at least it *was* somewhat relieved.

The hard part would be trying to forget what it had been like, being with him, feeling his heat and breathing his scent and... No. She wouldn't think about it. Not at all.

When Susan came out humming, looking for all the world like a young girl again, Josie lost her composure.

Self-recrimination was all well and good, and probably deserved. But what she'd done, she'd done unknowingly. Bob should have said something. So she'd more or less thrown herself at him? With his looks and body and charm, it probably happened to him all the time. He could have resisted her, could have been gentleman enough to tell her the truth, to explain that her own sister was interested in him. Susan certainly deserved better treatment than that. And not for a moment did she imagine Bob to be oblivious to Susan's interest. The man wasn't naive, and he had to have firsthand knowledge of female adoration.

As to that, why was he even accepting blind dates? He surely had his pick of women.

She thought about everything now and saw things in a different light. He'd said, several times, that they needed to talk. But she'd kept putting him off. Had he intended to tell her that what they'd shared had been no more than a wild fling for him? Just as she'd cut loose for once, maybe he had, too. Could she really fault him for that, when she knew firsthand how difficult it was always to be circumspect and conservative? Perhaps he'd even planned to explain the truth to her tomorrow. She hoped so, for Susan's sake. With all she knew now, she realized how ideally suited Bob and Susan were for each other.

When the delivery truck pulled up to collect all the flowers, Josie decided it was time to go home. Susan never noticed the extra basket. She merely signed the inventory form, moving in a fog as she made repeated trips to the back room for more chocolate in between singing Bob's praises. Josie gave the deliveryman an extra ten to make certain Bob's basket got delivered right away. She hoped he was still at the office, as Susan assumed, because she wanted him to get the thing today.

Susan stood staring out the front window, a small smile on her face. Josie couldn't help but smile, too. As heartsick and disillusioned as she felt, she was glad for her sister. Susan deserved a little happiness, regardless of the cost. "Hey, sis? Anyone home in there?"

Susan turned to her, one brow raised. "I'm sorry. I was thinking."

"Gee, I wonder about what."

Seeing Susan blush was a novelty. Normally Josie would have teased her endlessly. Today she just didn't have it in her. "Will you call him and thank him for the candy?"

Susan's blush vanished and her brows drew together in that stern look she had. "Of course not. Why don't you just thank him for me when you reset your date?"

"Susan…"

"Now, Josie, you promised you'd give him another chance. Don't back out on me now."

Josie rolled her eyes, trying to cover her discomfort. Susan could be so stubborn once she'd got her mind set. "Just once, why don't you do what *you* want instead of thinking about me?"

Susan looked nonplussed. "Why, because you're my sister, of course. And he'd make you the perfect husband, Josie. I just know it."

Josie quelled the churning in her belly and smiled. "You can't dictate love, Susan. It happens when you least expect it." If her words sounded a little uncertain, a little sad, Susan didn't notice.

"But you haven't even given him a chance!"

Josie closed her eyes, not wanting Susan to see the guilt there. She hated lying to her sister.

Susan huffed. "For the life of me I don't understand your attitude, Josie. He's a terrific man."

"I know. Perfect."

"Well, he is!" Susan crossed her arms over her chest and glared. Josie knew what that meant. "At least go out with him once. Just once. If you're truly not interested, then I'll accept it."

Though she knew it was a mistake, Josie saw no way around it. "And you'll admit that you're the one who's attracted?"

"I didn't say that."

"Susan." There was pure warning in Josie's tone.

Throwing up her arms, Susan conceded. "Oh, all right. If nothing comes of your date, I'll…consider him for myself. But trust me, Josie, you'll adore him. It's just that you don't know what you're missing."

But Josie did know. She only wished she didn't.

"I'M GLAD YOU DECIDED to come in for a few hours."

"A few minutes, not hours." Nick went past Bob, who

was lingering in the lobby of the building that housed their offices. Each of them had his own space, connected by a doorway that almost always remained open. They shared access to the numerous pieces of computer and graphic equipment they used. "Do I look like I'm dressed for the office?" he added.

Bob eyed his tan khaki slacks and polo shirt. "Not particularly, but with you I'm never sure."

Nick thought about being offended, since he always wore a suit to the office, but he didn't bother. At present, he had other things on his mind. "I'm only going to pick up the Ferguson file. I thought I'd look it over tonight and see if I come up with any ideas."

Bob trailed behind him, a fresh cup of coffee in his hand. "We don't have to make a presentation on that job for some time yet."

"I know, but I have the night free." Nick caught Bob's censuring look and shook his head. "Lighten up, Bob. It's Saturday. The work will still be here come Monday."

"Actually I was amazed you have Saturday night free. That's a rare occurrence, isn't it?"

Nick shrugged. He had no intention of explaining to Bob what he wasn't sure he understood himself. Josie hadn't in any way asked him to restrict his dating habits, but he'd done so anyway. And in the back of his mind lurked the worry that she might not be so considerate. He wasn't used to worrying about a woman, and he didn't like it. What pressing business did she have between now and Sunday?

Not that knowing would alter his decision. He didn't want to see anyone except Josie, and besides, after the day's activities, he was too tired to go out, but too restless to sleep. And sitting in his house had about driven him crazy. He kept remembering everything about her—her hot scent, the incredible feel of her skin, the way she moaned so sweetly when he—

He jerked open another drawer and shuffled files around.

He was damn tired of torturing himself with those memories. He needed a distraction in the worst way and the Ferguson account would have to be it.

With his head buried in a filing drawer, he heard a knock and then Bob opened the outer door to speak to someone. Nick twisted to try to see who had entered, but only managed to get a peek of a large basket of flowers and greenery. He blinked, lifted his head and smacked it hard on the open drawer above him. "Damn it!"

"You okay?"

"I'll live." Rubbing the top of his head, he sauntered over to where Bob stood opening a small envelope. "What's this?"

Bob grinned, still holding the card. "I sent Susan some chocolates. I guess she decided to send me flowers."

"Flowers, huh?" He looked at the basket with interest. No woman had ever sent him flowers. He fingered a bright green leaf, intrigued and a tad jealous. "Hey, the plants are alive. What do you know?"

"Umm…" Bob hastily stuck the card back in the envelope. "I think these were meant for you."

"Me?"

"Yeah. The card says, 'Bob,' but Josie sent them. I take it you didn't come clean with her yet?"

Half pleased over the gesture of the plant, and half embarrassed to still be caught in his lie, Nick rolled back on his heels and looked at the ceiling. "I tried. But she didn't want to do any serious talking. The timing wasn't right. We decided we'd clear the air tomorrow afternoon. We're doing lunch and a movie."

"But that's when we play poker. You've never missed a Sunday!"

Nick was well acquainted with his own routine; he didn't need Bob to run it into the ground. "I'll miss it tomorrow."

"But…this is unprecedented! You never change your plans for a woman!"

Nick ground his teeth, frustrated with the truth of that.

And it wasn't even Josie who had asked him to change his plans; he'd done so on his own. But he didn't regret it. And that was the strangest thing of all.

Bob was staring at him, assessing, and Nick forced a shrug, not about to reveal his discomfort. "So tomorrow will be a first."

It took him a second, and then Bob managed to collect himself. He looked away, and mumbled, "Maybe not. Here, you should probably read this."

Nick watched Bob hustle out of the room after thrusting the card at him. He discreetly closed the door behind him. Nick looked at the plant again. A live plant with flowers somehow stuck in it. It was pretty and he felt absurdly touched by the gesture.

He opened the envelope and began to read.

Dear Bob,
Yesterday I wasn't myself. If you ever met the real me, you'd understand what I'm telling you. It wouldn't be right for me to see you ever again. If you truly want a continuing relationship, I suggest you call on Susan.
All my best,
Josie

He read it twice, not quite believing the little fool would actually do such a thing, then he cursed. Storming out of the room, he went after Bob. He found him behind his desk, pretending to look over an ad campaign. "You sent Susan candy today, right?"

"Well..."

"And you had them delivered to her at her shop, am I right?"

"Well..."

"And you put your own damn name on it, instead of leaving it as a secret admirer like I suggested. *Right?*"

"Well..."

"Damn it, Bob, do you know what you've done? Do you know what that plant is? I'll tell you what it is. It's a damn *kiss off* plant. I'm getting dumped because Josie thinks I'm you and she apparently thinks I want Susan!"

Bob shot to his feet. "Well, whose brilliant idea was that? Not mine. I told you to tell her the truth."

"And you promised me you'd give me a little time. If you'd gone with our original plan and played the secret admirer, none of this would have happened."

"I'm no good at that stuff and you know it. I'd have been blushing every time I looked at her. It wouldn't have taken Susan five minutes tops to figure out the candy was from me. Then I'd have looked plain stupid."

"You would have looked like a romantic."

"Which I'm not. And I'd have ended up in the very position you're in right now."

He had a point. Nick supposed every speck of fault could be laid at his own big feet, but that didn't help him to figure out what to do next. A sense of panic began to swell around him. He had to do something. "I should go see her."

"Who, Susan?"

Frustration mounted. "No, not Susan." He ran a hand through his hair, leaving it on end. "That woman hates me, remember? I meant Josie."

"Do you know where she lives?"

"I know which condo complex she's in, but not which condo." He looked at Bob hopefully. "You could get her exact address for me."

"Forget it. Susan already thinks I should be interested in Josie, not her. The woman doesn't understand her own appeal. It took me forever this afternoon to get her to soften up a little, but she's still determined to get me and Josie together, no matter how I try to divert her. If I start asking for Josie's address now, she'll decide her intuition was right, and Susan will never give me the time of day. It'd be like taking three giant steps backward."

God, what a mess. Nick thumped his fist against the desk. "Think about it, Bob. Susan wants you to pursue Josie, but you want Susan. I want Josie, but she thinks I'm you and courting her sister." He groaned, his stomach knotting as he thought of how Josie must feel, how hurt she must be right now. Would she think he'd merely used her last night? Hell, she probably hated him, and he couldn't blame her. He'd been a total ass.

"So how are we going to fix things?"

Nick closed his eyes wearily. "You can't ask Susan for Josie's address because she'll think you're hung up on Josie. I can't very well ask her for it, because odds are she wouldn't give it to me. I suppose I'll just have to go over there and start knocking on doors."

"You're kidding, right?"

Nick glared at him. "No, I'm dead serious. Unless you have a better idea?"

"As a matter of fact, I do. I remember Susan mentioning a woman who heads up the decision committee for the condo. She has a nephew who does the yard work, and she monitors all the problems in the complex. She wanted some advice on inexpensive advertising for a small business she's recently started. She could probably tell you which condo is Josie's."

Nick rubbed his hands together, finally feeling a little of the bizarre panic recede. Things would work out. They had to. No woman had ever thrown him off balance this way, and he wasn't used to it. He didn't know how to react, that's all. He needed just a little more time.

He wanted to make love to her, to touch her. Her effect on him was unique, but considering how explosive they were together, it was understandable. At least to him. Hell, he got hot just thinking about her—yet she'd done the unprecedented and dumped him. "Give me her number."

"I can do better than that." Bob rummaged in his drawer and then withdrew a pink business card. He handed it to

Nick. "That's her address in the complex. From what I understood, she knows Josie pretty well. She can tell you which condo Josie lives in."

Nick snapped the card twice with a finger, then slipped it into his pocket. He felt filled with relief, and iron determination. "If you wouldn't think ill of me, I'd kiss you."

Bob pretended horror and ducked away. But Nick still managed to clap him on the shoulder, nearly knocking him into his desk.

Josie Jackson didn't stand a chance. She might think things were all over—damn her and her ridiculous *Dear John* plant—but she was in for a rude awakening. She'd started this game with her short sexy skirt and taunting smile and unmistakable come-on. She could damn well finish it. But this time they'd play by his rules. No more holding back, and no more being called by another man's name. He'd find out exactly why Josie had showed up in the bar looking like an experienced femme fatale, when in truth she was as innocent as a lamb. He'd find out why she'd chosen him, of all men, to be her first lover. And then he'd take over.

That had been his first mistake, giving up control. He'd let her think she was calling the shots and hadn't been up-front with her. Things had gotten way out of hand. But no more.

He went back to the inner offices, collected his plant with the big bow and colorful flowers and saluted Bob on his way out.

He left the Ferguson file behind.

EVERY NEIGHBOR in the complex had come to stare at him sometime during the day. But he hadn't buckled under, he simply stared back. They had the advantage, though, because most of them, he figured, had to be myopic—being stared at wasn't as personal for them, or as unsettling. That's if they could see him at all. Some of Josie's neighbors wore thick glasses, most of them had watery eyes of a pale shade.

Not a single one of them was under seventy.

At first he'd loitered around Josie's door, waiting, wishing he could peek in through a window, but not willing to risk having the neighbors converge on him in righteous indignation. But she hadn't come home. So he wandered around outside, looking at the neatly kept grounds, the symmetry of each building. He'd drawn too much attention there, so he'd waited for a while in his car. That got too hot, causing his frustration to escalate.

Where the hell was she? Mrs. Wiley, that little old white-haired grandma who wanted to advertise her Golden Goodies home parties for seniors, hadn't minded in the least if he waited. In fact, she'd wanted him to wait with her while she explained her home-sale ventures. He'd made a red-faced escape, unable to discuss with any dignity the prospects of advertising her product. She'd managed to press a colorful catalog on him before he got out, but he hadn't really looked at it yet. He couldn't quite work up the nerve.

Mrs. Wiley had seemed innocent enough, pleasantly plump in a voluptuous sort of way, with neatly styled silver-white hair and a smile that had probably melted many a man in her day. She'd used that damn smile to get him to agree to work on an advertising plan for her. Something simple and cheap, she'd said, and he'd known she was using her age to her advantage, trying to look old and frail. Nick had fallen for the ploy, hook, line and sinker. But how the hell did you advertise seductive novelties for the elderly?

He was sitting on the front stoop, staring out at the sunset and still pondering the issue of Mrs. Wiley's problem, when Josie finally pulled into the parking lot. He almost didn't recognize her at first, not in her small dull-brown car, with her hair pinned up and no makeup. She looked like a teenager, young and perky, not hot and sultry. He gawked, knew he gawked, but couldn't do a damn thing about it. In no way did she resemble the male fantasy that had turned him inside out last night.

He quirked a brow. In many ways, he admitted, she looked even better.

Josie Jackson made one hell of a good-looking frump.

He cleared his throat and stood. She hadn't yet noticed him. Stepping back from her car in her jeans and white sneakers, her arms filled with grocery bags, she looked like a typical homemaker. Not a sex symbol.

His muscles tightened. "Josie."

She stopped, but she couldn't see over the bags. Motionless for several moments, she finally lowered one of the bags enough to glare at him. Her expression didn't bode well. "What are you doing here?"

"Setting things straight."

Her cheeks colored and her beautiful eyes narrowed. "Didn't you get my message?"

His nod was slow and concise. "I got it. But I'm not letting you dump me with a damn plant."

The bags started to slip out of her arms and he made a grab for them. "Here, let me help you. We need to talk."

"There's nothing to talk about."

He took the bags despite her resistance. "Yes, there is. And we might as well do it inside rather than out here entertaining our audience."

Audience referred to three older women hiding behind some bushes and two men who pretended to be chatting with each other, but were keeping a close watch. Josie didn't seem to notice any of them. She looked blank-faced and flustered and hostile. After she closed up her car, she lifted one hand to her hair, but curled it into a fist and let it drop to her side. She seemed equal parts confused, angry and embarrassed.

"Josie?"

Her shoulders stiffened. "You've, um, taken me by surprise."

He grinned. "So I have." His voice dropped to an intimate level. "I missed you, honey. You look wonderful."

She snorted at that and started off for the condo at a brisk marching pace. He kept up, enjoying the sight of her backside in tight jeans, her exposed neck and the few stray curls that bounced with her every step. By the time she reached her door, a spot now very familiar to Nick, she had slowed to a crawl. She stood facing the door, not speaking, not looking at him.

His heart thudded and his determination doubled. "Unlock it, Josie."

Still with her back to him, she muttered, "The thing is, I really don't want you inside."

Brushing his lips against her nape, he felt her shiver. "I like your hair up like this. It's sexy." He kept his tone soft and convincing, reassuring her. "Of course, you could wear a ski mask and I'd think you were sexy."

A choked sound escaped her and she stiffened even more. "You're being ridiculous. I look like a...a..."

"A busy woman? Well, you are. Nothing wrong with that."

Her shoulders stiffened as she drew a deep breath. "I don't want to see you again."

The bottom dropped out of his stomach, but he pressed forward anyway. "I think I can change your mind. Just give me a chance to explain."

"You're not going to go away, are you?"

It was his turn to snort.

"Oh, all right." She jerked out the key and jammed it into the lock. "But don't say I didn't try to discourage you."

He stayed right on her heels in case she tried to slam the door in his face, and almost bumped into her cute little behind as she bent to put her purse on an entry table. He remembered that bottom fondly, petting it, kissing the soft mounds, gripping the silky flesh to hold her close.

He stifled a groan and followed her into the kitchen to put the bags on the counter. Josie stood with her arms crossed, facing him with an admirable show of challenge.

He looked around the condo, then nodded. "Waiting for my reaction, are you?"

She lifted her chin and tightened her mouth.

Her home was interesting. Domestic. Neat and well organized and cute. Everything seemed to be done in miniature. The living room had a love seat and a dainty chair, no sofa. The dinette table was barely big enough for a single plate and there were just two ice-cream parlor chairs, which looked as if they'd collapse under his weight.

The wallpaper design was tiny flowers and all the curtains had starched ruffles. A bright red cookie jar shaped like a giant apple served as a focal point.

"In a way I suppose it suits you."

Josie rolled her eyes. "You don't even know who I am, so how can you possibly make that judgment?"

He stepped close until mere inches separated them. Slowly, with the backs of his fingers, he stroked her abdomen. "I know you. Better than any other man."

Her eyes closed and she trembled. His fingers brushed higher, just under her breast. He was losing his grip, but couldn't stop. "Josie?"

She bit her lips and then caught his hand. "You have to listen to me, Bob. Yesterday was a mistake."

"No."

"Yes, it was." She waved a hand at the kitchen and beyond. "You see all this, and you think I'm as domestic as Susan, as conservative and contented as she. But I'm not content. I wanted—"

She broke off as he tugged her close, ignoring her frantic surprise. He tilted her chin and kissed her hard, without preamble or warning of his intent. When he thrust his tongue inside, he groaned at the same instant she did. Sliding his hands down her back, he cupped that adorable bottom and squeezed gently, lifting her up to her tiptoes and snuggling her close to his growing erection.

"You feel so good, Josie." Before she could object, he kissed her again, more leisurely this time—tasting, exploring, seducing her and himself. When he pulled back, she clung to him. "And you taste even better. Sweet and hot."

Slowly, she opened her eyes, then shook her head as if to clear it. "This will never work."

He saw the pulse racing in her throat. "It's already working."

"No." She tried to pull away, but he held her fast. "I want freedom, Bob. No ties, no commitments. I have no interest in marriage or settling down or starting a family. I—"

"Neither do I."

She frowned and her mouth opened, but he cut her short.

"And I'm not Bob, so please don't call me that again. I hate it."

Her expression froze for a single heartbeat, and then she jerked away. She stepped around the small table, putting it between them and glared at him in horror. "What are you talking about?"

He decided to take a chance on one of the little chairs. Tugging it out, he straddled it and then smiled at her. "I lied. I'm not Bob. I'm his partner, Nick."

She blinked, her lips slightly parted, her face pale.

"Thanks for the plant, by the way, but I refuse to get dumped. It's an experience I hope never to undergo."

"You're not Bob?"

"Naw. Bob is hung up on your sister. That's why *he* visited her this afternoon. I'm his evil partner, the no-talent, no-brain reprobate your sister took such an instant dislike to."

Her mouth fell open, but then instantly snapped shut. "You lied to me deliberately?" Her hands trembled, but it wasn't embarrassment causing the reaction. "All night last night, you let me believe you were a different man!"

"I hadn't intended to." He watched her eyes, fascinated with the way they slanted in anger, how the green seemed to sparkle and snap. Her cheeks were no longer pale, but blooming with outrage, making her freckles more pronounced. Her mouth was pulled into an indignant pout. He wanted to kiss her again; he wanted to devour her.

"Josie, I'd only gone to the bar to break the date for Bob because he wants Susan, not you. But when you showed up, looking so damn hot and sexy, my brain turned to mush and I just went for it. A typical male reaction. I'm sorry. It wasn't my most sterling moment, but it's the truth you threw me for a curve."

She took a menacing step forward. "You lied to me deliberately."

"Uh, I thought we already established that." He eyed her approach, wondering what she would do. "I'd like to get to the part about your little deception."

She came a halt. "My deception?"

"That's right. You led me to believe you were experienced when you were a virgin."

"I did no such thing."

"The way you looked, the way you spoke? No one would have guessed you could be innocent. Then you led me to believe you simply hadn't had the time to indulge your inclinations. You gave me that long story about being too busy studying and setting up your business." He looked around the condo again for good measure. "But it seems to me like you're some sort of Suzy Homemaker. I bet all your towels match and your shoes are lined up neatly in your closet. Am I right?"

The flush had faded from her face. Now she just looked angry. And determined.

Nick settled himself in to learn more about her.

She sent him a wicked smile that made his abdomen tighten in anticipation. "There was no deception, not really. You see, I was busy. Too busy. But I've decided to live on the wild side for a time. I want to be free, to date plenty of men, to expound on the realm of sensuality we touched on last night. Yes, I've led a quiet life, and it suited me for a while, but that's over now. I want fun, with no ties."

He spread his arms, benevolent. "Perfect. My sentiments exactly."

But Josie slowly shook her head, her smile now taunting. "You were just my starting point, so to speak. The tip of the iceberg." She tilted her head back, looking at him down her nose. "I intend to branch out."

He couldn't tell if she was serious or not, or if she only meant to punish him for lying. Women could be damn inventive in their means of torturing a man. They seemed to take great pleasure in it. He'd learned that little truism early on in life.

When she continued to smile, not backing down, he came to his feet and pushed the chair away. He'd intended to take control, and it was past time he got started. "Like hell."

"You have no say over it, *Nick.*"

"Like hell." He sounded like a damn parrot, but nothing more affirmative came to mind. She was mad and making him pay, and doing a damn good job of it. When he thought of another man touching her, a pounding started in the back of his skull, matching the rush of blood through his temples. It filled him with a black rage. Never in his life had he been jealous over a woman. He didn't like the feeling one bit.

Then finally salvation descended on him and he developed his own plan. He stared at her, working through the details in his mind, expounding on his idea. He nodded. "I'll make you a deal."

"What kind of deal?" She leaned against the counter, the picture of nonchalance—until he started toward her.

Holding her gaze, he stepped close until no space separated them. He could feel her every breath and the heat of her. She might be angry with him, but her body liked him just fine.

With the tips of his fingers he stroked her face, watching her, waiting for her to bolt. But she didn't even blink. His lips skimmed her forehead, then her jaw. His words were a mere whisper in her ear. "This is the deal, Josie. Are you listening?"

She gave a small nod.

"I'll show you more excitement, more sensual fun than your sweet little body can handle, honey. Every thrill there is I'll give to you until you cry mercy."

His fingers slid over her buttocks, then between, stroking and seeking before he nudged her legs apart and nestled himself between them. He levered his pelvis in, pinning her, pushing his erection against her soft belly in a tantalizing rhythm that made heat pulse beneath his skin and his muscles constrict. "I can do it, Josie. You already know that. I can show you things you haven't even imagined yet, things we both know you'll love. I can make you beg, and enjoy doing it.

"But it has to be exclusive. Just me. For as long as we're involved, for as long as we're both interested, there's no other men. You want something, you want to experiment or play, you come to me."

He held his breath, waiting, his body taut with lust, his mind swirling with a strange need he refused to contemplate. He didn't share, plain and simple.

She touched his chest, then her hands crept around his neck. With a small moan, she said, "I think we have a deal."

Chapter Six

WITHOUT EFFORT, Nick lifted her to the top of the counter. Josie felt his fingers on the hem of her T-shirt, tugging it upward, and she shivered. This was insane, outrageous, but she didn't stop him, didn't change her mind.

"Nick?"

"Finally." A rough groan escaped him and he squeezed her tight. "You don't how bad I hated being called another man's name." His mouth closed over her nipple through her bra and she dropped her head back, gasping. The gentle pull of his mouth could be felt everywhere, but especially low in her belly. When he pushed her bra aside, she knew she had to stop him before she was beyond the point of caring.

Panting, she managed to say, "I have a stipulation."

He surprised her by saying, "All right." Then he added, "But tell me quick. I'm dying here."

He lifted his head to look at her and she saw that the tops of his cheekbones were darkly flushed, his eyes slumberous but bright with heat. He looked so incredibly sexy, she almost forgot what she wanted to say. But it was important. He had lied to her and made a fool of her. When she thought of how she'd gone on and on about his partner Nick, she wanted to crawl away into a dark hole. And he'd let her discuss him as if he hadn't been sitting right beside her. He'd *let* her make a fool of herself.

She'd tried bluffing her way out of the embarrassment by claiming a determination to experiment, to experience life—and men—to the fullest. Only, he'd called her on it and made a counteroffer she couldn't possibly refuse. She knew how easily he could fulfill his end of the bargain, and knowing made her want him all the more. When he left, it would hurt; she didn't fool herself about that. But now, for at least a little while, she could have everything she'd ever dreamed of—all the excitement and whirling thrills. If she didn't grab this opportunity for herself, she'd regret it for the rest of her life.

But if she was going to play his game, then she had to have control, to make certain he would never again be in a position to deceive her. She'd take what he freely offered—but on her terms, not his.

Nick toyed with the snap on her jeans. "Is this your idea of foreplay, honey? Making me wait until I lose my mind? Believe me, with the way I feel right now, the wait won't be too long. After what I've been through today, insanity is just around the bend."

His teasing words brought her out of her stupor. "I have to be in charge."

He lifted one dark brow and his fingers stilled. "In charge of what?"

What kind of question was that? She tried to keep her chin raised, to maintain eye contact, but his slow grin did much to shake her resolve. "Things. What we're doing."

"So then this—" he dragged his knuckles from the snap of her jeans, along the fly and beyond until finally he cupped her boldly with his palm "—is what you would be in charge of? You want to control our relationship, what we do and don't do, where we do it...how we do it?"

She gulped, words escaping her. The man was every bit the scoundrel her sister accused him of being. Too blatant, too outrageous, too incredibly sure of himself and of his effect on her, probably on all women. She could feel his palm, so hot and firm against her, not moving, just holding her and making her nerve endings tingle in anticipation. And that tingling had become concentrated in one ultrasensitive spot.

"No? Did I misunderstand?" His gaze searched her face and she could see the humor in his dark eyes, the slight tilt of his sensual mouth. With his free hand, he took hers and kissed her fingers—then pressed her hand against his erection. He no longer smiled, and his expression seemed entirely too intent. "You want to control me like this, Josie?"

He felt huge and hard and alive. Instinctively she curled her fingers around him through the soft material of his khaki slacks.

"Women have been trying to control men since the beginning of time. This is the most tried and true method."

Her fingers tightened in reaction to his harsh words. She felt the lurch, the straining of his penis into her palm, and heat pounded beneath her skin, curled and uncurled until she felt wound too tight, ready to explode.

In a voice low and gravelly, he asked, "Is that what you want, sweetheart?" His breath came fast and low. "Because in this instance, I have no objections. Just lead the way."

Frozen, Josie could do no more than stare down at her hand where she held him. She licked her lips, trying to think of what to do, trying to remember her original intent in this awkward game.

"Josie?"

"I..." She shook her head, then carefully, slowly stroked him. His eyes closed as he groaned his encouragement. "I concede to your experience."

The sound he made was half laugh, half moan.

"But I want to do everything there is to do."

"Damn." His fingers flexed, teasing her. "I want that, too. Sounds to me like we're in agreement."

She shook her head. "You called what we have a...a relationship. But that's not what I'd consider it."

His answering gaze was frighteningly direct. "No?"

She looked away. "I'd call it a...a fling. With no strings

attached." When he got tired of her and walked away, she wanted him to know it was with her blessing. She was out of her league with Nick, coasting on dangerous ground. It was too tempting not to play, but she was too prudent not to take precautions.

She drew an unsteady breath. "I want—need—to be free to come and go as I please. No ties at all." He was the only person she'd ever felt tempted to do this with, but the same wasn't true of him. He'd been with many women, and he'd be with many more. She'd be a fool to expect anything else. "I can't agree to this exclusive stuff," she said. "I need to know you won't object if I decide to explore...elsewhere."

"Oh, but I do object. In fact, I refuse." His mouth smothered any comeback she might have made, not that she could think of any. The nature of his seduction suddenly became much more determined, almost ruthless. He lifted her off the counter and skimmed her shirt over her head.

"Nick..."

"I like hearing you say my name. Especially the way you say it." Her bra straps slipped down her arms when he unhooked it, then clasped her nipple with his hot and hungry mouth, sucking hard.

Her knees locked and her entire body jerked in reaction. *"Nick..."*

He switched to the other breast while undoing her jeans, and he hurriedly pushed them down to her knees. "Tell me you want me, Josie."

She made a sound of agreement, coherent words beyond her.

He dropped to one knee and kissed her through her panties—small, nipping kisses that had her gasping. Her legs went taut to support her, her fingers tangled in his dark silky hair. With a growl, he pulled her panties down and spread her with his thumbs, then treated her to the same delicious sucking he'd used on her nipple, only gentler, and with greater effect.

It was too much, but not quite enough, and she sobbed,

pressing closer, her eyes squeezed shut. His tongue rasped and she arched her body, tight and still, then suddenly climaxed with blinding force when he slid one long finger deep inside her.

The sharp edge of the counter dug into her back as she started to slide down to the floor. She needed to sit, to lie down; her limbs trembled, her vision was still fuzzy. Nick caught her against him and pressed a damp kiss to her temple. "Damn, that was good, Josie." His voice shook, low and sexy. "So damn good. For a virgin, you never cease to amaze me."

"I'm not a virgin anymore." The words sighed out of her, laced with her contentment.

His chuckle vibrated against her skin. "Ex-virgin, then."

Limp, she let him hold her for a few seconds, until he gently turned her to face the counter. She didn't understand what he was doing. Looking at him over her shoulder, she saw him smile. He took her hands and planted them wide on the countertop.

"Open your legs for me, Josie. As wide as your pants will allow."

The rush of heat to her face almost made her dizzy. He was looking at her behind, his hands touching, exploring, exposing, urging her legs even wider. She struggled with her embarrassment and the restriction of her jeans.

He made an approving sound. "That's nice. Now don't move." After laying his wallet out, he unsnapped his jeans and shoved them down his hips. Josie stared at his erection, her pulse pounding. "You've seen me before, honey. But I don't mind you looking. In fact, I like it."

He clasped her hips and brushed the tip of his penis against her buttocks, dipping along her cleft. He held her tight and pressed his cheek against her shoulder. "I like it a lot. Too damn much."

With a groan, he pulled a condom out of his wallet and slipped it on. Fascinated, Josie concentrated on holding herself upright, despite the shaking in her knees, and watched him closely so she didn't miss a thing.

But with his first, solid thrust into her body, she forgot about watching and closed her eyes against the too-intense pleasure of it.

"Ah. So wet and hot. You do want me, don't you, sweetheart? *Just me.*"

She rested her cheek on the cool countertop and curled her fingers over the edge, steadying herself. Nick's hand slid beneath her, then smoothed over her belly before dipping between her thighs.

"No…" She gasped, the pleasure too sharp after her recent orgasm, but he wouldn't relent. He continued to touch her in delicate little brushes, taunting her, forcing her to accept the acute sensations until her hips began to move with him.

He groaned with pleasure. "That's it. Relax, Josie. Trust me." He moved with purpose now in smooth determined strokes that rocked her body to a tantalizing rhythm. His forearm protected her hip bones from hard contact with the counter while his fingertips continued to drive her closer to the edge. Suddenly he stilled, his body rock hard, his breathing suspended. Josie could feel the heat pouring off him, the expectation of release.

He wrapped around her, his chest to her back and he hugged her tight. His heart pounded frantically and she felt it inside herself, reverberating with her own wild heartbeat. "Josie," he said on a whispered groan. And she knew he was coming, his thrusts more sporadic, deeper, and incredibly, she came with him, crying out her surprise.

Long minutes passed and neither of them moved. Josie was content. His body, his indescribable scent, surrounded her in gentle waves of pleasure. She could feel the calming of his heartbeat, his gentle, uneven breaths against her skin.

"Woman, you're something else."

She wondered how he could talk, even though his words had sounded weak and breathless. She relished his weight on her body, the soft kisses he pressed to her shoulders and nape and ear. He made a soft sound and said, "I could stay like this forever."

Mustering her strength, she managed to whisper, "That's because you're not the one being squashed into the cold counter."

He chuckled as he straightened and carefully stepped away. "Hey, you were the one in charge. You should have said something if you didn't like it."

Her sigh sounded entirely too much like satisfaction. "I liked it."

"I know."

She smiled at his teasing and forced herself to stand. "This is a downright ignominious position to find myself in."

She heard him zipping his pants, but couldn't quite find the courage to face him. Her fingers shook as she struggled with her panties, which seemed to be twisted around her knees.

"I think you look damn cute. And enticing." He patted her bare bottom with his large hand, then assisted her in straightening her clothes. "Are you okay?"

That brought her gaze to his face. "I'm...fine." She could feel the hot blush creeping up to her hairline. After all, she was still bare-breasted, and her hair was more down than up. She started to cross her arms over her chest, but hesitated when he covered them himself with his hot palms.

"I wish I had planned this better. But I only had the one condom with me."

"Oh." Her blushing face seemed to pulse, making her very aware of how obvious her embarrassment must be. He was so cavalier about it all, like making love in the kitchen was something he'd done dozens of times. And maybe it was, she admitted to herself, not liking the idea one bit.

Nick grinned, enjoying himself at her expense. "Of course, I could give you more pleasure, if that's what you want. I'm stoic and brave and all those other manly things. And we did have an agreement. I'll sacrifice my needs for yours if you're still feeling greedy. If you're in the mood for a little more *fun*."

She didn't quite know how to deal with him. He was all the things Susan claimed—arrogant and cocky, used to female adoration. She pulled away and slipped into her bra and T-shirt, then turned to the sink. As she ran water into the coffeepot, she could feel his gaze on her back, moving over her like a warm touch.

She drew a steadying breath and glanced back at him. "I think I can manage to be as stoic as you. But since you're here, we might as well get a few things straight."

His smile disappeared. "What things?"

"Our agreement, of course."

Disbelief spread over his face. "Little witch."

She ignored his muttered insult and measured out the coffee grains. Mustering her courage, she blurted, "Did you laugh at me after we made love on the boat?"

"As I remember, I was too busy trying to devise ways to keep from tripping myself up to find any humor in the situation."

Josie considered that. "You know, now that I think about it, a lot of things make sense. The way you kept insisting I not call you by name, your hesitance to take me to your house. Your surprise that I was willing to go with you at all."

"I thought you'd back down. Bob had repeated Susan's description of you—and you didn't look a damn thing like what I expected. It's for certain you didn't act the way I thought you would."

Knowing Susan, it wasn't difficult to imagine the picture she'd painted. "I thought you would be the way my sister described Bob. I expected you to run in the opposite direction when you saw what a wild woman I was."

He came to stand directly in front of her, and his large hot hand settled on her hip, his long fingers spread to caress her bottom. "A million ideas went through my mind when I first saw you, and running wasn't one of them." He leaned down and kissed her, gently, teasing. "Are we done talking now? I can think of better things we could be doing."

She faltered at his direct manner and provocative touch, but had the remaining wits to mention an irrefutable fact. "You said you were out of condoms."

He spoke in a low rumble against her lips. "I also said there were other things we could do, other ways for me to pleasure you without needing protection." His eyes met hers, bright and hot. "Right now, I'm more than willing to show you all of them. Tasting you, touching you, is incredibly sweet. Giving you pleasure gives me pleasure. And I love the way you moan, the way your belly tightens and your nipples—"

A soft moan escaped before she managed to turn her face away. "Nick."

With a huge, regretful sigh, he looped his arms around her and held her loosely. "All right, what were you saying?"

She gave him a disgruntled frown. "I don't remember."

"Oh, yeah. You thought I was Bob. And he probably would have been horrified to see you. Horrified and frightened half to death."

"That's what I figured."

"He's hung up on your sister, you know."

Having Nick so close made it difficult to carry on the casual conversation. But he seemed to have no problem with it, so she forged ahead; they really did need to get things straightened out. "He's the one who sent Susan the chocolates?"

"Yup."

"And he's probably the one who told her he didn't approve of my job."

"That'd be Bob. But I doubt he really cares one way or the other what you do. He's just willing to say anything to agree with Susan."

"Susan likes him, too. She was so pleased with his gift. When it arrived, she was all but jumping up and down."

Nick touched her hair, winding one long curl around his finger. "And what did you do?"

She wasn't about to tell him how hurt and betrayed she'd felt. That wouldn't have been in keeping with her new image. "I wasn't sure what to do, except that I knew I couldn't see you again."

"Hmm." He kissed her quickly and stepped away. "Finish the coffee and let's go sit in the other room. I don't trust these tiny kitchen chairs you have. I'm afraid they might collapse under me."

Josie eyed the delicate chairs and silently agreed.

It took an entire pot of coffee and a lot of explaining before they sorted out the whole confusing mess. By the end of the explanations, Nick had Josie mostly in his lap on the short love seat and he'd removed the pins from her hair so that he could play with it. In one way or another, he touched her constantly, his hands busy, his mouth hungry.

"I want to see you tomorrow, Josie. Will you go to the movies with me?"

She shook her head. As soon as she'd left Susan's shop, she'd accepted an invitation from one of her clients. She could have cancelled if she'd wanted to, but with everything she'd just learned, including his deception and her volatile reaction to him, she didn't trust herself to be with him again so soon. He was playing games while she was falling hard. She needed time to think, to regroup. "I already made other plans, Nick."

Through narrowed eyes, he studied her face a long moment, his gaze probing, then looked down at her clasped hands. "What about Monday?"

She shrugged helplessly. "I can't. Mondays are late nights for me."

He seemed disgruntled by her answer. Josie had the feeling few women ever turned him down. She almost relented; seeing the disappointment in his sensual gaze made her feel the same. But she had a responsibility to her patients, and as tempting as he was, her responsibilities took precedence over her newfound pleasure.

"How late?"

"It depends on who needs what done. But I can't rush my visits. For many of my clients, I'm the only company they get on a regular basis."

He sighed, obviously frustrated but willing to concede. He cupped her cheek and stared down at her. "You're pretty incredible. Do you know that?"

"It's not so much. I enjoy their company, and they enjoy mine."

"Does it involve much traveling?"

"Some. A lot of the people I work with now or worked with in the past, live in this complex, which is one reason I bought here. It's easier to keep an eye on things."

"You know, I did wonder about that. I had all these old folks staring me down, looking at me like I was an interloper. I didn't understand it at first."

"Young people in the complex are always a curiosity. I'm surprised Mrs. Wiley didn't come out and question you."

"She didn't need to. I went to her to find out which condo you lived in." He pulled the rolled catalog from his back pocket. "She gave me this and I promised to try to come up with some kind of inexpensive advertising promotion for her."

Josie stared down blankly at the Golden Goodies catalog, which had fallen open to show pictures of various-sized candles and love-inspired board games. She couldn't quite manage to pull her fascinated gaze away, even though she'd seen the thing dozens of times. The difference now, of course, was that she wondered if Nick would enjoy playing any of the inventive games, winning prizes that varied from kisses to "winner's choice." She had a feeling she knew what his choice would be.

Josie cleared her throat. "A supplier gives her the catalogs and fills the orders, then the selling is up to her. And she's pretty good at it. But I suppose she does need a wider audience than the complex allows."

Nick turned the page, perusing the items for sale. He

looked surprised. "Why, that old fraud. This stuff isn't X-rated. The way she carried on, I thought she was selling something really hot."

Tilting her head, Josie asked, "Like what?"

He opened his mouth, then faltered. "Never mind."

She smiled. "For most older folks, scented lotions and feather boas are pretty risqué. They love Mrs. Wiley's parties. It makes them feel young again, and daring."

"Have you ever been to one?"

Without looking at him, Josie flipped to another page, studying the variety of handheld fans and flavored lipsticks. "Once or twice." She cleared her throat. "There was a party here the night we met. I think I mentioned it—remember? That was one of Mrs. Wiley's."

"Ah. So that's the reason you didn't want to come back here."

Josie didn't correct him. But the truth was, she hadn't wanted to return because she hadn't wanted to see his disappointment when he realized what a domestic homebody she really was. She'd talked her way around that, but the risk was still there, because she knew from Susan's dire predictions that no man would tolerate her demanding schedule for long—certainly not a man used to female adoration, like Nick. Hopefully, before he grew tired of her harried schedule, she'd be able to glut herself on his unique charms and be sated. For a while.

Nick brought her out of her reverie with a gentle nudge. "Have you ever bought anything from her?"

"A few things."

His eyes glittered at her. "Show me."

"No."

He laughed at her cowardice. "Before we're through, I'll get you over your shyness." His taunting voice was low and sensual, and then he kissed her deeply.

Before we're through… Josie wondered how much or how little time she'd actually have with Nick. When he lifted his mouth from hers, it took her several moments to get her eyes to open. When she finally succeeded, he smiled.

"Sometime, if it's okay, I'd like to go with you to visit your friends."

That took her by surprise. In a way, his interest pleased her, but it wouldn't be a good idea to introduce him to too many people. The more he invaded her life, the harder it would be when he left, which would be sooner than later. Sounding as noncommittal as possible, she murmured, "We'll see."

He nodded. "Good. Now what about the rest of the week? When will you be free?"

"What do you have in mind?"

"We could go back to the boat, and this time I promise to show you the river at night. It's beautiful to look at all the lights on the water, to smell the moisture in the air and hear the sounds." He put his mouth to her ear and spoke in a rough whisper. "We could make love on the deck, Josie, under the stars. Mist rises off the river and everything gets covered in dew. Your skin would be slippery and..."

She shivered before she could stop herself, then remembered how he'd told her his parents were dead. Annoyance came back, but not quite as strong this time. Not with him so close. "Is it your boat?"

"I'm making love to you and you want to know who the damn boat belongs to?"

His feigned affront didn't deter her. "I'm just trying to figure out what's true and what you made up."

With an expression that showed his annoyance, Nick gave the shortest possible explanation. "It still legally belongs to my father. But when my parents divorced, it more or less became mine to use."

The sarcasm couldn't be missed, and Josie felt stung. Nick didn't want her to delve into his past, into his personal life. Their time together would center only on the physical. It was what she'd claimed to want, but now she felt uncomfortable.

She started to rise, but before she could move an inch, Nick's arms tightened around her.

"Damn it, Josie, do we really need to discuss this?"

She blinked, surprised by his outburst. "Of course not. I didn't mean to pry."

He reached for her hand and held it. "You're not prying. It's just…Your parents died when you were fifteen, and mine divorced. The effects were damn similar. They fought for years over everything material, and eventually, the boat was bestowed on me for lack of a better solution. Mother didn't want my father to have it, because then he might have shared it with Myra, the woman he married three months after the divorce became final. And my father didn't want my mother to have it because he was still too angry over her foisting me off on him."

"What…what do you mean?"

Nick sighed, then leaned his head back, his eyes closed. Josie realized he was shutting her out to some extent, but still he answered her question. "My mother thought it would be a cute trick to saddle my dad with me while he was trying to start a new life with his new wife. He saw through her, knew what she was doing, and pretty much resented us both. He tried to send me home, but Mom wouldn't let him."

Josie stared, speechless. She couldn't imagine him being treated like an unwelcome intruder by the very people who should have loved him most. For her, it had been just the opposite, and she suddenly wanted to tell Susan again how much she appreciated all she'd done. Careful to hide her sympathy, she asked, "That must have been pretty rough."

He shrugged, still not looking at her. "Naw. The only really tough part was putting up with Myra. For the most part, my mom and dad ignored me once everything was settled. But for some ridiculous reason, Myra saw me as competition. And she hated everything about me. She tried to change my friends, my clothes, even the school I attended. And she tried to make certain I stayed too busy to visit my grandfather."

"Why? What did it matter to her?"

"My grandfather had no use for her. And it bugged her. I used to spend two weeks every summer with him. But after Myra married my father, she convinced Dad that I needed some added responsibility and insisted I take on a summer job. It wasn't that I minded working, only that I missed Granddad."

"She sounds like a bitch."

He laughed with real humor, then opened his eyes and smiled down at her. "Myra wasn't unique. I haven't met a woman yet who didn't think she could improve me in one way or another."

Josie stiffened. "I like you just the way you are."

He didn't look as though he believed her. "I fought with Myra a lot, and likely made her more miserable than she made me. Graduation didn't come quick enough to suit either of us. The summer before my first year of college I moved out on my own. That's when I met Bob and we roomed together to share expenses. He got a job as an assistant to an accountant, and I got a job with the college newspaper. I did the layout on all the ads." He flashed her a grin, his pensive mood lifting. "And as your sister can attest, I'm damn good at what I do now."

It took her a moment, and then the words sank in. "Susan said Bob was the talented one. That he's solely responsible for making your business so successful."

Rather than looking insulted, he grinned. "Yeah, well, Susan refused to work with me. If she'd known I was handling her file, she wouldn't have given us her business."

Josie gasped. "You've lied to her, too! Oh my God, when Susan finds out you did her ads, she'll be furious. We'll all be running for cover."

Nick winced, though his grin was still in place. "Is it truly necessary to tell her, do you think? I mean, right now, she likes Bob, and he likes her. I wouldn't want to cause them any trouble."

Josie gave him a knowing look. "You just don't want Susan biting your face off. You're not fooling me."

"Your sister is enough to instill fright in even the stoutest of men." He kissed her, but it was a tickling kiss because he couldn't stop smiling. "She already despises me, Josie. If she knows I talked Bob into tricking her, she'll run me out of town. Is that what you want?"

As he asked it, his large hot hand smoothed over her abdomen and Josie inhaled. "No."

"Good. Then let's make a pact. We'll do all we can to get your sister and Bob together—before we drop any truthful bombshells on her. Okay?"

Since he was still stroking her, she nodded her agreement. Besides, if Susan knew the full truth, she would do her best to talk Josie out of spending time with Nick. That decided her more than anything else. "I don't suppose it will hurt to wait. As long as you eventually come clean. But Nick, you have to know, when she finds out Bob isn't all that's perfection, she won't be happy."

"Why don't we let Bob worry about that? Besides, he may not be perfect, but he is perfect for her. At least that's what he keeps assuring me."

"I hope he's right, because I don't want to see her hurt."

"Everything will work out as it should in the end." He smoothed the hair from her forehead, kissed her brow. "Now tell me about yourself."

"What do you want to know?"

"Everything. Yesterday we didn't exactly get around to talking all that much. I think we should get to know each other a little better, don't you?"

Josie blushed. Yesterday, words hadn't seemed all that important. "Do you really think it's necessary? I mean, for the purposes of a fling, do we need to know personal stuff?"

His expression darkened. "I don't like that word—fling." She started to reply to that, but he raised a hand. "Come on, Josie. Fair's fair. I confided in you."

She supposed he was right. But her story differed so much from his, she hesitated to tell it. She started slowly, trying to keep the focus on Susan's generosity, rather than her own grief. "After my parents died, Susan wouldn't even consider me getting a job. She sold our house so we'd have enough money for me to continue my education. It was a big, old-fashioned place with pillars in the front. It used to be our great-aunt's before she died and left it to my mother when we were just kids. We both still miss it, though Susan won't admit it. She doesn't want me to know how much it meant to her, or how hard it was for her to let it go."

With a thoughtful expression, Nick nodded his approval. "Susan did what any good big sister would do."

And Josie thought, *I had Susan. But who did you have?* Rather than say it, she touched his cheek and smiled. "Do you ever see your family now?"

He pretended a preoccupation with her fingertips, kissing each one. "Not often. Mother is always busy, which is a blessing since she's not an easy person to be around. And Myra still despises me, which makes it difficult for my father and me to get together." He sucked the tip of one finger between his teeth.

Feeling her stomach flutter, Josie wondered if she'd ever get used to all the erotic touching and kissing. She hoped not. "I imagine you must resent her a lot."

"Not really. If it hadn't been for Myra, I might never have hooked up with Bob, and he's great as both a friend and a partner. He's the one who suggested we go into business together. In fact, he's the one who got things started."

He deliberately lightened the mood, so Josie did the same. "Ah. So Bob really is the brains of the operation?"

He bit the tip of her finger, making her jump and pull away. Josie glared at him.

He grinned. "Sorry. But I hear enough of that derision from your sister."

"No doubt you'll hear a lot more of it from her when she finds out we're seeing each other."

He made a sour face. "Couldn't we skip telling her that, too?"

"You must not know my sister very well if you think I could keep it from her. She's like a mother hen, always checking up on me."

"Well, as I said, I'm stoic. I can put up with anything if the end result is rewarding enough." His thumb smoothed over her lips. "And you're definitely enough. Now, can you find any spare time this week to go to the boat with me?"

When Josie thought of all the women he must have taken there over the years, she couldn't quite stifle a touch of jealousy. She looked away, wondering how many women had observed the stars from the deck, the moisture rising from the water.

"Josie." As if he'd read her thoughts, he hugged her close again. His hand cuddled her breast possessively, and rather than meet her curious gaze, he stayed focused on the movement of his fingers over her body.

"Do you remember me telling you on the boat that I never take women there?"

"You took me there."

"And you're the only one. That wasn't a lie."

She wanted to believe him, but it seemed so unlikely.

Before she could decide what to say, Nick shook his head and continued. "I'm not claiming to have been a monk—far from it. I've always used the boat when I wanted to be alone. There's something peaceful about water, something calming, and I never wanted to share that with anyone, especially not a woman. With all the fighting that damn boat caused between my parents, it has a lot of memories attached to it, and most of them aren't very pleasant. I've never found it particularly conducive to romance." He made the admission reluctantly, his voice sounding a bit strained. He raised his eyes until he could look at her and that look started her heart racing. "Until I met you. Now I don't think I'll be able to see it any other way."

Emotion swelled, threatening to burst. Susan was wrong. Nick wasn't a self-centered womanizer. He wasn't a man without a care who would tromp on people's feelings. The special fondness he felt for his grandfather was easy to hear when Nick spoke of him. And his dedication to Bob went above and beyond the call of duty to a partner, to the point of silently accepting Susan's contempt. She'd accused him of having no talent; he *was* the talent. Nick had even agreed to work out an ad campaign for Mrs. Wiley, despite his reservations about her business. Though his adolescence had obviously been bereft of love and guidance, he was still a kind and generous man.

It would be all too easy to care about him.

"What are you thinking?" Nick smoothed the frown from her forehead.

"I'm thinking that you're a most remarkable man, Nick Harris."

He made a scoffing sound and started to kiss her, but Josie was familiar with that tactic now. Whenever he wanted to avoid a subject, he distracted her physically.

Teasing, he said, "I'm a scoundrel and a man of few principles. Just ask your sister."

"But Susan doesn't really know you, does she?" His gaze swept up to lock with hers. Josie lifted a hand to sift through his hair. "She's given me all these dire predictions, but I don't think you're nearly as reckless and wild as she'd like to think."

His expression froze for a heartbeat, then hardened. Before Josie could decipher his mood, he had her T-shirt pulled over her head and caught at her elbows, pinning her arms together, leaving her helpless. He studied her breasts with heated, deliberate intensity. When he spoke, his words were barely above a whisper.

"Don't, Josie. Don't think that because I had a few family problems, I'm this overly sensitive guy waiting to be saved by the right woman." His hand flattened on her belly and she trembled. "I want all the same things you want, honey. Fun, freedom, a little excitement. With no ties and no commitments. It'll be the perfect relationship between us, I promise you that. You won't be disappointed."

She wanted to yell that she was already disappointed. No, she hadn't ever considered a lasting relationship. But then, she hadn't met Nick. All by himself he was more excitement than most women could handle. And despite what she'd claimed, she wanted more out of life than a few thrills. So much more. But Nick had read her thoughts, and corrected them without hesitation. She'd dug a hole for herself with her own lies and deceptions, and she wasn't quite sure how to get out of it. She couldn't press him without chasing him away—and that was the very last thing she wanted to do.

Nick bent, treating one sensitive nipple to the hot, moist pressure of his mouth, and she decided any decisions could wait until later. He seemed determined now to show her all the ways he could enjoy her without the need for precautions, and at the moment, she didn't have the will to tell him no.

Minutes later, she didn't have the strength, either.

NICK WHISTLED as he entered the offices. He hadn't felt this good in a long time, though he wasn't sure exactly why he felt so content, and wasn't inclined to worry about it. Right now, he had better things to occupy his mind—like the coming night and the fact that he'd be alone with Josie again. His entire body tightened in anticipation of what he'd do with her and her sensual acceptance of him. It had been too long.

She hadn't been able to see him Tuesday, as he'd expected, because that, too, was a late night for her, and the needs of her patients came first—a fact that nettled since he wasn't used to playing second fiddle. So even though he'd had other plans for the night, he'd canceled them. Again. Josie didn't know he'd changed his plans for her, and he didn't intend to tell her. She might get it into her head that she could call all the shots, and he liked things better just the way they were.

Josie wanted to use him for sex, wanted him to be a sizzling male fantasy come to life, and if that wasn't worth a little compromise, he didn't know what was. It sure beat the hell out of anything he could think of.

Besides, she had given him a request, and it was to assist her in exploring the depths of herself as a woman, not to skim the surface with mere quickies. He could be patient until her time was freed up. He wanted to sleep with her again, to hold her small soft body close to his all night, to wake her up with warm wet kisses and the gentle slide of his body into hers. He shuddered at his own mental image.

As he entered the building, the sound of arguing interrupted his erotic thoughts. It was coming from Bob's office, and he started in that direction but drew up short in the doorway when he recognized Susan's virulent tones.

Since he enjoyed pricking her temper, and had from the moment he met her, he asked pleasantly, "Am I interrupting?"

Two pairs of eyes swung in his direction. "Nick," was said in relief at the same time "You!" was muttered with huge accusation.

Ignoring Bob for the moment, he directed his attention to Susan. "Miss Jackson. How are you today?"

"How am I?" She advanced on him and Bob rushed around his desk to keep pace with her. Nick had the feeling Bob intended to protect him. The idea almost made him smile.

"I was fine, that is until Bob confessed the rotten trick you played on my sister."

Turning his consideration to Bob, who looked slightly ill, Nick asked, "Had a baring of the soul, did you?"

"Actually," Susan said, staring up at him with a frown, "he did his best to cover for you after I forced him to confirm that you're seeing Josie. He's been explaining to me that you're a *reformed* womanizer, that you truly care for my sister. Not that I'm believing it." She pointed a rigid finger at his chest. "I know your kind. You're still a die-hard bachelor just out for some fun, and that's not what Josie needs in her life right now."

"You make *fun* sound like a dirty word," Nick muttered, but there was no heat in his comment. He was too distracted for heat. Did Bob really see him as *reformed?* The idea was totally repellent. For most of his life, certainly since Bob had known him, he'd avoided any attempts at serious relationships. Not because he was still troubled over his parents' divorce, or his father's remarriage. And not because his psyche had been damaged by his mother's rejection. Mostly he'd avoided attachments because he hadn't met a woman yet who didn't want to change everything about him. They'd profess unconditional love, then go about trying to get him to alter his life. His stepmother had been the queen of control, but at least she hadn't ever tried to hide her inclinations behind false caring.

No, he'd had enough of controlling females, and his life was as he wanted it to be. He didn't intend to change it for anyone. But he did want Josie, and he'd have her—on his terms, not Susan's.

Not about to explain himself to the sister, he halfheartedly addressed Susan's sputtering outrage, going on the offense. "You don't really understand Josie at all, do you?"

"She's my sister!"

"Yeah, but you would have hooked her up with Bob." He warmed to the subject, seeing Susan's face go red while Bob blustered in the background. He'd been coaching Bob for the better part of a week, getting him to send cards, to make phone calls late at night. To whisper the little romantic things women liked to hear. Susan appeared to be melting faster than an iceberg in the tropics. Though she hadn't as yet admitted it. According to Bob, all her considerable focus was still aimed at getting Josie *settled*. Damn irritating female. Josie didn't want to settle, and that suited Nick to perfection.

He grinned, feeling smug over the way both Susan and Bob

glanced at each other. "I'm sure you realize now what a mistake that might have been, for both Josie and Bob."

Susan thrust her chin into the air. "So she and Bob wouldn't have worked out. That doesn't mean I want her seeing you."

Softly he said, "But that's what Josie wants."

Susan bristled. "Josie is just going through a phase."

Damn right, he thought. A sensational stage of discovering her own sexuality, and he'd been lucky enough to be there when she'd decided to expand her horizons. He kept his expression serious. "She's discussed that with me, Miss Jackson. Josie and I understand each other, so you have no reason to worry." Nick not only understood, he encouraged her.

Agitated, Susan paced away. When she faced Nick again, her look was more serious than aggressive. "You think you understand, but you can't know what Josie's been through. When our parents died, everything changed. We lost our house, our car. There was never enough money for her to do the things most girls her age were doing. She didn't shop with her friends for trendy clothes, attend dances or school parties or date. At first she just became withdrawn. It scared me something fierce. But then she started college, and she put everything she had not just into succeeding but excelling. She's worked very hard at shutting out life, and now that she's ready to live again, she deserves the best."

"And to you, that means someone other than me?"

"Josie needs someone sensitive, someone who's stable and reliable."

His chest felt tight and his temples pounded. Susan was determined to replace him, but he wouldn't let her. For now, Josie wanted him, and that was all that mattered. "I won't hurt her. I promise."

"Coming from you, I am not reassured!"

Surely he wasn't *bad* for Josie, he thought with a frown. He was an experienced man, capable of giving her everything she wanted, and right now that meant freedom and excitement and fun, not love everlasting. He wasn't prudish and he wasn't selfish; he hadn't lied when he said he enjoyed giving her pleasure.

Susan assumed she knew what Josie needed, but Josie claimed the opposite. She'd made it clear she didn't want attachments, so he'd assured her there would be none. That had been her stipulation, but he'd gone along with the idea, even emphasized it, to keep her from backing out. Josie wanted a walk on the wild side, and he was more than prepared to indulge her. Especially if it kept her from seeking out other men, a notion he couldn't tolerate.

Susan was still glaring at him, and he sighed. "I'm really not so bad, Miss Jackson. Just ask Bob."

Bob nodded vigorously, but Susan ignored him. "Bob is sincere in what he does. His intentions are always honorable. But I'm finding he can be rather biased where you're concerned."

At that particular moment, Nick wanted nothing more than to escape Susan's scrutiny. But he had no intention of walking out on Josie now, so gaining her sister's approval might not be a bad thing. He sifted through all the readily available remarks to Susan's statement, none of them overly ingratiating, then settled on saying, "Bob is the most ethical and straightforward man I know."

Susan made the attempt, but couldn't come up with a response other than a suspicious nod of agreement.

"And yet he keeps me as his partner and his closest friend. Can you imagine that? Surely it says something for my character that Bob trusts me? Or is it that you think Bob is an idiot?" He waited while Susan narrowed her eyes—eyes just like Josie's, only at the moment they were filled with rancor rather than good humor. Bob sputtered in the background.

Through clenched teeth, Susan replied, "It might show that Bob is too trusting for his own good."

Nick almost laughed. Susan wasn't a woman to give up a bone once she got her sharp little teeth into it. Finally she sighed. "Though I don't think you're at all right for Josie, I'll concede the possibility that you might have a *few* redeeming qualities, Mr. Harris."

He gave her a wry nod. "I'm overwhelmed by your praise." Truth was, Susan had him worried. If she decided to harp on his shortcomings, would Josie think twice about seeing him? And if Susan kept marching marriage-minded men in front of Josie, would she one day surrender? He knew Susan had some influence on her—after all, Josie had been a twenty-five-year-old virgin!

He was distracted from his thoughts of being replaced, which enraged him, when Susan cleared her throat.

"Before I leave, Mr. Harris, I do have one last question for you."

He noted that Bob had begun to tug at his collar. Nick raised a brow, then flinched when Susan produced the damn catalog Josie's neighbor had given him.

She held it out by two fingers, as if reluctant to even touch it, and thrust it at his face. Her foot tapped the floor and she stared down her nose at him. "If you're truly as reformed as you claim, why do you have this floating around the office?"

She looked triumphant, as if she'd caught him with a girly magazine. Obviously she hadn't looked at the catalog or she'd have realized how innocent it was.

For a single heartbeat, Nick thought he would laugh. But he glanced at Bob and saw how red his face had turned. He grinned. "Bob's birthday is next month, you know. I was trying to find him something special. If you need any ideas on what to get him, feel free to look through the thing. I believe he might have dog-eared a few pages."

Susan stared at the catalog, stared at Bob, then amazingly, she flipped to the first bent page. Nick knew what she would find. After all, he was the one who had cornered the pages while searching for a hook on an ad campaign.

There was nothing even slightly offensive displayed on the

pages, but Susan's eyes widened and she dropped the catalog on Bob's desk. "I...uh, hmm."

"Find anything interesting?" Nick asked with false curiosity.

Susan made a small humming sound. "Ah... possibly." With a weak smile and a hasty goodbye, she made an unsteady exit.

"I'm going to kill you."

Nick slapped Bob on the shoulder. "Did you see her face? Sheer excitement, Bud. Take my word for it. She'll think about that damn catalog, and your romantic tendencies all night. It'll drive her wild."

Bob picked up the catalog and peered at the page Susan had turned to. He groaned. "Leopard print silk boxers?"

Nick raised his eyebrows, chuckling. "Real silk by the way. I was thinking of buying a pair." He turned to go into his own office. "But they'll look much cuter on you."

He barely ducked the catalog as it came flying past his head. Seconds later, he heard Bob cross the floor to pick it up again.

It seemed his efforts to bring Susan and Bob together were finally paying off. Maybe Bob could distract Susan from her campaign to marry off Josie. He didn't want Josie married. He didn't want her exploring elsewhere, either.

He decided he needed to ensure his position, and he could do that by driving her crazy with pleasure. After he finished, marriage and other men would be the farthest things from her mind.

Chapter Seven

"TELL ME IT'S NOT TRUE."

Josie had barely gotten the door open before Susan wailed out her plea.

"Uh—"

Susan pushed her way in and closed the door behind her, then fell against it in a tragic pose. "He's not Bob, Josie. He's not a man meant for a woman like you."

Josie didn't know if she should laugh at Susan's theatrics or wince at the unwelcome topic. "I take it we're talking about Nick."

"Yes!" Susan pushed away from the door. "Why didn't you tell me you were seeing him? Oh, this is all Bob's fault! If he hadn't stood you up in the first place, none of this would have happened."

"Then I'm glad Bob didn't show!"

They had both resorted to shouting, and that rarely happened. Susan blinked at Josie, then sank onto the edge of the couch. "Oh, God. You're infatuated with him, aren't you?"

Infatuation didn't come close to describing what she felt. But it wouldn't do to tell Susan that.

"Josie?"

Glancing at the clock, Josie realized she only had a little time left to get ready before Nick arrived. She wanted tonight to be special, for both of them.

She settled herself next to Susan and took her hands. "Susan, I know you mean well. You always do. But I'm not going to stop seeing Nick. At least, not as long as he's willing to see me." Susan shifted, and Josie squeezed her hands, silencing her automatic protest. "And yes, before you say it, I know what I'm getting into. Nick has been very up-front with me. I know he's not the marrying kind, and I can handle that." She would have to handle it; the only other option was to stop seeing him, which was no option at all.

"Can you?" Susan's smile was solemn. "When he walks away, do you have any idea how you'll feel?"

She had a pretty darn good idea, but she only smiled. "It'll be worth it. Even you have to admit, Nick is exactly the type of man any red-blooded woman wants to enjoy, with or without a wedding ring. And I plan to do just that, for as long as I possibly can."

Susan's blush was accompanied by a frown of concern. "You've always lived a sheltered life. You don't know his kind the way I do. They're arrogant and insufferable. They want everything their own way, and they don't care who they hurt in the process."

"Nick is different."

Susan snorted, causing Josie to smile.

"He may not want any permanent ties, but he's the most charming man I've ever met. If you got to know him, you'd probably like him. He's sweet and funny. He listens when I talk and he understands the priorities of my work. He doesn't pressure me, but he's so complimentary and gracious and attentive. He acts like I'm the only woman alive. He's...wonderful."

"Ha! He's a wolf on the prowl, so of course he's attentive. None of what you've said surprises me. It's just his way of keeping you hooked."

Josie knew it was true, knew Nick probably behaved exactly the same way with every woman he had an intimate relationship with. But for now she felt special, and almost loved. "Susan..."

"I don't want you to romanticize him, Josie. You'll only get crushed."

"That can only happen if I let it. But I know what I'm doing." Josie had at first been torn by mixed emotions. She wanted Nick, the excitement and the romance and the sexual chemistry that seemed to explode between them whenever they got close. It was so thrilling, making her feel alive and sexy and feminine. But she knew she wasn't the type of woman who could ever hold Nick for long. Her life was mundane and placid. She was a very common woman, while he was a wholly uncommon man.

But at the same time, the very things that made her and her life-style so unsuitable to him were things she wouldn't want to change. The friendship and kindness she received from working with the elderly, knowing she had made a difference in their lives, letting them make a difference in hers. All her life, Susan had been playing the big sister, taking care of her. But with the elderly, Josie got to be the caring one, the one who could give. They welcomed her into their homes and their hearts. They didn't judge her or frown on her conservative life-style. They didn't expect anything she couldn't give.

And there was the fact that Susan would never approve of Nick. But Susan had given up her own life for Josie, without complaint or remorse. She was the only family Josie had left, and she loved Susan dearly.

"I know this is all temporary, Susan. I won't be taken by surprise when Nick moves on. I have no illusions that I'll overwhelm him with my charms and he'll swear undying love."

"And why not? Nick Harris would be lucky to have you!"

Emotion nearly choked her. Though at times Susan could be abrasive, Josie never doubted her loyalty. "I know you can't approve, but will you please try to understand?"

Her sister's sigh was long and loud. "I do understand.

Maybe I wouldn't have before meeting Bob, but now I know what it is to get carried away. Bob is very special to me." She grinned. "I have to admit, I'm glad you didn't settle on him." Josie laughed out loud. "So you two are getting along?" Susan shook her head. "No, right now I'm furious with him. I do understand how you feel, honey, but I can't help worrying anyway. And I know if Bob hadn't lied to me from the start, if he'd gone to see you himself instead of sending Nick, we wouldn't be having this conversation."

Though she had promised Nick, Josie thought it was time to clear the air. She made her tone stern while she gave Susan a chiding look. "Do you even know why Bob lied?"

Susan lifted a brow.

"Because he cares about you. Bob did everything he could think of to keep you around. He even..." She hesitated, wondering if Susan would understand Bob's motives.

"He what?"

With a deep breath, Josie blurted, "He even told you he was the one who created your ads, just because he knew you didn't like Nick."

Susan's nostrils became pinched and her expression darkened. "Are you telling me Nick Harris is responsible for my advertisements? Are you telling me *he's* the one I should be grateful to?"

"Yes, that's what I'm telling you. Rather than let you go, Bob contrived to keep you around. And Nick, whom you seem to think is a total cad, let you revile him even though he could have taken credit all along."

"You're kidding."

"Nope. You can ask Bob, though I imagine it would embarrass him to no end."

Susan jerked to her feet. "I will ask him. But I have no doubt that damn partner of his is behind this somehow! That man is nothing but trouble."

With that, she stormed out of the condo, and Josie winced in sympathy for Bob. She hoped Susan wouldn't be too hard on him, but she had a feeling it was Nick who would feel the brunt of her anger.

Josie looked around her apartment, thinking how quiet it seemed without Susan there shaking things up. Her apartment always seemed empty, but somehow lonelier to her now. Before meeting Nick, she'd enjoyed her solitude and independence. But now, too much time alone only served to remind her of how she'd wasted her life, what a coward she'd been. She knew, even though Nick would never love her, she was doing the right thing. Her time with him was precious, and it filled up the holes in her life, the holes she hadn't even realized were there until recently. When he went away, she'd still have the memories. And for now, she had to believe memories would be enough.

An hour later, when the doorbell rang again, Josie was in front of her mirror, anxiously surveying herself. Knowing it was Nick, she pressed a fist to her pounding heart. She felt so incredibly nervous, this being the first time she and Nick would have extended time alone since that first night.

Moreover, it was the first time she'd dared to dress to please him. Though he hadn't said they'd be going anywhere except the boat, she had plans for the night, and her clothing played a part in it all.

The flowery dress was new, sheer and very daring, ending well above her knee. In the wraparound fashion, it buttoned at the side of her waist on the inside where no one could see. One button, the only thing holding the dress together other than the matching belt in the same material, which she'd loosely tied. Getting the dress off would be a very simple matter.

She'd left her hair hanging loose the way Nick preferred it. And this time, she had chosen red, strappy sandals with midhigh heels so she could walk without stumbling. She'd even painted her toenails bright red. She'd set the stage the best she could.

Beneath the dress, she hadn't bothered with sexy garters

or nylons; they would have been superfluous in this case. Other than her panties, she was naked.

She rubbed her bare arms, gave her image one more quick glance and went to open the door.

Nick lounged against the door frame. At least, he did until he saw her. Slowly, he straightened while his gaze traveled on a leisurely path down the length of her body and back up again. Without a word, he stepped forward, forcing her to back up, then kicked the door shut behind him.

"Damn, you look good enough to eat."

Her lips parted and heat washed her cheeks. He lifted one hand and traced the low vee of her neckline from one mostly bare shoulder to the other, then his hand cupped her neck and he drew her close. "Such a pretty blush. Whatever are you thinking, Josie?"

He must not have wanted an answer, because he kissed her, his mouth soft on hers while his tongue slowly explored. Josie gasped and clutched the front of his cotton shirt, almost forgetting what she intended. But she needed to wrest control from him, to play the game her own way before she lost her heart totally. As it was, her feelings for him were far too complicated. And Nick, well used to his effect on women, would recognize what she felt if she didn't take care to hide her emotions behind her strong physical attraction.

If he thought she was growing lovesick, he'd leave. And she wasn't ready for him to go. *Not yet.*

He slanted his head and the kiss deepened. One hand slid inside the top of her dress and when he found her bare breast, he pulled back.

"Damn." Hot and intent, his gaze moved over her mouth, her throat, the breast he smoothed so gently. "You're naked underneath, aren't you?"

"No." A mere squeak of sound and she cleared her throat, trying to sound more certain, more provocative—*more like the woman who had attracted him in the first place.* "No, but too many underthings would have ruined the lines of the dress." She tried a small smile, looking at him through her lashes. "I have on my panties."

"I'd like to see." No sooner did he say the words than he shook his head and took a step back. "No, we can't. There's not enough time. If I had you lifting your dress we'd never get out the door."

Josie tried not to gape at him, to accept his outlandish words with as much disregard as he'd given them. The thing to do would be to laugh, to tease. Instead she straightened her dress, covering herself, and tried to find a response.

Such an assumption he'd made! As if she'd just lift her skirt at his whim. Of course, she probably would. Nick had a way of getting her to do things she'd never considered doing before. It was both unnerving and exhilarating, the power he seemed to have over her. Now she wanted the same power.

"Are you ready to go? I've made a few plans."

He'd given up so easily. She hadn't expected that. "What plans?" She crossed to the couch to pick up her purse and her wrap. The September nights were starting to get cool.

"It's a surprise." He lifted his brows and once again scanned her body. "Not quite as pleasant as your surprise, which almost stopped my heart, by the way."

Feeling tentative, Josie smoothed the short skirt on the dress and peered at him. "So you like it?"

"Honey, only a dead man wouldn't. And I swear, I appreciate your efforts. I'll show you how much later, when we get to the boat." He reached for her hand and pulled her to the door. "But right now we're running a little late."

She had hoped their only destination would be the boat. "Where are we going?"

He looked uncertain, avoiding her gaze. "I told you, it's a surprise. Trust me."

She tried not to look too disappointed. "What if I'd had other plans?"

He smiled as they neared his truck. "It's obvious you did. And we'll get to that before the night is over." He opened the truck door and lifted her onto her seat. His gaze skimmed her legs while she crossed them. "That is, if I can wait that long. You are one hell of a temptation."

Josie wondered at his mood as he started the truck and pulled away from the parking lot. He kept glancing at her, his dark brows lowered slightly as if in thought.

The sky was overcast and cloudy and she knew a storm would hit before the night was over. She could smell the rain in the air, feel the electric charge on her skin, both from the weather and the anticipation. She welcomed the turbulence of it, took deep breaths and let it flow through her, adding to her bravado.

She had to follow through, had to make certain she got the most out of this unique situation before her time with him ended. In a low whisper, she said, "I'm not feeling nearly so secretive as you." She turned halfway in the seat to face him, aware that her position had slightly parted the skirt of her dress. "Would you like to know what my plans were?"

"I have a feeling you're just dying to tell me."

His smile showed his amusement, but it wasn't a steady smile and seemed a bit forced to Josie. So be it. He wouldn't be laughing at her for long. "I want to have my way with you."

He hesitated, and his gaze flew to her again. "You care to explain that?"

Using one finger, she traced the length of his hard thigh. "If you think it's necessary."

"I believe it is." His voice was deep, already aroused, and she drew strength from that; it took so little to make him want her.

"Tonight I want to know what *you* like, what your body reacts to. I want to drive you crazy the way you did me."

He laughed, the sound suddenly filled with purpose. "Men are embarrassingly obvious in what we like and need, honey. Unlike women, who are fashioned differently, men need very little stimulation to be ready."

Used to his blunt way of phrasing things, Josie didn't

mind his words. But she stiffened when they stopped at a red light and he was able to give her his full attention. His gaze was hot, intense. His hand slid over her knee and then upward and she sucked in a quick startled breath. "And you already make me crazy." He spoke in a low husky whisper, and his cheekbones were flushed. "You're so damn explosive. I've never known another woman who reacted the way you do. There's something called chemistry going on between us, and it works both ways. I've been different, too, if you want the truth."

"The truth would be nice for a change."

"Don't be a smart-ass." But now his grim tone had lightened and he relaxed. "We're hot together, Josie. Believe me, you make me lose control, too."

She'd seen no evidence of that, but she wanted to. It was her goal tonight to make Nick totally lose his head. Exactly how she'd do that, she wasn't sure. For now, though, a different topic would be in order. The present discussion had the very effect he'd predicted. Her pulse raced and she knew her cheeks were flushed. She wanted him, right now, and she was too new to wanting to be able to deal with it nonchalantly. "Do we have much farther to go?"

"We're two minutes away from where I'm taking you." He gave a strangled laugh. "And the way you affect me, I'm going to need five times that long to make myself presentable."

She glanced at his lap, knowing exactly what he spoke of. His erection was full, impossible to ignore. And the sight of his need quadrupled her own. She leaned toward him, imploring, letting the thin straps of her dress droop and fall over her shoulders. In low, hopefully seductive tones, she said, "Let's forget your plans. Let's just go to the boat." She reached for him, but he caught her hand and kissed the palm.

His gaze strayed to her cleavage, now more exposed, and he let out a low curse. "Sorry. But we can't." Incredibly, she saw sweat at his temples and watched as he clenched his jaw. He turned down a long gravel drive that led to a stately old farmhouse. It was a huge, sprawling, absolutely gorgeous home that looked as if it had been around and loved for ages. Josie hadn't been paying any attention to where they were going, but now she realized they were in a rural area and that Nick was taking her to a private residence. Horrified, she stiffened her back and frantically began to remedy the mess she'd made of her dress, smoothing the bodice and straightening the skirt, retightening her belt. "Oh my God, we're *meeting* people?" She thought of how she was dressed and wanted to disappear.

He jerked the truck to a stop beneath a large oak tree and turned off the ignition. "Calm down, Josie. It's okay." But he sounded agitated, too.

She gasped, then swatted at his hands when he reached out to help her straighten the shoulder straps of her dress. "Nick, stop it, don't touch me." She glanced around, afraid someone might see.

Her words had a startling effect on him. He grabbed her shoulders and yanked her close and when her eyes widened on his face, he growled, "I'm going to touch you, all right. In all the places you want to be touched, in all the ways I know you like best. With my hands and my mouth. Tonight…"

Her stomach flipped and her toes curled. "Nick—"

In the next heartbeat he kissed her—hard and hungry and devouring—and she kissed him back the same way, forgetting her embarrassment and where they were.

He groped for her breast and her moan encouraged him. But before he made contact there was a loud rapping on the driver's door and seconds later it was yanked open. They jumped apart, both looking guilty and abashed. Josie felt her mouth fall open at the sight that greeted her.

Standing beside the car, his grim countenance and apparent age doing nothing to detract from his air of command, stood a gray-haired man in a flannel shirt and tan slacks with suspenders. His scowl was darker than the blackening sky and his bark reverberated throughout the truck.

"If that's what you came for, you damn well should have stayed home. Now are you gettin' out to say your hellos and do your introductions, or not?"

Nick took a deep breath and turned to Josie, who was still wide-eyed with shock. Sending her a twisted smile of apology, he said, "Josie, I'd like you to meet my grandfather, Jeb Harris. Granddad, this is Josie Jackson."

With sharp eyes the man looked her over from the top of her tousled head to her feet in the strappy sandals. Josie felt mortified at the scrutiny and did her best not to squirm. He shook his head. "You can be the biggest damn fool, Nick." Then he laughed. "Well, get the young lady out of the truck before you forget your poor old granddad is even here."

And with that, he turned and headed to his front porch, leaning heavily on a cane and favoring one hip. Josie noticed his shoulders were hunched just enough to prove he tolerated a measure of pain with his movements. The caretaker in her kicked in, and she briefly wondered what injury he'd suffered.

Nick cleared his throat and she slowly brought her narrow-eyed gaze to his face. "This is your surprise?"

He kept his gaze focused on a spot just beyond her left shoulder. "Yeah. Granddad called, asked if I could visit tonight." He jutted out his chin, as if daring her to comment. "I didn't think it would do any harm to stop here for a bit first."

She opened her door and climbed out of the truck without his assistance. Nick was such a fraud. He didn't want her to think he was a softy, but the fact that he hadn't been able to refuse his grandfather only made her like him all the more. She glanced at him as he came to her side. "A little warning might have been nice, so I could have dressed appropriately instead of making a fool of myself."

"Josie, Granddad is getting older. He's not dead. He knows who the fool is, and he's already cast the blame. You he's simply charmed by."

Josie looked down at her dress, and decided there was no help for it. She sighed. "How do you know?"

"Because I know my grandfather." As Nick looked up at the house, Josie looked at him. There was a softness in his eyes she'd never seen before. "When I was a kid, I loved the times I spent with him here more than you can know."

Because he hadn't had anyone else. His mother had used him as a pawn and his stepmother and father had made him a stranger in his own home. She could have asked for better circumstances, but she wanted to meet his grandfather, knowing now that he was the only family Nick was close to.

Nick saw her frown ease and he leaned down to whisper in her ear. "You look beautiful. And I think you'll like my grandfather. He's the one who taught me everything I know."

Josie rolled her eyes. Somehow that didn't reassure her.

HE WAS LAYING IT ON a bit thick, Nick thought, as his grandfather said, once again, "Eh?" very loudly. Hell, the man's hearing was sharper than a dog's and not a single whisper went by that he didn't pick up on. But for some reason he was playing a poor old soul and Nick had to wonder at his motives.

At least Josie no longer seemed so flustered. She continued to fuss with that killer dress of hers—she'd almost given him a heart attack when he first saw her in it—but she had mostly relaxed and was simply enjoying his grandfather's embellished tales of life in years gone by.

The old bird was enjoying Nick's discomfort. The small smile that hovered on his mouth proved he was aware of Nick's predicament, but there wasn't a damn thing Nick could do about it. Not with Josie sitting there on the edge of the sofa, her legs primly pressed together, the bodice of her dress hiked as high as she could get it. She inspired an odd, volatile mixture of raging lust and quiet tenderness. It unnerved him, and at the same time, turned him on.

Right now he felt as if lava flowed through him, and the volcano was damn close to erupting.

He shot out of his seat, attracting two pairs of questioning eyes. His grandfather chuckled while Josie frowned.

"I, ah, I thought I'd go get us something to drink."

"Would you like me to help you, Nick?" Josie made to rise from her seat.

Before Nick could answer her, Granddad patted her hand and kept her still. "He can manage, can't you, Nick?"

"Yes, sir."

Granddad waved at Nick. "Fine, go on, then. Josie and I have things to chat about."

Exactly what that meant was anyone's guess. In the kitchen, he filled some glasses with ice tea, then stuck his ear to the door.

"I'm afraid you have the wrong impression, sir."

"Just call me Jeb or Granddad. I can't stand all that 'sir' nonsense."

There was a pause. "Really, Jeb, Nick and I are only friends."

"Ha!" Granddad made a thumping sound with his cane. "My old eyes might be rheumy, but I can still see what needs to be seen. And I ain't so old as to be dotty. That boy's got himself a bad case goin', and you're the cause. Probably the cure, too."

Nick groaned. At this rate, his grandfather would run Josie off even before Susan could. Josie didn't want the responsibility of another person, of permanence or commitment. This was her first chance to be free, and she wanted to widen her boundaries, to explore her sexual side.

Between Susan telling her how irresponsible Nick was and his grandfather trying to corner her, he probably wouldn't last through the week. The thought filled him with unreasonable anger. He didn't want things to end until he was damn good and ready.

His determination surprised him. He hadn't felt this strongly about anything since his mother had sent him home to live with his father, making it clear his presence was an intrusion. Not even Myra's ruthless attempts to alienate him had stirred so much turmoil inside him. Josie had tied him in so many knots, it was almost painful. But once he got her alone tonight, once he made love to her, everything would be all right.

"His mother and father are to blame for his wild ways, too caught up in pickin' at each other to remember they had a son. And that witch Myra—she let her jealousy rule her, though I doubt Nick knew that was the cause. But you see, she knew I had cut my son out of my will. After he married her, I left everything to Nick. And it ate Myra up, knowin' it. She couldn't do anything to me, so she took it out on the one person she knew I really cared about."

Nick groaned. Not only had his grandfather's impeccable speech deteriorated to some façade of what he considered appropriate dotage lingo, but now he'd gotten onto an issue better left unaddressed. Nick still felt foolish over his last bout of personal confession with her. Josie didn't want to get personal, but his grandfather was forcing the issue.

"I hear you're a home health caretaker? Nick said you run a nice little business called Home and Heart. Could use someone like you around here."

"Are you having some problems…Jeb?"

"Broken hip, didn't you know? Busted the damn thing months ago, but it still pains me on occasion. Front porch was slippery from the rain and down I went. Poor Nick near fussed himself to death—reminded me of an old woman with all that squawkin'. Wouldn't leave my side, no matter how I told him to."

"He did the right thing."

"There, you see? He knows right from wrong when it matters. It's just the women he's got a problem with."

Nick closed his eyes to the sound of Josie's disbelieving laughter.

Granddad ignored her hilarity. "Now to be truthful, I'm pretty much recovered, but I just don't get around the way

I used to. I could use someone to check up on me now and then, without me having to go all the way into town."

Nick used that as his cue to reenter the room. "Excellent idea, Granddad. Maybe Josie could help you out." If he got her involved with his grandfather, it would be difficult for her to dump him and find another man to experiment with. She'd be pretty much stuck with him, at least for the time being, until the excitement wore off.

Josie didn't look at all enthusiastic about the idea. "But don't you already have someone in place? I should think—"

Granddad waved her to a halt. "Didn't care for that woman they had coming here. She was too starchy for my taste. I discharged her. Told her to go and not come back."

Nick remembered the incident. Of course, Granddad had been officially released from care anyway, and the poor woman whom he'd harassed so badly was more than grateful to be done with her duties.

"I could find someone better suited to you if you have need of a nurse, Jeb."

Nick liked how she'd so quickly accustomed herself to speaking familiarly with his grandfather. He knew Granddad would appreciate it, too. It gave him a warm feeling deep inside his chest to see the two of them chatting. No matter how Granddad went on, Josie never lost her patience. She listened to him intently, laughed with him and teased him. Nick felt damn proud of her, and it was one more feeling to add to the confusion of all the others she inspired.

"Fine. Never mind. I didn't mean to be a burden."

Nick snorted, recognizing his grandfather's ploy, but Josie was instantly contrite. "You're not!"

"I know they said I was all recovered, that I didn't need any more help. And I live too far out for people to bother with. Should have sold this old house long ago."

Josie looked around. When she replied, her voice was filled with melancholy. "But it's such a beautiful house. It has charm, and it feels like a real home, not a temporary one.

Like generations could live here and be happy. They don't build them like this anymore."

Nick wondered if it reminded her of her own home, the one she'd lost after her parents' death. He watched her face and saw the sadness there. He didn't like it.

Granddad nodded. "It is a sturdy place. But it's getting to be too much for me. And it was made for a family, not one old man."

"You know," Josie said, setting her glass down with a thunk, "I don't think you need a caregiver, I think you just need to get out more. And I have the perfect idea. Why don't you come to this party my neighbor is having next week? She's a wonderful friend and I have the feeling, being that you're Nick's grandfather, you might like her."

Oh, hell, his grandfather would kill him. Josie was trying to play matchmaker and that was the one thing Granddad wouldn't tolerate. Since the death of his wife, Granddad was as protective of his freedom as Nick. But to Nick's surprise, he nodded agreement. "I'd love to. Haven't been to a party in a long time."

Covering his surprise with a cough, Nick watched Josie, wondering if she would invite *him* to the party, too. But she didn't say a word about it and his temper started a slow boil. Damn her, did she have some reason not to want him there? Had her sister gotten to her already?

"It's nice to have a young lady in the house again. First time, you know. For Nick to bring a woman here, I mean. 'Course, I wouldn't care to meet most of his dates." He leaned toward Josie, his bushy gray eyebrows bobbing. "Not at all nice, if you get my meaning."

"Granddad." Nick's tone held a wealth of warning.

In a stage whisper, Granddad said, "He don't like me telling tales on him, which makes it more fun to do so."

If his grandfather hadn't recently had a broken hip, Nick would have kicked him under the table.

When the evening finally wore down, his grandfather was

starting to look tired. Concerned, Nick took care of putting their empty tea glasses away and preparing his grandfather's bed in the room downstairs. He used to sleep upstairs, Jeb explained to Josie, before the hip accident. Now he did almost everything on the lower floors while the upstairs merely got cleaned once a week by the housekeeper.

"It's a waste of a good house, is what it is. I really ought to sell."

When Josie started to object once again, Nick shook his head. "He's always threatening that. But he won't ever leave this place."

By the time they walked outside, the sky had turned completely black and the air was turbulent. The storm still hovered, not quite letting go. Leaves from the large oaks lining the driveway blew up on the porch around Jeb's feet.

Nick watched Josie hug his grandfather and he experienced that damn pain again that didn't really hurt, but wanted to make itself known. Josie stepped a discreet distance away and Nick indulged in his own hug. He couldn't help but chuckle when his grandfather whispered, "Prove to me what a smart lad you are, Nick, and hang on to this one."

"She can't hear you, Granddad. You can quit with the 'lad' talk."

"I was pretty good at sounding like a grandpa, wasn't I? I hadn't realized I had so much talent."

"I hadn't realized you could be so long-winded."

"Stop worrying, Nick. I know what I'm doing."

Josie looked toward them, and Nick muttered, "Yeah? Well, I wish I did."

He took Josie's hand as he led her to the truck. The wind picked up her long hair and whipped it against his chest. "Are you tired?"

She smiled up at him. "Mmm. But not *too* tired."

Her response kick started a low thrumming of excitement in his heart. With his hands on her waist, he hoisted Josie up into the truck, then leaned on the seat toward her, resting one hand beside her, the other on her thigh. "What does that mean, Josie?"

"It means we made a deal earlier, and now I expect you to pay up."

He almost crumbled, the lust hit him so hard. It had been too long, much too long, since he'd made love to her. "It'll be my pleasure."

She shook her head and her fingertips trailed over his jaw. "No, it'll be mine. I want my fair turn, Nick. Tonight I want you to promise you won't move. Not a single muscle, not unless I give you permission."

He tried to laugh, but it came out sounding more like a groan. "Why, Ms. Jackson. What do you have planned?"

"I plan to make you every bit as crazy as you make me. This time I want you to be the one begging. Promise me, Nick."

He had no intention of promising her a damn thing. He wasn't fool enough to let a woman make demands on him. It would start with one request, and then she'd think she could run his life. He wouldn't let that happen.

Josie smiled a slow sinful smile, smoothed her hand down over his chest. "Promise me, Nick."

"All right, I promise."

Chapter Eight

"STAND RIGHT THERE."

Josie surveyed her handiwork and felt immense satisfaction at the picture Nick made. She'd stripped his shirt from his shoulders, unsnapped his jeans. He was almost too appealing to resist. Kneeling in front of him, she'd taken turns tugging his shoes and socks off. He even had beautiful feet. Strong, narrow. Right now those feet were braced apart while his hands clutched, as per her order, the shelving high above the berth where she sat. Her face was on a level with his tight abdomen and she could see the way he labored for breath.

She liked this game—she liked it very much.

Nick hadn't said much once he'd agreed to her terms. The storm had broken shortly after they gained the main road, lightning splitting the sky with great bursts of light, the heavy darkness pressing in on them. They'd ridden to the boat in virtual silence, other than the rumble of thunder and her humming, which she hadn't been able to stop. She put it down to a nervous reaction in the face of her plan. Nick's hands had repeatedly clenched the steering wheel, but he hadn't backed out, hadn't asked her about her plans. At one point he'd lowered his window a bit and let the rain breeze in on him. She appreciated his restraint, though now she hoped to help him lose it.

He stared down at her, his expression dark, his hair still damp from their mad dash to the boat through the rain. For a moment, Josie wondered once again why he'd taken her to see his grandfather. He'd even suggested Jeb hire her, but she couldn't go along with that idea. If she got entangled with the one person Nick was closest to, it would make it so difficult to bear when their affair was over. She needed to keep an emotional arm's length, but with every minute that passed, that became harder to do.

Determined on her course, she blew lightly on his belly and watched his muscles tighten and strain.

"I feel I have to get this right, you know." She stroked the hard muscles of his abdomen. "I don't want to disappoint you, or myself."

He made a rough sound, but otherwise he simply watched her as if daring her to continue. She smiled inside, more than ready to take up the challenge. She wanted to get everything she could from her time with him.

Using just the edge of one fingernail, she traced the length of his erection and heard him suck in a breath. Speaking in a mere whisper, she said, "You look uncomfortable, Nick. I suppose I should unzip you. But first, I want to make myself more comfortable, too."

Leaning back on the berth to make certain he could see her, she watched his face while she hooked her fingers in the top of her dress and tugged it below her breasts, slowly, so that the material rasped over her nipples and tightened them. She inhaled sharply, feeling her own blush but ignoring it. "That's better."

Nick's biceps bulged, his chest rose and fell. She cupped her breasts, offering them up, being more daring now that she could see how difficult control had become for him. She stroked her palms over her nipples and heard his soft hiss of approval.

"And back at the apartment, didn't you mention something about wanting me to lift my dress?" She flipped back the edges of the flowered skirt until her panties could be seen. "Is this what you had in mind?"

Nick's cheekbones were slashed with aroused color, and his eyes were so dark they looked almost black. The boat rocked and jerked with the storm, but he held his balance above her and smiled. "You're so hot."

"Hmm. Let's see if we can get you in a similar state." She eased the zipper down on his jeans and reveled in his low grunt of relief. "Better? You looked so...constrained."

His penis was fully erect and the very tip was visible from the waistband of his underwear. Enthralled, Josie ran a delicate fingertip over it and saw Nick jerk back in response, muttering a low curse.

She peered up at him, loving the sight of him, his reaction. "You didn't like that?"

He dropped his head forward, a half laugh escaping him. His dark, damp hair hung low over his brow. "That might not be the very best place to start." He looked at her, his face tilted to one side, and he grinned. "You're really pushing it now, aren't you?"

"Your control, you mean? I hope so."

"I meant your own daring. But have at it, honey." Though his voice sounded low and rough, his dark eyes glittered with command. "This is your show. I can hold out as long as you can."

"I'm so glad you think so." And with that, she leaned forward and this time it was her tongue she dragged over the tip of him, earning a dozen curses and a shuddering response from his body.

Holding himself stiff as a pike, Nick squeezed his eyes shut and breathed deeply through his nose. He seemed to have planted his legs in an effort to control the need to pull away— or push forward. Josie thought he was the most magnificent man she'd ever seen.

"Relax, Nick." She stroked his belly, his ribs, and his trembling increased. "It's not that I haven't enjoyed everything you've done to me. We both know I have. But I want to be free to do my own explorations."

He didn't answer and she grinned. "I think we need to get you out of these jeans. I want to see all of you."

He offered her no assistance as she tugged the snug jeans down his long legs. They were damp and clung to his hips and thighs. Crawling off the berth, she knelt behind him and instructed him to lift each foot as she worked the stiff material off him. That accomplished, she pressed her face to the small of his back and reached her arms around him. Using both hands, she cuddled him through the soft cotton of his shorts and discovered how nice that felt. He was soft and heavy in places, rock hard and trembling in others. She bit his back lightly, then one buttock, then the back of his thickly muscled thigh.

"You're so rigid, Nick. Try to relax." She couldn't quite keep the awe from her tone, or the sound of her own growing excitement. Her hands still stroked him, up and down, manipulating his length, until he groaned, his head falling back.

She let her nipples graze his spine as she slowly stood behind him. "I love your body."

"Josie..."

"Shh. I'm just getting started." She moved in front of him again, but this time she didn't sit. She insinuated herself in the narrow space between where he stood and the edge of the berth and she simply felt him. All of him. From his thick forearms to his biceps and wide shoulders, the soft tufts of hair under his arms to the banded muscles over his ribs and his erect nipples. She explored his hipbones and the smooth flesh of his taut buttocks. She pushed his underwear down and he kicked them off. "Do you remember what you did to me in my kitchen, Nick?"

"Damn it, Josie—"

"Shh. You said it was my show, remember?" She kissed one flat brown nipple, flicked it with her tongue and heard him draw in an uneven breath. "Tell me, Nick. Do you like that as much as I do?"

He narrowed his gaze on her face. "I doubt it. You nearly come just from me sucking your nipples. Not that I'm complaining. It really turns me on." His voice was low, seductive. "I've never known a woman with breasts as sensitive as yours."

Damn him, he made her want things just by saying them. Her breasts throbbed and her nipples tightened into painful points. She decided she wouldn't ask him any more questions. She could do better if he kept quiet.

"Maybe you're just more sensitive in other places." And that was all she said to warn of her intent.

She kissed his throat, breathing in his sexy male scent. "I love how you smell, Nick. It makes me almost light-headed. And it makes me want you, makes me feel swollen inside." Her mouth trailed down, over his ribs to his navel. She heard him swallow as she toyed with that part of him, dipping in her tongue while her hands caressed his hard backside, keeping him from moving away.

"Brace your legs farther apart."

He laughed, the sound strained. "You've got a bit of the tormentor in you, don't you, honey? It's kinky. I had no idea."

"Be quiet." But she blushed, just as he knew she would. She sat on the berth again, opening her legs around his, assuming a position she knew that would drive him wild. "I only want to try some of the things you've done to me. Why should you always be the one in control?"

"Because I'm the man," he said on a groan as she fondled him again, exploring, fascinated by the smooth feel of him, the velvety skin over hard-as-steel flesh.

"You certainly are. Do you like this, Nick?"

"Yes," he hissed.

She brushed her bare breasts against him. "And this?"

"Josie, honey..."

"And this?" Josie slid her mouth over him, taking him as

deep as she could and his hips jackknifed against her as a deep growl tore from his throat. She loved his reaction, the way he continued to groan, to shudder and tremble and curse while she did her best to drive him insane. She'd had no idea it could be so exciting to pleasure another person in such a way. Before Nick, the thought of doing such a thing not only seemed incredible, but unpleasant.

With Nick, she felt as if she couldn't get enough—and she made sure he knew it.

His breathing labored, he rasped out rough instructions, unable to remain still. He strained toward her, hard and poised on some secret male edge of control. Josie had never felt so triumphant in all her life, so confident of herself as a woman. She drew him deeper still, using her tongue to stroke, to tease. She made a small humming sound of pleasure when he broke the rules and released the shelf to cup her head in his hands and guide her.

But seconds later he stumbled away from her. Josie tried to protest, to reach for him, but Nick wouldn't give her a chance. He toppled her backward on the berth, tore her panties off and shoved her dress out of the way. He lifted her legs high to his shoulders, startling her, frightening her just a bit. His mouth clamped onto her breast at the same time he drove into her, hard, slamming them both backward on the berth. He went so deep, Josie felt alarmed by the hot pressure, then excited. She cried out and wrapped her arms around him, already so aroused by his reactions, she took him easily, willingly. Within moments, she felt the sweet internal tightening, the throbbing of hidden places as they seemed to swell and explode with sensations. It went on and on, too powerful, too much. She bit Nick's shoulder, muffling her shocked scream of pleasure against his skin.

He collapsed on top of her, still heaving, gasping, his body heavy but comforting.

They both labored for breath, their skin sweaty and too hot. "Josie."

He forced himself up, swallowing hard, and smoothed her wildly tangled hair from her face with trembling hands. "Josie, honey, are you all right?"

She didn't want to look at him, didn't want to move. It was all she could do to stay conscious with the delicious aftershocks of her release still making her body buzz.

"Josie." He kissed her mouth, her eyelids, the bridge of her nose. Carefully he lowered her thighs, but remained between them, still inside her. "Look at me, honey."

She managed to get one eye halfway open, but the effort was too much and she closed it again. Seeing him, the color still high on his cheekbones, his silky dark hair hanging over his brow, his temples damp and his mouth swollen, made her shudder with new feelings, and she couldn't, simply *couldn't* survive that kind of pleasure again so soon.

Nick managed a shaky laugh and kissed her on the mouth, a soft, mushy kiss that blossomed and went on until it dwindled into incredible tenderness, to concern and caring. He rolled, groaning as he did so, putting her on top.

"You're a naughty woman, Josie Jackson."

She smiled, kissed his shoulder and sighed.

"I didn't wear a condom."

Her eyes opened wide and she stared at the far wall, her cheek still pressed to his damp chest. His heartbeat hadn't slowed completely yet, and she felt the reverberations of it.

"I'm sorry, honey. No excuse except that I went a little nuts and it was a first for me. Going nuts, that is."

No condom. *Oh God.* She hadn't even thought of that in the scheme of her seduction. Her body felt lethargic, a little numb, and she mumbled, "My fault," more than willing to put the blame where it rightfully belonged. She had been in control this time, had manipulated the whole situation, and she was the one with no excuses.

Nick's arms tightened around her and he nuzzled his jaw into her hair. "We'll argue it out in the morning. Odds are, there won't be a problem. Not just that once."

She snuggled closer to him, her mind a whirlwind of worries, the major one being how she could ever let him go. For her, a baby wouldn't be a problem. It would be a gift of wonder, a treasure, a part of Nick. But she knew how wrong it would be and she couldn't help but shudder with realization. She'd set out to prove, to herself and to him, that their affair could remain strictly physical and she'd be satisfied. Instead, she'd proven something altogether different.

Damn but she'd done the dumbest thing. She'd fallen in love with Nick Harris, lady-killer, womanizer extraordinaire. Confirmed bachelor. Nick would probably never want a permanent relationship. And he might even see her forgetfulness with the condom as a deliberate ploy to snare him. So far, their time together had been spent on her wants, her needs, her *demands*. She'd gone on ordering him to show her a good time, on her schedule, without real thought to what he might want. But she knew; he wanted no ties, no commitments, a brief fling. She swallowed hard, feeling almost sick.

Now everything was threatened. If she hadn't pushed things today, the mishap might never have happened.

She realized where her thoughts had led her and she couldn't quite stifle a giggle. A possible pregnancy was far more than a mere mishap.

Nick lifted his head to try to see her face. "What tickles you now, woman? I hope you don't have more lascivious thoughts in your head, because I swear, I need at least an hour to recoup." The boat rocked with the storm and she could hear the rumble of thunder overhead. Nick held her closer. "I'm personally amazed that my poor heart continues to beat with the strain it's been under."

Josie kissed his collarbone. He didn't sound upset with her. So maybe now was the best time to find out if he planned to blame her. She didn't think she'd be able to sleep tonight if she had to worry about it. "Nick, I'm so sorry I forgot...myself. I should have been more responsible."

His hands on her back stilled just a moment, then he gave a huge sigh, nearly heaving her off his chest. "It probably won't even be an issue, Josie. But if it is, we'll figure something out together, okay?"

"I wouldn't want you to feel pressured. Or to think I did this deliberately."

"Hey—" he brought her face close to his and kissed her "—you're new at this. I'm the one who should have known better. I've never forgotten before, not that it matters now. But like I said, I've never felt quite this way before."

She wanted to ask him *what way,* but only said, "You're truly not angry?"

He smiled. "I'm not angry. Hell, I'm not even all that worried." His hand smoothed down her back to her bottom and he rolled to his side, keeping her close. They were nose to nose, and he yawned as if ready to sleep. "And I don't want you to worry, either. If anything comes of it, then we'll worry. But in the meantime, don't fret. Okay?"

"Okay," she said, but didn't feel completely reassured. Nick had never mentioned anything permanent between them, no matter how she'd wished it, and a baby would certainly be permanent. He was right, though. Worrying now was ridiculous. A waste of energy.

"Why don't you get this dress off, honey? You can't be comfortable like that."

She followed his gaze to where her dress was twisted around her upper arms and under her breasts. Her body was so numb with her release, she hadn't even noticed the restriction. She untied the belt, popped open the one button and slid it off. Nick took the dress from her and tossed it from the bed.

"That's better." He pulled her against his chest and closed his eyes once again. "Now let me sleep so I can recoup myself. There's the little matter of a payback for me to attend to, and I'll need some strength to see that the job's done properly."

To Josie's immense surprise, her body tingled in anticipation. She supposed she just had more stamina than Nick, because she was already looking forward to the payback.

NICK LOOKED AROUND the crowded room and wondered what the hell he was doing there. He'd get no time alone with Josie tonight. Every couch and chair was filled with an elderly person, and even standing room was limited. He'd barely gotten the door open and squeezed in past the loiterers.

He scanned the room, looking for Josie and trying to avoid all the prying eyes peering over the rims of their bifocals. It had been over a week since he'd seen her, a week since he'd given her control and she'd used it to drive him to distraction. But she hadn't tried in any way to abuse that control. She hadn't breached his privacy, crowded him in any way. He wanted to talk to her, damn it, but he doubted he'd get much private time with her here.

He headed toward the kitchen, hoping to find Josie there, and ran headlong into Susan. He caught her arms to steady her and accepted her severe frown. "Susan," he said by way of greeting.

"I want to talk to you."

He looked at her hands, which were behind her back.

"What are you doing?" she asked.

"Checking for concealed weapons. I want to make sure verbal abuse is all you have in mind." He flashed her a grin, which only made her stiffen up that much more. Damn prickly woman.

"What are you doing here?"

He crossed his arms and leaned against the wall. "That was going to be my question to you."

"I was invited!"

"And you think I snuck in through the bathroom window?"

Her face went red and she looked around the room, then took his arm and dragged him a short distance down the hall. "You've been seeing my sister some time now."

"And?"

"And you've had ample time to decide if you're serious about her or not. I don't want you to keep toying with her."

He thought of how Josie had toyed with him on the boat and couldn't quite repress his grin. To avoid replying to her statement, he asked, "How's Bob?"

Susan blushed. "He's...fine, I guess."

"You haven't seen him lately?"

"I'm still angry because he lied to me, letting you work on my campaign when he knew how I felt about that."

"Yes, you weren't exactly subtle." Before she could blast him, he added, "He cares about you, you know. He just didn't want to disappoint you."

"He lied to me."

"Only so you wouldn't go away. But I'm thinking it might have been better if you had. If you don't care about him..."

She narrowed her eyes at him and almost snarled. "I didn't say that."

"Ah, so you only want him to suffer? This is one of those female games, meant to prove a point?"

She flushed, which to Nick's mind revealed her guilty conscience. "Not that it's any of your business, but I was planning to talk to him about it tonight. He's here at the party."

Nick felt his jaw go slack. "You're kidding?"

"No." Then she flapped her hand. "Josie insisted. She's got some harebrained scheme to get me and Bob all made up."

"Is it working?"

She chewed her lip. "I suppose. Josie already explained Bob's reasons for the deception. In a way, even I understand them. And I hate to admit it, but you really are very talented."

Nick's grin was slow, and then he laughed full out, placing one widespread hand on his chest. "Be still, my heart."

Susan looked like she wanted to clout him. "The thing is, I don't know how to figure you anymore. Mrs. Wiley has been singing your praises ever since I got here. You're doing her work gratis, aren't you?"

"Our arrangement is private."

"Hogwash. Mrs. Wiley is telling anyone who'll listen what a *dear boy* you are." Susan stepped closer, causing Nick to back up until he hit the wall. "Well, *dear boy*, I want to know what your intentions are toward my sister."

Nick opened his mouth with no idea what he was going to say to Susan. Thankfully they were both sidetracked by his grandfather's booming voice coming from the living room. When Nick looked in that direction, he saw his grandfather standing next to Mrs. Wiley. He looked happy and he kept whispering in her ear, making her smack playfully at his arm. Nick shook his head in wonder.

"Your grandfather is charming."

"Ain't he though?"

"He's also very taken with Josie. He told me she's been out to see him twice this week."

That surprised him. No one had said a word to him, and his curiosity immediately swelled. What had they talked about? Him, no doubt. But what specifically? And where was Josie anyway? He needed to escape Susan's clutches. She wanted explanations, but he had no idea what to tell her. His arrangement with Josie was private; it was up to Josie to explain things to her nosy sister.

He nodded toward his grandfather. "I should go over and say hello."

"No need. He's headed this way." Susan gave him a searing look. "You and I will talk again later." With that rather blatant threat, she dismissed herself.

"Well, boy, about time you got here."

"I really didn't expect you to show, Granddad." Nick saw how Mrs. Wiley clung to his arm, and he couldn't help but wonder what his grandfather had been up to. Not since Jeb had been widowed years before had he shown interest in any woman.

"Josie brought me. Which reminds me, I've been meaning to speak to you about her."

Dropping back against the wall with a resigned sigh, Nick prepared himself for another lecture, but his grandfather wasn't quite as restrained as Susan. The man had a way of making his feelings known on a subject and he didn't cut any corners. Mrs. Wiley stood beside him, nodding her agreement at his every word.

"If you have half the brains in that handsome head of yours that I've always given you credit for, you'll tie that little girl up right and tight and make sure she doesn't get away."

Attempting to ignore Mrs. Wiley's presence—not an easy thing to do in the best of circumstances—Nick tried to stare his grandfather down. "We've had this discussion before, remember?"

"Damn right I do. But this is different." Jeb's eyes narrowed. "This isn't one of those other women. I *like* Josie."

"Granddad…"

"So what's it to be, boy? What exactly do you have planned here?" He raised his hand as if to ward off any insult. "I only ask because I hate to see you ruin things for yourself."

Nick looked across the room and found so many eyes boring into him, he flushed. With the music playing, no one could hear their conversation, but he had the feeling every one of them knew he'd just been chastised, and why.

How the hell had he gotten himself into this predicament? And how could he tell his grandfather that he didn't know what his plans were because he didn't know what Josie's were? She had insisted their time together be temporary, no strings, simple fun. Of course, he'd never betray her by saying so.

He ran a hand through his hair and silently cursed. He didn't like being bullied, not even by his grandfather. "Right now, my plans are to find Josie and tell her hello. So if you'll both excuse me…?"

He stepped away and heard Mrs. Wiley say, "Youth. They can be so pigheaded."

Jeb laughed. "He reminds me of myself at his age."

Mrs. Wiley cooed, "Oh, really?" There was a great deal of interest in her tone.

Nick finally found Josie in the kitchen. Once again, she took him by surprise with her appearance. He'd seen the sexy, femme fatale, the disheveled homemaker, the harried working woman.... Now she was the sweet girl next door. She wore a long tailored plaid skirt and flat oxford shoes. Her short-sleeve sweater fit her loosely.

She looked like a schoolgirl.

He grinned at the image and wondered what games he could come up with using that theme. She hadn't noticed his entrance. She seemed preoccupied, though she wasn't serving any particular function that he could tell. She stood at the counter, surveying the items Mrs. Wiley had laid out in a large display. Without disturbing her, Nick looked, too. There was an assortment of fancy bottled lotions, scented candles in various sizes, pink light bulbs and music meant to entice. He thought of the advertisement he had planned and felt good. He hoped Josie would be pleased.

He slipped his arms around her and nuzzled her neck. "Thinking of buying anything?"

She jerked against him and gasped. "Nick, for heaven's sake, you startled me."

He could feel her tension, her immediate withdrawal. His jaw tightened. Trying to dredge up an air of nonchalance, he asked, "What do you think I should buy?"

"You don't have to buy anything. You didn't even need to show up."

She'd shown so much reluctance to have him there, he'd perversely insisted on attending. And to ensure success, he'd gone to Mrs. Wiley. He didn't like being excluded from parts of Josie's life. Usually, women tried to reel him in, not push him away. He didn't like Josie's emotional distance; it made him almost frenzied with need.

"Of course I'll buy something," he said while searching

her face for a clue to her thoughts, but she was closed off to him. "Besides, I needed to be here to try to get a feel for the market I'll be appealing to. And I think I've come up with just the thing."

Slowly she started to pull away from him. He pretended not to notice. "Josie?"

Her smile was dim. "Tell me your plan."

He kissed her nose, her cheek. He couldn't be near her without wanting to touch her. He couldn't wait to get her alone. "I don't think so, not yet. I'll run my idea past Mrs. Wiley first. If she likes it, I'll let you know."

"I hate it when you're secretive."

She sounded so disgruntled that he kissed her again. He didn't want to stop kissing her, but he heard the sounds of the party in the other room and pulled back. Josie would be embarrassed to be caught necking in the kitchen. "How long do we need to stay here?"

If possible, she looked even more uncomfortable. "I'll be here till late. I want to help clean up afterward."

"I can help, too."

"No!" She looked at him then backed away. "No, you should head on home. I don't know how long it will take and there's no reason to waste your entire night."

Waste his night? His teeth nearly ground together as he pulled her close again. He tried to sound only mildly curious. Teasing. "Are you trying to get rid of me?"

Her head thumped against his breastbone, which offered not one ounce of reassurance.

"Hey," he said softly. "Josie?"

"The thing is," she said, her face still tucked close to his throat, "I'm a little indisposed tonight."

"Indisposed?" She was giving him the brush-off? Had she already found another man to experiment with? Anger and a tinge of fear ignited. He ignored the fear, refusing to even acknowledge it. "What the hell does that mean?"

He could almost hear her thinking, and it infuriated him.

"Damn it, Josie, will you look at me?" It seemed so long since he'd seen her, anything could have happened. Her sister could have gotten to her, or his grandfather. Hell, it seemed all the odds were against him. His blood burned and he knew there was no way he'd allow her to go to another man. Not that he had any authority over her, but...

"I can't have any *fun* with you tonight."

She blurted that out, then stared at him, waiting. He had the feeling he was supposed to understand, but damned if he did.

Josie rolled her eyes. She turned her back on him and began straightening the items on the counter, even though they were already in perfect alignment. Nick thought she wasn't even aware of what she did. He felt ridiculous.

"Honey, I'd really like an explana—"

"I'm not pregnant, okay?"

He stilled, letting her words sink in and slotting them with everything else she'd said so far. Realization dawned. On the heels of that came a vague disappointment that he quickly squelched. "You're on your period?"

She gave him a narrow-eyed glare that could have set fire to dry grass.

"Josie, honey, for crying out loud, I'm thirty-two years old. I understand how women's bodies work. You don't have to act like it's some big embarrassment." He knew he sounded harsh, but in the back of his mind had been the possibility that she'd be tied to him, that he might have compromised her and in the process produced some lasting results. He'd never even considered such a thing before, and he hadn't really consciously thought about it until now. But he couldn't deny the damning truth of what he felt: disappointment.

"Well, then, given your worldly experience, I'm sure you understand that there's no point in us seeing each other tonight." She started to march away, but he caught her arm and swung her back around.

These overwhelming emotions were new to him, and he

held her close so she couldn't see his expression or wiggle away. "I'd still like to see you tonight."

She forced her way back to look at him. "You're kidding?"

"No, I'm not kidding, damn it." He'd never had to beg for a date before. He didn't like the feeling. "I can settle for a late movie and conversation if you can."

She looked undecided and his annoyance grew. After what seemed an undue amount of thought, given the simplicity of his suggestion, she nodded. "All right."

He propped his hands on his hips. Her compliance had been grudging at best and it irked him. "Fine. And in the future, don't be so hesitant about discussing things with me. I don't like not knowing what you're thinking."

He waited to see if she would question his reference to the future. Their time together, according to her preposterous plan, was limited. At first, he'd been relieved by her edicts. But now, whenever he thought of that stipulation, his body and mind rebelled. Every day he wanted her more.

"I'll try to keep that in mind" was all she said. She picked up the tray of drinks and started for the door. Nick took one last peek at the display, decided his ad plan would be perfect and went in search of Mrs. Wiley. If everything worked out as he hoped, not only would Mrs. Wiley be able to expand her client list, Josie would also get some freed-up time.

Her dedication to the elderly who'd become her friends was admirable and he'd never interfere with her friendships. He wanted to support her in everything she did, everything she ever wanted to do. But now he wanted her to have more time for him, too. A lot more time.

The thought only caused a small prickle of alarm now. He was getting used to his possessive feelings. She would get used to them, too, despite her absurd notions of sowing wild oats. She could damn well sow her oats with him.

He caught up with her in the living room just as she finished handing out drinks, and when two older men scooted over on the couch to make room for her to sit, Nick wedged his way in, as well. The men glared at him and he smiled back, then leaned close to Josie to gain her attention and stake a claim. Ridiculous to do so when he was the only man in attendance under the age of sixty-five—besides Bob, who sure as hell didn't count. He felt the need regardless.

"Your grandfather seems smitten with Mrs. Wiley." Josie had leaned close to his ear to share that small tidbit of gossip. Her warm breath made him catch his.

"Smitten?"

"That's his word." She took his hand and laced their fingers together. "Mrs. Wiley went with me the other day to visit him, and when I was ready to leave, he asked her to stay. He said he'd call a cab for her when she had to go home."

"That smooth old dog."

Josie laughed. "I think he's adorable. And a fraud. Do you know, there isn't a thing in the world still wrong with his hip. He was limping around dramatically right up until he spied Mrs. Wiley, then he looked ready to strut."

Nick laughed at the picture she painted. "His hip still gives him a few pains in the nastier weather, but he gets around good enough. As long as he doesn't try climbing the stairs too often."

"Mrs. Wiley told him he needed a condo like hers, instead of that big house. He's been considering it."

Shocked, Nick turned to look at his grandfather. Not only Mrs. Wiley had made note of him. He was surrounded by women, all of them fawning on him. But he kept one arm around Mrs. Wiley. Nick snorted. He'd never have swallowed it if he hadn't seen it himself. "I do believe he's fallen for her. In all the years since my grandmother died, back when I was too young to even remember, I've never seen Granddad put his arm around a woman."

"Mrs. Wiley won't take no for an answer."

Nick stared at Josie's upturned face, her neatly braided hair and her small smile. He decided it might be a good rule for him to adopt.

By the end of the evening he was the proud owner of new boxers he planned to gift wrap for Bob, and richly scented bubble bath for Josie. What she might have bought, he didn't know. She'd kept her order form hidden from him.

He and his grandfather helped the two women clean up, and he presented his plan to Mrs. Wiley. She was thrilled.

"Advertising to the elderly in the retirement magazines! It's a wonderful idea. I can travel to their residences and put on the displays, or they can order directly from me."

"I checked around, and almost all of the retirement centers have a special hall for entertaining and events. We could call it Romance for Retirees. And each class of gifts will need a catchy name. Like I thought maybe the scented oils could be classified under Love Potions #99."

Jeb laughed. "And the silk boxers and robes could be listed, Rated S—for Seniors only."

Josie jumped into the game, her grin wide. "What about Senior Sensations for the candles? And the wines could be Aged to Perfection."

Nick looked down at her, one brow quirked high. "You're pretty good at this. You missed your calling."

Pride set a glow to her features, and that look, so warm and sweet, caused Nick's heart to thump heavily. He wanted to kiss her, to...

"Finish up the telling, boy, then you can see her home."

Roughly clearing his throat, Nick brought his attention back to Mrs. Wiley and his grandfather. "I thought you might want to make the parties a monthly event, open to all newcomers. That way more people would be inclined to join in and some of the retirement homes might be persuaded to make it part of a monthly outing."

Mrs. Wiley clapped her hands and gave him a huge grin. "That's wonderful! I love it."

"I can work up the ads later this week, then get them to you for approval."

Mrs. Wiley put on a stern face. "I'm overwhelmed. And

I insist on paying you something. I can't possibly let you go to all this trouble for free."

"'Course you can," Granddad insisted. "Let the boy do what he wants. He usually does anyway."

"That's right. Stubbornness runs in the family." Nick looked pointedly at his grandfather, then continued. "I'm thinking there's probably a lot of small, local publications where placing an ad won't be too costly, along with the insurance and retirement periodicals that go out. I'll call around on Monday and see what their advertising rates are."

Granddad took him by the arm and started leading him to the front door. Josie followed along, grinning. "You do that, Nick. Get right on it, Monday."

Mrs. Wiley was still thanking him when Jeb practically shoved him out the door. Josie cozied up to his side. "I think we need to get going, Nick."

"I think you may be right." As he finished speaking, the condo door closed in his face and he heard his grandfather's laugh—followed by Mrs. Wiley's very delighted squeal.

Chapter Nine

WHEN THEY REACHED Josie's condo, Nick offered to get the tape. "It's been a long day. Why don't you take a quick shower and get comfortable while I run down to the video store?"

Josie blinked up at him. "How do I know you'll pick out a tape I like?"

"Trust me." He tucked a wind-tossed curl behind her ear, struggling with his new feelings. He wanted to hold her close, keep her close. It was distracting, the way she made him feel complete with just a smile. "Give me your key and then you won't have to let me in."

To his surprise, she handed him the key without any hesitation. "I'll see you in just a little bit, then."

He rented two tapes, bought popcorn and colas, and returned not thirty minutes later to find Josie in the bathroom blow-drying her hair. She was bent over at the waist, her long red hair flipped forward to hang almost to her knees. Nick stared, mesmerized. She looked so young, with her face scrubbed clean and her baggy pajamas all but swallowing up her petite body.

She also looked sexy as hell.

Remarkable. No matter what she wore, what persona she presented, he found her irresistible. He wondered if she hadn't been dressed so sexily the first time he saw her, would he have reacted the same? It seemed entirely possible given the way his body responded to her now.

He stood there watching her for a good five minutes, wanting to touch her, to wrap her beautiful hair around his hands. Her movements were all intrinsically female and he loved how her bottom swayed as she moved the dryer, how her small bare feet poked out at the end of the pajama bottoms. Ridiculous things.

In such a short time, she'd come to occupy so much of his thoughts, and his thoughts were as often sweet, like Josie, as they were hot and wild like the way she made him feel when he was inside her.

She cared about people—her sister and her patients and even his grandfather whom she hardly knew. He hoped she cared for him, but he couldn't tell because she was so set on having a purely physical relationship. He'd encouraged her in that regard, but no more. Tonight would be a good place to start.

She turned off the dryer and straightened, noticing him at the same time. A soft blush colored her face. "Um, I didn't realize you were back." She started trying to smooth her hair, now tossed in wild profusion around her head.

Nick grinned, bursting with emotion too rare to keep inside. "You look beautiful."

"Uh-huh."

He crossed his heart and held up two fingers. "Scout's honor. I wouldn't lie to you."

She put away the discarded towel and started out of the bathroom around him. "You were never a Scout, Nick. Jeb would have told me if you were."

He followed close on her heels.

"True enough, but the theory's the same." He could smell the clean scent of her body, of flowery soap and powder softness. And Josie.

She headed to the couch, but as she started to sit, he pulled her into his lap, relishing the weight of her rounded bottom on his groin. The new position both eased and intensified the ache.

He caught her chin and turned her face toward him. Before he could even guess at his own thoughts, he heard himself ask, "Are you relieved you're not pregnant?"

He saw her chest expand as she caught her breath, saw her tender bottom lip caught between her teeth.

She looked down, apparently fascinated with his chin. After a moment, she whispered, "It's strange, really. I'd never before given babies much thought. There's always been a succession of priorities in my life that occupied my mind. Getting past my parents' deaths, getting through school, finding a job and then starting my own business. I suppose I'm fairly single-minded about things."

"But?"

Her gaze met his briefly, then skittered away. "There's really no room in my life right now for a child. But still, in my mind, I'd pictured what it would look like, if it would be a boy or a girl..."

He pictured a little girl who looked like Josie. An invisible fist squeezed his heart.

"Oh, good grief." She threw up her hands and forced a smile. "Luckily I'm not pregnant and so that's that. We've got nothing to worry about." Her smile didn't quite reach her eyes.

She was always so open with him. Yet he'd done nothing but be secretive and withdrawn. He'd manipulated her at every turn, even as he worried about her trying to control him.

Ha! Josie was unlike any woman he'd ever known. She wasn't like Myra, trying to run his life, or his mother, rejecting him, or any of the other women he'd known who'd tried so diligently to mold him into a marriageable man. No, Josie hadn't tried to change his life, and he'd been too busy trying to change hers to notice.

He was a total jerk. A fool, an idiot.

He'd lied to her from the start in order to get his way. Then he'd continued to lie to try to keep her interested, claiming he agreed with her short-term plan, when even at the beginning he'd known something about her was special. He'd even done his best to alter her job, just to make more time for himself. He'd forced his way in with her friends, but never introduced her to his. He didn't deserve her—but damned if he was letting her go.

Pulling her close and pressing his face into her hair, he asked, "Can I spend the night with you, Josie?"

She tensed, and he hugged her even tighter. "Just to sleep. It's late and I want to hold you."

In a tentative tone, she said, "I'd like to see your home sometime."

He'd avoided taking her there. He hadn't wanted her to see the way he lived, with everything set for his convenience. Women didn't appreciate the type of functional existence he'd created for himself, which was the whole point. More often than not, his shirts never made it into a drawer. He laid them out neatly, one atop the other on the dining-room table. His socks were in the buffet drawer, convenient to the shirts. He never bothered to make his bed, not when he only planned to use it every night, and he didn't put away his shaving cream or razor, but left them on the side of the sink, handy.

His small formal living room had gym equipment in it and he'd never quite gotten around to buying matching dishes. He'd set himself up as a bachelor through and through.

Once a week, he cleaned around everything. He remembered now why he'd started doing things that way—to annoy Myra, and on her rare visits, his mother. He laughed at himself and his immature reasoning. For Josie, he'd even put away his toothpaste.

"Nick?"

"I was just thinking about your reaction when you see my house."

One hand idly stroked his neck. "What's it look like?" She was warm and soft and he loved her—everything about her. The notion of something as potent as love should have scared him spitless, but instead it filled him with resolution. Damn her ridiculous plans; she could experiment all she wanted, as long as she only experimented with him.

"My house is small, not at all like Granddad's. It looks like every other house on the street, except that I've never planted any flowers or anything. I bought it because it's close to where I work, not because I particularly like it. You'd be shocked to see what a messy housekeeper I am. I can just imagine you fussing around and putting things away, trying to make it as neat and orderly as your own."

She leaned back to see his face. "You're kidding, right? I barely have time to straighten my own place. I'm not going to play maid for anyone." She kissed his chin. "Not even you."

Brutally honest, that was his Josie. He laughed, delighted with her. "So you wouldn't mind stepping over my mess?"

She stared at him, her expression having gone carefully blank. "I don't imagine it will be a problem very often. Do you?"

He didn't want to address that issue right now. He knew she wouldn't like his house because he didn't even like it. She wouldn't be enticed to spend much time there.

He kissed her again, then while holding her close, he said, "One of the movies I rented is a real screamer, a new release guaranteed to make your hair stand on end. What do you say we put it on?"

Greed shone from her eyes. "I'm certainly up to it if you are."

The movie was enough to make them both jump on several occasions, which repeatedly caused gales of laughter. At one point, Josie hid her face under his arm, her nose pressed to his ribs. They ate two huge bowls of popcorn and finished off their colas and by the time the movie was over, they were both ready for bed.

Josie looked hesitant as she crawled in under the covers. When Nick stripped naked to climb in beside her, she groaned and accused him of being a terrible tease.

It was the strangest feeling to sleep chastely with a woman, with no intention of making love. It was also damn pleasurable. Only Josie, he thought, could make a scary movie and popcorn seem so romantic, so tender. He pulled her up against his side, then sucked in his breath when her small hot fist closed gently around him. "Josie?"

She nestled against him. "I'm not a selfish woman, Nick. Just because I'm out of commission doesn't mean you should suffer."

He could find no argument with her reasoning while her slender fingers held him. "Sleeping with you isn't a hardship, honey. I think I can take the pressure."

"Nonsense." She kissed his shoulder, then propped herself up on one elbow to watch his face while she slowly stroked him. In a whisper, she told him all the things she wanted to do to him, all the things she wanted him to teach her about his body. "Will you groan for me, Nick?"

He groaned.

She kissed his ear, the corner of his mouth. She kept her voice low and her movements gentle. "I need more data for my experimentation, you see."

He refused to talk about that. If she even hinted at going to another man right now, he'd tie her to the bed.

"You can't continue to have your way with me without paying the piper, lady."

Her smile was sensual and superior. "Oh? And what does the piper charge?"

He ground his teeth together, trying to think through the erotic sensation of being led like a puppet. "I want a key to your condo."

Josie went still for just a heartbeat and Nick thought she would refuse. But she bent and kissed him, then whispered into his mouth, "Keep the one I gave you earlier. I have a spare."

"Josie..." He groaned again, wanting to discuss the ramifications of her easy surrender. Josie had other ideas.

And Nick, once again, gave her total control.

Almost two weeks later, he still had her key—and he'd all but moved in.

"GOOD GRIEF, JOSIE, you should get dressed before you answer the door."

Her sister's comment might have been laughable if she wasn't so incredibly nervous. Josie looked down at her short, snug skirt, the same one she'd worn the night she first met Nick, and stiffened her resolve. She had a new plan for changing her life, and this one suited her perfectly.

Keeping the door only halfway open, more or less blocking her sister, Josie said, "Hi, Susan."

Susan leveled a big sister, somewhat ironic look on her. "Aren't you going to invite me in?"

"I...uh, this isn't the best time."

Susan stiffened. "Oh? Is Nick in there? Is that it?" Susan tried to peek around her and Josie gave up.

"No, Nick isn't here. Come on in."

Josie turned away from her sister's curious, critical eye and went into the kitchen. She had to keep moving or she'd chicken out.

Susan followed close on her heels. "Why are you dressed like that?"

Because Nick likes me dressed this way. "What's wrong with how I'm dressed? I'm rather fond of this particular outfit."

Susan eyed the short skirt and skimpy blouse with acute dislike. "What's going on, Josie?"

"Nothing that you should worry about." Josie went through the motions of pouring her sister a cup of coffee. Nick would show up soon, and she needed to get Susan back out the door. What she planned required privacy, not her sister as a jaundiced audience. "So what brings you here on a workday, Susan? Is anything wrong?"

Susan chewed her lips, twitched in a wholly Susan-type fashion, then blurted, "Bob wants to marry me."

Josie stared at her sister, at first taken aback, and then so pleased, she squealed and threw herself into her sister's arms. Susan laughed, too, tears shining on her lashes, and the two women clutched each other and did circles in the kitchen.

"I'm so happy for you, Susan!"

"I'm happy for me, too, Josie! Bob is perfect for me. He's not the man I first thought him to be, but he's proved to be even better. And I love him so much." She wiped her cheeks with shaking hands and tried to collect herself, but she couldn't stop jiggling around. "He treats me like I'm special."

Josie knew the feeling well. Nick made her feel like she was the only woman alive—but he would never ask her to marry him. It was up to her to take the initiative. "You *are* special. Bob's a lucky man to have you."

"Bob told Nick this morning." Her tone suggested that Josie should be upset by that news.

Nick had gotten so comfortable with her, and every day it seemed he spent more and more time with her, sleeping with her at night, calling her during the day. He talked to her and confided in her. He'd taken her to his house and they'd laughed together at the unconventional steps he'd taken to simplify his life.

But inside, Josie's heart had nearly broken. By his own design, Nick had set up his life so there was no room for a permanent relationship. Jeb had warned her several times the effect his parents' divorce and his stepmother's spite had had on Nick. Not that Jeb wanted to discourage her from loving Nick. Just the opposite. Josie often had the feeling Jeb did his best hard sell on Nick, trying to maintain her interest.

"Don't you want to know what Nick had to say about it?"

"He's due home in just a little while. I'm sure we'll talk about it then."

Susan tilted her head in a curious way and then forced a laugh. "You say *home* as if Nick lives here now."

Josie sat in her chair, stirred her coffee, then put down the spoon. She looked around the kitchen for inspiration, but found nothing except her own nervousness.

"Josie?" Susan pulled out her own chair, then frowned. There was a heavy silence. Josie tugged at the edge of her miniskirt, knowing what was coming. Her relationship with Nick wasn't precisely a secret, not really. But it had been private.

Now, though, what did it matter? In a very short while, Nick would either decide to stay, or he'd go. "He's been sort of staying here, yes."

"Sort of? What the hell does that mean?"

Susan's voice had risen to a shout and Josie sighed. "It means I have my own private life to lead."

"In other words, you want me to butt out, even though I can see you're making a huge mistake?"

Josie refused to think of Nick as a mistake. He made her feel alive, special and whole. Even if he turned down her proposal, she'd never regret her time with him.

Josie was still formulating an answer when Susan's temper suddenly mushroomed like a nuclear cloud.

She launched from her seat and began pacing furiously around the kitchen. "I'll kill him! God, how that man can be so considerate and generous one minute and such an unconscionable bastard the next is beyond me!"

Josie glanced at the kitchen clock. She was running out of time. "Susan, I really can't let you insult Nick. It's not fair. We made an agreement and he's living up to his end of the bargain. I'm the one who stipulated no strings attached."

Susan slashed her hand in the air. "Only because you knew anything more was unlikely with a man like *him*." She thumped a fist onto the counter. "I asked him to leave you alone, but he wouldn't listen to me."

"You did what?"

"He told me he wouldn't hurt you."

"And he hasn't! Oh, Susan, you had no right. How dare you—"

But Susan wasn't listening. "And to think I was actually starting to like the big jerk."

"You were?" Then, "Damn it Susan, don't change the subject. When did you talk with Nick about me? *What did you say?*"

In the next instant, Bob stepped into the kitchen. "I knocked, but you two were arguing too loud to hear... me...." His voice trailed off as he stared at Josie in her killer outfit. After a stunned second, he gave a low whistle. "Wow."

Susan whirled to face him. Bob took one look at her piqued expression, quickly gathered himself, then pulled her close. He glared at Josie over Susan's head. "What did you say to upset her?"

Josie's mouth fell open in shock. She'd never before heard Bob use that tone. Before she could even begin to think of a reply, Susan jerked away from him.

"Don't you snap at my sister! It's not her fault. It's that degenerate friend of yours who's to blame."

Throwing up his hands, Bob asked, "What did Nick do now?"

To add to the ridiculous comedy, Nick walked in. "Yeah, what did I do? And who forgot to invite me to the party?" He grinned, caught sight of Josie and seemed to turn to stone. Only his eyes moved, and they traveled over her twice before he frowned and lifted his gaze to her face in accusation.

"We're not having a party," Josie informed him, feeling very put upon with the circumstances. She pulled two more coffee mugs down from the cabinet. "I'm just trying to convince Susan that I know what I'm doing."

Nick advanced on her, his stride slow and predatory. "I see. And what are you doing, dressed like that? Planning to expound on your experiences? Planning to breach new horizons?" He pointed a finger at her. "We had a deal, lady!"

"What in the world are you talking about?"

His cheekbones dark with color, his eyes narrow and his jaw set, he waved a hand to encompass her from head to toe. "Were you planning to go back to the same bar? Have I bored you already?"

Her plans were totally ruined, the moment lost, and now here was Nick, behaving like a jealous, accusing ass.

Her temper flared. "Actually," she growled, going on tiptoe to face him, "I thought I'd ask for your hand—or rather your whole body—in matrimony. So what do you think of *that*?"

She heard Susan's gasp, Bob's amused chuckle, but what really fascinated her was Nick's reaction. He grabbed her arms and pulled her closer still, not hurting her, but bringing her flush against his hard chest.

"You what?" he croaked.

"You heard me. I want to marry you."

A fascinating series of emotions ran over his face, then Nick turned, still holding her arm, and practically dragged her from the room. Josie had no idea what he was thinking, because the last expression he had was dark and severe and forbidding. In her high-heeled shoes, which still hampered her walk, she had no choice but to stumble along behind him.

Susan started to protest, but Bob hushed her. Josie could hear them both whispering.

Nick took her as far as her bedroom, locking the door behind them. Josie jerked away from him, but he simply picked her up and laid her on the bed, then carefully lowered his length over her, pinning her down from shoulders to knees. Josie struggled against him. "We have to talk, Nick. I've got a lot to say to you."

Still frowning, he said, "I love you, Josie."

Her eyes widened. Well, maybe she could wait her turn to talk. "Do you really?"

"Damn right."

She chewed her lip. "Do you love me enough to marry

me?" Before he could answer, she launched into her well-rehearsed arguments on marital bliss. "Because I love you that much. I had planned to ask you properly, after a special night out. Even though I'm not the sexy lady you met that first night at the bar, I can be her on occasion. I just can't be her all the time. I realize that now. I knew something was missing from my life, but it wasn't what I thought." She touched his jaw. "It was you."

His Adam's apple took a dip down his throat, and then Nick smiled, his eyes bright, filled with fierce tenderness. "You are that same, sexy lady, honey, and you make my muscles twitch with lust just looking at you. You're also the very sweet little sister who's spent years showing her appreciation, and the conscientious caretaker who makes people feel important again. I love all of you, everything about you." He kissed her quick and hard. "Were you serious about wanting to marry me?"

Josie threw her arms around him and squeezed him tight.

Nick laughed. "Talk to me, sweetheart. This is my first attempt at professing love and I'm in a welter of emotional agony here."

"You're very good at it, you know."

"At suffering?"

"At professing your love." She pushed him back enough to see his face. "Yes I want to marry you. And I want to buy a house and make babies and—"

"Whoa. About the house..."

His hesitation shook her and she cupped his face in her hands, hoping to soothe him. "A house is permanence, Nick, I know. But it's what I want. I don't expect you to change, to become someone else, because I love you just as you are. But you will have to meet me halfway on this."

"No more gym equipment in the dining room?"

"And no other women. Just me. Forever."

"I like the sound of that." He leaned down and nuzzled her chin. "Honey, we don't need to buy a house because we already have one. And no, don't look so horrified. I'm not talking about my house." He smoothed her hair from her forehead, his touch tender. "Granddad came to see me today. He's moving into the condominium with Mrs. Wiley and he wants us to have his house, if, as he put it, I was lucky enough to convince you to marry me."

The enormity of Jeb's gesture overwhelmed her and put a lump in her throat. She swallowed hard. "Oh."

"Granddad knows you love that house almost as much as he does. He insists it has to stay in the family, and he said it might help my case in persuading you to the altar. Wait until I tell him you proposed and all I had to do was say yes."

"So you are saying yes?"

"How could I not when I'm so crazy about you?"

Josie contemplated a lifetime with Nick and felt so full of happiness, it almost hurt. "I can't believe I'll get to do anything and everything to you that I've ever imagined."

He froze over her, groaned, then settled his mouth, hot and wet, possessively over hers. Josie had just decided she didn't care if Bob and Susan were in the kitchen when Nick pulled back.

"I have a few confessions to make."

She bit his lip, his chin. Her breathing was unsteady. "Not now, Nick."

He caught her hands and held them over her head. "It has to be now. I don't want to mess up anymore. So just be still and listen."

Since he wasn't giving her much choice, she listened.

"I didn't realize it at the time, but I took you with me to see my grandfather because I knew he'd talk me up to you. I suppose I wanted you to like me as more than a damn fling, and Granddad seemed like the perfect solution."

Tenderness swelled in her heart. "You've never needed any help with that one. I've always liked you."

"I wasn't thinking of anything permanent when I did that, Josie. I just wanted more time with you, and I knew I couldn't let you start experimenting with any other guy. The thought makes me nuts."

"I never intended to. I just told you that so you'd agree to hang around. I knew it was what you wanted to hear."

He stared at her with widened eyes. "You lied?"

"Mmm-hmm." She touched his jaw, his throat. His familiar weight pressed her down and had her body warming in very sensitive places. "I'd have done anything to keep you around a while."

"Damn it, Josie, do you have any idea what you've put me through?"

"Are you talking about on the boat?" She dragged one foot up his calf, then wrapped both legs around him. "I remember it very well."

His expression changed from annoyance to interest, then to grudging respect. "You know damn well that wasn't what I was talking about, you just said it to distract me. You're such a little tease."

"I learned from a master."

His grin was slow and filled with wickedness. "A master, huh? But I haven't even come close to showing you everything yet."

Though his words caused a definite hot thrill to shimmer through her belly, she hid her reaction and smiled. "And I haven't even come close to testing the limits of your restraint. Do you know what I'd like to do to you next?"

"I don't want to know. Not yet."

She leaned up and whispered in his ear anyway. He groaned, pressed his hips closer to hers and asked, "When?"

Epilogue

NICK..." Josie's groan echoed around the large bedroom and Nick slowed his pace even more, loving the sound of her pleas, loving her. For almost six months now they'd been married and living in what he still called Granddad's house— and Nick knew he couldn't have been happier.

"Tell me what you want, sweetheart."

For an answer, she dug her fingers into the muscles of his shoulders and tried to squirm beneath him.

"Uh, uh, uh." He pressed down, making her gasp. "You promised to hold perfectly still."

"I can't, Nick."

His lips grazed her cheek. "You always say that, honey. I always prove you wrong." He chuckled softly at her low moan. "Trust me. You'll enjoy this."

He slipped his hand down between their bodies and pressed his thumb where she needed it most. "Easy..." But this time his words did no good. Josie arched off the bed, her head back, her cries deep and real and she took him with her as she climaxed.

Long minutes later, he managed a dry chuckle and a mild scolding. "You're too easy, Josie. And you need to learn to slow down. I'm going to get conceited if you don't stop trying so hard to convince me what a wonderful lover I am."

Without bothering to open her eyes, she lifted a limp hand and patted his cheek. "You're the very best."

He laid his hand on her belly and watched her shiver. "I love you, Josie."

A smile tilted her mouth. "I've been thinking about cutting back at work some. With the way Granddad and Grandmom run things, I don't need to make my rounds to visit nearly so often anymore. No one is lonely, not with those two always throwing a party of one kind or another."

Nick still had a hard time thinking of Mrs. Wiley—now Mrs. Harris—as *Grandmom*. But he called her that because she asked him to and because he loved the way she pleased his grandfather, doting on him and putting the glow back in his eyes. She doted on Nick and Josie, as well, treating them as if they were her own grandchildren. The elders had married about a month ago, and were the epitome of lovesick newlyweds.

Nick dragged his fingers down Josie's belly to her hipbones. He explored there, watching gooseflesh rise on her smooth skin. "If you want to work less, you know I won't complain. But why the sudden decision?"

She turned to look at him and she caught his hand, bringing it to her lips. "Susan is pregnant."

He stared at her for a long minute, then broke into a huge smile. "Well, I'll be damned. Bob hasn't said a thing."

"Susan was going to tell him tonight."

"He'll be thrilled. And Susan will make a wonderful mother. Maybe it'll keep her from checking up on you so often."

Josie smacked at him. "You know she's cut way back on that since we got married. She even likes you now."

"Yeah, but she pretends she doesn't. I think she just got used to hassling me."

Josie shook her head. "She knows how much you enjoy arguing with her." Then she bit her lip and tucked her face into his shoulder. "Nick?"

"Hmm?"

"What would you think about having a baby?"

His heart almost punched out of his chest. It took him thirty seconds and two strangled breaths to say, "Are you...?"

"Not yet. But I think I'd like to be."

He fell back on the bed and groaned. "Don't do that to me. I almost had a heart attack."

Josie didn't move. "So you don't like the idea?"

He came back up over her and rested his large hand on her soft belly. He stroked. "I love you, honey. I didn't think I'd ever feel this way about a woman, and now I can't imagine how I ever got by without you."

"Oh, Nick."

"And I'd love a baby." His rough fingertips smoothed her skin, teasing. "I'd love three or four of them, actually. God knows this house is big enough for a battalion, and nothing would make Granddad happier."

She chuckled and reached her hand down to his thigh. "Let's concentrate on just one, for now. I promise to make the endeavor pleasurable."

"I await your every effort."

Josie laughed at his hedonistic sigh. "You're so bad."

With one move, he flipped her over and pinned her beneath him. "You just got done telling me how good I am."

She lowered her eyes and flashed an impish grin. "Hmm. Then that must mean it's my turn to show you how good I can be."

"You're not done experimenting yet?"

She trailed a fingernail over his collarbone. "Nick, I've barely just begun."

HIS EVERY FANTASY
Janelle Denison

Chapter One

LEAH BURTON stood just outside of Jace Rutledge's auto shop, her heart beating triple time in her chest as she gathered the courage to approach Jace with her shameless proposition.

In all of her twenty-five years, she'd never been so brazen. But in the span of a few hours she'd gone for broke. First, she'd daringly stolen a page out of the *Sexcapades* book she'd found on the coffee table at the wedding planner's office. Then she'd made a spontaneous decision to seek out what really should go on between a man and woman in the bedroom. Because she certainly wasn't getting anything in that department from her soon-to-be fiancé, Brent. In fact, he seemed immune to her efforts to tempt him beyond luke-warm kisses, affectionate hugs and his gentle insistence that he respected her. He had no doubts that it was best to wait for their wedding night to make love.

If she accepted his offer of marriage, she thought, and leaned wearily against the cool metal siding of the building. She'd been stunned by his unexpected proposal a week ago during a candlelit dinner at one of Chicago's finest restaurants, since after all, they'd only been dating for six months. Though she had to admit, from the moment they'd met, Brent had swept her up into a whirlwind courtship that included expensive dinners, lavish dates and social events, and extravagant gifts. Including the gorgeous, two-karat diamond engagement ring he'd presented her with when he'd asked her to marry him.

Even though at times she felt more like a convenient social hostess than a true girlfriend, and she knew their relationship was based more on a subdued compatibility than on passion, she couldn't help but consider his proposal. Despite being a bit on the staid side, Brent was offering her that elusive something she'd spent the past few years searching for—a man who wanted to settle down and get married.

As an investment banker, Brent's career was stable and secure, which she considered a bonus. She loved kids and couldn't wait to have a family of her own, and she wasn't getting any younger. Brent had assured her that he wanted the same. He'd said all the right words during his proposal, and while she told herself her emotions for him would flourish as time passed, she hadn't been able to bring herself to answer with an unconditional yes. Instead she had given him a quiet, solemn, "I'm not sure."

Leah winced as she recalled the disappointment she'd seen in Brent's gaze, but he'd been incredibly gracious and understanding about her uncertainty. He'd reached across the table, squeezed her hand and told her to think about his offer while he was out of town for a week-long business trip. She could give him her answer when he returned on Sunday afternoon.

Which left her with only this weekend to figure out what she wanted in her life and in her future.

But one thing was clear—that missing intimacy between herself and Brent was causing a whole lot of doubts about herself and their relationship. And his lack of sexual interest made her painfully aware that she wasn't inspiring wild passion in Brent, nor was he doing it for her, either. Not in the way a certain someone else could light a fire within her with just a glance.

She exhaled a deep breath and at the same time damned that book of erotic invitations she'd come across. The contents of the book had played on all her feminine insecurities and had compounded the doubts in her mind about herself and Brent. She'd gone into Divine Events that afternoon hoping that being surrounded by every aspect of planning a wedding would give her the boost of excitement and feeling of absolute certainty she needed to accept Brent's engagement ring.

Unfortunately, her impromptu trip to the wedding planners had only increased her anxiety.

While she'd been waiting in the reception area to meet with Cecily Divine, a red leather-bound book on one of the tables in the entryway had caught her attention. There was no title on the outside of the volume, and curiosity had gotten the best of her. She'd opened the cover and discovered the titillating world of *Sexcapades,* a sizzling-hot book for lovers all about shedding inhibitions, pushing boundaries and taking risks.

Inside, there were sealed pages of provocative, daring invitations. Some were even missing, as if other customers had helped themselves to a page to spice up their sex life. Right then and there, Leah took a risk of her own, and when no one was looking, she'd ripped out an invitation and had come away with "The Dance of the Seven Veils."

Once she'd reached the safety and privacy of her car, she'd opened the sealed page and read the provocative instructions, which included baring herself to her lover, body and soul. She'd shivered, certain she didn't have the nerve to pull off such a bold stunt, but the fantasies dancing in her head had taken on a life of their own. Except, in her mind it hadn't been Brent whom she'd performed the seductive striptease for. It had been Jace Rutledge, her brother's best friend since junior high, and a man she'd been half in love with for years.

That's when she realized her feelings for Jace were partly contributing to her inability to make a firm decision about Brent. And she knew that before she could commit herself to Brent—or any other man—for the rest of her life, she had to get Jace out of her system once and for all, so she could move on without any "what ifs" or regrets haunting her.

Jace was the guy she'd always desired from afar, but could never have. Not in the emotional, forever way that mattered, regardless of her strong attraction to him. Over the years they'd become good friends and spent time together on a casual basis. But ultimately, he was a bad boy who'd always played the field, who was content to remain a confirmed bachelor. And she'd heard enough talk between Jace and her brother to learn his MO when it came to dating. No strings attached. No commitments involved. And he'd made it clear that he had absolutely no interest in marriage.

Which actually made him the perfect candidate for what she had in mind. After having her sexual advances toward Brent subtly turned down with placating excuses, she was determined to validate her sexuality. She also needed to know that she had the nerve and fortitude necessary not only to seduce a man, but to strip for him as well.

With an erotic invitation tucked into her purse, she intended to learn what men really wanted from women, what turned them on, and to uncover what *she* found sexy and arousing. In the process, she hoped to find out what kind of man she wanted in her life. And there was no one better to experiment and indulge in those seductive desires with than Jace. Not only because she had the hots for him, in a way she didn't for Brent, but also despite his playboy reputation, he was one of her best friends, and someone she trusted with sexual tutoring and advice. She also trusted him to keep everything private between the two of them.

One weekend of Jace's time was all she'd ask. One weekend was all she'd give herself to be free and to satisfy the fantasies about him that slipped through her mind on a too-frequent basis. Then, armed with new knowledge, skills and confidence, she'd reevaluate her relationship with Brent. Her obsession with Jace would be behind her, so thoughts of him would no longer cloud her decision.

But, first, he had to agree to her request.

Biting her lower lip, she considered every last detail of her plan. So far, she hadn't told a soul about Brent's proposal— not even her best friend, her brother or her family, and she didn't intend to enlighten Jace either, or mention all her thwarted attempts to entice Brent. No, she'd tell Jace she just wanted the male point of view on how to spice things up sexually.

Squaring her shoulders, she turned the corner of the building and stepped into the auto repair garage Jace had bought six years ago and had since cultivated into a very successful business. There were eight bays, all filled with various vehicles in different stages of repair, and she glanced down the line of cars and the mechanics working in the garage in her search for Jace.

She waved to Gavin, one of Jace's workers and the garage manager, who smiled at her and pointed toward the front end of a BMW. She followed his directions and found Jace with the top half of his body bent over the engine, a wrench in hand as he worked on tightening a bolt.

Stopping a few feet behind him, Leah gave in to the pure pleasure of admiring his fine backside and decided that no one filled out a pair of faded jeans like Jace Rutledge. The soft, well-worn denim, complete with streaks of grease where he'd absently wiped his hands, molded to his toned butt and hard thighs, and the waistband rode low on his lean hips in a very enticing way. The blue work shirt he wore stretched over the muscles bisecting his back and bunching across his broad shoulders as he gave the wrench another firm tug.

He was an earthy, physical kind of man, in every way that mattered. He didn't mind getting down and dirty to get the job done, and he seemed to enjoy the exertion and labor involved in his line of work. Unlike Brent, who was polished and meticulous and wouldn't be caught dead with grease on his hands.

Jace straightened, six-feet-two of impressive, overwhelming male, and turned around to reach for a different-size wrench. He came to an abrupt stop when he caught sight of her, and a slow grin lifted the corners of his mouth, accentuated by a disarming dimple that had been charming those of the female gender since middle school.

Her pulse fluttered and a slow heat thrummed through her veins, a normal reaction whenever she was around Jace. He was so breathtakingly gorgeous, so inherently sexual, that any woman would have to be blind not to be affected by his virile good looks and confidence.

His facial features were Brad Pitt handsome, and his deep-green eyes lit up with genuine delight upon seeing her. "Hey, Leah," he drawled, his voice low and smooth and incredibly sexy. "How long have you been standing there?"

Long enough to look my fill of you. "Not long," she replied, and returned his smile with a casual one of her own, though she was feeling anything but nonchalant, considering the reason for her visit.

Grabbing a rag instead of one of the tools lined up on the workbench, he wiped his big, callused, working-man's hands on the towel, leaving dark smudges behind. "What's up?" He tipped his head, causing his roguishly long, sandy-blond hair to fall across his brow as he studied her for a quick moment. "Is everything okay, Leah?"

Depends on whether you'll agree to my proposition, she thought, and shifted nervously on her feet. "Would you happen to have a few spare minutes to talk?"

"For you, I have all the time in the world." He winked at her. "Just let me get cleaned up a bit, and I'll meet you back in my office."

"Thanks." She watched him disappear down a hallway that led to the men's room before she headed into the adjoining reception area of Jace's Auto Repair.

Leah said hello to his longtime secretary, Lynn, and continued on to the back room where Jace had set up a small but efficient office for himself. Other than the chair behind his desk, there was no place to sit, but she had too much restless energy swirling inside her to be idle. So, instead, she paced along the small strip of gray industrial carpet in front of his desk and in her mind rehearsed her request.

He entered the office minutes later, all cleaned up in a different T-shirt and jeans, and all traces of grease gone from his forearms and hands. The familiar, arousing scent of orange citrus clung to him, which was from the special solvent he used to cut through the grime that came from working on engines and automotive parts.

He handed her a bottle of chilled water, which he knew she preferred over soda, and popped open his own can of cola. "So, what brings you by?" he asked, his warm gaze connecting with hers. "Not that I'm not glad to see you, but you seem...distracted. Like something's on your mind."

As a longtime friend, he'd always had the uncanny ability to read her moods. "There is something on my mind," she admitted. He waited patiently for her to continue, and she rolled the cold bottle of water between her warm palms. "Actually, I need your help. That is, if you're willing to...assist me."

Setting his drink on his desk, he turned back toward her

and gently grasped her shoulders, his attention undivided and direct. His touch was firm, and the way his thumbs idly stroked the bare skin of her arms caused an insidious, forbidden heat to steal through her and settle in her belly.

She'd always known that Jace's touch was enough to ignite sexual sparks...and his ability to do so was a blatant reminder of what was lacking between herself and Brent. The distinct contrast was one she couldn't deny, and one which made today's quest more important than ever.

Concern creased Jace's brows, and, luckily, the silk blouse she wore was loose enough that he couldn't see the way her nipples had puckered tight. And if he noticed the goose bumps that had risen on her arms from the soft scrape of his fingers, he didn't mention the telltale sign.

"Honey, whatever it is, you know I'm here for you," he said, reminding her of the reason why she was there. "All you have to do is tell me what you need."

She met Jace's gaze, gulped for air and courage and, remembering the *Sexcapades* invitation that had set her on this course, she took her second risk of the day. "I want you to show me what turns a man on, and how to satisfy him in bed."

JACE BLINKED at the woman standing in front of him, certain the words he'd just heard slip past those soft, full lips of hers were part of one of his deepest, fondest dreams.

She was a far cry from what he'd consider a vixen, especially one who'd initiate such a sinful advance. No, Leah was more the traditional type, inside and out. The simple cream silk blouse and navy skirt she was wearing backed up his image of her, and also told him she'd just come from her job as a secretary for an engineering firm. But as conservatively as she dressed, he couldn't deny that he'd spent many pleasurable hours imagining her naked beneath all those buttoned-up outfits, wondering what it would be like to skim his hands over the firmness of her small breasts, the delicate curve of her waist and hips, the silky softness of her bared skin...

He shook his head, hard. Obviously, his imagination was spinning fantasies, because there was no way sweet, sensible, good-girl Leah Burton would ever issue him the tempting offer of being her tutor in the finer art of seduction, no matter how much he might have wished for such an opportunity.

When he'd first met her as the sister of his friend in middle school, Leah had been a young girl, and through the many years that he'd known her she'd become his good friend as well. He'd watched as she'd blossomed into a beautiful, desirable young woman with thick, shiny chestnut-brown hair that reached her shoulders, and a slender figure with just the right amount of curves to complement her petite frame. A woman completely and totally off-limits to him—in deference to his friendship with her brother, and in respect for her parents, who'd accepted him into their lives despite his questionable background.

His father had walked out on him when he was five and had never looked back, and he'd been raised by a mother who'd spent more of her time cruising bars for men and booze than with her son who'd needed her the most. The Burtons had fed him when he'd been hungry and had given him a safe place to sleep when he'd been too scared to stay the night alone in the ramshackle house his mother had rented. They'd bought him new shoes and clothes when his few pairs of secondhand jeans and shirts had been too threadbare to wear, expecting nothing in return. And when he'd gone through a rebellious stage, straying to the wrong side of the law and getting picked up for shoplifting, it had been Leah's father who'd met him at the police station, not his own mother. Jace had gotten a lecture on responsibility from Mr.

Burton and a tour of the local prison, which had scared the hell out of him and straightened him out real quick.

He'd always be eternally grateful for their generosity and guidance, and for being a part of Leah's family, and he'd never jeopardize his relationship with the Burtons by getting involved with their daughter. As a product of a dysfunctional family, he didn't do intimate relationships, not the kind that included an emotional commitment, because he just didn't know how to give to another person that way. But that knowledge didn't stop him from thinking about Leah beyond the friendship they shared. Her warmth and unconditional affection drew him and appealed to the loner he'd become, and the confirmed bachelor he'd sworn to be.

At the moment, though, the only thing that mattered was clearing up the misunderstanding that was wreaking havoc with his head and hormones.

"Want to run that request by me again?" He grinned ruefully, stroked his palms down her arms to her wrists and brushed his thumb over the thrumming pulse there, just to keep the connection between them. "I think my brain is working overtime today and I'm sure I didn't hear you correctly."

"I'm sure you did," she said with a slow, deliberately sensual smile, more bold than she'd ever been with him before. Then she repeated the same proposition that had tied him up in knots the first time. "I want you to show me what turns a man on, and how to satisfy him in bed."

Oh, shit. His stomach clenched, and he immediately dropped her hands and took a huge step back, the bond between them no longer the gesture of comfort it had once been. Heated, rippling overtures of keen awareness surged between them, the kind of attraction he'd been fighting for too many years now. He wanted Leah, but he'd also taught himself to keep his desire and need for her buried deep down into his soul, so no one would ever know.

And in one breathy statement she'd made him feel defenseless to resist her, and all too eager to accommodate her invitation to show her the ways of pleasuring a man—and eager to please her in return.

He exhaled hard and searched for a logical explanation to this bizarre, and far-too-arousing situation. "Leah...tell me this is some kind of joke that your brother cooked up to get even with me for getting him toasted when we went out drinking last weekend."

"I swear this isn't a joke, Jace," she said softly, her big blue eyes searching his, hopeful and daring at the same time. "I'm completely serious. I want you to be the one to tell me what fantasies men find exciting, and show me what drives them crazy with lust."

Licking her lips, she closed the distance he'd put between them and placed her hand on his chest, right over his rapidly beating heart. "I want to learn how to touch and caress a man in the most effective, arousing way," she said huskily as her palm slid lower, along his ribs to his belly. "And I wouldn't mind discovering a thing or two about what *I* like, either."

She was doing a damn good job of inflaming him right now. His skin felt hot and feverish, the muscles in his stomach coiled tight. And lower, his penis lengthened and strained against the fly of his jeans. It took every ounce of strength he possessed not to grab her hand, cup her fingers against his erection, and give her ample proof of just how much she turned him on.

Leaning his backside against his desk, he crossed his arms over his chest, trying to take a more logical, reasonable approach. "Why do you need me to teach you these things?"

She shrugged a slender shoulder and opened the cap on her bottled water. "I want a better understanding of men and what they like sexually."

He watched her tip her head back and take a drink of the cool liquid. "And what about you and what you like sexually?"

She licked a droplet of water off the corner of her mouth, and a light blush swept across her cheeks. But his straight-forward question didn't deter her at all. "I figure I'll discover that along the way," she said, playful and teasing.

A stunning thought slammed into him, and he abruptly straightened. "Good God, Leah, you're not a…" He couldn't even bring himself to say the word.

"A virgin?" she supplied for him, and laughed lightly. "No, I've been with two other men, neither of whom rocked my world in bed, or out of it even. So, that leads me to believe that I'm missing out on some crucial element when it comes to sexual pleasure and seduction."

He rubbed a hand across his forehead. He couldn't believe he was having such an intimate conversation with Leah. Sure, as friends they'd discussed a variety of topics, but nothing so personal as her sex life. Or his for that matter. But that hadn't stopped him from thinking about her and the men she dated, which brought to mind the executive-type guy she was currently seeing.

"Why not ask Brent to help you with your…research?"

For the first time since propositioning him, she glanced away, but only for a few seconds before her gaze meet his again, more determined than before. "Because, quite honestly, he doesn't always do it for me in that way, and he doesn't have the kind of reputation you do."

He lifted a brow. Her comment flashed him back to the scruffy, insecure teenager he'd once been, and possibly always would be deep down inside, though he'd managed to build a façade of confidence around himself over the years. "Ahh, so you'd rather get down-and-dirty hands-on training from a bad boy from the wrong side of the tracks?" She wouldn't be the first woman who'd considered a fling with him in those terms.

She looked startled by the bite in his tone, but quickly recovered. "That's not what I meant, and you know I've never thought of you that way," she said adamantly.

He couldn't argue her point, because she was one of the few people in his life who'd accepted him for who and what he was—before he'd become a successful businessman.

"As for your reputation," she went on, "you've been with a lot of women, so I'd think you'd have a whole lot of experience in this area."

She flattered him, and he did his best to hold back a snort of derision. Lots of women, hardly. Maybe half a dozen that he'd actually slept with over the years, and with age he'd grown more discriminating and hadn't found anyone who'd interested him beyond a date or two. He'd hardly label himself a Don Juan who'd been with a slew of women.

Reaching out, he trailed the back of his hand along her smooth cheek, watched her eyes catch fire from his touch, and a part of him was gratified to know that while she might question her ability to respond to other men, it was obvious she was incredibly responsive to him.

"Honey," he murmured huskily, "I don't know what other men like, or what turns them on. I only know what *I* like."

"That's good enough for me." Her voice was breathless, her breasts rising and falling heavily. "I'm asking you to do this for me, with me, because I trust you to show me everything from the basics to the more erotic, and to keep everything between us discreet and private. All I want, all I need from you, is this one weekend."

She was offering him two nights of anything goes. Judging by everything he'd learned thus far, Brent wasn't giving her the attention she needed to satisfy her more feminine desires. Otherwise she wouldn't be here right now, asking him for lessons in foreplay and mating rituals.

She tempted him like no other, yet he managed, just barely, to remain chivalrous enough to try and dissuade her from this wild idea. "And if I say no?"

Her chin lifted a fraction, a defiance and rebellious spirit so contradictory to her normal agreeable personality. "Then I guess I'll have to find someone else who *is* willing."

He knew a direct challenge when he heard one, and she was blatantly provoking him to accept her dare. She seemed hell-bent on following through with her impulsive plan, and the thought of her finding another man to agree to her proposition sent a jolt of jealous heat shooting through his veins.

And considering how bold and brazen she was being with him, he didn't doubt she *would* sway another man into agreeing to give her a crash course in how to please a man in bed and out.

He struggled with doing the right thing, the *noble* thing that even her own brother would expect him to do, but he just couldn't bring himself to push her into the arms of another man for something he was all too willing and eager to give her. And then there was the possessive emotion twisting low in his gut that took him by surprise, as well.

Sure, he'd always been protective of Leah given they were friends and his situation with her brother and family, but this feeling was different—a completely physical and intimate need to take charge and show Leah everything she wanted to learn.

Yes, he'd be her weekend lover. This way, he'd be in control of the situation, whereas there was no telling how another man, a stranger possibly, might take advantage of her. If anyone was going to satisfy her erotic curiosity, it would be him, he decided. No one else.

He could have Leah for one weekend. His every fantasy

fulfilled, and hers, too. A perfect secret arrangement with no entanglements or expectations—just a hot mutual affair that would remain completely private between the two of them.

It really was an ideal arrangement.

Anticipation pumped through him, and he pushed his fingers through his already mussed hair and gave her what she'd come there for. "Fine, I'll do it."

She released a sigh that was pure relief. "Thank you, Jace."

She was smiling up at him, looking extremely pleased with herself, her eyes sparkling with unabashed excitement. He wondered if she realized what she was really getting herself into, and decided to give her one last chance to change her mind about this crazy plan of hers before she did something she'd regret later. He owed her, and himself, that much.

Yes, she trusted him, and he'd never, ever do anything to hurt her, but if he showed her exactly what to expect and how demanding and aggressive he could be when it came to getting what *he* wanted, maybe she'd come to her senses and realize just how potent and dangerous her scheme could be to them both.

"Since we have an agreement, are you ready for your first lesson?" he asked.

Startled surprise etched her expression, and she cast a quick glance out the window behind him, overlooking the building's parking lot. "Right here? Right now?"

She was shocked, possibly uncertain about getting caught. Good. He was about to shake her up even more.

He backed her up against the nearest wall and flattened his hands on either side of her head, trapping her in the cage of his body and allowing her no escape...not unless she asked to be set free.

His gaze dropped to her soft, pink, glossy lips, then slowly, lazily lifted once again. "Sure. Why not right here, right now?" he drawled impudently.

The thrill of the forbidden flashed in her eyes. "Whatever the first lesson may be, I'm game," she whispered, teasing him with her words, her eagerness to explore anything and everything with him. "Let's go for it."

"Yes, let's." He lowered his head, took her mouth with his, and finally kissed her as he'd been wanting to kiss her for what seemed like forever.

Chapter Two

LEAH HAD DREAMED of this moment for years, but her fantasies didn't even come close to the reality of having Jace's mouth on hers, the pressure of his lips parting hers so that he could slip deep inside and taste and stroke and tangle his tongue with her own. The kiss was hot and greedy and wickedly aggressive, bypassing all the gentlemanly preliminaries she was used to with Brent.

Jace was no gentleman, not when it came to kissing her, and his response excited her as nothing else had in a very long time, if ever. This was exactly what she craved. To be possessed by a man, and to experience passion in its most raw, untamed form.

One kiss, and she felt alive as a woman and a sexual creature with feminine desires and needs. And it felt amazingly, gloriously wonderful to experience such an instantaneous surge of lust for a man.

But as much as kissing him thrilled her, it wasn't enough. She ached for a more intimate contact with him, but other than their clinging lips, he wasn't touching her anywhere else. His hands were still braced firmly on the wall next to her head, and six inches of space separated their bodies. Embracing the assertive woman she was determined to be this weekend with Jace, she sought to remedy that problem, to break any last threads of restraint in him and let him know that she wanted no reservations between them.

Dropping her hands to the waistband of his jeans, she hooked her fingers into the belt loops at his sides and slowly, inexorably, pulled him toward her, until her soft, female curves molded to his hard, masculine contours. Their hips met, and the impressively thick, solid erection nestling against her belly surprised her in a very good way.

Knowing she was responsible for his state of arousal boosted her confidence, made her burn for him, and she slid her hands around to his backside and cupped his taut buttocks in her palms. She instinctively arched into him, shamelessly rubbed her mound against that solid ridge of flesh, and reveled in the low groan of need that rumbled up from his chest.

He threaded his fingers through the strands of her hair and slanted her head to better fit their mouths together for a warm, wet, and wonderfully erotic kiss. His free hand caressed her jaw and trailed down the side of her neck, until his thumb found the erratic pulse at the base of her throat, though he didn't linger there long. Releasing the first button on her blouse, he slipped his splayed palm into the loose, open collar. His roughened fingertips abraded her smooth skin, and her breathing deepened as he slid lower and nestled her small breast in his hand. The material of her bra was thin and insubstantial, all sheer fabric and lace, and when he grazed her tight, sensitive nipple with his thumb, she shuddered and nearly came apart.

He seemed just as lost in the heady pleasure of the kiss, just as sexually charged. The long fingers wrapped in her hair tightened, and he pressed her more fully against the wall with the lean, powerful length of his frame. Grinding his hips hard against hers, he thrust his tongue deeper into her mouth. Aggressive male heat radiated off him in waves, and her body grew pliant and damp, aching for his touch in places too long denied.

The phone on his desk buzzed, and he jerked away and stumbled back, nearly falling on his ass in his haste to put distance between them. His breathing was shallow and quick, and she almost laughed at the incredulous look on his face. Too incredulous, as if he couldn't quite believe that she'd allowed him to go so far.

And then it dawned on her. Obviously, Jace had meant to change her mind with that explosive, dominant kiss, but his plan had backfired. She wanted him now more than ever. He was everything she'd ever desired, and their sizzling encounter proved just how much he wanted her, too.

Abruptly, he rounded his desk and punched the intercom button on his phone, all the while his gaze remaining riveted on her flushed face. "What is it, Lynn?"

"Mr. Dawson is here to drop off his Porsche for servicing," his secretary said, her voice filling the small office. "And he wanted to talk to you about the repairs he's having done."

"Offer him something to drink, and tell him I'll be there in a minute." He disconnected the line, but remained behind the barrier of his desk.

Leah lightly brushed her fingers along her mouth, and watched his eyes dilate with a renewed hunger. Her lips felt wet, swollen, deliciously ravished. After experiencing too many of Brent's quick, passionless kisses, the lush sensation felt so, so good, as did witnessing Jace's heated reaction to the seductive way she touched her mouth.

She lowered her hand and was the first to break the silence that had descended between them. "I think you just covered first, second and third base in that lesson." A smile quirked her lips and humor laced her voice.

"Close, but not quite. There's still a whole lot more to learn," he returned with a slow, lazy grin of his own. "That is, if you're still interested."

Did he really think she'd refuse? "More than ever. I'm looking forward to every single minute of your private lessons."

"Then I'll be at your place tonight, 7:00 p.m. sharp, and I want you to wear something short and revealing."

She lifted a brow curiously. "Another lesson?"

"You could call it that, yes." He finally rounded his desk, his gaze glittering purposefully, his demeanor just as sinfully direct. "If you want to know what men find sexy, then there's one thing you should keep in mind."

"And what's that?" she asked, wide-eyed and eager.

"Most men like visual stimulation when it comes to the opposite sex." Gathering the sides of her loose blouse in his fists, he gradually tightened the material across her chest. "Initially, if you want to turn our heads and keep our attention, then you need to give us an incentive to look. Bait the hook, so to speak. And a more formfitting outfit will do that every time."

The fabric was now taut in his hands and cool across her flesh, revealing her small, pert breasts crowned with pointed nipples and the indentation of her waist and hips. He looked his fill, his ravenous gaze causing a delicious heat to spread through her veins.

"You have a nice body, Leah," he murmured huskily. "Don't be afraid to put it on display every once in a while. And since this weekend is all about executing lessons, I want you to wear something enticing for me."

He released her blouse, but her breasts remained tight and aching. "I'll see what I can do," she managed to murmur. If he wanted enticing, she'd definitely deliver on his request.

Picking up her purse, she left his office, her stomach fluttering with the exciting knowledge that sexy bad-boy Jace

Rutledge belonged to her for the next forty-eight hours. And she was all his.

She only hoped that was enough time to satisfy her longing for him, and finally get him out of her mind and heart, once and for all.

AT FIVE MINUTES to seven, Jace made his way up to Leah's apartment, the anticipation of what the night might hold kicking up his adrenaline a few notches.

This was it, he thought. Once he stepped into Leah's place there would be no turning back—because his presence was just as good as a promise. His arrival meant he had every intention of following through on the pact they'd made.

He'd given her one last chance to change her mind. Considering the uninhibited way she'd responded to the hot, combustible kiss they'd shared, and her sassy attitude afterward, it was safe to say that she knew exactly what she was getting herself into, and her mind was made up.

Well, so was his.

From his perspective, all bets were off, and from here on he wasn't holding back with Leah. He'd selfishly accept anything she offered, take her as far as she dared to go sexually, and do his best to boost her confidence along the way. This weekend was for him just as much as it was for her, and he intended to give her an affair to remember.

He knocked on her door to announce his presence and used the key she'd given him months ago to enter her apartment. "Hey, Leah, it's Jace," he said, and closed the door behind him.

"I'm in my bedroom," she called out. "Come on back."

For as many times as he'd been in her apartment over the years, he'd never been in her bedroom before. There had never been any reason to traverse into that feminine domain. And now she'd issued a personal invitation he wasn't about to refuse.

"Hey there," she said, greeting him with a smile as she slipped into a pair of strappy, high-heeled sandals. "I'm almost done getting ready."

Jace stared at the vision before him, his every fantasy come to life. Leah's transformation from conservative to knockout gorgeous made his mouth go dry and awareness surge through his bloodstream. He'd always known that beneath the sensible, practical clothing she normally wore, she had the potential to be a sexy siren, and the alluring outfit she'd changed into confirmed his hunch.

The dress was thigh-length short with a flirty, ruffled hem and a bodice that nipped in at her slender waist. A gathered, scooped neckline tied together with a small bow between her breasts, and it was all he could do to stop himself from reaching out and tugging on that string and baring all her luscious assets to his gaze.

"Wow, you look...*incredible,*" he rasped as he took in the way she'd piled her hair on top of her head in a messy topknot, exposing the elegant line of her throat for the stroke of his fingers, the caress of his mouth. He shook himself mentally and cleared his throat. "How long have you been hiding *that* outfit?"

"For a few weeks now." She shrugged a shoulder and smiled tentatively as she picked up a pair of gold hoop earrings from her dresser and pushed them through her lobes. "It looked so cute on the mannequin in the store, and so I bought the dress, but I haven't had the opportunity to wear it."

He lifted a brow and felt compelled to ask about her boyfriend's opinion on the matter. "Not even for Brent?"

"I wasn't sure that Brent would like it since it's so...different," she said, shades of uncertainty creeping into her voice. "He's more on the conservative side, and he doesn't think it's appropriate to have so much skin showing in public."

Jace stared at her, feeling both stunned and disgusted. Did

Brent have rocks in his head? Or, more appropriately, in his pants? He doubted that Leah wanted to hear his point of view on Brent's way of thinking, so he kept his sentiments to himself. He hoped the lessons she learned this weekend would knock some sense into Leah about her significant other.

"Anyway, the dress has been hanging in my closet, and tonight just became the perfect opportunity to put it to good use." She twirled around, giving him a 360-degree view of her new outfit. "So, what do you think? Do you like it?"

"What's not to like?" he said, his gaze drawn to her supple thighs where the swirling hemline ended.

Brent's unappreciative attitude made Jace want to pull out all the stops with Leah, to make her feel desirable and sexy in every way. "You're a beautiful woman in a hot dress, and I, for one, love how much of your skin is showing. It makes me want to touch you all over, just to feel how soft and smooth all that skin really is."

Her cheeks flushed a becoming shade of pink that spread down to the small swells of her breasts, but her eyes shone with a come-hither dare. "Then do it."

Without hesitating, he crossed the bedroom, closing the short distance between them. The dresser was right behind her, and he grasped her waist and lifted her so she was sitting on the smooth surface. Pressing his hands against her knees, he widened her legs and moved in between.

He'd definitely surprised her with his aggressive move, but she didn't object to their intimate position, and he considered skipping all the preliminaries of seduction and getting right down to the raw, primal need of making love to her. She'd made him excruciatingly hard, and he ached to feel her liquid and lush around him, the soft cushion of her naked breasts pressing into his chest. He thought about pushing up her dress, pulling down her panties, and sinking into her slick body. He imagined how she'd wrap her legs high around his waist, urging him deeper, and how she'd scream his name when she came.

The thought made him shudder.

He fingered an errant strand of hair that had fallen from her topknot, the silken texture teasing his senses, as did the soft, feminine scent emanating from her. "I like your hair up like this." Cupping her smooth cheek in his callused palm, he tipped her head and nuzzled the side of her throat, and felt her shiver in response. "It gives me access to some of the most sensitive spots on your body...like right here," he murmured. He skimmed his open mouth up to her ear and laved the spot just below her lobe with his tongue.

She gasped and curled her fingers around his upper arms for support. "I...I like that."

He did, too. "Mmm, and right here," he went on, and gently sank his teeth into a tendon at the base of her neck, branding her with a love bite.

Her breathing deepened. "Oh, Jace..."

He smiled knowingly and whispered in her ear, "I'm betting you felt that biting sensation in other places, too, didn't you?" Like the tips of her breasts, her belly, between her thighs.

She managed a jerky nod and clenched her knees against his hips. "Yes."

Satisfied with her answer and the slumberous heat of desire in her gaze, he continued to tempt her and himself. "As much as I like your hair up, I love it down even more."

Releasing the clasp holding the chestnut tresses atop her head, he watched as the thick mass spilled free, then buried his hands up to his wrists in the luxurious strands. "I love it tousled around your shoulders and pretty face, and how warm and silky it feels wrapping around my fingers and against my skin."

"I like your hands in my hair," she admitted, and groaned

when he massaged her scalp, then glided his thumbs along her jawline. "It feels so sensual and arousing."

"I agree." He was equally seduced by her, and the moment he'd created.

She was staring at his lips, so he crushed his mouth to hers and gave her what she wanted, what he craved, knowing that, soon, kissing her would no longer be enough to satisfy him. They'd boldly stepped over a line they'd never before crossed with this provocative proposition of hers, and being with her in so many intimate ways was unearthing a slew of emotions and needs he'd kept deeply buried for years.

He kissed her, long and slow and deep, her mouth so hot and soft and sweet under his, just as he imagined her body would be as he moved over her, inside her. With that arousing thought dancing in his head, he swept a hand down her back and shifted her bottom closer to the edge of the dresser, until the only thing separating their bodies were her insubstantial panties, and his khaki trousers. She locked her ankles against the backs of his thighs, rocked her pelvis against his erection in a natural, unconscious invitation, and his shaft swelled to the point of bursting.

With every kiss, he was slowly, gradually becoming addicted to her, and he wondered in the back of his mind if after this weekend he'd be able to let her go and watch her be with another man. The practical side of his brain said he had no choice, but his body and heart struggled to convince him otherwise.

One last lingering taste and he lifted his mouth from hers. But he still held her close, his fingers tangled in her hair, disheveling the strands even more. Her beautiful blue eyes were heavy-lidded, and a dreamy smile curved her puffy, well-kissed lips.

The pleasure she gave him was immense, beyond physical, and more than he had ever dreamed possible. "If you were mine, and you wore this dress out with me, I'd make damn sure you looked just like this before we left the house, so that every man who glanced your way would know without a doubt that you were taken."

The pulse at the base of her throat fluttered wildly. "And how do I look?" she asked curiously, guilelessly.

He brushed the back of his knuckles over the soft, heaving swells of her breasts. "With your hair down and rumpled, your lips pink and wet and parted, and your eyes soft and unfocused, you look like a woman who just came from my bed after a long, hot session of mindless sex."

Her brows rose, shock mingling with sexy overtones of confidence. "Except I'm far from satisfied."

He groaned. She was going to kill him before the weekend was through. "That was just a sample to whet your appetite for more," he promised. "It's called the slow, gradual buildup of sexual tension that leads to the main event, and we've got the whole night ahead of us, sweetheart."

She laughed, the sound filled with low, throaty affection. "I can't decide if you're very bad for teasing me like that, or very good, Jace."

He grinned and helped her scoot off the dresser. "How about a little of both?"

"I'll give you that." Bemusement and eager anticipation etched her expression. "So, where are you taking me tonight?"

"Out dancing," he said, and twirled her playfully in his arms. "Where you can put that racy outfit to good use and drive a few men crazy with lust."

Placing a hand on his chest, she lifted up onto the tips of her shoes and nipped gently at his bottom lip. "The only one I want to drive crazy tonight with lust is you." With a sassy smile, she turned and sashayed out of the bedroom.

Jace didn't think that was going to be a problem. He was already there.

LEAH HAD NEVER BEEN to a nightclub before, at least not one as upscale and dynamic as Chicago's Red No. Five. Wearing a fun, sexy dress, and having a gorgeous guy on her arm, she was determined to enjoy the new and unique experience to its fullest potential.

Jace held her hand securely in his as he cut a path through the crowd, while she took in the seductive ambience, complete with laser lights, a huge dance floor, and intimate seating areas with private, secluded booths and couches swathed in rich velvet. They passed a cluster of women who were undoubtedly on the make, and there was no mistaking the appreciative, interested looks they cast Jace's way. He merely smiled politely and continued toward the back of the lounge.

The place was packed, the music loud with a distinct techno beat she found sensual and exciting, and thrummed rhythmically through her body. The people out on the dance floor were loose-limbed and uninhibited in their movements, and she envied their ability to just let go and enjoy themselves and their undulating bodies, uncaring of who watched. Which made her think of that *Sexcapades* invitation she'd taken, and how she needed to learn to be just as daring so she could strip with the same unreserved ease.

Jace found a vacant booth and let Leah slide across the seat first before he settled himself beside her. While the spot he'd chosen was dimly lit, they had a perfect view of the bar area and the packed-to-capacity dance floor.

He leaned close and said loud enough for her to hear over the blaring music, "So, what do you think?"

"I like it." So far, she was fascinated by the sexually charged atmosphere, and wanted to be a part of it. "It's also a good place to watch men and women flirt and interact with one another. You know, the seduction thing?"

He grinned wryly. "I'm sure you'll get a good feel for the various kinds of mating rituals between couples."

A bar waitress came up to their table, set down napkins in front of them, and bent low to be heard. "What can I get the two of you to drink?"

Jace glanced at Leah, indicating that she should order first. If she were with Brent, she would have ordered a glass of chardonnay without hesitating. But she wasn't with Brent, and she definitely wasn't in a wine mood tonight.

"I want the most outrageous drink your bartender can make," she decided. "Something fun and exotic and uncivilized."

The pretty blonde thought for a moment, then her eyes sparkled in female camaraderie as she extended her suggestions. "Well, you've got your choice between a Blow Job, an Orgasm, or a Deep Throat."

They all sounded perfect for her wild, liberating weekend with Jace, and Leah definitely wanted to experience all three. "I think I'll start with an Orgasm and go from there."

"Good choice." The woman jotted down her drink preference and glanced at Jace, who looked taken aback by Leah's bold pursuit of the ultimate festive cocktail. "And for you, sir?"

"Since I'm the designated driver for the evening, and my date here is going to be enjoying orgasms, I'll take a cola." He flashed the waitress a grin.

Laughter danced in the woman's eyes. "You got it."

Minutes later, their drinks were delivered, and Leah anxiously sampled the smooth concoction flavored with Amaretto, vodka and rich cream. The drink was delicious, unlike anything she'd ever indulged in, and a moan of appreciation and pleasure rolled up from her throat.

Jace watched her, arresting her with his hot stare and the wicked slant to his smile. "Better watch out, sweetheart. Those orgasms are potent stuff."

She didn't miss the double entendre woven into his playful warning, and tossed out a sexy innuendo of her own.

"Mmm, but they sure do go down easy." Enjoying the sensation of being naughty, of feeling sensual and wanton, she swirled her finger into the sweetened cream and slowly licked it off. "Would you like to taste my orgasm?" she asked, not so innocently.

He choked on the drink of soda he was swallowing, and it took him a moment to recover. And when he did, he leaned in close, filling her vision with his bold, masculine features. "There's nothing I'd like more than to taste your orgasm," he said, his voice rough around the edges. "But *alcohol* is out of the question since I'm driving tonight."

The man's willpower and restraint amazed her. Undaunted, she dipped her finger into her drink once more, but this time she rubbed the creamy substance along *his* bottom lip. "Then let me taste it on you," she whispered, and grasping his jaw between her palms, she brought his mouth to hers and slowly lapped and nibbled away the heady flavors along with the pure male essence that was Jace.

She felt him shudder, felt that control of his slip a notch, and continued to tease him with her tongue and the arousing scrape of her teeth, relishing a feminine power that she had never before realized she possessed. Or maybe it was a matter of being with the right man, one who made her feel free to be assertive and confident.

In their dimly lit corner booth they were afforded a semblance of privacy, not that anyone would care if they were making out, because she'd seen a few couples doing just that when they'd entered the lounge. She was out with Jace tonight to test her sensuality, to seduce him, in a place where no one knew her. The exciting thought was more intoxicating than the drink she'd just consumed.

With one last leisurely lick, she lifted her mouth from his and slowly dragged her tongue across her own bottom lip. "Now *that* was potent."

Blazing heat flared in his gaze, so hot she felt scorched to her toes. The warmth of the liquor flowed through her limbs and unfurled in her belly, and the vibrating beat of the music pulsed within her, low and deep, adding to the sense of freedom she'd embraced for the weekend.

She glanced out at the other couples enjoying the lively music and wanted to be right in the middle of it all. "Let's dance," she said enthusiastically, and he didn't refuse her request.

Time passed quickly, and Leah couldn't ever remember having as good a time as she had flirting with Jace, dancing with him and teasing him. That luscious sexual tension between them built with every brush of their bodies, every heated look, every provocative comment that passed between them.

This, she realized, was the kind of seduction she'd craved.

Thirsty from dancing, she ordered the Deep Throat drink the waitress had mentioned earlier—this one a shot glass of vodka and Kahlua, topped with whipped cream. She downed the drink as the bartender instructed. Jace watched in amusement, and Leah fleetingly thought how appalled Brent would be to learn how well educated she was becoming when it came to cocktails. And she wasn't talking the dry martinis he preferred.

She finished off the exotic drink and kissed Jace on the lips, uncaring of anything but their time together. She refused to let thoughts of Brent ruin her short time with Jace.

An hour later, the ladies' room beckoned, and she excused herself to take care of personal business. When she returned minutes later, she couldn't find Jace where she'd left him at the bar. She searched the lounge, but no luck there, either.

Still curious about that last drink she'd yet to try, she made her way back to the bar and ordered a Blow Job, giggling as she did so because it felt so wonderfully wicked to say such an outrageous thing out loud. She felt just as naughty drinking the concoction in a quick shot, the liquid sliding down her throat in a rush of coffee-flavored brandy and more whipped cream.

When a friendly, nice-looking guy asked her to dance, she was flattered by the interest in his gaze and figured what could it hurt to enjoy another man's attention for a few minutes?

She followed him out into the crush of people gyrating to the beat rumbling through the speakers. The drinks she'd consumed relaxed her body and mind, allowing her to let go of any last inhibitions and move to the provocative tempo of the music.

JACE GLANCED toward the ladies' restroom one last time, fairly certain he'd missed Leah's exit while another woman had been diverting his attention with her numerous attempts to convince him to join her for a good time. He'd forgotten what ruthless pickup joints nightclubs could be, and that thought worried him for Leah, wherever she might have disappeared to.

Despite how she'd shamelessly flirted, touched and toyed with him the past few hours, she was inexperienced when it came to the kind of brazen games these singles played, and much too vulnerable to a sophisticated guy who could see past the eye-catching dress and vivacious attitude to the sexually naive woman beneath. Mix in a few potent drinks, and she was ripe for the picking, just waiting to be taken advantage of.

His stomach cramped, and he knew he'd never forgive himself if something happened to her. Neither would her brother, he thought with a grimace. Undoubtedly, if John ever discovered that he'd introduced his sister to such iniquity and left her unchaperoned, he'd not only be disappointed in Jace, but more than a little furious.

Jace continued his search through the club, and finally learned from the bartender that she'd enjoyed a Blow Job before heading out to the dance floor with another guy. While the bartender's statement held overtones of amusement, Jace couldn't bring himself to laugh at how sexual his comment sounded. And he certainly didn't like that she'd so easily gone off with another man.

Minutes later, as one song segued into another, he finally found Leah in the partying throng of people on the dance floor. Her face was flushed and her eyes were bright and sparkling. A light sheen of perspiration gathered on her throat and chest, damp tendrils of hair clung to her temples, and she was laughing and smiling at the good-looking guy she was with, who seemed completely smitten with her. Jace was unprepared for the sharp kick of jealousy that flared through him, but he welcomed the white-hot possessive streak as he made his way toward Leah and her temporary date. He stepped between them, and Leah's sultry grin widened when she saw him.

"Jace!" she said breathlessly. "I was wondering where you'd disappeared to."

"I think *you're* the one who disappeared, sweetheart," he drawled, then glanced back at the other man who didn't seem at all surprised that Jace had cut in. "Sorry, buddy, but she's with me tonight."

A wry grin tipped the man's mouth. "Yeah, she told me she was with someone else for the evening, but I was hoping maybe you'd forget about her and I'd get lucky."

Jace's jaw clenched, though he couldn't fault the guy for being so honest in his interest in Leah. "Not a chance. She's mine, and I don't share."

The man backed down gracefully and left the dance floor to find another willing partner. Leah continued to sway provocatively to the beat of the music, then leaned close and said into Jace's ear, "I like you being all macho like that."

He grunted in reply because he'd never, ever acted so territorially before with a woman, then he groaned when she turned around and shimmied her bottom against his groin with utter abandon. The wanton movement made him instantly hard, and before she could spin around again he wrapped an arm around her waist, splayed his hand on her belly, and pulled her close, until her sweet backside aligned with his chest, stomach, and thighs.

Submerged in the middle of the crowded dance floor, he followed Leah's lead and rolled his hips against hers, showing her exactly what she did to him, letting her feel every thick, powerful inch of him. Having his rigid erection nestled against her bottom was sheer torture and exquisite pleasure, all rolled into one.

She glanced over her shoulder at him, her gaze brimming with a sexual energy that was nearly palpable. With his arm secured around her waist, he could feel her rapid breaths, could sense the need building within her, as strong and undeniable as the tempo of the music pulsing through them. Boldly, she grabbed his free hand and slowly, daringly, skimmed his flattened palm up her bare thigh and beneath the short hem of her dress, until his fingers encountered the damp crotch of her panties.

Slick, wet heat scalded the tips of his fingers. She was just as aroused as he was, and he instinctively pressed deeper, sliding the silky fabric between the soft, swollen lips of her sex. Her head fell back against his chest, her lashes drifted closed, and her lips parted as her entire body shuddered along the length of his. Her orgasm was only a stroke or two away, he knew, and her gyrating hips beckoned for him to give her that release.

The insane madness of the moment struck him and brought him back to where they were with a jolt of reality. Apparently, those drinks she'd indulged in had stripped away her inhibitions, and while Jace wanted nothing more than to give her body what it craved, he wasn't about to allow her first climax with him to happen in such a public place.

That was a fantasy he didn't intend to share with anyone.

He swore, low and succinct, and grabbed her wrist. "Let's get the hell out of here," he growled, and pulled her through the nightclub to the exit, not giving her a chance to refuse his spontaneous decision.

Not that he believed a protest was forthcoming. One quick glance at the soft, expectant smile on her face, and he knew she was just as anxious to be alone with him, to finish the seduction flowing hot and illicit between them.

Chapter Three

THE DRIVE BACK to Leah's apartment was as insane as their erotic encounter out on the dance floor at Red No. Five. Leah couldn't keep her mouth or her hands to herself and, while Jace kept his fingers wrapped tightly around the steering wheel, she leaned across the console and nuzzled, nipped, and licked the side of his neck in the most incredibly wicked way.

Her breath was warm and sweetly scented as she placed a damp kiss on the corner of his mouth and her fingers fumbled to unbutton his shirt. Once she managed the feat, she slipped her hand inside the parted material and caressed his chest, plucked at his stiff nipples with exploring fingers, and slid her palm lower, over his abdomen. His stomach muscles contracted in response, and he drew in a quick, harsh breath.

Her hand stilled. "Can I touch you?" she whispered, and he heard the threads of uncertainty in her voice.

His mouth lifted in a sinful grin he tossed her way. "Sweetheart, you *are* touching me."

"I want…" Her voice faded away, and she swallowed, then tried again, this time with more determination. "I want to touch you the way you touched me out on the dance floor."

His pulse raced, and his groin throbbed, recognizing the pleasurable ramifications inherent in her request. He'd agreed to show her how to satisfy a man, but he'd never expected her curiosity to emerge while he was attempting to drive a car. Yet he couldn't bring himself to refuse her request because he ached to feel her hands on him—all over.

Lifting her hand, he drew her palm down to the rock-hard bulge straining against the fly of his pants and curled her fingers tightly around his erection. "This is what you do to me," he said, wanting to make sure she was well aware of her effect on him.

She looked into his eyes with something akin to wonder and fascination before he had to return his attention to the road. But that glimpse of enchantment was nearly his undoing, as was the tentative way she squeezed and fondled him through his slacks. She seemed unsure at first, but all it took was a low, encouraging groan from him to persuade her to be more assertive—to stroke the hot, rigid length of his erection against her palm, and learn the size and shape of him with the slow, firm slide of her fingers along his confined shaft.

By the time they arrived at her place, his blood was running hot and thick in his veins, his breath was coming fast and shallow, and he was damn close to erupting into a scalding release. He shut down the engine, removed her hand from his lap, and glanced her way.

A full moon glowed in the night sky and illuminated the interior of the vehicle, tipping the ends of Leah's tousled hair in a silver halo effect. Except, at the moment, she didn't look at all angelic. Her lips were parted and damp, her eyes shone with unquenched lust, and her expectant expression was turning him inside out with wanting her.

The modest, conservative girl he'd known for years had seemingly overnight evolved into a woman on a mission to destroy his restraint, and she'd nearly done just that!

"Will you come upstairs with me?" she asked huskily.

He'd nearly come right there, he thought, but kept the remark to himself. He'd promised Leah a sensual, uninhibited weekend filled with passion and seduction, and while he wanted her to remember everything about the first time they made love, he wasn't about to take advantage of her inebriated state. However, there were many other pleasurable lessons to teach her that didn't include actual consummation.

Besides, they had unfinished business to take care of that she'd started out on the dance floor right before they'd left. He could at least take the edge off all that suppressed desire stringing *her* tight. As for him, he'd have to take matters into his own hands later.

"Yeah, I'll come upstairs with you," he said, and buttoned up his shirt before they exited the vehicle.

Once they were inside her apartment with the door shut and locked behind them, she flicked on the living-room lamp and kicked off her strappy sandals. She leaned against the wall with a languid sigh and a naughty smile curving her lips, then reached for him. Grabbing him by the shirt, she pulled him close, giving him no choice but to brace his hands on the wall on either side of her head to keep from crushing her with his body.

She tipped her chin up so that her eyes met his and her delectable mouth was positioned inches below his. "I have to tell you, that last Blow Job I had was scrumptious."

The sexual insinuation in her comment was like a well-placed stroke along his shaft, instigating vivid and arousing images of her tending to him in such a carnal way. The woman was too adept at throwing him curves when he least expected them, but he most definitely liked this improper side to Leah and had no qualms about playing along.

He raised a brow curiously. "What do you know about blow jobs?"

"I know they taste good," she murmured, and licked her lips. "*Real* good. See for yourself."

Curling a hand around the nape of his neck, she drew his mouth down to hers. She kissed him, openmouthed, hot, and deep, sharing the delicious flavor of the rich, sweet, coffee liqueur still lingering on her tongue.

Minutes later, she finally let their lips drift apart, and he grinned down at her. "That did taste good," he agreed. "Now, what do you *really* know about blow jobs? The real thing and not the drink?" While his tone was teasing, he was extremely interested in hearing her answer.

She blinked at him, feigning confusion. "What do you mean?"

Oh, she knew exactly what he was referring to, and after her brazenness tonight, he wasn't about to let her evade the risqué topic or slip behind a shield of modesty. "I mean oral sex, sweetheart," he said, so there would be no misconstruing his meaning. "Pleasuring a man with your mouth, and vice versa. How much experience have you had?"

"Not much," she said, a flush of embarrassment staining her cheeks, along with an endearing amount of vulnerability. She glanced away for a brief second before returning her gaze to his and lifting her chin to a rebellious slant. "All right, 'not much' is a lie. I don't have any experience in oral sex at all."

Chuckling at her indignation, he touched the pads of his fingers to her soft mouth. He skimmed his thumb across her plump bottom lip and was gratified to feel a tremor of response ripple through her. "Ahh, so you're a virgin, at least in that respect." He was amazed and ridiculously pleased by the notion.

"So I am," she admitted, more easily this time. "But I'd like to learn. Will you teach me?"

Her eager request nearly brought him to his knees,

literally, which would put him in the perfect position to worship her body with his mouth and tongue and fingers and give her a mindless lesson in those provocative pleasures. But as much as that fantasy excited him, he wasn't sure she was in the right frame of mind to make that leap to such an intimate act so soon. So he decided to improvise.

"I promised to teach you whatever you want to know," he said, and led her to the couch in the living room. "So, if you're ready for a lesson in oral sex, and what a real blow job is like, then let's do it."

She sat down, an avid student, and he settled in close beside her, making sure she was relaxed against the soft sofa cushions. "We'll start with you first." Because there was no way in hell he'd last with her mouth and tongue on any part of his anatomy.

Picking up her hand, he skimmed his finger along the webbing of skin between her thumb and forefinger. "Imagine, for the sake of this lesson, that this crease right here is the lips of your sex."

His frank monologue didn't shock her, and she shivered as he stroked that spot again. "It's very sensitive."

"It should be," he said, and gently bit down on the pad of skin just below her thumb, making her gasp. "Imagine how sensitive you are between your legs, along your cleft, and when you add lots of wetness and lots of tongue, like a French kiss, it feels incredibly good." Fastening his mouth along that ridge of flesh between her fingers, he simulated the technique, licking slowly, sucking gently and using his tongue to stroke and lap softly.

Her arm went lax, and her eyes rolled back as a low, throaty moan escaped her. "Jace..."

The one word was filled with such aching need, matching the same hunger pulsing through his shaft. But he wasn't done with this particular lesson, not until she learned what it was like to give him the same kind of erotic attention.

Releasing her hand, he touched his index finger to her lips and exerted a gentle, persistent pressure. "Now it's my turn," he said huskily, and eased closer so he could kiss her cheek, her jaw. "Open your mouth and let me inside."

Her eyes smoldered with blue fire as she parted her lips and let him slip his finger into the warm, sleek, wetness of her mouth.

His stomach and thighs tightened reflexively, and he forced himself to concentrate on instructing her. "When it comes to pleasuring a man with your mouth, the best way to describe what you're going to do is pretend his erect penis is your favorite flavor of Popsicle. You're going to lick and suck and swirl your tongue along the length and over the tip."

Grasping his wrist, she pushed his finger deeper into her mouth, then slowly withdrew the length along the tantalizing stroke of her tongue. His cock stiffened painfully, all hot, thick sensation gathering between his legs.

"Mmm, cherry," she whispered, a sensual smile curving her lips as she immersed herself in the lesson.

He let her take over, let her experiment any way she wished, and imagined her mouth elsewhere, where he was excruciatingly hard and throbbing for release. And what she lacked in experience, she more than made up for in eagerness. She teased him with her tongue and lightly grazed his taut skin with her teeth, then sucked him back into the silky depths of her mouth and flicked and swirled her tongue along the sides and tip of his finger. Her eyes fluttered closed, her rapturous expression reflecting her enjoyment of the act as she continued to increase his excitement and whittle away at his restraint.

She didn't think she had what it took to seduce a man, yet

he was drowning in her innate sensuality, dying to rip off her panties and just take her right then and there, with little finesse. When she adopted an instinctive up and down rhythm while sucking him, his control completely shattered.

Pulling his finger from her mouth, he replaced it with the heat of his lips on hers and kissed her urgently, insistently. Deeply. She whimpered and speared her fingers into the hair at the nape of his neck as her mouth opened wider beneath his for the hot, sexual thrust of his tongue.

She was just as wild and feverish as he felt. Knowing what her body craved after all that mental and physical stimulation, he shifted closer, pressing his aroused body against hers, and eased her down so that she was stretched out on the couch beneath him. With his mouth still fastened to hers, he wedged his knee between her legs, opening them for him, and slid a hand beneath the hem of her dress and up the back of her thigh. He smoothed his palm over a rounded hip, followed the elastic band of her panties downward to the very heart of her femininity. Then he slipped his fingers beneath the thin barrier of silk so he could graze his thumb along the soft, swollen folds of her sex.

She was hot and wet, drenched with desire, and her low moan and the way she arched into his touch were all the permission he needed to finish what he'd started with her. Wrenching his mouth from hers, he stared down into her beautiful face, and her trusting expression caused his heart to punch hard in his chest.

With effort, he continued. "Imagine my mouth right here," he murmured, and caressed her slowly, spreading her wetness upward, over her clitoris. "My soft tongue teasing, then pressing deeper…"

She tossed her head back and rolled her hips sinuously against his fingers, and then she was unraveling, coming in soft pants that turned into a long, ragged groan as her body shook from the force of her orgasm. But instead of her climax sating her, it seemed to inflame her even more. Within moments of her release she was shifting beneath him on the couch, spreading her legs wider, urging him between.

Before he realized her intent, she reached for the waistband of his pants, unzipped his fly, and tugged his slacks over his hips to his thighs. She cupped his erection in her hand through his briefs and, amazingly, he grew longer and thicker with each stroke of her fingers.

His breath hissed out between his teeth and barely able to hold back his own needs any longer, he caught her wrist, then her other hand, and pinned them both above her head to keep him in control. He knew the drinks she'd had at the night club were partly responsible for loosening her inhibitions, and while he refused to make love to her without her being completely lucid, there was no denying what both of them wanted. He could at least give her, and himself, this bit of pleasure.

Capturing her mouth with his, he rubbed his shaft against her cleft, deeply and rhythmically. Instinctively, she wrapped her legs around his waist and arched up into him, causing wet silk to rasp against the soft cotton briefs confining his swollen penis. He imagined thrusting inside her without the barrier of clothing between them, imagined being surrounded by her slick heat and softness, and when she strained against him and cried out as she climaxed a second time, that's all it took to send him right over the edge with her.

His breath hissed out between his teeth, and he shuddered as he came, his own release pumping out hard and fast and scalding hot, draining him, more than just physically. He buried his face against her neck with a groan, and it took a few minutes for him to regain his bearings. When he finally lifted his head and met her gaze, she smiled up at him, her features replete and content.

"Thank you for that very enlightening and enjoyable lesson," she said softly, her lashes falling slumberously.

"It was my pleasure." He kissed her on the lips and eased up off her. "I'll be right back," he said, and made a quick trip to the bathroom.

When he returned, she was right where he'd left her, with her hands still above her head, the hem of her dress bunched around her hips, and her thighs splayed. She looked deliciously rumpled, and if it wasn't for the fact that she'd fallen asleep, he wouldn't have had the willpower to resist her a second time.

But the night's events had finally caught up to her, and it was time for him to go, no matter how much he wanted to stay.

"Come on, Sleeping Beauty," he murmured as he scooped her up from the couch and adjusted her in his arms. "Let's get you into bed where you belong."

With a soft sigh, she snuggled against his chest as he carried her into her bedroom, and damn if she didn't feel as though she belonged in his arms, and in his solitary life, as more than just a friend. As more than just a temporary, weekend lover.

He helped her remove her dress and bra, and smiled when he realized that he hadn't spent much time on those small, perfectly shaped breasts. But there was still tomorrow and more lessons to teach her, and he'd be sure to give those sweet mounds of flesh the attention they deserved.

By the time he pulled the covers up around Leah and tucked her in, she was already fast asleep, her breathing deep and even. He stood there and watched her for a few minutes longer, aching to crawl into that bed beside her and hold her close instead of heading back to his own quiet, lonely house and equally empty, lonely bed.

He was in way over his head, deeper than he'd ever allowed himself to admit to before. And he was no longer sure what to do about those growing feelings that made him wish for the impossible with her.

LEAH WALKED into Jace's Auto Repair the following afternoon with a light bounce to her step and a sensual confidence she'd lacked the day before when she'd come to proposition him. In the span of twenty-four hours, she'd gone from a woman who hadn't had the nerve to seduce a man with a *Sexcapades* invitation, to an impetuous female who was going after what she wanted, without guilt or regrets, and was reaping the pleasurable benefits of being so spontaneous and unreserved.

Last night with Jace, at the nightclub and then later at her apartment, she'd been daring and adventurous and willing to experiment, in a way she'd never been able to with any other man. Jace had brought out the wanton in her, and it had felt amazingly wonderful to be so fearlessly sexual, to openly enjoy his attention and his tutoring—and to know that she had the ability to tie him up in knots, as well.

She strolled through the quiet, empty reception area and into the back garages, a smile on her lips as she recalled how she'd touched and stroked Jace through his briefs, and that's all it had taken for him to lose control with her. She'd been awed by that feat. Watching him let go of his precious restraint, and feeling the extent of his need for her, had brought her to climax—a second glorious time in a row.

Tonight, she wanted to feel every inch of his shaft inside her, wanted to experience being filled to overflowing with the heat and strength and scent of him, with nothing between them. She wanted that intimacy, needed that unforgettable memory, before she had to let him go.

Since closing time on Saturday for Jace's shop was in a half an hour, at one o'clock, there were only a few mechanics on duty who were finishing up basic vehicle services, such as rotating tires and oil changes.

"Hey, Gavin," Leah said, approaching the garage manager from behind as he tightened the lug nuts on a tire. "Do you know where I can find Jace? He's not in his office."

Gavin cast a quick glance over his shoulder at her, then did a double take—obviously stunned by the difference from yesterday's conservative secretarial outfit to the formfitting jeans that laced up at the front, and the peach-colored top that crossed snugly over her breasts and nipped in at the waist—revealing that she did, indeed, have a bit of cleavage when the right kind of push-up bra was worn. Gavin abruptly lifted his gaze from her chest to her face, his expression suddenly sheepish. "I'm sorry, what did you ask me?"

Leah bit back a grin. The other man's reaction definitely backed up Jace's claim that men were visual creatures. For her, dressing this way was about self-assurance and presentation. There was a certain satisfaction in knowing that she did have what it took to capture more than a passing glance from those of the male gender.

She'd applied Jace's advice about "baiting the hook" when it came to turning a man's head, and she was prepared to show him that she was a quick learner. Last night she'd worn a dress that had garnered its fair share of attention at Red No. Five, and this morning she'd gone shopping and bought a few fun weekend outfits. And it appeared that other men weren't immune to her transformation, either, though she was certain that Brent would be less than thrilled with her new selection of playwear, since he preferred her to dress more on the subdued side.

She knew she ought to feel a twinge of guilt about that, but this weekend wasn't about Brent, she reminded herself. It was strictly about *her* and what she wanted, and she intended to enjoy her newfound sensuality to its maximum potential.

Geared up even more now by her thoughts, she was anxious to find her weekend lover. "Do you know where I can find Jace?" she asked again, and lifted the white deli bag she held in her hand. "I brought him lunch."

Gavin cleared his throat, recomposed himself, and hooked his finger toward the back of the establishment. "Uh, yeah, he's out in his private garage."

"Thanks." She sauntered past the other man, and feeling his eyes on her as she walked away, she put an extra feminine sway into her hips.

Jace's private garage was located at the far end of the shop, separate from the other bays. Normally, he stored his Chevy Blazer there during the day while he worked. But she'd seen the vehicle parked out front, which was odd, since Jace was so finicky about his meticulously detailed SUV, and liked to keep it covered as much as possible.

As soon as she entered the last adjoining building, she realized why his Blazer hadn't been parked in the garage. Another vehicle had taken its place. And just like yesterday, she found Jace bent over the hood of a car as he worked on the engine—this one an old sporty classic Chevy Camaro that had been restored to its former beauty.

"Time for a break," she said lightly, announcing her presence. "And I hope you're hungry."

Jace ducked his head out from beneath the hood, straightened, and turned around. "I'm starved, actually..." His cheerful voice trailed off as his surprised gaze took in her new and improved outfit. His smile faded into a frown. "Jesus, Leah, you can't come through here looking like *that*."

She lifted a brow, amused by his disconcerted attitude. "Like what?" she prompted, curious to know what he found so objectionable about her fashionable jeans and top.

"Like...like..." Frustration edged his tone, and he waved his hand in the air between them and shook his head, clearly at a loss for words.

She set the deli bag on a nearby workbench, refusing to let him off the hook so easily. "What happened to your lecture about giving men an incentive to look? I was just applying what you taught me, and I thought you'd be impressed by the results."

"I am," he said, his reluctance to admit as much obvious. Heading to the sink at the back of the garage, he vigorously scrubbed his hands and arms up to the elbows with cleaning solvent, and glanced back at her. "It's just that… that my guys aren't used to women traipsing through the garage wearing something so…so provocative and tempting."

She smiled, undaunted by Jace's forthright remark. On the contrary, it delighted her. "Yeah, Gavin's jaw did drop a little bit when he saw me."

"And you seem pleased by that."

She shrugged unapologetically. "It was flattering."

Jace grumbled something beneath his breath as he ripped off a roll of paper towels and dried his hands.

She batted her lashes playfully at him. "Why, Jace, I do believe you're acting jealous, and a bit possessive." And it seemed much more like a lover's jealousy than brotherly protectiveness; she liked that change.

He drew a long, slow breath and pitched the wadded paper towel into a nearby trash can. "I just don't think you want to give guys the wrong impression, especially by wearing a pair of jeans that look like with one tug of that leather tie, they'd slide right off your hips and drop to your knees, and a top that makes your breasts look like they're going to spill out of that bra you're wearing."

So, he'd noticed, which made the bra well worth the astronomical price she'd paid for it. "It's amazing what underwire and a bit of push-up support can do for a woman's figure, don't you think?"

He grunted in response and came to a stop in front of her, bringing with him the clean, delicious scent of orange-citrus.

She sought to understand why he seemed so piqued with her, when he'd been the one to suggest a more visually appealing package to tantalize a guy's senses. "So, are you trying to say in that roundabout way of yours that you just want me to look sexy for you, and no other man?"

He lifted a finger between them, and his lips pursed. "I didn't say that."

No, he hadn't, but she would have been thrilled if he had.

"I just don't want you to take these lessons to the extreme, because there are men out there who'll misinterpret your signals." His tone gentled, and he brushed tousled strands of hair off her cheek. "You come across sensual and confident, and guys see that as a huge turn-on and a green light to proceed."

She relished his touch, and felt his caress all the way down to the tips of her breasts. "All I care about is whether I'm turning *you* on. I'm not out to deliberately impress anyone else, but I'd be lying if I didn't say that the attention doesn't feel good for a change. I just want to enjoy it for a little while with you."

With a sigh of defeat, he pressed his forehead to hers and hooked a finger into the front waistband of her jeans, drawing her hips closer to his. "Fair enough, but I have to warn you, if anyone is going to be pulling these ties of yours open, it's going to be me. At least for this weekend."

She laughed at his low, possessive growl, even as that qualifier, *at least for this weekend,* became a vivid reminder of where she stood with Jace—that he was hers for a very short time, for an exciting, forbidden fling that would inevitably end and become nothing more than a sensual memory, one she'd always treasure. And she hoped she'd become a fond recollection for him, too.

Her initial goal for this weekend had been to indulge her desires for Jace, to fulfill the fantasies that crowded her head at night, and ultimately to shake him from her mind and her heart. Unfortunately, with every lesson they engaged in, with every touch and kiss and illicit caress they shared, she wanted him even more, not less.

Refusing to let those tangled emotions encroach on her time with Jace, she rerouted her thoughts back to his sexy threat. "Since I don't think it would be too appropriate having my pants drop to my knees with your mechanics still on duty, let's eat lunch."

Jace let Leah slip from his embrace and watched as she cleared a spot on the workbench to make room for their meal. She set tools aside and spread out paper towels over the wooden surface, seemingly unaffected by the less-than-sterile environment.

He came up beside her and stopped her before she could set out their lunch. "You know, we can eat in my office where it's fairly clean."

"I kind of like it back here." Brushing his hand aside, she continued with her task, placing a wrapped sandwich on his place setting, then hers. "It's quiet and private and I feel like I'm inside some secret male domain." Her eyes sparkled with fun-loving amusement.

"You are," he admitted, and accepting that she was truly okay with eating in his garage, he retrieved a soda and water from his stock of drinks in the fridge beneath the workbench. "Not many people, other than my mechanics, come in here."

She slanted him a curious look that caused her hair to tumble temptingly over her shoulder. "And why is that?"

"Because this garage is mine, and it's quiet and private," he said, using her own words as he dragged a padded stool over for her to sit on. "It's a sanctuary for me in here, a place where I can escape to immerse myself in what I love the most."

A knowing smile tipped the corners of her glossy lips. "Tinkering with cars?"

"Yep." He unwrapped his sandwich, not at all surprised to discover that it was pastrami with mustard and pickles, his favorite. "This private garage also reminds me of who and what I am, and all that I've accomplished."

"And you've definitely come a long way," she said, then took a bite of her own turkey and cheese sandwich.

"I'm constantly amazed how taking on a job at a gas station as a grease monkey at the age of sixteen led to owning my own car repair business." It was a venture he hadn't been able to accomplish alone, though, and he was well aware of the people who'd made such a difference in his young, undisciplined life. "I was fortunate I had a lot of mentors along the way who saw potential in me, and kept me on the straight and narrow. Teachers, employers and your family, too."

"I've always been very proud of you, Jace," she said softly. "And my parents have, too."

He met her gaze and held it. "I owe them a lot." He certainly owed them much more than fooling around with their daughter, yet no matter how selfish, he knew there was no way he could have refused Leah, or himself, this weekend together.

"You owe them nothing." She rewrapped her half-eaten sandwich, and stuffed it back in the deli bag. "They love you as if you were their own son. Don't ever doubt that."

Yet despite the Burtons' unconditional acceptance, he'd always been plagued with deeper uncertainties instilled by a mother who'd never been there for him when he was growing up. Jace had wanted her love first and foremost, and it had never been forthcoming. If anything, she'd resented his presence, especially after his father had walked out on them. According to Lisa Rutledge, Jace looked just like his father, and that had been enough for her to ignore his existence and drown her bitterness with alcohol and faceless, nameless men.

Now, she was dead and gone, and he was left with the deep-rooted inability to sustain a long-term commitment with a woman, an inability to love strongly enough, because a part of him feared the same kind of rejection. Over the years, it had been easier and less painful to keep women at a distance and remain a bachelor than to take that emotional leap.

Yet sitting beside him was the one person who made him ache for that intimate emotional bond, who tempted him to take those risks. But Leah deserved more than he could ever give her and, regardless of their sensual weekend together, she had Brent—a polished, sophisticated executive type who was more suited to Leah than the simple, ordinary kind of guy Jace would always be.

"If it wasn't for your brother's friendship so early on in my life, and your family's unconditional support and guidance, God only knows where I'd be right now," he said, and shook his head. "I'd probably be some hoodlum evading the law."

"But you're not," she said, and rested her palm against his jaw. The tender gesture told him how much she'd always believed in him—possibly more than he'd ever believed in himself. "You're a talented mechanic and a successful businessman, Jace."

Still, insecurities lingered. "What I am is a man who is usually covered from wrist to elbow in grease." That was his daily reality, and one that turned most women off when they realized what his work entailed.

She smiled at him, a lilting, flirtatious grin that caused a rush of heated awareness to surge through him. "And when you wash it all off, you smell like a big, juicy orange that I want to take a big bite out of."

Finished with his sandwich, he crumpled up the wrapper, tossed it into the trash, and slanted her a searching glance. "And what would you do if I missed a spot of grease and smudged some on you?"

She looked at him oddly. "I'd wash it off," she said, as if the answer to his question was a simple one.

He downed a long drink of his soda, then said, "Grease doesn't wash off silk at all. It stains permanently."

Brows raised inquisitively, Leah crossed her arms over her chest, which served to prominently display the upper swells of her small, firm breasts. "And how would you know that?"

The tips of his fingers itched to caress the soft, plump upper curves spilling from the neckline of her blouse, but instead he crushed the empty aluminum can in his hand and pitched it into a recycle bin. "Experience, unfortunately."

"Hmm," she replied thoughtfully. "Do tell."

He hadn't meant to share details of that humiliating ordeal, but even now it served as a reminder that he was and always would be a blue-collar mechanic. "A woman I was dating a while back was impressed to learn that I owned my own business, until she unexpectedly stopped by one day and realized that I actually work on the cars in my shop," he said wryly. "When I accidentally brushed against her arm, you'd think I'd committed murder by the way she shrieked and carried on about her designer silk blouse being streaked and ruined by grease." His tone was harsher than he'd expected, and he cleared his throat. "Pretty nice, huh?"

"Pretty shallow," she countered, and gave a snort of disgust.

He smiled, appreciating the way she so vehemently defended him. "Women are initially impressed that I run my own business, but once they learn I repair cars for a living and maintain a modest lifestyle, they tend to become completely disenchanted. The fact that I work in the garages turns them off, and they move on to someone more exciting."

"They obviously weren't in the relationship for *you*." With a sexy glimmer in her eyes, Leah closed the short distance between them, her chin lifting sassily. "Unlike myself, who wouldn't mind having a handprint or two on my person as a sign of your possession...right here—" she grasped his wrist and placed his big palm on her jeans-clad bottom "—and here," she said, and curled his long fingers around the lush softness of her breast.

He skimmed his thumb over the tight nipple beading against his hand, and kneaded the luscious curve of her ass, thrilled by her brazen and arousing advances. Luckily, he didn't have any grease left on his hands, but a part of him wished he did, just to be able to mark her as his in a very elemental, territorial way. But, since permanent handprints weren't possible, he'd just have to claim her in the only other way available.

Squeezing her bottom, he drew her hips to his and bent his head for the deep, hungry kiss he'd been craving since she'd first walked into his private garage. But before their lips could so much as touch, the intercom on the wall buzzed, interrupting the moment and causing Leah to jump out of his embrace, her eyes wide and startled.

"Jace, it's after one, and we're closing up the shop," Gavin announced. "Do you need anything else before we leave?"

Jace pressed the connect button as Leah moved away toward the Camaro parked in the garage. "Just make sure the bays are secure, and lock up the front on your way out."

"Will do," his manager said. "Have a good weekend, and I'll see you early Monday morning."

Jace disconnected the call and returned his attention to Leah, more than a little disappointed that the sensual mood between them had been shattered. So, instead, he watched as she caressed her hand lovingly over the smooth, glossy hood of the vintage vehicle, painted a bright red with two white racing stripes down the center.

"When did your auto shop start working on classics?" she asked curiously.

"We don't. This is mine. I just got it." He came up beside her, wishing those hands of hers were on his body instead of the car. "I've wanted a '67 Chevy Camaro since I was a teenager, and this muscle car was too good a deal to pass up. What do you think?"

"I think it's hot, and a total chick magnet," she said teasingly. "Do you mind if I test it out?"

"Not at all." He opened the driver's side door for her, but instead of sliding behind the wheel, she pushed the front seat forward and crawled into the back. "There's not a whole lot to see and do back there," he said, ducking low to see her.

She reclined against the upholstered seat and shook her head in disagreement. "Don't you think, as a teenager, you would have found plenty of things to do back here with a girl who was hot for you?"

Excitement pumped through him, and he grinned like a fool. "Ahh, so, are you offering to fulfill a teenage boy's fantasy?"

"Absolutely." She crooked her finger at him, a comehither dare etching her features. "Care to join me?"

Unable to resist such a tempting overture, he slid into the back seat and shut the door behind him, enveloping him in the warmth inside the car, the heady scent of Leah, and the promise of seduction glimmering in her bright-blue eyes.

Chapter Four

LEAH HAD Jace right where she wanted him. Okay, so maybe the small, cramped back seat of his classic Camaro wasn't as comfortable as a bed but, for the moment, it was absolutely perfect for what she had in mind.

Pressing her hand in the center of his chest, she pushed him back, so that he was reclining against the side of the car. Then she boldly straddled his waist and sat her bottom on his muscular thighs.

"I've never made out in the back of a car before," she said huskily, and scooted closer so that the hard bulge behind the fly of his jeans pressed firmly against the crux of her thighs. "Care to broaden my lessons a little bit?"

He settled his hands at her waist, and ever so slowly tugged the hem of her top out of the waistband of her jeans, his irises turning dark and hot. "Honestly, this is a first for me, too, but I'm sure I can still offer some guidance."

Leah shivered as his fingers strummed across her ribs, and decided if this was his first time making out in the back seat of a car, too—and his newly restored Camaro at that—then she wanted the encounter to be exciting and memorable for him. A treasured recollection that would bring a smile to his face whenever he happened to glance in his rearview mirror.

"Actually, would you mind if *I* took the lead this time, and you just followed along?" she asked.

He grinned indulgently, causing that disarming dimple of his to make an appearance. "God, Leah, that's a request few men could resist."

She pushed his shirt up his torso, and he helped her pull it over his head. "You included?" A hint of insecurity crept into her voice—not many men, if any, had found her sexually irresistible.

He suddenly grew as serious as the question she'd just asked, and it amazed her just how in tune to her feelings he was.

"Especially me, sweetheart," he murmured, and trailed a finger down the low-cut V of her blouse, leaving a tingling sensation in the wake of his heated touch. "Resisting you is becoming damn near impossible."

And for her final day and night with him, that's all she cared about. "Good."

Splaying her hands on his bare chest, she leaned forward and kissed him. Their lips met and meshed damply, and she slipped her tongue inside his mouth to lazily tease and explore and chase his tongue with her own.

His warm palms tunneled beneath her top again, this time to move restlessly up and down her back, then around to her breasts. With her bra still on, he fondled the small, taut mounds of flesh with his hands and lightly pinched her nipples through the material—pleasuring her, yet still allowing her to be the one to dictate the direction of the unfolding seduction.

The rigid length of his erection pressed hard against her sex, and she rocked her hips, creating a pleasurable friction that made him growl deep in his throat and deepen the kiss even more.

Knowing what he wanted, what he craved, she moved her mouth to his jaw, nuzzled his neck, and let her lips and tongue traverse their way lower. She laved his nipples, and his fingers threaded through her hair as her teeth grazed his belly and her tongue dipped into his navel. With his body angled across the back seat, she found a relatively comfortable position between his legs and fumbled with the button on his jeans until she managed to unfasten them. Then, with utmost care, she slowly lowered his zipper, relishing the anticipation of touching him so intimately, of learning his shape and texture and taste without any barriers of clothing between her hands and his flesh.

He caught her wrist before she could go any further, and when she looked up into his face, his expression was taut with restraint, dark with desire and need. "Are you absolutely sure about this?"

"Absolutely, positively." She nipped at him though his cotton briefs, and watched in fascination as his impressive erection twitched. "I want to apply what you taught me last night about a blow job. Not the drink, but the real thing."

His answer was a full-body shudder, and he released her, allowing her to proceed. She grasped the waistband of his jeans and briefs, and he lifted his hips so she could pull them down to his thighs, freeing his shaft. Dampening her lips with her tongue, she touched her fingers to the engorged head of his penis and marveled at how smooth and velvety soft the tip was—a contrast to the hot, hard length of the thick stem.

The sight of him—all virile, aroused male—made her equally hot, and wet too, but this afternoon tryst was solely for him, and she'd get hers later, tonight. Wrapping her fingers tightly around him, she gently fondled the swollen sacs between his legs with her other hand. His breathing quickened and the muscles in his thighs tensed as she parted her lips and enveloped him in the wet heat of her mouth, deeply, eagerly, all the way down to the base of his shaft.

There was something powerfully invigorating about holding the most masculine part of Jace in her mouth and being in complete control of his pleasure. And something wonderfully provocative about him trusting her so unconditionally with the most vulnerable part of his anatomy.

She felt incredibly sexual, so wicked and uninhibited, and her own pulse raced in growing excitement. She wanted desperately to make him come, just like this.

Remembering the techniques he'd taught her the night before, her lips and tongue joined in on the foray, licking and swirling, stroking rhythmically, then finally she added a slick, steady suction that made his hips buck upward and a raw expletive escape his throat.

His fingers tangled in the strands of her hair, alternately pulling her close, then trying to push her away as his climax neared. *"Leah,"* he whispered gruffly, her name a husky warning.

She ignored him and continued resolutely, drawing him deeper and sliding her mouth and tongue wetly down the length of him, then sucking strongly. With a primal groan that rumbled up from his chest, he came, his body taut, his hips arching, as he gave himself over to his release. She stayed with him all the way, until the last tremors ebbed and he slumped back, his head resting against the back of his seat. His eyes were closed, and he was breathing hard, as if he'd just completed a two-mile sprint.

He looked totally, deliciously wasted, and that satisfied Leah more than an orgasm of her own, because she'd been the one to put that dazed look on his face. She moved up beside him and noticed that the windows were steamed from the heat they'd generated. She experienced the girlish impulse to write an intimate note in that fog, an I Love Jace message that would claim him as her own.

Her stomach took a deep free-fall, then her heart followed with erratic pounding as the truth shook her to the core. As a teenager, she'd been infatuated with Jace and had cloaked her attraction to him in friendship. As a woman who was learning about intimacy and passion and experiencing an emotional connection with a man for the very first time, she knew she was falling deeply, irrevocably in love with Jace.

She swallowed hard, knowing she'd never reveal her feelings to him—the last thing she ever wanted was for him to feel forced or obligated to return the sentiment. Their time together was about sex, not love, and she wasn't about to throw him such an unexpected, and likely unwanted, curve halfway through their weekend.

"Well?" she prompted, and nestled against his neck, determined to keep things light and playful and fun. "Did I pass?"

He laughed, the sound low and rough, as if expressing his amusement took effort. "You're a quick learner." He pried open his eyes to look at her. "You definitely earned an A-plus."

She couldn't stop the silly grin that lifted her lips. "You're a great teacher," she said, returning the compliment. "You do realize, don't you, that we're going to have to make sure that stellar grade-point average doesn't falter."

"Then let's go for some extra credit by letting me return the favor." He fingered the leather ties securing the front placket of her jeans.

Before he could tug open the fly of her pants and make her melt with his deft, skillful touch, she reluctantly moved back, just out of his reach. "As tempting as that sounds, I've got to go."

A frown marred his brow and added to his perplexed expression. "Go where?"

"Shopping."

He pulled his pants back up and fastened them. "Shopping?" he repeated, sounding dumbfounded.

"Yes, shopping." Finding his T-shirt on the seat beside her, she handed it back to him to put on. "I still need to buy a few things for tonight, especially something to wear."

His gaze drifted lazily, hotly, down the length of her as he undressed her with his eyes. "What if I don't want you wearing anything at all?"

Heat sizzled along her nerve endings, rousing her libido all over again, enticing her to stay and take him up on his offer to return the favor. "Now what fun would that be?" she said with effort. "I want to buy something that teases and tantalizes, and drives you crazy with lust."

He groaned like a dying man. "Ahh, we're back to that again, are we?"

She planted a quick kiss on his lips. "Yep." She was looking forward to finding an outfit that would turn him inside out with burning desire. "If it makes you feel any better, I promise you can have your wicked way with me tonight."

A slow, sinful grin eased up the corner of his mouth, and his green eyes gleamed with anticipation. "You can count on that, sweetheart, because tonight, *I'm* calling the shots."

LATER THAT EVENING, Jace reclined against the sofa in Leah's apartment, watching as she slipped a CD into the stereo player. Within moments, the soft strains of Enya filled the living room and added to the romantic, provocative atmosphere Leah had created for the two of them.

True to her word, Leah had found herself an outfit that had made him instantly hard the moment she'd opened the door and greeted him. The vivid purple silk, lace-edged camisole molded to her breasts, and the matching drawstring pants shimmered along her hips and slender thighs whenever she moved and walked. She'd called the two-piece set a casual lounging outfit, and he countered that the sexy lingerie was downright illegal for any viewing purposes outside of the house.

Not that they were going anywhere tonight, thank God, because he wasn't in the mood to share Leah with anyone.

She lit the half-dozen pillar candles scattered on the nearby tables, wall unit, and shelves, then switched off the lights except for a lamp in the corner. She turned toward him, and the luminescent glow of the candlelight made all her bare skin shimmer with warmth. She'd worn her hair down, and the chestnut strands fell in soft waves to her shoulders. Her eyes held the self-assurance of a woman who knew how the night was going to end.

It was a heady thought to know that the confidence in this exciting woman in front of him was partly a result of their weekend together. Jace suspected she'd always harbored those sensual tendencies; they were just waiting to break free under the right circumstances. With the right man. One who'd take the time and care and allow her to embrace her uninhibited side and indulge in erotic whims and fantasies.

She'd chosen him to be the lucky man to take her on this journey of discovery, and while he accepted that their agreement had included no entanglements or expectations beyond their brief weekend affair, he never would have guessed that he'd become so addicted to everything about her. Like her sweet smiles and infectious laughter. The soft, feminine way she smelled, and how she so effortlessly seduced him in spite of her mistaken impression that she needed lessons to tempt a man. Then there was the way she understood him as had no other woman he'd ever known, and most especially the way she accepted him.

She sat on the cushion next to his, facing him, and curled her legs beneath her. "So, what's on tonight's agenda?" she asked eagerly.

You. Me. Together. Finally, he thought. "Foreplay," he drawled.

A naughty smile canted the corners of her full, glossy lips. "It seems like this weekend has been one long session of foreplay. Not that I'm complaining, mind you."

"Then consider tonight an overview, an enticing and final seduction leading up to the main event." Stretching his arm along the top of the sofa, he rubbed soft strands of her hair between his fingers, which brought back memories of their afternoon together, and how he'd wrapped his hand in those silken tresses while she'd pleasured him with her mouth.

"You have my full attention," she said, prompting him to go on.

He inhaled a slow breath, and focused on the lesson at hand. "Foreplay is the most important part of making love. It's all about taking the time to learn what excites your partner, what makes them hot and bothered, what turns them on. It's all the touching, fondling and kissing that gets your juices flowing and leads up to the actual act of sex."

Placing his free hand on her silk-clad knee, he feathered his thumb along the inside of her leg, demonstrating the arousing effect of an illicit caress. Her breath caught, desire darkened her eyes, and the tips of her breasts tightened against the thin silk of her camisole.

Satisfied with that reaction, he continued. "Foreplay is all about that tickle you feel in your belly when you're excited, and the way your nipples pull tight and ache for the wet heat of my mouth, the soft stroke of my tongue," he murmured, aching to do just that. "It's about you getting wet, and me getting hard."

His blatant description caused her to shiver, but he wasn't done stimulating her mind and body with his monologue just yet.

"Foreplay is about pushing each other to the absolute

limit and sharing mutual pleasure before letting your part-ner come," he said, and slowly glided his hand higher up her thigh, watching as her lashes fell to half mast and the pulse in her throat quickened. "And there are dozens of different ways to do that."

A lazy smile tipped her lips. "Which begs the question burn-ing in my mind. What excites *you*, Jace?" she asked brazenly.

"Anything that excites *you*," he returned, refusing to let her turn the tables on him. After her generosity with him that afternoon, tonight was all about her sensual gratification, first and foremost, and he meant what he'd said about him being in charge this time.

Deciding it was time to move on to the next phase of their lesson, he slid off the couch and knelt on the plush carpet in front of her. "There's nothing sexier to me than a woman who enjoys the pleasure her own body has to offer, and doesn't hold back in what she wants or needs."

"Right now, I need you to touch me," she whispered. "All over."

"I will," he promised, and pushed her knees wide apart so he could fit in between her spread thighs. "But first, I want you to scoot your bottom to the edge of the couch."

She obeyed, the intimate position forcing her to straddle his waist until the most feminine part of her pressed against his belly and he was eye level with her luscious breasts. Their clothing separated them, but not for long.

He stripped off his shirt and tossed it aside, but left his jeans on for now. She placed her cool palms on his shoul-ders and let her fingers drift down to his nipples to tease the erect disks. Knowing he'd never last with her touching him so enthusiastically, he gently removed her hands and flat-tened them on either side of her legs on the couch.

She looked confused, and he sought to reassure her. "Keep your hands to yourself for a little while, and just *feel*."

An adorable pout puffed out her lower lip. "But I want you to enjoy this, too."

"Trust me, I will." Smiling, he leaned forward and gently, softly, kissed her mouth. "Just watching and feeling the way your body responds to me makes me hard, so don't hold back. And don't hesitate to let me know that what I'm doing to you feels good, or to tell me what you want."

He skimmed his damp, open mouth along the side of her neck, and she moaned in encouragement and tipped her chin back to give him better access to her throat.

"Yeah, just like that," he praised and marked her with a love bite right at the sensitive curve of her shoulder, making her gasp in delight. Slipping his fingers beneath the thin straps of her camisole, he pushed them down her arms, causing the silky fabric to pool around her waist. Aching to see her naked, he lifted his head, awed by the beauty of the small but firm rose-tipped breasts that strained toward him, so lush and ripe.

His mouth watered for a taste, and this time when she delved her fingers through his hair and pulled him forward, he didn't have it in him to chastise her for not keeping her hands to herself. She brushed a peaked nipple against his parted lips, and he teased her with a leisurely lick of his tongue over the swollen crest, and the warmth of his breath along her damp skin.

She moved restlessly against him and her thighs clenched at his hips. "Take me in your mouth, all the way," she begged.

He kneaded her breasts, closed his lips over the engorged flesh and all but devoured her with his hot, hungry mouth. And still, it wasn't enough for either of them. He sucked her deeply, strongly, using his teeth and tongue to heighten the sensations rippling through her and increasing the heat burning him up inside.

She arched into him, breathless and impatient, and tried to pull him on top of her.

Instead, he pressed her back against the sofa, let his mouth move down to her stomach, and rasped, "I'm not done with you yet."

He dipped his tongue into her navel for a leisurely taste, and she squirmed and groaned restlessly. He pulled at the ties of her silky pants, loosening the waistband. Then he tugged the bottoms down her long legs and off. He removed her camisole as well, leaving her scantily clad in a pair of insubstantial lace panties. The deep shade of purple was an erotic contrast to her pale skin.

He looked up and met her drowsy gaze, glittering from the candlelight. He took in her flushed face, waiting to find a trace of modesty, possibly even a bit of reserve, but finding none.

"Take them off," she said, granting him her consent, her ultimate acquiescence, and letting him know she was in this all the way.

Relief surged through him, and he hooked his thumbs into the elastic leg bands of her panties and peeled the scrap of damp fabric off. He splayed his hand on her belly and slowly dragged his palm downward, until his thumb grazed across her tight clit, then burrowed between her slick folds. She was hot and wet, and so incredibly sexy, her delectable body all his for the taking.

Soon.

She closed her eyes, clutched at the edge of the sofa cushion, and gyrated her hips against his hand. He stroked her rhythmically, watching as she let every one of her inhibitions slip away, watching as she tried to grasp that illusive orgasm he deliberately kept just out of her reach.

"Jace...*please.*"

He eased one finger, then two, deep inside her, and her

inner muscles instantly contracted around him. "*This* is fore-play, sweetheart."

She made a low, raw sound of need. "This is sheer torture."

His cock throbbed painfully against the confines of the denim, echoing her sentiment, but he'd ignore his own discomfort until he'd satisfied her. "Tell me what you want, and I'll give it to you."

"Let me come." She bit her bottom lip, then revealed more tentatively, "I want to feel your mouth on me."

There was no denying Leah anything, and this was something he wanted just as badly. Withdrawing his fingers, and ignoring her moan of protest, he grasped her bottom and pulled her closer to the edge of the sofa. He draped her legs over his shoulders and lowered his head, rubbed his stubbled cheek against the inside of her smooth thigh, and let his open mouth drift upward as he licked and kissed and gently bit her flesh along the way.

By the time he reached her core, her hands were tangled in his hair and she was panting in anticipation. He inhaled the heady, rich scent of her, all aroused woman, then closed his mouth over her sex and pressed his tongue deep, swirling and teasing and suckling greedily on her hot, sweet flesh.

Her back bowed and she released a ragged moan as she erupted into a shattering climax. Sheer primal lust reared through Jace, along with the desperate urgency to possess her in the most elemental, physical way possible. He wanted Leah so much that he shook with the force of his need. He couldn't wait another minute to have her—as hard and fast and deep as she'd allow.

Leah gasped for breath, still trembling from the aftershocks of her orgasm as the sensual haze clouding her mind dissipated and her surroundings, and Jace, gradually came back into focus. He was still kneeling in front of her, and she watched as he dug a condom from the front pocket of his pants, then unfastened his jeans and shoved them down to his thighs, freeing his thick erection. Ripping open the foil packet, he gritted his teeth as he rolled the snug latex over his shaft, then glanced back up at her, his eyes hot and hungry and demanding.

Leah fully expected him to take her on the couch, but instead he pulled her down to the floor with him and gently turned her around so that she was facing the sofa and her arms were braced on the cushions. He kneed her legs apart and pressed his groin against her bottom. She swallowed hard as she felt the head of his penis nudge along the wet, swollen tissues of her sex, and knew he was going to take her in this untamed, primitive way. It was what she wanted, too—to be thoroughly possessed by Jace and be the recipient of his wild passion. It was a heady thought to realize that she'd driven him to this extreme.

The thrill of the forbidden beckoned, and she glanced over her shoulder at him, letting him know that she trusted him, with her body, her heart, her soul. She was all his for the taking.

With a low, rumbling growl, he gripped her waist and entered her in one long, driving stroke that made Leah toss her head back and gasp as he filled her to the hilt. Then there was only pleasure and friction and heat as he pumped harder, faster, deeper, and she undulated her hips sinuously and instinctively pushed back against him, matching the frenzied rhythm of his thrusts.

He leaned more fully into her, covering her from behind. He grazed his mouth across her shoulder and sank his teeth into the taut tendons along her neck, adding to the erotic sensations spiraling within her. His movements became more frantic, more urgent. His hands slipped around to her breasts, fondling them, rolling her nipples between his fingers, then he stroked her belly and lower, where they were joined.

Another firm stroke, another sleek caress, and she arched against his hips as her climax hit and she contracted and convulsed around his shaft. Her breath came out on a low, earthy moan that seemingly obliterated the last thin thread of his restraint. Jace's entire body stiffened then shuddered as he rode out the pulsating waves of his own orgasm.

He slumped against her, a quivering mass of spent energy. Remaining inside her, he nuzzled her neck, placed a sweet kiss on her cheek, and murmured, "I can't believe I took you like an animal."

She glanced over her shoulder and met his contrite gaze. Knowing he was about to plead for her forgiveness, she refused to allow him the opportunity to dilute what they'd just shared. "Don't you dare apologize for the best sex I've ever had," she said adamantly.

Jace chuckled, grateful that Leah was open to a bit of sexual adventure. "All right, I won't apologize because that was the best sex I can remember ever having, too."

Which said a helluva lot for the woman he was with. He'd had good sex before, but he'd never lost control as he had with Leah. And even though he'd just had her, he was far from sated. He feared it would take him a lifetime to get his fill of her.

Unfortunately, he only had this one night left to satisfy any and all cravings he had for Leah. And he planned to take full advantage of that fact.

Despite her assurance that she didn't mind his more aggressive side when it came to sex, he didn't want to leave her with that unrefined impression of him. "At least let me make love to you properly on a soft, warm mattress instead of both of us kneeling on your living-room floor."

She sighed, her smile as intimate as a kiss. "Now that's an offer I'm not about to refuse. My knees do feel a bit rug-burned."

He laughed in agreement and, minutes later, after she'd blown out all the candles and he'd made a quick trip to the bathroom, he met Leah in her bedroom. She was already lying on the bed waiting for him, beautifully naked and temptingly tousled. With a sultry look in her eyes, she feathered the tips of her fingers along her flat belly and strummed them up to her breasts, arousing herself with that lazy caress.

Mesmerized, he strolled to the foot of the mattress. The lamp on the nightstand allowed him to view every intimate dip, curve, and feminine swell of her body. And just looking at her made him so damn hard he hurt—from his chest all the way down to his groin.

"It appears you're very happy to see me," she teased, her gaze riveted to the erection nearly parallel to his stomach.

"You're beautiful," he said huskily, branding this moment in his mind for those long, lonely nights ahead.

"So are you," she replied just as reverently.

He'd brought with him the other prophylactics he'd had in his jeans pocket, and he tossed all but one of them on the vacant pillow next to Leah, knowing he'd likely use every single condom before the night was through.

He sheathed his shaft and crawled up onto the mattress. Starting at Leah's ankles, he leisurely worked his way upward, worshiping every inch of her body with his mouth and his hands, intending to make this time around a long, slow buildup of pleasure. Easing her legs apart, he grazed her inner thigh with his lips, his warm breath, and let his tongue stroke and gently explore her tender flesh before moving on. His palms caressed her hips, he kissed her quivering belly, and paid homage to both breasts, then suckled Leah's jutting nipples until she writhed restlessly beneath him and he knew she was more than ready for him.

He moved over her, positioned himself between her spread thighs, and groaned when she wrapped her legs around his waist and pulled him forward. He was poised at her hot, wet center, a thrust away from being inside her liquid heat. He wanted her so desperately, far beyond this physical joining, and the depth of his need made him feel stripped down to his soul, for the first time in his entire life.

Oh, God he loved her.

Bracing his arms at the sides of her head, he stared deep into her eyes, his heart pounding relentlessly in his chest as he let the realization settle over him. Out of all the lessons he'd taught Leah this weekend, this joining was by far the most profound, and he wanted to be sure she knew it, too.

"*This* is the way it's supposed to be between a man and a woman," he murmured. *Magical. Sublime. Emotional.*

He slowly pressed deep into the tight heat of her body, and she clenched around him, so soft and giving, and so incredibly, perfectly right.

"Oh, Jace," she whispered, and he could have sworn he saw tears gather in her eyes before she pulled his mouth down to hers for a searing, tongue-tangling kiss.

This time around, he took her on a slow, sweet journey, the intensity of it rising steadily, leisurely. She climaxed first, and only then did he let go and lose himself in the ecstasy and pure emotion of being such an intrinsic part of her.

Chapter Five

LEAH KNEW the moment she awoke the following morning that there was no way she'd be able to accept Brent's proposal. Not when she'd spent the most glorious night of her life with another man. Jace had shown her how hot passion could burn between a man and woman, had spent the weekend teaching her that she was irresistible and desirable. Just thinking of how thoroughly Jace had made love to her last night, and again earlier this morning, made her body tingle with renewed heat.

She rolled over in her bed and discovered she was alone, but the muted sounds coming from the kitchen and the scent of freshly percolated coffee assured her that Jace was still there. She was comforted by the fact that he hadn't skipped out on her, even as she dreaded facing him this morning, knowing that their affair was over.

Just as her relationship with Brent was over. As soon as he returned from his business trip this afternoon, she'd not only tell him that she could not marry him, but she'd also explain that their relationship was lacking all the important elements she now knew were necessary to sustain a lasting marriage. Not just fantastic sex, but the kind of emotional bond that had been missing between them—the kind of intimate connection she'd experienced with Jace last night, when he'd been buried deep inside her, and when he'd held her so securely while she'd slept.

She cared for Brent, and in hindsight she knew he'd done her a huge favor by putting off a physical relationship with her. If they had slept together, she never would have pursued Jace, and she never would have known how amazing and unforgettable their time together would be. And, quite possibly, she would have accepted Brent's proposal for all the wrong reasons, mostly because he was offering her all the things she wanted in her life.

Yes, she wanted to get married. Yes, she wanted kids and a family of her own. None of those dreams had changed, but she, as a person, had evolved because of Jace's belief in her, and she liked the sensual, self-assured woman she'd become. One determined not to settle for anything less than honesty, mutual attraction and unconditional love. Which was everything she felt for Jace.

The realization made her heart hurt, because he was the one man she wanted for a lifetime but would never have. He'd given her exactly what she'd asked for—lessons on how to arouse a man and two nights of incredible passion. He'd made her no promises beyond this weekend, and she'd known from the beginning that he had no interest in being involved in a committed relationship. She wasn't about to break the rules they'd established and pressure him for anything more than what they'd agreed to. Their friendship was too important to her to risk, and she'd make the transition from lovers back to friends as smooth as possible for both of them.

With an aching sigh, she drew his pillow to her chest, buried her face in the softness, and inhaled the purely masculine scent of Jace. She closed her eyes, trying to squelch the misery working its way to the surface, and instead focused on gathering the fortitude to face him after last night and not give away how much she loved him.

Oh, Lord, getting Jace out of her system had been a good idea at the time, but never would she have guessed her plan would backfire and leave her so heartsick and emotionally devastated. And feeling more alone than she'd ever felt before.

Knowing she couldn't stall the inevitable forever, she got out of bed, slipped into her favorite chenille robe, then brushed her teeth and attempted to restore some order to her wild, disheveled hair. Heading down the hall, she entered her small kitchen and found Jace sitting at the table, drinking a cup of coffee and perusing a piece of paper in his hand. A slight frown marred his dark brows.

She was disappointed to discover that he was already dressed in his jeans, shirt and shoes, as if last night had never happened. As if he didn't plan on sticking around for long. It was obvious there would be no morning-after intimacy between them, and she berated herself for wanting a few more moments with him when she had no right to expect anything more than he'd already given her.

"Good morning," she said softly, and padded the rest of the way into the kitchen.

He glanced up and smiled. "Hi."

She thought she saw a glimmer of yearning in his eyes, but it was quickly masked by a reserve that made Leah's stomach twist with dread. She hated that a part of him had withdrawn from her, but she couldn't blame him for being cautious, for making the end to their affair as cut-and-dried as possible.

She ought to do the same, mostly to preserve their friendship, and that meant holding her emotions in check until he left.

"What's this?" he asked curiously, and turned the paper in his hand around for her to see.

Ahh, she thought, recognizing the *Sexcapades* invitation she'd taken from Divine Events two days ago that had prompted her to proposition Jace. She'd left the paper on the table, on top of a pile of magazines and mail, never thinking that he might find it or question her about it.

She bit her bottom lip as the words "The Dance of the Seven Veils" mocked her, forcing her to remember her inability to test out her feminine wiles on Brent. All for good reason, she realized now, and was grateful she hadn't attempted to try and seduce him when he wasn't the right man for her. On the other hand, she would have been more than willing to perform the dance for Jace, given the chance. He'd given her that confidence, had coaxed her to embrace her uninhibited side and enjoy the pleasures her body had to offer.

"*That* is a provocative invitation I took from a book I found at the wedding planner's boutique last Friday," she replied, and headed over to the counter to pour herself a cup of coffee.

"What were you doing at a wedding planner's?" he asked with tension in his voice as she filled his mug with the steaming brew, too, then returned the carafe back to the burner.

With her back facing him, she stirred cream and sugar into her coffee and drew a deep breath, knowing Jace deserved to hear the truth. All of it. About her and Brent. About the invitation that had played on her insecurities, and Jace's part in it all. She owed him that much.

Cradling the warmth of the mug in her hands, she turned back around. "I was at a wedding planners because Brent asked me to marry him."

Jace stared at her in incredulous shock. "He did?"

She nodded and took a sip of her coffee, unable to look Jace in the eyes, afraid to see condemnation in them for the weekend she'd spent with him now that he knew the truth. "I asked him to give me some time to think about his proposal, and he gave it to me. He's been out of town, and I thought maybe going to see a wedding planner might help with my decision." She left out the part about her experiencing a bout of anxiety the moment she'd walked into Divine Events, opting to keep those uncertainties to herself. "But, instead, I found an erotic book of invitations titled *Sexcapades,* and I took one of the pages inside."

Finally, she glanced at him and wanted to weep with relief when she saw no signs of censure or criticism in his expression. He sat there patiently, waiting for her to continue.

"When I read the invitation, my first thought was that I couldn't imagine performing that intimate dance for Brent." She let Jace come to his own conclusions about those reasons. "So, I enlisted your help to teach me how to please and arouse a man, and to show me what they find exciting and—"

"—what drives them crazy with lust," he finished for her, a wry grin tipping the corners of his mouth.

"Yes, that too," she said quietly.

He stood and strolled across the kitchen, bringing his mug with him and setting it in the sink. "You're a natural, Leah. Don't ever doubt what a sensual, desirable woman you are."

Maybe we're just great together, and you bring out the best in me, she thought, but kept the comment to herself.

Jace moved in front of Leah and brushed his knuckles across her warm, soft cheek, unable to resist touching her any longer. He felt so torn up inside, aching to take Leah back to bed and keep her there forever, yet knowing he didn't have that right.

"Tell me something," he murmured, following the lapels of her robe down to where it crisscrossed over her breasts. Jace had to forcibly hold back the urge to strip her bare and take her right there on the kitchen counter one last time. "After this weekend, do you have the confidence to perform that Dance of the Seven Veils?"

"Yeah," she whispered huskily. "Yeah, I do. *You* gave me

the confidence, and I appreciate everything you taught me this weekend, most especially to believe in myself and to embrace my sensual side."

And now he was going to send her back to Brent, armed with all the seductive knowledge he'd taught her, and he wanted to roar with the injustice of it all. Except he'd gotten exactly what he'd agreed to, and she'd gotten precisely what she'd asked for.

Good God, when had the arrangement gone so emotionally awry?

"I have to go," he said abruptly. His chest felt tight, and he desperately needed air and space. He had to get the hell out of there.

He turned to leave, but made it only as far as the living room before Leah chased after him. She clutched his arm, giving him no choice but to stop. He caught the hopeful look in her eyes and his heart leapt up into his throat, nearly strangling him.

"Jace..." Her voice trailed off, but there was no mistaking the uncertainty in her tone, as if she were afraid to speak what was truly on her mind.

"Yes?" he asked, his voice rough and gravely like never before.

"I..."

He held his breath, waiting, a part of him praying for the impossible.

"Thank you," she finally said instead, and followed that up with what appeared to be a forced, and very brave, smile. "For everything."

"You're welcome...for everything," he replied, and gently kissed her temple one last time before heading out the door.

JACE GAVE the wrench another forceful push and ended up stripping the bolt, causing his knuckles to scrape along the edge of the exhaust manifold.

"Shit," he cursed, and tossed the tool onto the bench with a loud clatter. He glanced down at his hand and winced at the two knuckles he'd skinned, now bleeding. Stalking to the first-aid kit on the wall next to the back sink, he opened it and withdrew the medicinal aids he needed to disinfect the cuts.

After leaving Leah's several hours ago, he'd come directly to his shop to do more engine repairs on his Camaro. Normally, working on cars proved soothing to him, a way to calm his nerves when he was feeling uptight, but nothing could shake the agitation riding him hard.

No matter what he did, Jace couldn't keep his mind off Leah. Couldn't stop thinking about her going back to Brent, accepting his proposal, and doing that veil striptease for him—a preppy executive who didn't seem to appreciate Leah for the woman she was. And, mostly, he couldn't stop berating himself for being such an idiot and walking out on her earlier. He'd left because of the promise he'd made before their weekend together, and because he believed it was the right thing to do.

He wasn't so sure anymore.

Taking out the small bottle of antiseptic, he clenched his jaw as he scrubbed his wounds with the astringent, wondering when he, someone who'd always been a fighter, had become such a coward. He was so hung up on the fact that Leah deserved better than a kid who'd grown up on the wrong side of the tracks, a mechanic who spent his days elbow-deep in grease, that he couldn't get past the possibility that maybe, just maybe, she'd take him, as is…. Yet he'd done nothing, absolutely nothing, to sway her to take a chance on him.

His heart thudded hard in his chest as he cast a quick glance around his private garage, seeing all that he'd accomplished over the years, and realized that *he* was the one with the hang-ups. And that meant he was going to have to step up to the plate and get over the insecurities he'd lived with since childhood. He might not be some fancy-schmancy executive, but he owned his own business and supported himself with plenty left over. It was about damn time he had more faith in himself, and if there was going to be a man in Leah's life, it was going to be him.

Because that man certainly wasn't Brent.

He patched up his knuckles with a few Band-Aids, now mentally prepared to fight for Leah, and to hell with the consequences he might have to suffer with her family and her brother—his best friend. He'd deal with them later, and make sure they knew he'd never, ever hurt Leah. That she was incredibly precious to him, and he'd do whatever it took to make her happy.

But first, he had to stop her from making the biggest mistake of her life—and his. As he locked up the shop, he prayed he wasn't too late.

IT WAS OVER with Brent, and Leah was more relieved than she'd ever thought possible. She was also grateful that he'd taken the breakup so well, but his lack of anger or hurt feelings just reinforced the fact that he hadn't had a whole lot invested in their relationship—emotionally or physically.

Yes, he'd been disappointed, but he'd wished her well and seemed to mean it. The whole encounter had been disturbing because she'd seen so clearly that she would have been nothing more than a convenient wife and social hostess for him had she accepted his proposal. Ending their relationship had, undoubtedly, been the right thing to do.

And she had Jace to thank for that. For making her realize she didn't have to settle for less than the real thing. Now, as she stared at her reflection in her dresser mirror, scantily clad in a sexy bra and panties and sheer, colorful scarves, she was a nervous wreck. More so than she'd been breaking off her relationship with Brent. Her stomach was in knots, her heart was a tangled mess. So much was riding on this, because she intended to seduce Jace back into her life on a permanent basis. He'd been the one to teach her all about the power and sensuality of being a woman, and it was only fitting that she return the favor by showing him what an avid student she'd been—by performing the Dance of the Seven Veils for his eyes only.

Tonight, she'd not only give him her body, but her heart and soul, as well.

A knock on the door startled her, since she wasn't expecting company. She quickly grabbed a knee-length coat from the coat closet to cover her skimpy, barely-there outfit, and tightened the sash. One quick glance through the peephole revealed Jace standing on the other side of the threshold.

Surprised by his unexpected visit, she opened the door, taking in his fierce expression. His thick hair was mussed as though he'd repeatedly finger-combed it. Restless energy seemed to radiate off him.

"Jace," she said breathlessly, and with more than a little uncertainty. "I was just coming to see you."

"Good, then I saved you a trip," he replied, all dominant male, and moved past her to enter without an invitation. As if she'd ever deny him entrance into any part of her life.

"You certainly did." Closing the door, she leaned against the hard slab of wood, trying like mad to figure out why he'd returned and failing to come up with any answer that made sense.

So, she asked outright. "What are you doing here?"

He jammed his hands on his lean hips, his stance uncompromising. "You can't marry Brent."

His order was the last thing she'd expected to hear pop out of his mouth, but his possessive demand made her feel giddy and kicked up her pulse an optimistic notch. But before she relieved Jace of his mistaken assumption, she needed to hear the reasons behind his adamant request.

"Why not?" she asked.

"Because for as long as I can remember, I've wanted you, and after this weekend, I can't let you go off and marry another man, especially one who doesn't appreciate you in all the ways that matter."

Her breath caught and held in her throat, cutting off her ability to speak. But he seemed to have plenty to say, so she remained where she was against the door and just listened.

"I've been running from any kind of emotional commitment since I was a kid, first because of my father's abandonment, then my mother's rejection, and I just didn't believe I had what it took to give to another person in that way. It was so much easier, and simpler, to remain single and alone than to let anyone close." He took a step toward her, closing the distance separating them, filling the air she breathed with the intoxicating scent of orange. "Except you always had a way of being there for me," he murmured gently, "even when I didn't realize how much I needed you in my life."

She melted inside, his words touching her deeply, profoundly. "That's what a friend is for."

"Yes, you're a friend, but you've always tempted me, Leah, and I've fought my attraction to you for years."

Her eyes widened. "You have?"

"More than you'll ever know." Bracing an arm on the door behind her, he lowered his head and skimmed his lips along her throat, making her shiver from the delicious, intimate contact. "You understand who I am and where I've come from, and you accept me for the person I've become—you did that even before I did. I want to learn to give in return, to be the kind of man you want and need in your life. Just give me that chance."

"It's yours, Jace," she said huskily, and, framing his face in her hands, she pulled him back so she could look into his eyes. "*I'm* yours."

He pressed his forehead against hers. "Then tell Brent no." His tone was ragged, desperate.

She smiled and kissed his lips. "I already have. I had doubts before our weekend together, but after being with you, I knew I couldn't marry Brent."

He shuddered, his relief palpable. "Thank God." Then another round of doubts darkened his gaze. "Your family has been so good to me, and I don't want to disappoint your parents or your brother by getting involved with you."

"Oh, Jace...disappointing them is impossible. They love you as much as I do, and you're already a part of the family."

He reared back, caught her under the chin with his fingers, and stared deeply into her eyes, watching her face carefully. "You love me?"

She nodded jerkily, her heart swelling with the emotion. "For longer than I can remember."

"I love you, too," he said and flashed her a dimpled grin as he tugged on the ties of her coat, loosening them. "And I think we've wasted way too much time being friends, and have a helluva lot of loving to make up for."

Desire rippled through her, warm and exciting. "I couldn't agree with you more." Cool air washed over Leah's bare skin as he opened the lapels of her coat and pushed them wide apart.

He gaped at the sheer outfit she wore, and his brows snapped into a protective frown. "Jesus, Leah, where in the hell were you going dressed like this?"

"To see you. To dance and strip for you. To be your every fantasy. To tempt you to enjoy an invitation to seduction and put to good use everything you've taught me this weekend." Grabbing his hand, she led him into the living room and pushed him down onto the easy chair, then she dimmed the lights and switched on the stereo, which still held the Enya CD. "But since you came to me, I'll just have to improvise."

The soft strains of music filled the room, and she let the sensual beat infuse her mind and soul and stimulate the confidence Jace had instilled in her. Then, to an avid audience of one, she began moving slowly, gyrating gracefully, her body picking up on the evocative rhythm and making it her own.

As she lost herself in the music and the hot look in Jace's eyes as he watched her, she pulled away one of the scarves she'd tucked into her lacy bra and let it flow over her curves, across her belly, and along her thighs before dropping the silky fabric to the floor at her feet. Then she started the process again, gracefully twisting and turning—methodically, temptingly, stripping away the veils and creating an aura of sexual excitement with each scarf she removed.

She shimmied out of her bra and panties too, and smiled as he tugged off his shirt and skinned out of his jeans so he was just as naked as she was. His need for her was visible, and she went to him without hesitation. She straddled his hips and sank down on his shaft, taking him all the way. They moaned simultaneously, letting the pleasure of the moment gradually, leisurely sweep them away. Wonderful minutes later, Leah slumped against Jace's chest and rested her cheek against his shoulder, replete and happy, their heartbeats mingling.

"That was nice," Jace murmured as he caressed a hand along her spine, holding her close. "Very nice. I taught you well."

She laughed. "Yes, you did."

His fingers slid into the hair at the nape of her neck and gently drew her head back so that she was looking into his eyes, which had grown serious and searching.

"What is it?" she asked.

He exhaled a deep breath. "Being friends and all, I think we know just about everything we could possibly know about each other, don't you?"

She thought about all the years between them. "Pretty close, but I'm sure there're a few surprises that will crop up along the way." She grinned. "Luckily, I like surprises."

"Me, too." And then he gave her the biggest surprise of all. "Marry me, Leah. I love you and I swear I'll do everything in my power to make you happy. And I want babies with you, a family—"

She covered his mouth with her hand to cut off his rambling so she could get a word in edgewise. "Yes, Jace," she said, amazed at how an erotic invitation had changed the course of her future and had given her her heart's desire. "Yes, I'll marry you."

And as he kissed her again, long and slow and deep, Leah knew their lessons weren't over, that they'd only just begun. She was certain it was going to take a lifetime for them to teach one another all the pleasures of satisfying one another...in bed, in life and in love. And she was more than up for the adventure.

PLAYMATES
Crystal Green

To Lulu and Scott Shields.
Thanks for your knowledge, guidance
and love of a good time!

Chapter One

WHEN SEAN MCINTYRE first saw her, his sex drive let out an endless, shuddering wolf whistle. One that would've brought down the high-rise building if Los Angeles hadn't been so strict about fortifying the place against occasional earthquakes.

Or another natural disaster trigger, like his new co-worker.

He settled back in his leather office chair, just taking in the show, a grin easing over his mouth as she leaned against the door frame. All long legs, curves and catnip.

Dark gypsy hair waved softly past her shoulders, matching the black smoke of her eyes. She aimed a lowered gaze at him, the tips of her red lips swooping upward in a gesture more suited to a wet dream than the business offices of Stellar Public Relations, Incorporated.

Sean raised an eyebrow, amused. Intrigued.

But, as usual, Louis Martin screwed up the moment, bursting past the woman in a flutter of kinetic overload.

"There she is. Didn't know where you disappeared to," said the short, balding boss man. "One second I'm giving you the tour, the next you're…"

The woman interrupted him with one sultry glance. Louis almost fell backward from the force of it.

"Sorry," she said, her voice as thick and slow as honey dripping from a fingertip. She nodded toward the window while returning her gaze to Sean. "I prefer the view in this office."

He bit back a laugh. Cheeky. Already he liked her. Already he wanted to peel off that slightly see-through, butterfly-sleeved red suit that pushed the limits of professional wear. Sharp, flashy, powerful. All the things a PR representative should be.

And then some.

Louis fidgeted with his tie. "The view. Right. Your office'll be down the hall, though."

Time to open his mouth, Sean supposed. "This is my lion's den. Not fit for a lady."

"No wonder I feel right at home." She flashed him that cool/hot gaze again.

Sean shifted. Nice. A thirty-two-year-old schoolboy with a hard-on. Should he grab a textbook and hide behind it while he got to his feet to shake hands? No English Lit or Trig tomes available, you say? Then maybe he could just stay seated and zoom his wheeled office chair on over to her, introducing himself as half the cad he actually was.

That's right. A gentleman would stand up, take a woman's hand, pay her proper respect. But gentlemen probably refrained from popping wood the second a beautiful female came within range.

He flicked a manila folder off the desk to his lap—the better to fool you with, my dear—and performed the chair slide.

But his cautious move didn't throw her off, not if that knowing gleam in her eyes was any indication.

What the hell, thought Sean. He grinned as he stood, flipping aside the folder, extending his hand. "Sean McIntyre."

The woman perused his outstretched palm, her gaze slipping to the front of his pants, her mouth still heated by that lazy grin. She knew he was turned on. Not that it made her a genius.

She tucked her fingers into his hand, sliding a nail along his thumb in a wickedly disguised shake. "Fiona Cruz. Pleased to meet you."

Cruz. The name rang an alarm. He'd heard of her successes as a marketing machine for actors. She was good. Damned good. But hadn't there been some hint of scandal surrounding her...?

Time seemed to furl around itself as their skin pulsed with the contact, touches languishing, almost as if both of them wanted to see who would let go first.

Louis's voice sawed apart their grip, but not their sustained eye contact.

"We brought on Fiona because she's gangbusters."

Sean coolly acknowledged the weasel's remark. This introduction was Louis's way of turning on the burner under Sean's chair, wasn't it?

"Got that covered, Martie," he said, knowing the nickname would piss off the other guy.

The boss man's cheeks reddened. "It's Louis. As in Martin."

Fiona Cruz had started to wander around Sean's office, trailing her hand over the rigid, metal bookshelves, the writhing steel sculpture in the corner. A flame in the center of a frozen twist of furniture.

He couldn't help admiring her beautiful ass, wanting to cup the curves of it, rocking her against his groin, feeling every voluptuous inch of her opening for him....

"McIntyre?"

Louis again.

"What?"

"Fiona's brought her rising star with her to the firm. Lincoln Castle."

Sean blanched. "The soap star? *That* Lincoln Castle?"

As Fiona stopped by the window, which overlooked Wilshire Boulevard with its palm trees and summer-in-the-city streets, she tossed her words over a shoulder. "There's only one man with a name that... singular."

Rage kicked him into gear, forcing his footsteps over to Louis, where he shadowed the boss with his height. "Look, do you have any idea how Castle is connected to my new client?"

Louis shrugged. "Of course. Say, McIntyre, I've got a conference call with Edgar Lux and his publishing house. Can you show Fiona to her office when she's ready?" Then he lowered his voice. "That is, unless she gets comfortable in *your* chair."

Rather than saying something that would cause Louis to fly into a fit, Sean kept his mouth shut, electing instead to usher his boss from the room with a thanks-a-lot glare.

Louis dashed away, leaving Sean alone with a woman who could very well be the end of his career at Stellar. If you could call it a career anymore.

He turned his attention to Fiona, trying to focus his anger. But he was distracted by the way her dress caught the sun through its sheer material, a dreamcatcher winding darker hopes through the threads of red while allowing fantasies to pass through.

"Let me guess," she said, her back still to him, "watch out for Louis Martin."

"The guy's harmless, unless you don't know how to play office politics."

She turned around with a smile, leaning against the window frame, shifting the sunlight and blinding him with another jab of pure lust.

"I know how to play," she said. "Do you?"

He couldn't hold back a sardonic laugh. Another sweeping gaze over that jazz-baby body. "Listen, Ms. Cruz—"

"Call me Fiona."

"Fiona." The purr of her name caught in his throat. A professional-suicide hairball.

To compensate, he sauntered nearer to her, hovering. Her chin lifted as she stood her ground, tension snapping between their bodies while he leaned in close enough to catch her scent. A tang of fruit—fresh, exotic.

"Let's be direct. You're here to bust my balls," he murmured.

She reached out with both hands, gripping the ends of his undone tie—that and his rolled-up sleeves evidence of a hard-knock day—and pulled down gently. A hitched breath separated their faces, their mouths.

"Bust your balls? Oh, no, sir." She laughed softly. "I'll be more gentle than that."

Her hands floated downward, one knuckle brushing against the reawakening bulge in his pants. Or maybe she hadn't touched him at all and he was just wishing she had.

At any rate, she stepped away from him, shoulder sliding against his arm with lackadaisical disregard. Then she took a stand, hands on hips, a challenge in her raised eyebrows.

A player. Fiona Cruz was obviously one of those teases in a suit, one who flaunted her femininity around the boys' locker room, working them with a come-hither/hands-off strategy. Controlling.

The female version of him.

There was one way to handle the Fionas of the world. Get down to business first, then… What would she do if he took her up on those silent, raw-edged invitations?

He leaned against the back of a leather couch, folded his arms over his chest. "You came fully loaded to Stellar, didn't you? Lincoln Castle, the Brad Pitt of daytime soaps."

"He's a good friend. We've known each other since college. Besides, I excel at what I do."

"You'll need to. His star's not so golden anymore. And he was going places, too, with that Aaron Spelling gig he used to have."

There. A flinch. A different tilt of the hip. And, damn her, even though she wasn't smiling anymore, her lips still tipped up at the ends, giving her an I-know-something-you-don't-know upper hand.

"Linc missed daytime acting, and *Flamingo Beach* made an offer he couldn't refuse," Fiona said.

"Yeah," Sean replied, "he's so thrilled to be back on a soap that he's hired his own private publicist."

She acknowledged his point by staying cool and silent. Many soap actors made good use of the PR rep the soap employed—unless they decided to go "big time."

Finally, after a sufficiently maddening pause, she responded. "Lincoln's always been in demand, but he wants the security of being in a soap right now. That's all."

"Good try, Dr. Spin." He almost mentioned the actor's rumored time in rehab, and how no one outside the soaps—where Lincoln had a strong fan base—would probably ever take a chance on him. But he didn't say a word.

Sean could relate to Castle, because he knew a lot about seeing your professional star fall from the highest point, knew a lot about battling one unworkable PR disaster after another: rising stars who enjoyed "working girls," fading actresses who climbed on political soap boxes and aired extremely conservative opinions. Sean McIntyre, as good as he was, couldn't save every reputation.

But he'd get back on top, especially with his new account.

He continued. "You know I handle Lakota Lang's publicity now?"

"Ah." Fiona was grinning again.

"I can't believe Louis didn't sense a conflict of interest."

"Why, because Lakota and Linc once slept together?"

"*Once* slept together?" Sean chuffed. "They burned the sheets from coast to coast. In several very public positions, too."

"I know. Passion." Fiona's gaze drifted to the ceiling, all Cinderella soap dreams and glass slippers. But as quick as the pop of a bubble, the soft sparkle in her eyes disappeared. Right back to the career woman. "Isn't it convenient that they're on the same show again? Imagine the publicity we could work, the possibilities."

"For what? Them killing each other?" Sean shook his head. "This is trouble waiting to happen, and you're having delusions of grandeur."

"Pshaw." Fiona moved to his desk, sat on the edge of it, rankling Sean with the territorial gesture. "You need to look at the bright side, Mac. We've got a gold mine."

Mac? "So we're pals already," he said dryly.

"Hey, you scratch my back, I'll scratch yours."

A hunger stretched in his belly, pawing at the inside of his skin.

He grinned. "Does the offer extend to—"

"—Bad boy." She wagged her finger at him. "We're talking business."

"You do *business* with all the shy delicacy of Anna Nicole Smith."

She watched him, tracking his movements as he rose from the couch. "I can tell you're going to keep me on my toes."

Right. Either there or on her back.

That wolfish howl screamed through his veins once again. Jerk.

Not that he'd ever heard any complaints about his libido and its excesses. He loved women: their slippery skin after a bout of sex, their sighs of pleasure in his ear, their muscles clenching around his cock as they came. But sometimes Sean wondered if he'd be married with kids by now, happy as the families in a fast-food commercial, if it hadn't been for the way he was brought up.

Forget all that. He had business to do.

He brushed by her, trying not to let her mouth-watering perfume get the best of him, then sat in his chair. Claiming it.

Fiona scanned him over her shoulder, eyes unreadable. "I like a guy who can give me a run for my money. We're going to be quite a team."

"I work alone."

She stood, started to leave. "That's not what I heard."

"You've done your research with me, huh?" He laughed. "I guess I won't make the mistake of underestimating you."

She turned around, holding up a finger. "That's right. And the same goes for me. I know you're tops. Three years ago, you engineered the Yum Gum blitz campaign winning the Guerilla Marketers of the Year award from *Brandweek* magazine. Not bad. Not bad at all."

Sean wasn't fool enough to swell with pride. Three years was a long time. Time enough to lose your footing.

"Oh, before I leave you in peace," she added, "that children's charity event you have Lakota attending tomorrow night? Linc's going, too. He's got a big heart and wants to help raise money."

"Is his heart as big as his ambition?"

He wanted to know the same about her, too. Not that heart mattered much in this business.

Fiona lifted her hands in a gracefully dramatic gesture. "I've sent out press releases hinting that Linc's an all-around enormous man. Not that I've seen anything firsthand."

Cheeky. "Uh-huh, right, you're college friends. FYI, Lakota Lang's a micromanaging superstar in the making, and that means she wants me at the event to oversee her moment in the spotlight."

"I'm sure she'll be more comfortable flying solo once she gets used to her diva role." Was that a proxy swipe at his client, establishing the ill will between Lakota and Lincoln?

Sean's voice took on an edge of sarcasm. "All the same, I'll report back to you, boss."

"No need. I'll be there. Linc's escorting me. More social than business, but I'll be wearing my professional demeanor."

Friends, huh? A claw of jealousy scored Sean, but he ignored it. Sure, he'd love to see what Fiona Cruz was made of when she stepped *out* of the office, but the fulfillment of his curiosity might blow his career to smithereens.

"Great," he said, pausing when she didn't move completely out of his domain. "Need me to show you to your dungeon?"

"No." She took pains to adjust her sleeves, the filmy material breezing over her dusky skin. "I already know where it is. Remember, I've done my research, Mac."

And, without further ado, she left him sitting behind the desk, his emerging grin beating back a more prudent frown.

Sure, he was hungry for more, but that didn't mean he was happy about it.

THE NEXT NIGHT, at the fund-raiser in the Renaissance Hollywood Hotel, Lincoln Castle was reluctant to come out of the men's rest room.

So, naturally, Fiona went in.

"Linc?" She poked her head around the door.

Two men stood before the urinal, mouths agape. One zipped up and deserted the room, shooting Fiona a dirty glare, which she answered with her best charmingly apologetic smile. The other man took his time, nodding at her and leering.

She ignored him, slipping farther into the forbidden space. "Linc, I know you're in here."

"Stage fright." His words echoed off the tile. "I'll get over it."

Fiona's nerves jumped in sympathy for her friend. He was fine in front of the cameras, but live audiences? Another beast all together.

She followed his voice to a stall. The door creaked open to reveal her college pal. Lincoln Castle—a stage name for Kevin Lincoln. He was a composite of every heartthrob cliché imaginable, with a six-foot tall, freestyle-weight physique, tanned skin, blond hair and blue eyes. All of that in a tux, besides.

"Hey," she said.

He looked so lost and pathetic propped up by the wall, eyes closed. "Just waiting for the Alka-Seltzer to take hold."

"Do you think that 'plop-plop-fizz-fizz' will chase away more than your anxiety?"

Linc blinked his eyes open after the other bathroom patron slammed the door on his way out. "Thanks. I needed to be reminded of Lakota. That, coupled with this bid for comeback success, really makes my night."

Still, he managed a grin.

It was the same disarmingly sensitive gesture she'd known

throughout her early twenties. Same guy, even though soap stardom, a featured role on a hot prime-time drama then a brief, mortifying obscurity had claimed him.

"See," she said, "you're better already. Let's go."

"You in some kind of rush?"

Fiona raised her brows. "Why would I be?"

Why? Could it be the fact that Sean McIntyre—Mac—would be in the Grand Ballroom?

When she focused again, Linc was assessing her.

"You're putting off steam, Fi."

"Me?" Fiona walked away, propelled by a nervous, sexual energy. She could almost feel Mac in the building, could almost hunt him down with her awakened senses.

Without warning, the bathroom door crashed against the wall. Security guard. Wonderful.

"Miss," said the tidy little uniformed man, "this ain't the ladies' john."

Linc half stumbled out of the stall, revealing himself. Fiona discreetly checked his eyes, his scent. Good. Not drunk.

The guard held up his hands. "Hey! My girlfriend used to watch you on that Thursday night show!"

Linc modestly shrugged, and Fiona's heart went out to him. Though daytime soaps were filled with solid actors, the genre was considered a step down from prime time. But Linc didn't seem to mind right now. Like most soap actors, he genuinely loved the fans, relished the contact.

As the man asked for an autograph and repeated over and over how his honey wouldn't believe this, Fiona stood by. Linc's connection with the public was one of his strengths.

Soon, they were on their way to the fund-raiser. The festivities were being held down the boulevard from the legendary cemented hand and footprints and refurbished glamour of the Chinese Theatre. The hotel was tucked next to the Kodak Theatre, the most recent home of the Academy Awards. Dazzle and sophistication cloaked the black-tie guests.

When she and her friend walked into the Grand Ballroom arm in arm, lulled by the DJ's background-volume techno music, blinded by photo-op flashbulbs and fake silver stars hanging from the ceiling, the first person who caught her eye was Mac.

And he was worth the wait. The man shouldn't be allowed anywhere near a tuxedo. The sight was enough to make every woman in the room implode. The way he filled out the dark, suave cut of his jacket with those steel-beam shoulders, that broad chest, those hefting-the-weight-of-the-world arms...

How would the female race survive if they were all spontaneously combusting? It just didn't seem fair.

While Linc led her farther into the roar of the party, she allowed her gaze to linger on Mac a decadent moment longer. She couldn't stop herself.

Shaded blond hair, razored to just above the collar, green eyes with a sharp-shooter squint, the rakish hint of stubbled mustache and half beard surrounding a full mouth slanted in wary repose. If you took all his features and inspected them one by one—as she'd slyly done today during a firm meeting—they'd be slightly off-kilter. Especially the subtly crooked nose and the too-strong chin.

But all together....

Whoo doggie.

As Fiona and Linc moved past the summer-night decorations featuring simulated moons glinting over the sea, past the auction items and information tables, she realized Mac wasn't alone.

The vampish Lakota Lang was leeched onto him.

After refusing drinks from a passing waiter, Linc's arm stiffened as they came to a stop on the opposite side of the empty dance floor.

She squeezed his solid bicep, hopefully lending him reassurance. "Steady."

The emotion in his voice belied his polished, pretty-boy exterior. "I'm good."

Gorgeous Linc. Not like Mac, who seemed to wear that worn-and-torn attitude like it was an outlaw's faded duster, edges shredded and beaten by a run of bad luck. You had to look past the rough smirk, the creviced slant of his cheekbones to see the bruised beauty of him.

Hey, cool it with the Snow White la-de-da fantasies, she told herself. *Get your mind back on Linc. Back on business.*

Fiona patted her friend's wrist. "Ignore Lakota, just like you've been doing."

"She doesn't make it easy."

"At least you don't have scenes together."

"Yet. And who's the guy she's salivating over?"

Fiona tried not to react, to light up inside at the mention of Mac. Instead, she playfully pulled Linc away from the dance floor, but he wouldn't budge.

"No competition. You are a demigod," she said. "I'm telling you so. All the soap magazines tell you so."

He laughed, thank goodness. "I appreciate that, but I'm in trouble when I start believing my own press."

Fiona barely heard him. What was that woman doing to Mac, rubbing her hand up and down his arm? And…was he smiling? Reacting to the way she arched her neck when she giggled?

Oh, and she supposed that her co-worker was probably

making the most of his low, sexy voice. Its touch of snake-charmer trust.

Well, yesterday's flirtatious introduction had been her fault, really. She'd come on strong, immediately drawn to him as he'd assessed her from his chair, his long legs stretched out in front of him, cocky as you please. She loved a man who had the talent to banter, to tease. To tower over her until her body almost melted right into his.

He's a co-worker, a competitor, Fi. Don't forget it.

Right. Right. Her conscience was absolutely right. And her pride couldn't afford to lose another PR gig.

Even from across the room, Fiona felt his rifle-sight gaze on her before actually meeting his eyes. They hadn't said a word to each other in the office today, both consumed with arranging photo shoots, media interviews and guest appearances for other clients. But, right now, the awareness was flammable. Unavoidable.

A quaking need roared through her, tearing through every inch of skin until it splashed into her belly, dripping into a steady pulse between her legs. God, the ache. The want.

He must have seen the desire in the angle of her body. With a devilish grin, he toasted her from across the floor. She returned a jaunty salute with her own champagne flute.

Lakota must have seen their exchange, because the redhead latched onto Mac's muscular arm, staring stilettos at Fiona.

Linc walked away, taking her with him. "More Alka-Selzter."

Fiona tugged him back, gently, so no one would notice the tension. "Don't go drama on me. You didn't keep me on as your publicist so I could look the other way as you make a scene."

"You're my employee, Fi."

His tone was light, but she knew better. Before rehab, when Lincoln got agitated, he got into trouble. That was the problem with being talented and catered to. But she loved him enough to continue keeping him in line. He'd almost ruined his career after the breakup with Lakota, who was at the time an extra on Linc's daytime set. His broken heart had led to an excess of drinking, partying, getting into scrapes that Fiona and Linc's manager constantly got him out of.

And she cared too much to see him fall apart again.

"Listen," she said, "I appreciate how you stuck by me after I got fired at the last firm, but their lack of faith doesn't mean I don't know what I'm doing now. Don't falter. You're going to have to put up with Lakota every day."

She could feel his struggle in the ticking muscles of his arm, but she knew he'd pull through. She'd make sure of it.

"I can't believe she's the star of *Flamingo Beach*," he said, acknowledging a female fan who made it clear she recognized him by pointing and squealing. "How the tables have turned, huh? Now *I'm* the new guy."

Fiona flicked another gaze to Mac again, discovered that he'd left Lakota all alone, and breathed a sigh of relief. "Don't sweat it. You'll do fine."

He nodded, squeezed her hand. "I suppose I will. Now if you could only keep your mind on your publicity stunts...."

She didn't have to ask what he meant. "That man with Lakota, Sean McIntyre, works with me. There's a little flirting going on, but..."

"...But?"

Lying to Linc, to herself was useless. "Okay, he's my kind of poison. True. But I'll be good."

"Good? You actually know that word?" Linc's laughter rose above the fresh set of reggae music. "That's a new one.

I thought girls with your body and appetite weren't built for flowers and valentines."

Fiona's heart fisted, bleeding out every stupid romantic dream she hid from the world. She had no use for roses and sweet nothings anyway. Hadn't needed them for a long time, after being slammed by Ted, the ex.

Nope. Now she was in control of her life, every aspect. Her career, her family, her love…

…Or lack *of* love life.

Didn't matter. Not in the least. She got along just fine with men, keeping relationships to the essentials—sex and…well, sex. She didn't hurt anyone, they didn't hurt her. It was all fun and games, light and laughter.

No more sitting at home, crying because her man had done her wrong.

Never again.

"Fi?" said Lincoln, rubbing a hand along her bare arm. "You know *I* don't believe you're heartless."

Fiona manufactured a smile, beaming at him. "You're the only one. And you're wrong, besides."

Her friend stared at her a moment longer. He'd been there when Ted had dumped her, and she'd returned the favor with Lakota. That's what glued them together—their failures and, soon, triumphs.

"Soap hunk," she said, "there's a group of women waving you over to them. Probably for autographs and a picture or two. And I see your manager and personal assistant making a beeline for you. Escape to the fans while you can."

He straightened his bow tie, his debonair jacket, and with an amiable wink, he was off. Fiona diligently tried to keep her mind on business—damn, it was hard watching her charge like a proud mama seeing her child off to the first day of school, when Mac was somewhere around. As Linc's mini-entourage controlled the growing crowd surrounding him, he proceeded to charm the ladies, posing for photos, signing autograph books.

The night wore on, and she stayed on the outskirts of the festivities while Linc bid adieu to his fans and led the auction. He helped raise several thousand dollars for the children's charity, while a distant Lakota and other cast members from *Flamingo Beach* joined him onstage to entertain the masses.

As the presentation wound down, Fiona glanced around the ballroom, discovering that Lakota Lang was holding hands with Brendon Fillmore, a fading young James-Dean-type actor who still had enough drawing power to attract attention and probably a gossip mention in the fan magazines. Had Mac arranged their liaison, manipulating every shared laugh, every hug for the camera?

Good publicity move. But Fiona wanted to be sure Linc didn't notice. Her friend didn't need another dart to the ego.

When she checked on him, he was busy with a gaggle of adoring fans and seemingly having the time of his life. Some security guards now flanked him.

Maybe now was a good time to visit the powder room, to freshen up.

She set down her champagne and walked toward the rest room, entering a shady hall crammed with gossiping women and soap-star wannabes. Just as she spotted the ladies' room ahead, a young girl crashed into her, yelling, "I think that's Deirdre Hall! Oh. My. God." Then the fan took off, bumping Fiona into the nearest body.

A broad-shouldered, hard-chested body.

"Packed house," said a deep voice. A pair of large hands closed over her arms, steadying her, charging shock waves through the top layer of her skin.

Sucking in a breath, she looked closer, finding Mac standing over her, smiling, challenging her to pass in the limited space.

"Not much room to maneuver." She nodded her head toward the ladies' door. "Do you mind?"

He didn't move. "Go right ahead."

All right. She wouldn't be able to get by him without some full frontal contact, the jerk.

So be it. With a saucy glance, she slid her body over his. Too close. The tips of her breasts hardened and dragged against his jacket, the thin linen of his shirt, slipping over the bulk of his powerful chest, the ridges of his upper abs. At the same time, her hips swayed over his, the hitch in his crotch making her pause and hold her breath. As they stared at each other, she grew moist, achy with the possibilities.

He bent his head, his lips near her forehead, a whisper stirring her hair with warmth.

"Can't move?" he asked.

No. She wouldn't mind nestling against him for the next hour, either, his arousal tucked into her as random people shifted around them, the crowd unaware of Fiona's desire to flow into his fire like glass over flame. She could imagine being in this same position in the dark of night, her legs wrapped around him, urging him inside, moving with every thrust, every slick demand.

She hadn't been attracted to anyone like this in years. Hadn't wanted to rub against them in a packed room, hardly caring what anyone else thought.

For a second, Fiona dipped against him, struggling against the thick moisture of a people-choked room, the overwhelming buzz of being touched so intimately. She was dizzy with the faint scent of leather jacket and…what? Enjoying the fantasy? Fighting to keep her breathing even? Liking the fact that she couldn't manage to gain the upper hand?

But then someone crashed into them, banging Fiona's head against the wall. Knocking some sense into her. *Get a hold of yourself, Fi.*

"Excuse me," she said, trying to make her way past Mac, cold air nibbling at her skin, at the regretful loss of contact.

He gripped her arms tighter. The blood expanded in her veins, thudding, echoing jungle drums, primal and mysterious.

A silly thought occurred to her. What if he didn't let go?

Ridiculous. And tempting, too. But she should have been more worried about other questions.

What if she allowed him to keep her restrained?

It wouldn't happen. Fiona would never fall prey to the whims of anyone—not even this man—again.

She shot a lethal smile at her amused captor. "I'm leaving," she said. "Game over."

"Actually…" Sean McIntyre returned her own slash of a grin. "It's just starting."

Chapter Two

"WHAT'S JUST STARTING?" she asked, dark eyes cautious, smudged with a hint of something like interest.

"The game."

His grip on her arms tightened even more, and Fiona gasped. Sweet sound, that gasp, making Sean's pulse tumble and growl.

He didn't know she could seem so vulnerable, with her lips parted, her hands grasping at his biceps, clenching, then relaxing.

Releasing.

He didn't want her to go, didn't want to return alone to that party with its confetti-colored balloons and forced gaiety, with Lakota Lang and her spunky ambition.

Instead of letting Fiona escape, he took her by the elbow, away from the crowd to an empty table, where he pulled out a chair for her. With cautious acceptance, she sat, leaning her elbows on the surface, her dress sleeves spreading over the linen like yawning black ink stains.

"What game?" Fiona asked, as he took his own seat.

"The battle of wills between our clients. Or haven't you noticed the storm brewing?"

"Oh, I caught a groan of thunder in the air, all right."

He leaned toward her, close enough so he could feel the

wisp of her clothing as it moved against his thigh. "Usually I leave the baby-sitting to the managers, but with these two, I think reconnaissance might not be a bad idea."

And, he added silently, he kind of felt protective toward Lakota Lang. There was still some innocence wrapped in all that tight satin and bravado.

Her date, Brendon Fillmore, was another of Sean's clients. It seemed logical to get both of them some exposure by setting the two strangers up for the night. Brendon's TV show had just been canceled and he needed to stay in the public eye. Lakota needed to cultivate a prime-time image because, with a few night-slot TV cameos under her belt, that's where her career was headed. Up.

The kid definitely needed some of Sean's guidance, not that Fiona had to know this.

Her leg moved beneath the table. Back and forth, teasing him with the languid flow of imagination: Her bare thigh skimming up the side of his, her hips grinding against him...

He'd gotten a taste of her body in the hall, when she'd tried to get by him. If he didn't know better, he would have said that Fiona's incidental contact had been just that—a happy accident. But Sean did know better.

She was playing with him.

Voice as low as a murmur of night wind, she said, "I like the way you think. I want to get a feel for how those two react to each other, just to see if we need to worry about a PR explosion. We don't want Linc and Lakota making a scene—unless it's during *Flamingo Beach,* of course."

"Right." Sean glided his forefinger beneath Fiona's chin, directing her gaze across the room. "Watch."

Her breath sighed over the skin of his hand as he lingered, then stroked the side of her neck on his way down.

Damn, he wanted so much more.

Restraining himself—he was on the clock, not a mattress—Sean looked across the room, as well. There, near the very visible dance floor, Lakota and Lincoln worked the crowd, mingling with fans and the press, their backs to each other.

"You have to know they're aware of every move the other one makes," Fiona said.

Just as Sean, himself, was. Every time she swayed her leg so it breezed near his, every time she inhaled and exhaled, for God's sake.

She continued. "What are we watching for?"

"Wicked glances, a foot stuck out just in time to trip another body. They're getting closer and closer to each other. My sixth sense is vibrating."

And that wasn't all.

She turned to him, her voice close enough to buzz around his ear. "I bet Lakota strikes first."

"Lakota? She's got no reason." He turned his head, bringing his lips closer to Fiona's cheek. "Lincoln's the one who got dumped. I'm sure he's up for a little revenge."

"Linc?" Her warm laugh sizzled his skin. "He's harmless. She's the one who's almost quaking with pent-up hostility. Look at the way she keeps flicking a gaze over her shoulder. She knows he's there, can probably hear his jokes, and I'm betting that his popularity with the fans is killing her."

He tensed, wanting to defend his client, but Fiona's knee had just scratched along his thigh, a slow and deliberate move leaving a wake of burning need in his belly.

Concentration wasn't in the cards tonight.

"Lakota's got enough confidence to keep Lincoln from getting to her," he said.

She slanted her body toward him, bringing her knee back

into contact with his body. She nudged it over the top of his shin, then in between his legs.

In reaction, he trailed a hand over her thigh, resting it on that naughty knee. She laughed, a throaty touché from the master.

"Lakota's going to be the first one to cause trouble," she said. "Mark my words."

He glanced at his client. Slinky Versace dress, bed-head red hair, siren makeup. Sure, he wouldn't put it past Lakota Lang to mess with Lincoln Castle, but with Fiona's thigh underneath his hand, with his thumb easing along the inside, seeking a hint of toned muscle, of moist acceptance, he wasn't in a cut-and-dry mood.

He wanted amusement.

"Care to bet on that?" Sean asked, loyal to his client.

"What? That Lakota's going to rile Lincoln first?" Her smile blossomed. "What's the winner get?"

He pressed his hand higher, fingers creeping to her mid-thigh. Fiona stretched her leg, leaning into him, biting her lip and lowering her gaze in a steamy pause of expectation.

"When I win," he said, "you'll do a task of my bidding."

"Or vice versa."

She removed his touch by sweeping her leg over the other one, crossing them at the knees, keeping him out of further trouble.

A rusty laugh escaped him. "You think Lincoln will keep his cool and ignore Lakota."

She sat a little straighter, and he could tell that she wasn't quite as cocky as she wanted to let on.

"He never fails me," she said.

The blood beat through his hands, filling their emptiness. What he'd give to cup her curves against his palms.

He leaned back in his chair, trying to pretend Fiona didn't

affect him. But the awareness between them was too potent to ignore.

It was bad form to be screwing a co-worker. But at this point, he didn't care.

As he chided himself, he found that they didn't have to wait long for the fireworks to start. A paparazzi photographer whom Sean had arranged to stir up some visibility for his clients appeared, urging the soap stars together for a picture. Lakota cozied up to Lincoln as if they were still lovers.

Pop! After the flash faded, she kept her hold on Lincoln's tuxedo jacket. The man's discomfort was clear—the pained expression, the wooden posture.

Sean perched on the edge of his chair, ready to swing into action if anything happened. The managers were at the stars' sides in an instant, but not before Lincoln lost his cool and liberated himself by shrugging out of his jacket, tossing it over a still-clinging Lakota's head.

As he stalked away, several photographers caught her flipping the clothing off her head and bundling into it, then rubbing her hands up and down her arms as if she'd been cold and Lincoln had lovingly loaned her some warmth.

Fiona made a sound of disgust. "You know she started that. Probably said something to goad him."

"Hey," Sean said, grinning. "The only evidence I saw was Lincoln's tux flying through the air to land on my poor client. Quick thinking on her part, huh? She almost does our jobs for us. I'll make sure *Soap Opera Digest* or *US Magazine* has a picture of Lakota in Lincoln's jacket. I can see the caption now—'She's got his love to keep her warm!'"

"Spare me. I'll arrange it so Lincoln is linked with Nicole Kidman, a much classier redhead."

By the tone of her voice, he knew she wasn't thrilled about losing this battle.

"I'll ignore that slight and go easy on you," he said. "What did the winner of our wager get? Oh, yeah. You have to cater to my whims."

He paused, taking great pleasure at how her dark eyes widened, then narrowed.

A grin quirked his mouth. "Fetch me a drink. Whisky on the rocks."

Fiona stiffened, apparently affronted by the command in his voice.

Sean lifted up his hands, such the good guy. "I could've called in a much more...interesting...prize."

She hesitated, then swept a long look over his body, her gaze like feathers winging from his toes to his neck, leaving a trail of rough tickles.

"I suppose you're right," she said. "But this isn't the end of it. I don't like to lose."

As she left, she winked, her thick eyelashes lending an air of wanton flirtation.

He watched her walk away, unable to tear his eyes off her, off the clingy material of her dress and how it molded those thighs he'd explored, that *ass*.

There was no way he'd get through this night, not without some kind of sexual release. And if getting her into bed made for a tougher workplace tomorrow, then that's how it'd be. He was willing to sacrifice p.c. office protocol for Fiona.

God, she'd be worth it.

This had never happened before, him pursuing someone in the office. Sure, there had been the occasional loaded gesture with an administrative assistant, with a client. But he'd never crossed the line professionally.

Until now.

Work had always mattered too much. He'd spent years being myopic in his pursuit of success. But lately...

Lately it didn't seem to matter as much as the fulfillment of all the fantasies he'd conjured about Fiona Cruz since she'd va-va-voomed into his life yesterday.

Soon, she returned with a flute of champagne for her, a martini for him.

He lifted an eyebrow as she sat. "Not whisky."

A tart smile. "The occasion—and that hot tux—calls for a more sophisticated cocktail. Hollywood's all about image."

"You didn't follow my orders. That means you still owe me."

"Do I?" She watched him over the rim of her glass as she took a sip.

He shrugged, swigged from his drink. Not bad. She knew his tastes, didn't she?

"You always rebel against authority in this way?" he asked.

"I told you, Lakota was the instigator. You didn't win anything."

And she didn't like losing. "Go on. We both know better."

She oh-so-gently set down her flute, so slowly that Sean knew he was in trouble.

"I propose a new bet."

"Clearly losing rankles you more than you'll admit."

"I've got Linc in my sights right now," she said, ignoring his jibe. "He's fully in control and unruffled. Lakota didn't get to him, you see. But I'm going to bet your client is so hot under the collar she'll try to make Linc jealous. I hear that's her modus operandi."

He couldn't dispute her comment, but he still knew Lakota had ample brains and wouldn't make him lose. "And I'm supposed to wager that Lincoln does something to make Lakota jealous first? Hell, yeah, my money's on him to blow it."

"We'll see. Linc's a *professional.*"

With practiced skill, Sean reached out, running a thumb over her collarbone as she watched him. He dipped the thumb under her bra strap. Toyed with it. Her pulse fluttered against his skin.

"What does the winner get?" he asked.

She glanced at his hand, then back at him. "When I win, you tell me something secret about yourself."

"Or the other way around. I've been wondering what you wear to bed anyway."

It was out there now. She could either tell him to back off and he'd respect her wishes, or she could take up the gauntlet. Her call.

Fiona's eyes went soft, and Sean could have sworn that he'd passed some test. Did she appreciate that he'd laid the choice in her lap?

Instead, she said, "Lakota's got fifteen minutes to lose the bet for you, Mac."

A smile spread over his mouth, and they locked gazes, the promise of tonight and what could happen in the wee hours after the party stretching between them.

As Fiona coolly glanced away from him, making it a point to watch Lincoln and Lakota across the room, the DJ put the pedal to the metal with the music, cranking up the volume. People gradually wandered onto the floor, shedding jackets, dancing, bumping against each other.

Ten minutes passed, but Lakota and Lincoln remained apart. Good girl. She wouldn't do anything to jeopardize her cultivated image, not after he'd put her through all that media combat training.

Then again, maybe he'd spoken too soon. In the near distance, Lakota was arrowing a sly glare in her ex-boyfriend's direction.

It was as if Lincoln felt the sting of Lakota's eyes, because he glanced over at her, their gazes meeting. Sean knew that look.

Wounded, open.

The kind of expression his dad had worn for years, sitting across from his mom's empty chair at the dinner table while Sean and his two sisters took care of the food, the bills, the anguish.

Across the room, Lakota smirked, then turned back to her crowd of admirers, leaving Lincoln hanging.

Sean refrained from toasting her expertise. Clever woman, toying with Lincoln. A lot like Fiona.

Lincoln grabbed a nearby woman's hand and led her to the dance floor, provoking Lakota first, thus assuring Sean's victory in his wager with Fiona. Obviously affronted, Lakota followed suit, partnered with her own weapon of choice—Brendon Fillmore, who'd been courting his own fans with his soft-rebel persona.

Great.

"Dance off," said Sean.

"Let me guess. Lakota's the Shark, Lincoln's the Jet." Her voice was resigned.

He shrugged.

She sighed, a clear white flag of surrender. "I wear girls' tighty-whitie undies."

"You wear ugly underwear to bed?"

"They're made for women, and they're extremely cute. You know, bun-huggers?"

Lust sucker punched him once again. "Fiona, I'm surprised. I expected you to confess a fondness for black-net bodysuits or satin nightgowns. But..."

The image clouded his mind. Fiona, with her long legs showcased by a pair of those clinging panties. With her torso bare, breasts full and throbbing for his touch.

She mock-glared at him. "You're developing a nasty habit of winning."

"That's the way I like it."

Though she seemed to be joking, Sean wondered if she wasn't telling the truth.

"You know," he said, "there's a hole-in-the-wall bar on the corner. Quiet. Secluded."

"Meaning?"

"You're a smart woman."

Fiona stared at him, as if considering the offer. Self-aware ladies knew a night like this probably wouldn't end with a drink. Not with the way he and Fiona were offering those testing swipes.

But before she could answer, Sean felt the frigid fingers of his business sense strumming the back of his neck. He contained a shiver, then turned around.

Lakota and Lincoln had come toe-to-toe on the dance floor, and it wasn't a *West Side Story* moment, either. She'd left Brendon dancing by himself in order to confront Lincoln, her hand splayed over her ex's chest, nails bared like claws. For his part, Lincoln was holding strong, trying to play off the contact. But before Sean could get out of his chair, the managers had pulled the two apart.

Lakota's handler, Carmella Shears, shot him a glare. Back to the ever-present office.

"Looks like I need to get busy seeing that Lakota smiles for the cameras on the way out." He rose from his chair. "I'm off to help her handler lock her away for the night."

Fiona followed his example and stood. "Have fun tucking her in."

"I don't get involved with clients." But he would mix business with pleasure if given the chance. With Fiona, that is.

He started to leave, then on the spur of the moment,

turned back around. "Bailey's. That's what the place on the corner is called."

And, without waiting for her answer, Sean moved toward his troublemaking soap star, feeling Fiona's eyes track him with every step he took away from her.

HE'D WON EVERY BET, damn him.

Fiona had hailed a cab from Linc's house near Griffith Park, where she'd comforted him and talked him down from his doomed meeting with Lakota. Now, as she traveled to her apartment by The Farmer's Market, she stewed over Mac's victory streak.

Sure, he could've really fried her over the flames if he were less of a gentleman. Could've asked her to do something deliciously ridiculous, like flash her breasts in the crowded room. Or was that *her* fantasy machine at work?

Whatever the case, she'd told him she didn't like to lose, and that had been the truth. Fiona had been raised to compete, growing up in a household of three brothers, where they'd all had to vie for attention. Maybe she'd absorbed a lot of testosterone over the course of the years. Who knew?

But she certainly didn't like sitting in the loser's column.

They were approaching Hollywood Boulevard and Bailey's, the bar Mac had mentioned. Her body sang with longing as they got closer. Closer. Passing it by.

Was he waiting there?

And what would happen if she walked in? Sat down?

They'd end up in someone's bed.

A tremble of remembrance riffled through her body, recalling his hand on her leg, in between her thighs.

She wanted him there. Everywhere.

Handling him at work wouldn't be a problem. She'd enjoyed an office affair or two and had always controlled the situation with discreet grace. No one got hurt; that was her mantra.

So why was this any different? Because she needed this gig? Needed to feel successful again?

She was on her way up, and nothing, not even Sean McIntyre, was going to stop her. She could have her cake and eat it, too, just like any man in her business.

"Please turn around," she said to the driver. "There's a bar. Bailey's."

"I know it." The man whipped around the cab, probably thinking she was indecisive, mind-scrambled.

And she was, wasn't she? Deliriously, ecstatically giddy with flashbacks of Mac's corded chest against hers, the chiseled bulges of his arms holding her captive. Controlling her when *she'd* always been the one calling the shots.

The driver dropped her off in front of a sign with a neon-lined martini and olive, and she paid him. As he left, the motor revving into the distance, Fiona took a deep breath, walked into the dark recesses of the bar.

It was a real funky joint: a slim cigarette case lined with half-empty bottles, the aroma of salt and gin, anonymously low lighting and faux-leather upholstery gleaming in the shadows. The jukebox near the back played a Doors tune— "People Are Strange"—and a few suited patrons splayed their bodies over bar stools.

A dead-end weeknight. Her dead end, too.

Mac was among the barflies, ensconced in a booth, discarded tuxedo jacket slouched over the seat, his expansive back to the door. She knew his choice of location was purposeful—not too eager, not too concerned if she showed up or not.

She laughed to herself, then took the first confident step

toward him, feeling the gazes of the male customers. Her power grew with every collected, silent compliment.

When she arrived at his seat, he didn't acknowledge her at first. Part of the game, she knew, the pretense of not having the other person on your mind for the past hour and a half. Instead, he kept his eyes on the wall across from him, gaze trained on a picture of a man who could've been the bar's owner posing with Marcus Allen in a Raider's football uniform. One of Mac's hands enfolded a glass of amber liquid—probably that damned whisky he'd wanted her to fetch earlier.

"Drinking alone?" she asked.

Finally, he glanced up. "Thought I would be."

Was that relief written in the tough-life lines of his face? There was something about his expression—the stumbling slant of his mouth, the laconic curve of an eyebrow... She didn't dare hope he was that happy to see her.

His mien returned to its regular programming: gunslinger calm mixed with roguish promise. Then he motioned to the space opposite. "Did you sing Lincoln a few lullabies?"

She slid into the booth. "He's a big boy. Lakota didn't rattle him as much as his manager did, lecturing him about comebacks and all that fun stuff."

"Right." Mac turned to the bartender and ordered her a sour apple martini. Turned back around to flash her a shit-eating grin.

So he was returning the favor from their first bet, flying against her wishes just to get the best of her. Playful boy. Luckily she liked his choice in beverages.

"You actually showed up," he said.

The words had a lonely ring to them, and Fiona's heart tilted on its axis. Lopsided, off center.

"How could I resist?" she asked. "You practically begged."

He laughed, probably not feeling the need to correct her. Fiona was certain that Sean McIntyre never had to plead with a woman, but she could see how it might be the other way around.

"So..." she said.

Silence, as the bartender slid her drink onto the table. She didn't touch it.

Mac waited for the man to leave, then reclined against the seat's cracked leather, narrowing his sharp green eyes. Assessing her intentions?

"Tell me why you're here, Fiona Cruz."

Her breath caught in her throat. Then, she eased her arms onto the table, leaning toward him, knowing good and well that she was showing cleavage, reveling in the power as his eyes strayed there.

"You asked," she said, "and I came."

He grinned again, and her heart did a belly flop, a scalding, breathtaking plunge.

"And come you did. But hopefully not for the last time tonight."

Highly entertained, she smiled right back at him.

Chapter Three

FIONA SHOOK HER HEAD. "You think I'm going to hop right into the sack with you."

"You haven't thought about it?"

The crimson light from a vintage beer sign fizzed on, suffusing Mac's steady gaze. A second later, it blinked off, as if too weary to put out the effort.

She pressed her breasts against the table, rubbing a little, watching the undisguised hunger of his posture: his wide shoulders arched forward, arm muscles straining against the white of his rolled-up shirtsleeves. Poised like a predator. Practiced and ready.

"Mac," she said, "let's stop circling each other and be direct. I like men. I like those ridges right above the hipbones. I like kissing my way down a hard chest until I get to the belly button, where I can feel the ab muscles clench with each touch of my lips. I like the feel of a man's back as his shoulders bunch and flex." She paused. "But there are also things I don't like. Pretty words designed to get me into bed. Speedos at the beach. Commitment."

He didn't say anything for a moment. Instead, he ran a finger around the rim of his glass, still watching her.

She tried not to think about what that finger could be doing to her body within the next hour.

Finally, he spoke. "I don't wear Speedos."

"Not many American men make that mistake."

"And I'm wondering how we're going to manage the boss man when he finds out that I made you purr tonight."

Oh.

"Are you assuming that you're going to have the chance?"

He lifted his drink, toasted her. "I'm banking on it."

Cocky. God, she liked that in a man.

As he swigged his whisky, she suggestively ran a finger along the stem of her own martini glass. "Just so we have an understanding, we wouldn't talk about our...extracurricular activities...inside the office. *If* it were to happen."

He pushed his glass away, though it still had plenty in it. "Discretion is the better part of fooling around."

She couldn't believe they were sitting here, talking about this so calmly, not yet tearing each other's clothes off and rolling over the intimate, scarred table. But the verbal foreplay was nice, making her swollen, wet, in need of release.

She wiggled in her seat a bit. "So I can count on you to keep this quiet?"

"As long as we know what to expect of each other, I think we'll do fine."

Expectations. Back when she'd been in love with Ted, she'd cherished a lot of those. Fidelity, everlasting love. Things you saw in romantic movies. Things fairy tales trained young girls to require in a relationship.

She had no expectations now. None except secrecy and lack of commitment.

"If we're laying down some ground rules here, what do you want from me?" she asked.

He reached across the table, positioning a long finger over the one she was using to fondle the martini glass's stem.

"From you?" A graveled chuckle. "Don't worry, Fiona. I'm not the house-in-the-suburbs, two-point-three children and an SUV-in-the-garage type. I'd want to love you for the moment, but nothing beyond that."

The words dug into her, left her hollow. Though she'd been encouraging him to tell her he didn't want anything serious, some tiny, princess-hopeful cell in her body hungered to be romanced, valued in the long run.

Maybe even loved.

But she was beyond that. Love was in the cards for some people—they were meant for marriage, babies. Fiona Cruz was the exception, the yin to normalcy's yang.

"I appreciate your honesty," she said, forcing some moxie into her tone.

He took both of her hands, and she sat up from her cleavage-show hunch. Here it went, the seduction. The part where he sketched patterns over her skin, warmed her palms with temporary affection.

Good. As always, the predictable contact would take away the sting. Would help her refocus on physical pleasure, pure and simple.

Nevertheless, excitement beat in her chest, lower, where it pooled, boiled, bubbled.

"Is there anything you want from me?" he asked, a glint in his eyes.

She hesitated. "Just your vow that when it's over, it's over. No randy winks as you pass my office, no veiled comments to colleagues."

"Can do."

"Good." A quiver passed through her, twanging, vibrating. "I don't ever want to end up like Lakota and Linc."

"What? Warped from the illusion of love?"

Damaged? she added silently.

His comment had a biting snap to it, like the business end of a whip. Did Mac hide his own disappointments, his own reasons for playing the field without settling?

"Something like warped," she said. "I know Linc was over the moon for Lakota. She was more open in those days, and I think there was genuine affection there. But Linc had a complex. 'What if she loves the star and not me?' he'd always ask."

"Lakota seems viperish, but I think she wasn't always that way. She's a sweet girl underneath it all."

Fiona smiled. "A fresh-scrubbed innocent?"

"Believe it or not."

All this talking was killing her, but Fiona didn't want to seem desperate, yanking him out of the bar as if she hadn't had sex in months. Which she actually hadn't. After miscalculating what her client needed during her last job, she'd concentrated on succeeding in a new one, putting sex...and emotions, she supposed...on the back burner.

Now, she'd wait for *him* to make the first move. After all, there was pride to consider.

Mac threaded his fingers through hers. The gesture touched her, striking her as somewhat tender, testing. Without thinking, she tightened her grip on him, then loosened it, ashamed of being so needy, so easily charmed.

"Lakota," she said, swallowing away the surge of feeling, "called off the relationship because she thought Linc was cheating. He wasn't, of course. You'll never find a more constant guy than he is. But she got territorial and overreacted by leaving him altogether."

"Par for the course," said Mac, focusing attention on just one of her hands now, stroking the rough tips of his fingers up the inside of her arm, back down.

White heat spiraled through her bloodstream, infecting her with passionate discomfort.

"What do you mean?" she asked, slightly breathless. "Are you saying women can't get through a liaison without some measure of possessiveness?"

"That's right."

"You're wrong."

He cocked a golden brow. "Am I?"

"Absolutely." Fiona pushed away his fingers. "There're women who can be just as cavalier as men. Not in a relationship necessarily, because, by definition, those are supposed to be based on feelings. But when it comes to sex, females don't necessarily have to get attached."

"I've never seen evidence of that." He glanced at her arm, then brazenly slid his finger down one of her veins until he came back to her palm. "Every woman I've been with has shown some sign of wanting to go beyond sex, even if it's a hesitation as you kiss good-night."

"Did you ever take them up on their willingness, subtle as it might be?"

"No." The word grated out. Then he grinned. "That's where the liaison ends, when someone gets ideas. Cut it out before she gets her heart broken, I say."

"I agree." She really did. Absolutely.

"Sounds like you think the rule doesn't apply to you. That you can escape unscathed after sex."

"I can."

"Bullshit."

Fiona shook her head. "Poor guy. You operate under some fearful misconceptions."

"You're telling me that, after having sex with a man for, say a month, you could leave the affair without..."

"...becoming possessive or territorial? Yes, I can. I *have*."

He laughed again, combing his other hand through his dark blond hair, the strands sticking up, ruffled and boyishly attractive, contrasting with the darkness in the center of his irises. "If you hadn't lost every bet we initiated tonight, I'd wager that, given one month with me, you'd become emotionally attached."

Her heart chopped against her ribs, and her hand inadvertently fisted around his busy finger. "Well, that's damn arrogant."

He cast a pointed glance at the intensified contact, and she let go.

But even after a second, she missed the feel of him. His callused skin. The way he was big enough to hide her fingers in his grasp, cradling her. Just holding her.

"Wouldn't you love to see me lose?" he asked.

Yes, she would, so much she could almost do a victory dance right now. And she *could* win. No problem. She'd spent the past few years being emotionally distant, if not physically warm and willing, after sex.

"If we embarked on such a philosophical experiment," she said, "what would the winner get? Wait. I'd love to go to the Caribbean. It's time for a vacation."

"Sounds good. A Caribbean getaway of the winner's choice, all expenses paid by the loser."

"This is getting interesting, because I could kick your ass in this bet."

He seemed grandly amused, his full mouth tilted at an angle, half-hidden by the scruffy drifter's stubble surrounding his lips. "You'd be in love with me before you knew it."

Though his comment came off jokingly, Fiona wasn't so

sure he didn't mean what he said. Then again, hadn't he mentioned he ended his affairs before they went too far?

Not that it mattered. Fiona didn't do love. Wouldn't happen. She had this wired.

"So," he said, "how will I know I've won the bet?"

She laughed low in her throat, a hint of the purr he'd promised her earlier. "You'll see it in my eyes, Mac. The fact that you've lost, I mean."

"Then we do this scientific eye check after every time I've been inside you?"

She could almost feel him now, filling her, slipping in and out while the sheets got torn off the bed corners. "That's logical enough."

Silence, punctuated by another jukebox Doors song. "The End."

Which should have told her something.

A wave of yearning stretched Fiona out of the booth, bringing her to her feet. She started to walk away from him, slowly, zinging that extra sway into her stride.

She glanced over her shoulder, discovering his gaze on her derriere. The naked desire in his look turned her blood to steam.

"The bet starts now," she said, crooking her finger at him in summons. "Game on."

She turned around, moving away, knowing he was going to follow.

THEY'D TAKEN A TAXI to his rented place off Melrose Avenue because she'd requested they go where he lived.

He understood her reasoning, because he liked to go to his lover's place, as well. It gave a person control.

Done with the sex? Hey, I've got an early meeting tomorrow, time for me to leave.

The visitor dictated the schedule.

But, with Fiona, Sean didn't mind. He wanted her in his bed as soon as possible, no matter the location.

Hell, he'd have taken her on the way to his home if he hadn't wanted to make a point.

To show her he had patience and would win the bet.

Yeah, the wager was a good way to get Fiona to do what he wanted. And, no, he had no intention of making her fall for him. As usual, the second he saw emotion, he'd stop the affair.

A sultry midnight mist had fallen over the streets, lamps casting a bourbon tinge over the sidewalks. Jazz music—heavy on the drumbeats—beckoned from the open windows of a neighbor's house. When they walked through the gate to his Spanish Renaissance Revival home with the palms and Birds of Paradise plants lining the sidewalk, Sean tried not to rush through the door. Instead, he took his time, allowing her to walk in front of him, her hips ticking back and forth like a pendulum, counting down the moments.

She sauntered up the steps, leaning against the stucco wall near the door, waiting for him to unlock the iron grating.

They hadn't said a damned word all the way here, and the silence ate at him.

He pulled open the iron, then pushed in the heavy wood door. His pulse thudded in his ears as she glided past, the swish of her black, airy dress coaxing him to follow her inside.

As he reached for the lights, Fiona grasped his wrist, pulling him away from the entrance, bolting him against the wall. The door slapped shut, darkening the room further. But the sheer-gold moonlight allowed him a peek of her while she pressed against him, body to body.

White curtains billowed away from his open window, the

linen flirting, dancing over her dusky skin. Her eyes wide, black as a dreamless sleep, she asked, "Ready for me, Mac?"

Tousled voodoo hair. Jazz drums. The smoldering aroma of her mango-scented skin reminding him of lush breezes and oceans lapping at the sand.

In response he planted a hand in her loose curls, tightened gently, guided her mouth to his in a searing kiss.

She moaned against his lips, opening, rubbing, nipping at him. And, as he devoured her in return, he slipped a hand to the small of her back, tracing the curve of spine, trailing downward. His fingers sketched over her fruit-plump ass, palming it under the cheek and thrusting her against his growing erection.

Damn, he was hard—too ready and willing. If he wasn't careful, he was going to spill himself all over the carpet like a twelve-year-old on his first date with a *Playboy* centerfold.

Sean slowed the pace. Tilting Fiona's head with his other hand, he eased his tongue into her mouth, running it over the edge of her teeth, circling, tasting a memory of champagne sweetness.

She came up for air, leaning her head against his jaw. "Your stubble burns," she said. "But in a good way."

"I'm not about to stop and shave it off."

"Even if I asked you to?"

"You really—"

She pounced, cut him off with her lips.

They sipped at each other, chafing against the wall, knocking into end tables and anemic wooden chairs.

The force of their kiss heating up again, he whipped her around, gently yet firmly placing her against the wall now. Raising her arms above her head, he stared down at her.

"You're a damn good kisser, Fiona," he said around the holes of his breathing.

She panted, too. "And vice versa. I like a good, old-fashioned lip lock. Did I leave that off my list?"

The list. Images of her skimming her lips down the length of him shuddered an emergency alarm through every cell of his body.

Unable to hold back, he rocked against her, urging his cock into the crevice between her legs.

Her arms lost their bone structure, melted down until they rested on top of her head.

Seizing the opportunity, he roamed south, thumbs dragging over the pounding column of her neck, over her swollen breasts, the softness of her stomach, to her thighs. There, he slid upward, under her dress.

Garters. He should've known she'd be wearing thigh-high stockings and a belt. A woman with fire like Fiona's wouldn't settle for less, not even on a weeknight.

Sean leveled out his breathing. *Take it easy, man.*

With hard-won deliberation, he unsnapped one garter. Then the other. Lifted her skirt so he could glimpse the retro-sexy lingerie.

Oh, yeah. Dark lace and long legs.

"Men are so visual," she said on a sigh.

"And you use that to your advantage."

He pushed the dress to her waist, slipped a thumb between her legs to slide against her damp panties. He pressed against her clit, massaging, daring her to explode before he did.

She sank against the wall, biting her lip as she smiled and squeezed her eyes shut. As he exerted more pressure, Fiona started to move her hips, swaying in time to the stimulation.

How was he going to last? Already moisture was building on the tip of his penis. He could feel it.

With something close to a groan, he stroked his fingers

into her underwear, eased them inside of her. In, out, faster, thumb working her, moaning, sliding...

She embraced him again, bit his ear, making him dizzy, disoriented. His lobe was his Achilles' heel.

Without warning, she'd forced him backward, and he held on to her, backing into a chair. She pushed off with a triumphant gasp, and before he knew it, he was seated, pulse pounding in his crotch.

He laughed, intrigued by this tug-of-war. "The wall wasn't comfortable enough for you?"

Her smile echoed his mirth. Instead of answering, she plucked off her ankle-strap heels, propped her foot on the chair's arm and slicked off one stocking, dangling it in front of him. Moonlight filtered through it, clouding his vision. She allowed the silk to shiver to the ground.

He stretched in the chair, accommodating her stripteasing, wishing she'd get on his lap so he could thrust himself inside her.

When the other stocking was done for, she wiggled out of the garter belt, kicking it behind her. His hands itched for her to join him on the chair, but she pulled another fast one by turning around, shimmying, glancing over her shoulder.

"Get over here," he said, the words graveled with raw need.

She sent him a saucy glance, resting her chin on her shoulder as she appeared to unbutton the front of her dress. A faint jazz-drum tattoo accompanied her, lending a laconic sensuality to her undulating hips.

Encouraged, Sean unbuttoned the top of his pants. With a teasing laugh, she reversed onto his lap, smoothing her rump back over his thighs until he had his chest near her spine. Her legs were spread apart, straddling him.

"Ever had a lap dance?" she asked.

The breath whooshed out of him. "You think I'm a monk or something?"

"Do you like lap dances?"

He muttered a frustrated curse, hating and loving her playful pokes at seduction. With one smooth scoop, he had her flush against him, one leg over the chair's arm, his fingers tracing the inside of her thighs.

"Wanna tease me some more?" he asked, urging her back against his arousal. It beat against her rear, pounding out its demands.

She wiggled in answer, exciting him to the point of bursting. But he controlled himself, wanting to win this power struggle, wanting to end the contest while enfolded in her spasming, slippery heat.

As she gyrated, grinding up, then down his lap, reaching back to caress his hair, his face, he held on to her hips, working them to and fro. She arched away from him, causing him to reach up, cup her lacy-bra-bound breasts, feel her nipples harden between his fingers, under his thumbs.

One last brush of her ass against his crotch, and he'd had enough.

He picked her up, laying her face up on the floor. "I'm taking over now."

"So you think."

With skillful finesse, he delved inside her dress, undoing her bra, freeing her breasts. He took one in his mouth, sucking, tonguing it.

"Dammit," she said, threading her fingers through his hair. Pressing herself to him, she wrapped her legs around his body.

He'd imagined the cage of her legs, the strain of their bodies absorbing each other's sweat. And fantasy wasn't nearly as good as this.

They kissed again, pausing only to tear Fiona out of her dress, panties and bra, to pull him out of his shirt and pants. Bare naked, both of them.

She breathed into his ear. "Got a—?"

"—Yeah."

He attacked his pants pocket, fought with his wallet, took out the condom.

She tugged it away from him, running a finger under his cock, making him grab for the carpet with the lightning-flash electricity of her touch. Then she paused to rub her thumb over the tip of him, spreading the beads of semen that had accumulated.

"You're gonna feel so good, Mac."

Her fingers traced his balls, and he tilted back his head, fighting for restraint.

She pushed him backward, until he lay prone on the carpet, then slid the rubber over him with a single, smooth caress.

Legs encasing him, she rested her hands on his shoulders, using her nails to abrade him. Then she sat on his belly, her nether lips opening over his skin, sticking to him with her juices. She moved her mouth up to his head, slicking down his body with the laziness of a summer cloud traveling the sky. Her dark hair rained over his face, his chest, his lower stomach.

He shuddered deep within his belly, and the violence of his reaction spurred him into motion. He grasped her hips, urgently leading her onto his shaft, impaling her.

She sucked in a breath, bending back her head, body waving to and fro. Then she flipped her hair, leaned forward, furling and unfurling over him, working him to a frenzy with increasing thrusts.

While she pulsated against him, he watched her breasts move with every thrash, her hair swing and mingle with the sweat on her shoulders, her arms and chest.

He tore into her, their bodies drumming and stretching to the saxophone rhythm of a July night, skin misted, slick, sensitive. Inside, she was hot and fluid, a vortex of fluttering muscles that swallowed him in a roar.

But he held back, straining for control, as she moved on top of him, churning, grasping for satisfaction.

He plunged deeper, watching her face, the silent *o* of her mouth, the lazy roll of her neck. Fascinated, he added the play of his fingers to her mounting orgasm, working her, delving between her wet lips. Pressing, on, off, around, up, feeling the base of his cock as it slipped in and out of her. Getting even more turned on by the thought of disappearing, being enfolded by her heat, being sucked in and out.

In.

Out.

She shuddered, arched backward until her long hair winged over his legs, then she groaned, a long, sated signal of fiery contentment. After a jagged breath, she prowled back over him until she lay flush against his length, eye to eye, predator to predator.

It was all he could stand.

A growl wrenched from his lungs as he turned her over, her back on the carpet. She laughed and circled him with her endless legs. Beyond restraint, he hammered into her, hearing her breathe a soft, instinctive "oh" every time he drove home. Deeper.

They were a tangle of arms and legs. She bit into his neck, climaxing again and spearing an aching spasm through his dick.

"Oh, yeah," she said, grinding hard against him, encouraging his own implosion. "Come on."

He burst, spilling himself into the rubber in a swirl of mindless light, filling the condom. Filling her.

He was spent, but he didn't want to leave. She was holding him there, wrapped around every aftermath throb. It was the only kind of embrace he could bring himself to accept, and Fiona seemed to understand that as she held him inside her, their muscles clenching, unclenching, weakening. Letting go.

They lay side by side, panting, skin-slicked and intimate, watching each other. He'd found a perfect partner, hadn't he?

Sean smoothed back her hair, peered into her eyes with taunting exaggeration.

He froze. Did he see a flicker, a flame?

Whatever it was, the warmth was doused in an instant.

Sighing, she shut her lids, turned away her face. "The bet." She blinked open again, all of a sudden coy, playful. "What do you find, Sherlock?"

Now? Nothing but a wink and a smile. Nothing more than he'd asked for at the bar. "A whirlpool of emotion," he said, trying to play it off as if it didn't matter.

And it didn't. That tiny seed of disappointment in his belly, growing among the awakening aftershock shivers, didn't mean anything. He wanted it this way. No attachment, no bonding.

But wasn't she feeling anything? Hadn't he seen *something?*

She rose to an elbow, her breasts moving, tempting him to regroup and go another round with her. But she was having none of it, apparently, because she got to her knees, reached for her clothes.

"That was amazing," she said, chipper as a Girl Scout who'd just gotten a badge for creating rug burn.

Maybe too chipper?

Shifting position, he felt the carpet beneath him stroke his tender backside. He'd pay for this later.

He murmured an agreement to her "amazing" comment, leaning his head back into the cradle of his arms.

She was actually leaving.

Her efficiency was astounding. She called for a cab, then started to get into her clothes.

"Since you haven't won any Caribbean vacations yet," she said, "when do we try this again?"

In a half hour? "Whenever you want."

"Okay." She finished dressing. "I'll catch you bright and early tomorrow at work. We'll see what happens afterward."

She swept one last look over his sweat-decorated body then made for the door. There, she hesitated, and he propped himself on an elbow, waiting.

When she opened her mouth, no words came out. Instead, her gaze fell to the floor, and she laughed a little.

"You can't hear it, but I really am purring inside," she said softly.

"Isn't that what I promised?" He ignored the spark in his chest. "Wait for the cab in here."

For a second, she didn't move. Then, "No. It's one of those beautiful, warm California nights. I'll be fine."

She opened the door, stepped outside. Through the thin dress, he could see her legs, her curvy figure. Then she left. Done. Gone.

His conscience tried to placate him:

Let them go before they start to care. Keep it light. No strings attached.

Sean McIntyre closed his eyes, shutting out the longing for something more.

Chapter Four

THE TWINGE in Fiona's conscience—as well as the faint vibrations tickling her skin—lasted into the next evening.

And, dammit all if she couldn't keep her mind off Mac. The stiff, damp throb between her legs, the constant replay of their night together, invaded her with intangible heat. Reminding her. Thrilling her.

Taunting her.

In spite of the air-conditioning, Fiona fanned herself, surveying the scene at the Goddess Gallery on Beverly Boulevard. She'd put together a photography show for one of the clients who had been assigned to her by the firm. Terry Oatman, the artist in question, was a washed-up actor who'd done several straight-to-video bombs during the past few years. Two decades ago, he'd been the hippest Ray•Ban-wearing man on the scene, but now, after a bout with drugs and a freefall from fame, he was sober. Ready to reinvent his image.

And it was her job to make sure he made it again.

Things looked good so far. A few A-list rockers and movie stars had made it to opening night; they wandered through the incense-scented gallery, mingling, drinking the gratis champagne, perusing the black-and-white portraits only when they thought it would matter. Fiona had persuaded a movie magazine to do a layout of Oatman's work and, every few minutes, another flash would light up the white-walled room.

The only person who seemed genuinely interested in something other than being noticed or eating their fill of hors d'oevres was Lincoln, the lone soap star, isolated by his low position on the Hollywood food chain. He wandered the exhibit, considering each photo.

Her throat tightened. He hadn't wanted to talk about last night and what had happened with Lakota, so she'd decided to give him space until he was ready. Give him space because he knew something was up with her, also.

Brother. Could she stop thinking about Mac? She'd managed to extinguish all the sparks he'd ignited in her. Sort of. It was necessary though, because those dangerous bursts of hope and connection rubbed against the emptiness of her better judgment, shocking her system.

Had Mac seen what she'd felt, even for that terrifying second? It'd been a mix of instinctive optimism, the utter happiness of contentment. Of finding an equal.

Fiona leaned against the wall, the black-garbed gallery crowd blurring into one big empty hole.

At least she'd gotten out of his house before she'd surrendered to the moment altogether. The cab had arrived within ten minutes and, with every moment that ticked by, she hoped Mac wasn't looking out the window, seeing her standing by herself. Seeing how much she'd wanted to go back inside to be with him again.

Thank God he'd been called out of the office today, overseeing a star-studded fashion show sponsored by Stellar, making sure all their top talent got tickets, got noticed.

And she'd definitely felt his absence. But only because sex was still on her brain—the comfort of a near stranger, the warmth of another body reassuring her that she was wanted, if only for a short time.

She had everything under control now. Mac was nothing more to her than a bet. An intense flirtation. A day-after, first burn of sensual awareness that cried out for more.

And if he hadn't called her yet, so what? It didn't matter. Nothing to get territorial about.

Fiona focused again, the room returning to normal, the black hole vanishing, morphing back into her glamour-and-grunge clients. Her real life.

A petite woman clutching a clipboard parted the crowd, rolling her eyes in exasperation as she reached Fiona. Rosie, her assistant.

"Trouble?" asked Fiona.

Rosie's pale cheeks were splotched pink, and strands of her strawberry-blond hair spiked out from the tight bun she wore. Even her off-the-rack suit was a little rumpled. Fiona would have to take the enthusiastic girl shopping if she wanted to get ahead.

"Fiona, Jerry Rute's had too much to drink again, and he's starting to hit on the movie magazine photographer." Rosie adjusted her wire-rimmed glasses. "His handler just took him out the back door."

Jerry Rute. One of those boy band singers who'd turned movie star and didn't quite know how to handle his middling fame.

Fiona kept frustration at bay. "His manager should've taken all those drinks out of his greedy little hands. Isn't that why these stars have entourages? To keep them out of trouble?"

"Or to get them into it."

She stepped out of her corner. "You're learning quickly. Are you sure you want a job that usually requires cleaning up messes instead of preventing them?"

The assistant brightened. Like everyone else in this town, she wore her ambition in her gaze. "I'm sure. Oh, and I'll let the caterers know that we need more fontina risotto balls with that marinara sauce. They're going like hotcakes."

"Thanks, Rosie."

"No problem." The young girl started to dash away, then turned around again, holding up a finger. "By the way, those premiere tickets came through."

A bolt of adrenaline shot through Fiona. Score one for her. This was where she'd regain her shine. If she pleased the ragtag bunch of clients Stellar had dumped on her, more powerful talent would gravitate her way.

She could win their game.

"Excellent work," she said to her assistant, making her glow.

As the young woman darted behind a white wall covered by a mammoth image of an abandoned filling station on Route 66, Fiona couldn't stop an emerging grin.

Let's see, she thought. A limited number of tickets to the hottest movie premiere in town next week. Who would benefit the most? The actress who was living down a very public struggle with anorexia? The actor whose last film bombed during opening weekend? Or all the B-listers who wanted so desperately to be A-list?

She hated choosing. Hated hearing the client's voice on the phone when they realized they weren't important enough to score the most sought-after prizes of fame.

If only she could please them all.

Lincoln passed into her view as he moved to a new picture.

His posture tore at her: the slightly slouched shoulders of someone who knows he's not wanted at the popular kids' party, the too-intense scrutiny of the art.

Fiona slid up next to him. "See anything you like?"

Linc didn't say anything for a second, then he shrugged, his classy-cool bomber jacket creaking.

"Oatman's got a good eye. Not that any of these people would care."

"It might help if you mingled with 'these people.' Schmoozing is worth its weight in gold. Come on, let's work the room."

He shot her a wry glance. "I'm in soaps. And, guess what? I kind of like being there. You're the one with all the high hopes for me."

Was he angry with her? "You deserve the best, Linc. That's what I want for you."

She felt him take her hand, squeeze it, then let go. "I know."

"Something else is bugging you though."

"Not here, Fi."

"Okay. I got it. You're fine. You big he-man who no want to deal with woman problem."

Another partygoer who happened to be interested in the actual display wandered by them, lingered, then moved on.

Linc stirred, moved closer to Fiona. "I need to stop throwing my whole heart into relationships. It kills me."

Not that he fell in love with every woman he met, but when Lincoln was smitten, he was gone. Completely devoted to the point of *becoming* the other person. His love wasn't of the healthy variety, yet she'd done her best to support him throughout the years.

"You're just that way," she said, keeping her voice low enough to avoid announcing their conversation, loud enough to overcome the soft, live acoustic guitar music being played in the corner by yet another client.

She continued. "You're intense, and someday you'll find a woman who'll accept all your love. But she's not going to be easy to find."

"I smother them, don't I?"

They'd had this heart-to-heart before. "If you're talking about Lakota..."

"Lakota's a free bird, not a clinging vine." He laughed without humor. "The whole 'other woman' deal provided an excuse for her to leave. That's that."

The other woman. The phrase reminded her of Ted, her ex. But in Linc's case, there had been no other. Only Lakota.

Was there more than one woman in Mac's life?

The thought caused Fiona to cross her arms over her chest, but once she realized what she'd done, she returned to her relaxed, isn't-this-a-great-party? position.

Fiona lightly bumped into Linc. "Don't let your intensity do you in now. Okay? I've told you before to keep your distance from Miss Thang."

"Not likely." He turned away from the picture: two fluffy, coy Maltese dogs sitting in a rusted-out car. "The next script has our first scene together and, surprise! The writers are pairing us up again."

"Ooo. Well, it was inevitable, wasn't it? The fans will go nuts for you two, and the network knows it."

"Fame costs too much. Maybe I should retire." He jerked his chin toward an Oatman portrait of a desert landscape. "I'd like to be this guy, taking pictures for a living. That'd make me happy."

Fiona remembered how he used to take off some weekends just to capture photos. He'd skid back Monday morning in time for class, then develop his own pictures, never showing anyone else but her.

"You can do anything you want to, Linc."

He laughed, dismissed the idea by turning away from the exhibit. "Now that we've hashed out my angst, how about that spark in your eye?"

Fiona took a step back, laughed. "What're you talking about?"

"All right. Have it your way."

"No, I mean…" God, she wanted to talk to him about Mac. Talk to anyone about him. Being naturally more comfortable with guys, she wasn't close to any women, and she definitely wouldn't tell her family. The only confidant she really responded to was Lincoln. "We…"

Another art gazer happened by.

When she was gone, Fiona added, "…You know."

"It's been so long that I don't think I know. Is it love?" he joked.

"Of course not."

"That's right. Love will never again find Fiona Cruz. You'll make sure of it."

The truth pinched at her. "Thanks for being direct."

"Someone needs to be with you. You were wearing more than your sex drive on your sleeve last night."

"That's how I look at all my victims, so don't misinterpret lust as something more."

"Whatever you say."

The movie mag photographer walked by them, obviously searching for a worthy subject. Linc straightened, flashed his brightest, sexiest smile.

The woman reacted to his gesture—what female could resist?—but passed by without a request for a photo.

The snub knocked the breath out of Fiona.

Though Lincoln kept his eyes on the crowd, scanning it as if he'd turned around for that very purpose, she could see the pain floating below the surface. He slowly put his hands in his jacket pockets. He maintained that lethal smile, even though Fiona knew it wasn't real.

"We'll get you there," she said softly.

The smile dimmed, revealing a streak of vulnerability. "If anyone can dig me out of my hole, you can."

Fiona clasped his hands in hers, hardly caring who saw, hardly caring what they would speculate.

And caring way too much that they probably wouldn't bother.

"Six months of staying out of trouble, Lincoln. You've already helped yourself back to the top."

They stayed connected for a moment, until Fiona, thinking she shouldn't stay that way for too long, finally let go.

THREE DAYS and he hadn't called her. Did that make him a creep?

As Sean hopped out of his Jeep and made his way across Pasadena's gas-lamp-lined Colorado Bridge, he stifled the urge to toss his damned cell phone off the side of it.

Lakota's manager had kept calling him while he was arranging an *Entertainment Tonight* interview for another client; she'd insisted that he get himself over to a photo shoot he'd secured for Lakota. A shoot for *People* magazine's "50 Most Beautiful" issue. What a coup. Unfortunately, they'd requested that she pose with Lincoln Castle, thus upping the interest level for the audience. Ex-lovers reunited on their soap.

He and Fiona had managed to work out the details via their assistants, but this current situation required his personal attention. Probably Fiona's, too.

Dammit, should he have sent flowers? Tapped on her office door to say, "Hey, had a great tumble with you. Wanna go again?"

Did wager etiquette require that sort of thing? Or should he take it at face value—an affair of convenience. Nothing more.

Hell, their bet hadn't said anything about him becoming territorial. And...

You know, he wasn't even going to think along those lines. It'd been a good time. Period.

So why was he so reluctant to see her? To ask when they would resume the contest?

They'd both been too busy to come face-to-face in the office. Or maybe he'd made sure that he was buried under more field work than he could stand.

Damn, he *was* a jerk. A jerk who couldn't stop thinking about her.

Sean approached the screens and lights, the crowd composed of makeup artists, the photographer, the actors and their employees and...

Damn. Fiona *was* here.

She was the only sight he could focus on.

Drawing nearer, he grinned. Summer sunlight gleamed off her dark hair, the subtle wind blowing a strand across her eyes, masking her. She wore a curve-hugging black suit, propping her hands on her hips, but not in a defensive way. As usual, she was cocked at a provocative angle, loose-limbed. Inviting as hell.

As he came to stand in front of her, he thought she sucked in a breath. But then her confident business smile took over, erasing any hint of what had happened between them.

"I knew Lakota would call you, just to one-up Linc."

Cool as the smooth edges of an ice cube, wasn't she?

He sidled closer, forcing her to tilt up her chin so she could meet his gaze. It reminded him of how she'd stood on her toes, flush against his wall, as he'd pressed her upward, onto him.

When he didn't answer, she whipped the hair out of her eyes. *Pow.* Her glare sent a punch of need right through him, a reminder of how she'd met him thrust for thrust, driving him further into madness every time she'd urged him, countered him.

"Well, Fiona," he said, dragging out her name just enough to establish the upper hand, "when my client tells me that her demanding co-star won't be photographed from his left side, it tends to throw a kink in the smooth shoot I had planned."

"Did your dainty angel mention that she's been just as ornery?" Fiona faced him straight on. "Linc wanted me here to sort things out, to make sure the crew knows that he's willing to cooperate. Lakota's not his boss. Today, he's taking orders from the magazine. If she continues to bark out commands—"

"—He'll call in the cavalry."

A muscle in Fiona's jaw twitched. "Listen, Mac. Linc's got more fan mail than anyone else on the soap now, including Lakota. I'm not saying she's jealous—"

"—No?—"

"—but we need to work together on this nightmare. Can we deal with it?"

It. Was she talking about Lakota's and Linc's stubbornness? Or was she referring to the heat that hung over them?

Sean glanced at Lakota, who was surrounded by her minions, clearly at home with her diva role. Three lampposts down the bridge, Lincoln leaned over the rail, ignoring his own exhausted manager.

These two were going to take up too much of his precious time, weren't they?

Sean didn't turn back to her. "He called and you came running. Either you don't know how to manage your time, or you're the ultimate friend."

She paused. "That's right. He called, I came. What can I say?"

They weren't talking about Lincoln anymore.

Suddenly, Sean's shirt collar felt too tight, the air caught in his windpipe, choking him.

"Sean!"

Lakota had discovered his presence, and he had to admit that her timing was exceptional.

She wiggled on over to him in high heels, a tight red dress that complemented her Jessica Rabbit hair. Makeup was caked on her face, adding years of sophistication.

"Will you set things straight?" she asked, keeping Fiona in her sights.

Fiona merely sighed and nodded in Lincoln's direction, beckoning to him. "We're going to take care of this ridiculous pissing contest right now."

Lakota's mouth opened, then shut. When she glanced at Sean, he didn't react.

"You and Lincoln can make the image spinning easier for all of us," he said. "Prime-time producers won't want to hire a troublemaker as a regular for their shows. Remember that."

This kept Lakota in check. She desperately wanted to get out of the soaps someday. The sooner the better.

Lincoln came to stand between Fiona and Sean. "Sorry about this, guys."

Sean almost felt sorry for him. He knew how it was when a woman got her dander up. There was no pleasing them. And if you catered to them too much, they took advantage, sometimes even left. Ask his father about that.

"Now," said Fiona. "We're going to get something straight. You two need to think about how you're coming off to the magazine people and all the other professionals you're ticking off."

Lakota watched the ground. "But he—"

"—Oh, no." Fiona wagged a finger. "Don't go all junior high on me."

"Fi," said Lincoln, "this won't happen again. Will it, Kota?"

Kota? Nicknames?

The starlet's head shot up and, for a second, Sean thought he saw her lips flutter into a half smile. Then the tenderness disappeared, replaced by a tight line.

"If you can manage to let me show my best side to the camera without insisting that you show yours, it won't happen again."

Fiona shook her head and spoke to Sean as if the others weren't even there. In a mock-ecstatic voice, she said, "They're both blessed with a perfect right profile. Isn't that convenient?"

The two stars shot a miffed glance at Fiona.

Why was it she'd left her last PR firm? Had she rubbed a client the wrong way? One thing Sean increasingly hated about this job was the amount of butt kissing that went on. What happened to the days when he used to thrive on the fast pace, the accomplishment of seeing his work rise to great heights?

His stars weren't the only things that had lost their luster.

But not Lakota Lang. Not his last chance. "Luckily," he said, "those profiles will get them bigger contracts, better projects."

Fiona pulled an impressed face, still in full sarcastic mode. "I might add that it'll take more than profiles to climb their way up the Hollywood ladder. Talent, bankability, strong work ethic, thinking about how their co-workers might feel... All of those qualities make for a well-rounded entertainer."

Had the co-worker reference been aimed at him? Dammit, she had no idea how many times he'd reached for the phone, wanting to hear her husky voice again, wanting to ask her for another night. Any night.

Without thinking, he said, "Maybe co-workers need to worry about their own business and not bring feelings into it."

Her chin lifted, then lowered. Lakota and Lincoln were strangely silent.

"Well," said Fiona, those plump lips turned up in her permanent smile, "I guess if co-workers had agreed to keep feelings out of the 'office,' so to speak, then it's not a problem."

Lincoln pointed toward the waiting cameras. "I think—"

But Sean couldn't hold back a retort. "Great. If the co-workers understand each other, there's no harm done."

"None at all."

Lakota locked gazes with Lincoln, and they both left without saying goodbye.

Not that Sean or Fiona noticed.

She'd crossed her arms over her chest, inadvertently pushing up her breasts. Or did she know exactly what she was doing?

Blood pumped to his crotch, beating out images of their night together, touch by touch: her smooth skin, whispering under his fingertips. Her nipple, beading against his tongue. The wet folds of her sex, slipping against him.

He watched their clients go back to work, both of them shifting into acting gear, smiling at each other every time the camera flashed.

Liars. But good ones.

He didn't move, just fixed his gaze on the pseudolovers. "I guess I should've called."

Fiona sighed, and even that sounded like an invitation. "That wasn't the deal. I'm just surprised—"

She cut herself off.

"I didn't ask for more?" he finished for her. He faced her, tucking his hands in his pants pockets.

Maybe he'd caught her unaware, but she had a strange look on her face.

Territorial? Possessive?

She made a show of squeezing shut her eyes, smiling. "It doesn't matter. We're mature adults. We can go on with our jobs and forget about what happened after the charity auction."

"Fiona." His voice had a scratch to it, a scraped need.

Her dark eyes widened.

"Dinner," he said, stepping closer to her. "Tonight."

A sidelong glance. A return to the old Fiona, the charmer. The metamorphosis left him dazed.

"Was having me at your beck and call a part of the bet?" she asked.

She ran a hand along her skirt-covered thigh, rendering him capable of nothing but the simplest of sentences.

"I'll pick you up at eight."

"No." Fiona turned, started to walk away. "I'll pick *you* up."

Who was he to argue? "Any way you want it."

Another grin, this one kittenish. Hungry for some cream. "I'll remember that."

With a lingering glance over her shoulder, Fiona tracked him as she left. "One more thing," she said.

He shook his head, caught up in the sway of her voluptuous hips, the length of her legs in that clinging black suit.

She winked. "How about you finish smoothing things over with our stars? I've got other matters to take care of."

Like what? Soaking herself in mango-scented water, preparing to drive him nuts? Picking out another pair of filmy stockings to slide up those curvy legs?

Before he could ask, she was gone, getting into her Miata and zooming out of Pasadena. Back to the office.

Back to their bet.

Sean swallowed, coating a mouth that had gone dry.

Chapter Five

TONIGHT, TONIGHT, won't be just any...

Oh, can the hysterical musical monologue, Fiona thought for about the fiftieth time since she'd gone home to shower and primp for dinner.

Dinner. A slight understatement. Mac had made arrangements for a picnic to be served on a rented boat. Talk about going all out.

They'd anchored off the night-blanketed coast of Santa Monica, where the city lights sparkled from the hills, winking like a sky full of wishes. Or of ill-conceived love songs.

Tonight, tonight...

Stop it.

She diverted her attention to the black water that surrounded them. The boat cut through the swells, distancing them from the Santa Monica pier, with its colorful Ferris wheel and roller coaster, which soon looked like the smears of a child's finger painting.

Fiona held her glass of Chardonnay by the stem, judging its pale hue from the light of a tiny lantern Mac had positioned on the cabin's top. She breathed in the tang of ocean mist, enjoying the scene. Mac had spread a linen cloth over the opposite bench, topping it with an assortment of strawberries, watermelon and honeydew melon, shrimp cocktail, various panini sandwiches and baby spinach salad.

"A man of many talents," she said, leaning back on a cushioned bench and crossing her bare feet at the ankles. She'd chosen a gold chain to complement red toenail polish and a lavender skirt with a slit running along her leg. She'd discarded her light coat in order to reveal a matching long-sleeved Lycra shirt, one which fit every curve with near-sheer willingness. "I had no idea you cooked or played Popeye."

He finished tying off a sail, then filled a plate for her. "One out of two ain't bad. But there's a lot about me you don't know."

Smackdown. She curled her legs beneath her, took a sip of wine to fill the silence. Then, "You don't go near a kitchen?"

"Not unless I'm forced to." He handed her the food. "I've got a good corner grocery near my place."

She accepted the loaded plate, trying hard to still the slight tremble of her hand. He stood over her, so powerful with his shoulders blocking the moonlight, their width covered by a dark T-shirt. Jeans completed his uniform, casting him in the role of a bad guy—stubbled, troubled and misunderstood.

Today, when he'd showed up at the photo shoot, she'd been shaking inside, too. She'd planted her hands on her hips, hoping to anchor herself, to regain some semblance of control.

Now, as he stepped closer to her, her skin tightened, extra sensitive under the sticky assault of marine air. She set the plate on the bench beside her while he returned to the other side and piled food onto his own.

She caught her breath, half-relieved by the space he'd created.

Calm down, Fi, she thought. If you can't get a handle on yourself, the bet's dust.

"You know why I'm here?" she asked, her tone light and playful.

His shadowed profile—or maybe it was his deep voice— revealed a grin. "To get laid."

She drew back a little. But it was true, wasn't it? She wasn't in this for anything more. "Partly."

"You've got motivations beyond sex?" He stood again, came to sit beside her.

The shivers started up again. God, she hoped they wouldn't claim her voice. "In spite of this seductive setup, there's nothing beyond orgasm for me tonight."

"That's just fine. I'm a very patient man."

His words rolled over her, and her nipples contracted, braless, nudging her top. Inspired, she repositioned herself so that he'd have full view of her breasts, which she knew were completely visible under her formfitting, filmy top.

Hey, if he could try to up the stakes with a sexy dinner, she could play by the same rules.

And it worked. His gaze settled on her chest, caressed it. She took another sip of wine, and the warmth flowed downward, pooling low in her belly.

She breathed deeply, chasing away the funny feeling.

"I'm here," she said, "because I'm going to win."

He reached out, ran a thumb over a crested nipple. Fiona gasped, then moaned, her free hand instinctively seeking his fingers, brushing over them.

He continued rubbing. "Aren't you being premature?"

The boat bobbed with extra vigor, and she suddenly felt dizzy.

In spite of the dangerous spasms of yearning that speared through her, Fiona gathered all her strength, taking her hand from his, trying to wear a serenely composed facade while moving with his every stroke.

"I've got all the confidence in the world," she said, schooling the breathiness out of her tone. "It's not about the prize, you know."

"The Caribbean isn't good enough for you?"

"Oh, no." She bit her lip, then recovered as he cupped underneath her breast, kneading it. "My victory will be more symbolic."

He didn't say anything, just watched her, probably waiting for her to break open, allowing him inside where he didn't belong.

Not in her brain, anyway.

"It's a triumph for all women," she said, smiling at him with sleepy emphasis.

A grin slanted over his mouth, his hand trailing down her ribs, thumb etching the line of her inner thigh. Then he stood, going to the opposite side of the boat, sitting on the edge of it while digging into his food with relish.

Excuse me? Here she was, her heart pounding through her body like it was a bass drum, and he'd left her?

So that's how it'd be, huh? She'd show him what it was like to be left in the lurch.

Lurch. The boat nodded, and Fiona closed her eyes.

Recovering, she thought that now it was really about winning, toying with him as he was with her. She only wished she'd had this same opportunity with Ted, before he'd run off with Crissy Banks.

Her best friend.

Oh, if she could've wrapped Ted around her little finger and peeled him off with deliberate payback, she would've. Would've teased him to the point of suffering. Would've let him know what he would miss for the rest of his life.

Now, if she could stay strong with Mac...

She stopped, exhaling, head beginning to ache. This was wrong, using him as a substitute for her resentment.

It was only about sex. It had been for years.

Fiona calmed herself, dipping a piece of shrimp into the cocktail sauce. Even if she'd lost her appetite, she couldn't help licking off the spicy concoction when Mac glanced over. Couldn't help laving the curve of the meat, hinting at what she'd be doing to him later.

His response was somewhere between a chuckle and a grunt. "You're a competitor, all right."

"Hey. Tit for tat. You'll be difficult, I'll be more difficult. I was raised to win."

"Whoa. Do we want to go there?"

She made a show of devouring the shrimp, then prepared another one. "Family talk is fine. Likes, dislikes—okay by me. Past relationships—definitely off-limits."

"Agreed." He drained his own wine, returned his attention to eating. "You a California girl?"

What an appetite the man had. It was fitting, though, judging by his stamina in other areas.

She pretended not to notice. "I moved here for college."

"And you've got siblings. That explains your competitive nature."

"Well read, Mac." She sucked on a strawberry until he glanced away, shaking his head. Ha ha... Oooo, the waves were getting choppy. "Three brothers. The oldest ones are twins. Hellraisers, those guys, both sporty types. My other older brother is a high school basketball coach."

"You're just one of the boys, aren't you?"

Sometimes she felt like it. In fact, she'd always done her best to be in the boys' clubs at work. That's how a lady succeeded in this business. "I used to play Little League because I wanted to do everything my brothers did. I was a pitcher."

Mac set down his empty plate, leaned a muscled arm on his thigh. "You're kidding."

She delicately set aside her own plate, unable to deal with food any more. "Don't sound so patronizing. I pitched my team to a championship."

Mac held up his hands. "Hey, didn't mean to offend you. My mom would've had a coronary if my sisters played ball."

"My mother died when I was young, so she wasn't around to chastise me."

A swell of emotion washed over her, pressing down on her chest. She cleansed herself of it, knowing this wasn't the time or the place.

Mac paused. "I'm sorry to hear that. I really didn't have a mom, either."

Sean didn't want to talk about this. Didn't want to tell her how the woman known as "mother" had deserted the family and left a mess known as "dad" behind.

Fiona considered him, dark eyes boring into his soul. In that incredibly hot outfit, she resembled a contented cat lounging on a couch, licking its paws with lazy strokes, planning its next move.

Damn, she had him dancing on his last nerve. That's why he'd retreated to this side of the boat. Because he didn't know what he'd do next.

Could she win, not by staying detached, but by effortlessly possessing *him?*

Wouldn't happen.

"But," he said, stretching up to a stance, tucking his hands under his arms to keep everything inside, "I do have two pain-in-the-butt sisters. Both are married, of course and, in their tormented state of matrimony, both want to see me tie the knot, too."

"Misery does love company."

He hadn't been joking about the torment. Katie and Colleen constantly complained about their husbands, reaffirming Sean's belief that love wasn't worth it.

His first clue had come in the form of his mom.

Echoing his body language, Fiona unsteadily got to her bare feet, her ankle bracelet shining in the lantern light. Her dress absorbed the glow, revealing the dark centers of her breasts, the hint of a caressable stomach, her belly button.

Sean's muscles clenched, imprisoning him.

He fought to be released. "Wait," he said. "Don't move."

She didn't, except for the fingers that were plucking the sides of her skirt. Nerves? He wished. Her anxiety meant something more than pure lust was happening, and that would lead to victory for him.

He brushed aside the curiosity, knowing anything beyond sex wasn't in the plan.

"What?" A wobbly laugh rode the end of her question.

He stared a moment longer, consuming her. "I'm putting you in my mental scrapbook."

"Oh." She exhaled, looked away, put a hand on her tummy. "Are you done now?"

"You don't like to be looked at?" He never would have expected this from a beautiful woman like Fiona.

Her slight smile made him forget every other image in the bulging memory tome of his brain. Women: petite, long-limbed, brunette, blond, redheaded... They were all there, asking him what they'd done wrong.

"Are you through?" she asked, her grin wobbling.

He pushed aside the other women, their questions. "You're eager."

Fiona reached for the cabin, slumping against it.

"Looking a little pale there. You okay?" he asked.

"I think I'm a bit seasick," she said, rubbing a hand over her temple.

"Do you need help?"

She shook her head. "Sorry about the bad timing, but I'm not feeling well right now. Maybe it was the motion of the ocean."

As she closed her eyes and held her stomach, Sean realized she wasn't putting on a show. Looks like he'd lost tonight's battle.

But definitely not the war.

FORGET THE WAR.

Sean couldn't get back to work because he was too concerned about Fiona. Last night, she'd gotten sick. Yeah. Throwing-up-over-the-side-of-the-boat sick.

He'd held back her hair and smoothed a hand over her spine as she'd cleared her stomach, apologizing the whole time.

"I hate having you see me like this," she'd said, voice wavering.

Sure, she'd been at her worst but in a weird way, Sean hadn't minded so much. She'd clung to him, not in passion, but in a different kind of need. He'd been around to help and it felt kind of decent.

Even as he'd motored the boat to shore and driven her back home, catching a taxi to return to his place, Sean hadn't minded the night's outcome.

He shook himself to the present and caught himself smiling like a dope. What the hell?

Getting out of his chair, he paced to the window which showcased the Boulevard. Upscale clothing stores and talent agency offices stretched down the pavement. Tourists and locals bustled down the sidewalks.

He barely saw them. All that mattered was Fiona. Erudite,

saucy, completely compatible with his needs in bed. When he could get her there.

He'd never met a woman like her before, and probably never would again. Maybe he should get out of their affair now, before he really lost it.

If he hadn't already.

Oh. Hell, no. He wasn't capable of feeling. Didn't want to be. Would never be.

His father had taught him well. Not that Jimmy McIntyre had made it a point to show his son how much love hurt. In fact, the man had tried to hide it for a while.

After Mom had left because of all those arguments about money and other things Sean didn't grasp, his dad had continued with life for a while—marching into his Chicago law firm on a daily basis with his morning cup of coffee in hand, making sure Sean and his sisters were well-provided for. But one day, when Sean had ditched high school early, he'd found out that Jimmy Mac had been living a lie.

He'd discovered his father at twelve noon, sitting in a kitchen chair near a window that overlooked the driveway, dressed in his business suit, obviously watching for Mom. He'd avoided all questions and, when Sean had asked one of his father's business associates what was going on, the man had told him that Jimmy had been fired from the firm a few weeks ago.

From that point on, Sean and his sisters had done their best to run the household, living off their father's unemployment while it lasted. Then they'd moved on to his sister's paychecks for the next few years until they married their way out of the household.

Sean had eventually gone to a local college where he could keep an eye on his father, who continued to wait for Mom, no matter how many years passed. His time in front of the window decreased, but the look in his eyes never changed. In his mind, he was obviously still watching for her.

Now, years later, Sean continued to send money home while Katie and Colleen took turns checking on Dad. Sean visited once in a while, but he couldn't stand to see his father still waiting in front of that window.

He backed away from his own view, shaken. There was work to do. Lots of it.

"Sean?" asked a voice through his speakerphone. Carly, his trusty assistant.

He pressed the answer button. "Yeah?"

"Fiona Cruz wants to know if you're available."

His stomach jumped. She'd come to work? "Tell her to get in line."

"Um…" Pause. "Okay."

He shouldn't have growled at Carly. The poor girl had nothing to do with his thwarted sex drive.

He left his office and passed Carly at her desk on his way down the hall to Fiona's, nodding to the assistant. Note: Get the woman some flowers to tell her how much he appreciated her hard work, then their slate would be clean again.

As he walked the hall, he caught the aroma of lunch: hot dogs, burritos, hamburgers. Heart attack food. Come to think of it, he needed a meal himself. Might as well encourage the inevitable.

When he drew up to Fiona's office, he stopped short.

There she was, one long, black-stockinged leg thrown over the other, body encased in a deep purple suit with gypsy ruffles. The only reminder of last night's tummy troubles was a trace of white tinting her skin. Was she trying to ignore the weakness she'd shown?

A healthy lunch—salad, chilled water and fish tacos—

waited on the opposite side of her desk. And she was read-ing something, hardly bothering to hide the book cover.

The Sensuous Woman, by "J."

"You've clearly recovered," he said.

"Fit as a fiddle." She stretched a little, her supple body re-minding him of what he'd missed out on.

That's okay. He could contain himself. "I thought you'd stay home today."

She pulled an unconcerned face. "Not to worry. I'm a trouper." She smiled a little. "Thanks for...well, helping me out."

"All in a night's work."

She hesitated, as if wanting to say something else. But in-stead, she set down *The Sensuous Woman,* gave it a gentle pat.

Sean shook his head, then took a chair.

"This is nice," Fiona said, tearing off a slice of flour tor-tilla and putting it in her mouth. She squinched her face. "Lunching with you. Braving the corporate atmosphere."

He watched her chew with that disgusted expression on her face. "What happened to 'let's keep sex out of the office'?"

"I am."

He grabbed a taco, decided he might as well eat. "Come on. You're making damned sure I know you're reading that book."

"Oh. *That.*"

"You're not going to break me down, no matter what you have up your..." He grinned. "Sleeve."

"I've got more than you bargained for." She ran her fin-gers over the book's nondescript cover. "When I was about twelve, I found a drawer in our living room that had all these naughty novels in it. All I remember now was *Mandingo* and this one."

"*Mandingo?*" He polished off the first taco.

"Long story. Anyway, I used to sneak into the living room

and pretend to be listening to the stereo while I was really reading." She tilted her head, lifting one eyebrow. "And learning."

"Twelve years old?"

"Don't worry. I didn't start putting my knowledge into practice until college. But we're not going there, remember?"

"Especially here."

"Exactly."

Forget past relationships. Were they even supposed to be talking about dirty books? Sean definitely didn't want to ask. This was too entertaining. Besides, he could handle the erotic prodding.

Really.

"Where was I?" She tapped a red nail against her lips, drawing his attention to them.

Lips. The ones he hadn't felt since…

"The book," he choked out.

"Right. When you came in the office, I was just reading about a little something called The Butterfly Flick."

Oh, damn.

"Stop," he said.

"I'm discussing literature with you over lunch."

"Fiona…"

She sent a wicked grin at him. "Just reminding you that I'm in charge, Charles."

Sean lifted a finger to make another point. Something about her not being the one who was driving this revved-up bus to hard-on-ville, but his cell phone rang before he had the chance to say it.

He glanced at her, and she gave him an unconcerned shrug. Go for it.

After unholstering the phone, he answered. "McIntyre, here."

"It's Lakota."

Great. He shot a look to Fiona, and she knew who it was right away. She leaned forward, narrowing her eyes.

"What can I do for you?" he asked, raising a wry brow at his co-worker.

She smiled in appreciation, nodding at his double talk.

"Well…" Lakota hesitated, and he knew this wasn't going to be good. "I was wondering if we could meet today. You know. Right now, actually. To plan strategy."

Good God. Did Lakota think she was his only client? "Know what? I can put your manager through to Carly, and she can make an appointment. I'm swamped today with the work I should've been doing yesterday. You know, when you called me to the photo shoot."

"Oh, that." Another pause. "Um…"

Fiona's phone rang, and she picked up. "Hello?"

Lakota spoke. "I'd really like to talk to you. Show my appreciation for all the work you've done. You deserve a bonus for putting up with me."

Fiona leaned back in her chair, gesturing toward her phone while she listened to her caller. Clearly it was either Lincoln or his manager.

"What's going on?" Sean asked Lakota.

"All right. Lincoln Castle and I got into a bit of a tiff at a restaurant near the studio."

"And…?"

"And a columnist for Soap Serial Online was there. Karen Carlisle."

Sean cursed. "When is this crap going to stop, Lakota?"

"It was a long day and…" She started to cry.

Cry?

Why couldn't she bother her manager with this garbage?

"Calm down," he said, gentling his tone.

"I hate Lincoln Castle. Do you know what it's like having to work with him?"

As she bitched further, Sean glanced at Fiona, but she'd gotten out of her chair, all business, and was pacing the carpet. He grabbed a pen from her desk, a piece of paper. Then he wrote, "We'll talk about literature later. Lots to work out."

With a burst of resigned frustration, he got out of the chair, leaving the rest of his lunch. Fiona turned around, and he pointed to the note.

She lifted her hand at him in a lazy goodbye, then returned to her call.

Sean stood there for a moment, emptiness lining the pit of his stomach.

Lakota's voice intensified. "So what should I do?"

He turned to go, chancing one last glance at Fiona, who still had her back to him. Dismissed.

As he made his way through the halls, back to an office filled with work he'd have to ignore until he returned tonight, he clutched the phone, almost to the point of throttling it.

"Let me contact Karen Carlisle while I drive to meet you. We're going to talk this out. Once and for all."

"Thanks, Sean. You're the best, and I won't forget this."

He hoped she wouldn't. If she became the star he thought she could be, her devotion would amount to his comeback.

She continued. "Meet me at Moulin Rouge Lingerie on Abbot Kinney Boulevard in Venice. I'm on my way."

And he was, too, even though he'd left Fiona and last night's strange bond behind.

Chapter Six

LAKOTA STOOD in front of the cute cottage that housed Moulin Rouge Lingerie, knowing she'd messed up yet again.

What was it about Lincoln that drove her nuts? The fact that he'd so quickly gotten back into the good graces of the soap fans while she'd had to work her butt off to merely garner their attention? The way everyone on the set seemed to love him and cater to him, even though he hadn't earned it yet?

Or maybe she was so upset with him because she still had a tender spot in her heart for the guy.

There. She'd admitted it. She'd never gotten over Lincoln. Even after that horrific breakup, where she'd accused him of stepping out on her and he'd denied it, she still adored him.

Why? It wasn't logical, wasn't smart.

Sean McIntyre pulled into a curbed parking space in his timeworn gray Jeep. Thank goodness he was here. She could always count on her publicist, even more than her co-workers and friends, manager, agent, personal assistant, makeup artist...

Okay. So maybe he looked a little put out.

"Hey," she said, smiling brightly, peeking out at him from underneath the baseball cap she used as camouflage.

He didn't answer, just ambled toward her, features etched in bristled weariness.

A little nervous now that he was actually here—boy, had she been putting him through the wringer—Lakota started to climb the steps that led into the shop.

"Thanks for meeting me."

"I'm not going in there." Sean rested one hand on his holstered cell phone, immovable.

Lakota stuck out her bottom lip in a pout. It didn't work with Sean, of course. "They've got the cutest selection. Indulge me? Please?"

With a disbelieving chuff, he walked away from her. Lakota hopped off the stairs, intent on catching up to his long stride.

"I talked to Karen Carlisle on the way over," he said. "She's not going to report your spat with Lincoln."

"Oh. That's good news. Isn't it? I mean, he and I are supposed to adore each other and—"

"—You're giving her a tour of your house next week. You'll have tea on the balcony and reveal all the sweet dreams that dance around in your head. You'll tell her how much you respect and *adore* your co-star."

Lakota stopped in her steps, but Sean kept going.

"Wait!"

"I'm not licking your boots, Lakota."

She used her sweetheart voice. "But I pay you to do that."

This time he did halt. Even though he wore a starkly chic Armani suit, he still seemed scruffy around the edges. A wild card.

He held up a finger, leaned toward her. Ten feet away, and she shrank back anyway.

"There comes a point in a man's life where he doesn't give a shit anymore." The finger came down, and he should've seemed less intimidating. But he wasn't. Not with that bar-brawl gaze he was leveling at her.

"I've reached my limit," he said, resuming his unhurried gait. "At least for today."

Had he just told her off? Ever since months ago, when Lakota had started inching up the fan marketing polls and getting guest spots on prime time, no one had talked to her like this. Could PR people do that? She'd never had her own rep before, and *Flamingo Beach*'s publicist was too busy to sass her.

Maybe Sean McIntyre really didn't care about kissing his clients' butts. She'd heard about his fire-in-the-belly ambition from another actress and, in an effort to spin herself into a starring nighttime role soon, she'd seized the opportunity to work with him.

Thank goodness. With his guidance, her numbers had exploded, allowing her to recently renegotiate for an unbelievably lucrative contract. Prime time was around the corner. Just as it'd once been for Linc.

Her manager and agent told her that a hungry, ambitious man like McIntyre would come cheaper than the rest, that he'd work his tush off for her in order to get back on top. And he did work like a madman. But she'd never expected to feel so comfortable with him—like she was the little sister and he was the big brother who gave all her prom dates the third degree.

He was a keeper, all right.

Sean was about a block away now, and he hadn't back-tracked. Left her behind, had he?

Hmm. Maybe she *was* only twenty-two, pretty much a kid in many ways. But couldn't he take her seriously?

Lakota speed-walked after him, taking care to appear that she wasn't exerting herself in the least. As she closed the distance, two teenage girls did a double take at her. She chanced a quick smile at them then ducked under the bill of her hat.

Maybe Sean had superhero senses, because he glanced over his shoulder, hardly surprised she'd run after him.

"You left me standing there," she said.

"I suppose I did."

Out of the corner of her eye, Lakota caught sight of the teenagers, who were huddled together, whispering.

Sean nodded approvingly. "Recognition. Good. But I'm surprised they know it's you."

"Why?" Usually, she loved to chat with her fans. But she wanted to be herself right now—not Rita Wilde, her soap character. Lakota started speed walking in the other direction.

Sean easily kept up. "It's that sophisticated stage makeup you wear on the show. Without it, you look about seven years younger. And, anyway, who'd expect *Flamingo Beach* vixen Rita Wilde to be walking around in a flannel shirt and jeans?"

Lakota felt herself blush. Most actresses wore full makeup and a snazzy wardrobe in public. Not her. "Once I take off the slinky dresses and get back into my street clothes, I leave the soap behind. Just like I thought I'd left Lincoln."

"Ah."

He didn't say anything more, and she didn't know if she wanted to, either. Would he laugh himself silly if he knew she still carried a torch for Linc?

Well, she wouldn't tell him, that was for sure. Nobody needed to know about that particular embarrassment. Their time together had been brief—an emotion-packed two months—but it'd marked her forever.

They passed Abbot Kinney's funky boutiques, art galleries, neon green fliers taped to the lampposts announcing a clean needle program for drug users. L.A. rocked.

A particularly attractive vintage shop caught Lakota's eye, and she tugged on Sean's sleeve to guide him inside.

"I thought you wanted to talk game plans, not piddle around," he said, crusty as ever.

"Admit it. You're crazy about me, just like siblings in the back seat of a car during the family trip. Sure, you want to kill me right now, but if I really did end up getting hurt, you'd be all torn apart."

Lakota finished with one of her perky grins. A real one.

He relented, and once inside the vintage shop, Sean, seemingly bored, muttered something beneath his breath and got busy lounging next to a wicker basket overflowing with faded pictures. She poked through the lot of them, snapshots of more interesting lives than hers. Family vacations, children with slicked-back hair and lacy collars smiling into the camera.

She grabbed one. A girl from the sixties, wearing a pageboy, a graduation gown and a dazzling smile. She stood between her parents, holding a diploma.

Flashing it to Sean, she said, "Might as well get a life, right?" Her voice cracked.

Concern cocked his brow. "You okay?"

"Oh, sure." Lakota impulsively grabbed a pair of cranberry suede boots. Too big, but maybe she could stuff the toes with newspaper. Then she fingered some neckties dangling from a hanger, choosing a vivid peacock-blue one. She could be so Annie Hall.

She unloaded the items on a glass-topped counter, and the owner smiled at her from under his salt-and-pepper mustache. When she glanced back down, the photo consumed her focus.

A family. A mom and dad who cared, who were proud of their diploma girl.

Lakota's midwestern mom had always said she was an idiot. Pretty, but how far was that going to get you? Her father... Let's just say he'd never been in the picture. Any picture.

Agitated, she proceeded to flit around the shop. Lakota could feel Sean watching her while she inspected brooches, bridesmaid dresses, pillbox hats and a shiny Boba Fett lunchbox. In a dusty corner, she even found a music box that played the theme from *Love Story.*

Music boxes.

She swallowed, cradled it to her chest with the other purchases.

When she returned to the counter, she caught Sean staring at a 40s movie star nightgown, his gaze naked with repressed fire.

"Buy it for her," she said, wiggling her eyebrows.

Sean's jaw unclenched in apparent surprise.

Lakota turned to the owner, who was standing by patiently, adding up her purchases. "Men. They think girls have no clue."

The clerk didn't say anything. Maybe he knew better than to get into these sorts of conversations.

"And what is it you've figured out?" Sean asked, slightly less annoyed than fifteen minutes ago, thank goodness.

Lakota inspected the chokers hanging on a rack in front of her. "You think we don't know what's going on inside your heads, but it's painfully obvious."

"Hate to tell you, but a lot of our thoughts center around one thing."

"I know." The backs of her eyelids pricked, signaling the start of tears she'd already cried. "Unfortunately, sometimes one woman isn't enough for a guy."

Sean came up behind her, and she immediately felt safer, more comfortable. Protected.

"This is about Lincoln, isn't it?"

"I can't stand him. You know, I was thinking, can you spin some bad publicity his way? He's making me look like a viper."

Shut up, Lakota, she thought. *You don't really mean it.*

Sean didn't say anything, probably because he was thinking she was doing a good job of ruining her image on her own.

Instead, Lakota heaved out a breath, moisture stinging one corner of an eye as she turned to him. "I'm so in love with him, and there's no chance he's ever going to feel the same. To top it off, I'm being such a jerk about it."

At first, Sean made a you-got-that-right expression, but it turned into a look of pity instead.

See? Her publicist was more than worth what she paid him.

She sniffed, shrugging. "I suppose I want to put the screws to him before he puts them to me this time."

"What did he do wrong?"

A chopped laugh, full of regret. "I thought he was cheating, even though I didn't have any evidence. I don't know. I was a nobody, and he was... God. Lincoln Castle, the soap star. It's hard to live with a guy who's the fantasy of so many women. He could have his pick."

"But he wanted you."

"Hard to believe." That stubborn tear finally welled, tumbled down her cheek. She swiped at it, bucking up to show that Lincoln didn't affect her. "Have you ever felt this way? Crummy and ecstatic to be around a certain person, all at the same time?"

An antique clock ticked on the wall behind Sean. Then, "Sometimes we make it harder than it needs to be, I suppose."

The shopkeeper had sneaked away to the other side of the store, leaving them alone. Embarrassment swallowed her up. Why couldn't she have kept this angst to herself instead of letting it all out? She'd also let fly today in the restaurant, and it hadn't been pretty.

Sean had shoved his hands in his pockets, glancing away from her. Hard as a profile on Mount Rushmore, wasn't he?

"Once," he said, voice low, barely there, "I was with a woman. I couldn't think of anything but her, during work, when I got home...always. Neither of us was looking for anything serious, so we messed around, kidded each other. Made a bet that she wouldn't get emotionally involved during the course of our affair."

"Did she?"

"No." Sean turned his back on her, ran a hand over a pile of outdated records. Lakota noticed that his fingers were curled, as if wanting to tear at something.

"How could you do that?" she asked. "Make a bet about love?"

"Not love."

She couldn't see his face, but his voice told her more than he'd probably wanted to reveal.

Sean tensed up, left the shop.

Lakota watched him go, frowning. There was a glitch in his story, something out of place, as if...

Her own problems shoved to the back of her mind, she grabbed the nightie he'd been ogling. It flowed like olive oil over her fingers, the amber color rich and heavy.

"Excuse me?" she said to the shopkeeper. "Will you ring this up, too, please?"

Five minutes later, lingerie hidden in her bag and a devious spring in her step, she emerged from the store. She headed toward her favorite shop, a boutique that sold flower essences. Keeping his distance, Sean loitered while the assistant used a pendulum to lead them to the proper brandy/water potions, much like one would use a divining rod to locate water. Lakota had requested something to help with her career, and she walked out with three bottles that would do just that if taken internally two times a day.

"You believe in this?" he asked.

"Absolutely. Mind over matter. Oh!" She took his hand, walked him across the mellow street to another quaint cottage. This one had Perfumery written on a sign in the yard. "I'm out of my fragrance."

"Order it online."

"It's personalized. They mix it for me."

"You have your own perfume?" His mind really wasn't on the question or the shopping. He'd felt sorry for Lakota, with her scrubbed face and tomboy baseball cap. Felt sorry enough to talk where he shouldn't have been talking.

That damned nightgown had softened him up. He'd pictured Fiona underneath the silk. Curves lit by warm, licking flame, his fingers slipping the material up, over her body.

He fisted his hands.

"Just come in," said Lakota. "They've got a lounge, and we'll have a drink. Then we can get down to business. And..." She shook her massive purchase bag. "I've got something for you."

"Don't tell me."

She opened the top, giving him a peek of smooth silk. "We can talk advice, if you want. I owe you."

Advice? Who was this kid to be offering it?

She gave a little hop of excitement, and he couldn't deny her the satisfaction of giving him a present. Hell, maybe he would end up giving the gown to Fiona, but without the gift wrap of emotion.

Why not?

Sean held out his arm, and Lakota took it. Together, they walked up the cottage stairs.

BACK AT Stellar Public Relations, Fiona was still on the phone. This time, instead of Linc's manager, she was talking with the man himself.

She'd already chastised him for the restaurant argument with Lakota, and Mac's assistant had told her that he'd taken care of Karen Carlisle on his end. For her part, Fiona had spent about a half hour guaranteeing the online reporter exclusive interviews with Lincoln for the next couple of months.

Bribery, the foundation of the entertainment business. But they called it "leverage."

Fiona's stomach coiled and she reached for a water bottle on her desk, finding only the crushed remains of three other containers. Last night hadn't only left her dehydrated, it'd caused her to go back to square one with Mac. Frustration, anyone?

"Lincoln," she said into the phone, "I'm about to send you to military school, you know. You need some discipline."

"I can't help myself." He sounded agitated, and she hoped he didn't have any liquor handy. "When I get around Lakota, my circuits go haywire."

"Self-accountability. Remember that phrase?"

"Yeah, I do. From months of rehab."

"Good boy." She couldn't help the fondness from overwhelming her tone. "If I didn't know any better, I'd say you were still in love with Lakota, and that's why you can't contain yourself."

Pure, utter silence.

"Oh, no."

"Fi, don't sound so disappointed. It's being near her again that's doing me in."

She remembered when Lincoln had first started seeing Lakota a year ago. How they'd gone to restaurants and nuzzled in the corner booths, so consumed with each other that they'd shut the places down without knowing how much time had passed. She remembered when the relationship had exploded—not burned out. He'd spent seven nights on Fiona's couch, not wanting to go home to an empty bed.

Then the real trouble had started. He'd just begun working on his prime-time show—acting by day, carousing in the bars by night, picking up the random women who reminded him of Lakota. Crashing his motorcycle into a guardrail on the 405 Freeway one foggy evening, his blood alcohol level at twice the legal limit.

The show had fired him then, killing off his character after only three months.

"I've grown up," he said, clearly knowing what she was thinking.

"I hope so, Linc. God, I really hope so."

"Are you mad at me?"

The question took her aback. "For what?"

"Nothing."

The one word said it all. "What, you think I'm jealous because you're in the throes of love and I'm... not?"

Why had she hesitated? What she had going with Mac had nothing to do with tender declarations of forever, even after the way he'd held her head last night.

Great, she thought. Barfing, the language of modern romance.

Linc sighed. "You could be happy. If you didn't believe you'd had your moment with Ted and it'll never happen again, you could—"

"—What I had with Ted can hardly be described in Shakespearean sonnets. It'd take something more like a tragedy to fill in those blanks."

"Ted was a loser. I've told you that a million times."

So why didn't she believe it? "I thought I was the person who lost in that scenario," she said softly.

Images assaulted her: Ted holding her hand while they watched the Dodgers playing the Padres, the two of them feeding each other hot pretzels and snuggling throughout the game. Ted taking her for a ride to rural Ramona, just outside of San Diego, where he'd asked her if she could imagine living with him on a small ranch, where he'd slipped the ring onto her finger. Ted holding her after they'd made love behind a cove of rocks on a blanket at the beach, counting the stars with her, making her wish on each one. Ted calling her in a hotel room one night to say that he and Crissy had gone to Vegas during one of Fiona's many business trips.

That they'd gotten married.

She'd never seen it coming, him and Crissy. She'd been putting in too many hours at her new publicist's job. But she should have. Even Linc had commented about how Crissy looked at Ted. How Ted always affectionately kidded Crissy about how she'd managed to retain her small-town innocence, even in L.A.

God, she'd never be that stupid again. Would never open herself up to that sort of anguish.

"Fiona?" Linc, probably thinking she'd jumped out the high-rise window.

"I'm here." She blindly shuffled through some papers on her desk.

"You'll find the one," he said.

Fiona forced a light laugh. "Spoken like a man in love."

"Right. How am I going to handle this with Lakota?"

"Be careful," she said. She put all those meaningless papers to the side of her desk. "Just…"

"Watch out. I know." He chuckled. "Will do."

They blabbed a few more minutes, then said their good-byes. As the sun set over Wilshire Boulevard, Fiona leaned back in her chair, the light from the window listing over her blank walls. She hadn't decorated yet. Hadn't had the time. But she would soon.

That's what she always said.

An hour could've passed. Maybe two. Whatever the case, most everyone had gone home. It was dark when Mac's assistant tapped on Fiona's door, a plain box in hand.

"Fiona? Sean asked me to run this down the hall to you."

Her pulse skittered. "He's in his office?"

"Working like a demon, playing catch-up." Carly set the box on Fiona's desk. "I think this has something to do with the whole *Flamingo Beach* thing."

Business. Of course. "Thank you," she said as Carly left, waving good-night.

The minute the assistant disappeared, Fiona attacked the delivery, peeking under the lid before throwing it away altogether.

She sucked in a breath at the sight of the gown. Then she darted over to her office door, closing it. Back to the lovely piece of work.

It reminded her of a gin joint, an evening of Cotton Club seduction. If she put it on, would the material curl around her skin like smoke dancing from the tip of a lit cigarette?

Oh, Mac.

Mac. Damn him. This wasn't playing fair.

She picked up her phone, rang his extension.

"Sean McIntyre."

Again, with the accelerated pulse, the tingles and anticipation. "What's this all about?"

She could hear him switch off the speakerphone, and his tone lowered to a graveled drag. "You like it?"

She loved it. Loved all pretty things, even if she had pitched a no-hitter when she was ten years old. "It's very sweet of you, but what's it for?"

"Tonight."

Tonight, tonight...

Nuh-uh.

She mewed into the phone. "Let me check my social calendar. Oh, now, I don't see you penciled in."

"Then get to penciling."

"This has to be against the rules."

She could picture him leaning back in his seat, muscles rippling up his long body.

"What rules?" he asked.

What rules, indeed? "All right. Your place again. Say, eleven?"

Always his place. Always in control of when she left.

"As long as I can sleep in on my Saturday morning," he said. "But I am coming into the office tomorrow."

"Glutton. And don't worry. I won't inconvenience you by overstaying my welcome."

Neither of them said anything, and Fiona took that as approval on his end. The silence stung.

She lowered her tone to a whisper, ignoring the slight. "Be ready for my mouth all over your body."

He gave a strangled moan. Good, back in the driver's seat.

When she hung up, she dropped the phone.

What was this?

She stared at the handle, at her trembling hand.

Nerves. Excitement. That's all.

She put the piece back in its cradle, taking a deep breath.

Mental foreplay. Nothing more.

That's what she kept telling herself as she took the back way out of the office.

Chapter Seven

MARINA DEL REY was an upscale area where the houses piled on top of themselves as they perched on the banks of the boat-lined bay. Lincoln cut his Harley's engine as he drove onto a quiet street. At 10:30 p.m., it was rude to shatter the peace with his growling machine, and the last thing he wanted to do was draw attention to himself.

Except in the eyes of one person.

Lakota lived by the canal in a Venetian-inspired two-story home. He secured his bike below her dark window, took out the flashlight.

His thumb rested on the activation switch. No turning back if he flicked it forward.

What was he doing here? His impulsiveness had overstepped its bounds this time, but he couldn't sleep, knowing he'd fallen for her again. Knowing he'd fought with her today.

Did he want to revisit all the pain? The keening hollowness of knowing he'd failed her during their first go-around? Did he want the temper, the stubborn ambition that went with Lakota?

He beat the flashlight against his leg. Why was he here anyway?

When he glanced toward her balcony, a curtain rustled

through the open French doors. It was like she stood right next to him—orange-blossom perfume mixed with the ocean breeze.

Not long ago, she'd rested her head against his chest after making love. Content in the afterglow, he'd close his eyes, taking on the weight of her slight body, wrapping his arms around her like knotted ropes, burying his nose in her hair, drawing her into him. Making them one person.

God, he wanted her back. Linc aimed the light at her window, turned it on, played the beam over the misty curtains, realizing it probably wouldn't be enough to attract her attention.

Well, it'd been a good idea when he'd hopped on his Harley.

"Lakota," he said in a harsh stage whisper.

No answer. Well, maybe he'd have to get practical rather than romantic. He reached into his bomber jacket pocket, took out his cell phone, speed-dialed her. He'd never removed her number.

One ring. Two rings. Breathe, man, breathe.

She answered on the third. "Yes?" Sleep weighed down her voice.

He didn't know if he was relieved or concerned that she was in bed so early on a Friday night. Where was the Lakota who worked her connections at The Sky Bar? The Viper Room?

Linc didn't say anything, just used a point of light to write her name on the curtains.

Seconds later, she peeked around the material. "Lincoln? Is that you?"

She knew who it was. He shut off the flashlight, waited, but she didn't move. "Come out, Kota."

The sound of a nearby car traveling the streets stretched the awkward moment.

Was she still angry at him?

Linc stepped closer to the balcony, speaking softly into the phone. "I hear Karen Carlisle's going to visit you next week, compliments of your publicist."

"I hear you've got the same punishment."

Odd, how he'd been inside her only months ago, only to be talking to her from a distance right now. Sure, fame isolated him. So did failure, to an even greater degree. But not being able to get close to the woman he still loved...jeez, that's right, *loved*...put him in the middle of a wasteland, made Linc feel like a remnant, a bleached bone stranded in a place no one would ever find him.

"Please come out," he said.

This time, all the contained anguish throttled his voice. And she must've heard it, too, because she did as he asked, slipping around the curtain, revealing a petite, fawn-legged body barely hidden by white babydoll pajamas. She wore her red hair in a ponytail and, even from this distance, he could catch the pale of the moon in her blue eyes.

"Hi," he whispered.

She moved closer, leaning an elbow on the balcony railing in order to fix the phone to her ear. She stood right above him, and he closed his eyes, savoring her.

"I'm sorry about lunch," she said.

He could hear her real voice and the phone voice at the same time. Still, if he hung up, he was afraid he'd lose her, afraid he'd jinx this run of civil interaction.

"I apologize, too," he said, opening his gaze again, gulping at the way the moonlight filtered through her pajamas. The material draped over those small, beautiful breasts— breasts that had filled the cup of his hands, sustaining him.

His palms tingled from the want of her.

"You know," she said, oblivious, "at that restaurant, I was talking extra loudly about your beer belly because I half hoped you'd hear and I'd get a rise out of you." Lakota shook her head. "Isn't that stupid?"

"Stupid? That's something your mother would say. Never me. And you did provoke me into facing off with you, so your grand plan worked."

"Too well. I didn't mean any of it."

"Not the cracks about the extra pounds? Or the bags under my eyes?"

Lakota covered her face with her free hand. "You don't have either. It's just that…"

Say something personal, he thought. *I don't want to be the first one to put myself out there. Not this time.*

The warm night air hung between them. No words. No chances.

So, she wasn't going to take a risk, either. That's the way it was, then. Probably for the best anyway.

Her body angled away from him. "I can't believe we haven't talked since that night."

An opening. *That night.* The breakup. He'd desperately tried to reach her after she'd left their house, but to no avail. That'd led to him trashing his life, ending up in jail, in rehab, back home with the loving family who'd supported him through thick and thin. They'd healed him, encouraged him to go back to what he loved doing.

Acting. In a soap, on TV. Wherever.

"We can hash it all out now." Linc craved one more look, one more glance that would tell him they were done fighting. For good. "If we can manage not to tear each other up."

But, frankly, fighting had been the basis for their passion. His body remembered it all too well: her sweat on his tongue, salty and thirst-inducing. His skin under her fingernails, a piece of him for her to keep.

If they got near each other again, what would happen?

Would they make the same mistakes? Was there a chance of having something more?

Just look at me, he thought. *Please.*

She did, and his heart swelled in his throat.

"You know," she said, the phone mouthpiece so close to her mouth that he could imagine her lips brushing against his, "the fans are right to love you again. In our scene today, when you found Rita Wilde on your doorstep, her clothes messed up from that bad date with Forrest Rockridge…"

Great. She wanted to talk business. Okay, fine by him. All he wanted was to make up with her. Couldn't he settle for that?

She continued, watching him. "…God, the way you looked at Rita brought me into the moment. Won me over."

Me. Her.

A sharp intake of breath signaled that she realized her error. Or was it the truth?

What if she wanted him back as much as he wanted her?

He reached up a hand, beckoning, inviting more than just business. "This storyline's going to bring you an Emmy."

"You think so?" She sounded so young, so unsure.

"Come down here."

Take it slowly, Lincoln.

She backed away from the railing. "I'm not sure this is a good idea. Maybe we'd better keep things…"

His hand fell to his side. "You're right. Bad idea. But maybe we could just drive around on the bike, like we used to. Go wherever we want." It didn't matter where they ended up. He only wanted to be with her again.

"And that's all?" she asked, suspicious.

"That's all."

Moving too fast had been their problem before. They'd shoved a lifetime of need and raging love into two months.

There hadn't been trust, just desire, cooling their hungers with each other's bodies.

Lakota turned off the phone, stared at him for a moment, then went back inside, shutting the French doors.

Linc did away with his phone, too. Was this a good or bad sign? Had she locked him out? Would Monday at work be a lower circle of hell for him?

A few minutes passed. Then a few more. He'd blown it, pushed too hard, hadn't he? Damn, he should have apologized and gone. Wiped his hands clean and left well enough alone.

Aching, he righted his Harley, prepared to wheel it out of sight. That's when she sprinted through the front door, dressed in jeans and a sweatshirt.

She came to stand next to him, her head barely reaching his shoulder. Her scent made him dizzy with memories, with new opportunities.

"You were leaving without me," she said. "I hate being left behind."

"I thought you weren't coming."

Gravel crackled under the bike's wheels as they began to walk it out of the neighborhood, their stride matching each other's. Why was this so clumsy? Why was it hard to get a sentence out when, once, they'd pillow talked about everything that mattered at the moment?

Away from the houses, he hid the flashlight, took out their helmets, and gave her one. Straddling the bike, he helped her onto the back seat.

"Remember," she said, "take the ride slow." She popped her helmet on her head, settled her hands on his waist, grooving into the natural fit.

He would take it slow, because this time, he wanted to get it right with Lakota.

Lincoln started the engine, revving it to life.

This time, he'd make sure it was about more than sex.

SEAN WISHED she'd hurry up and get here already.

Finally, at twenty after eleven, he opened the door to find Fiona. She was dressed in a long trench coat, the buttons firmly done up, black-fantasy hair spilling over her shoulders.

His house was in near-darkness, lit only by a dim lamp in the corner of the TV room. Eclipsed, she shot him that wicked smile, her lips pulsing with deep red lipstick.

"Hi," she said. "I'm the Sensuous Woman, and I'm here to practice pages 120 through 121 on you."

The Butterfly Flick? Images of what it might be twisted his veins to the point of popping.

Sean leaned against the door frame, pressing his forehead against a fist. Sheer agony. "You're late."

"The better to keep you in the palm of my hand, my dear."

He ran a rough gaze over her, seeking visual fulfillment from under lowered brows. His nostrils flared, detecting the musk of her own excitement under that coat.

Today, in the perfume shop, Lakota had told him five hundred dollars would buy a consultation. She'd begged him, no joke, to let her get him one. So, he'd thought, why not give Fiona perfume *and* the nightgown? He'd have the bet cinched.

The perfumer had asked him a lot of questions. What food does your woman like? What spices? Music? Flowers? Era?

Whoa. He knew her complexion and hair color, but when it came to anything else, Sean was sorely lacking.

The realization had jolted him. What did he know about this woman he was screwing?

Did he want to know more?

Fiona sauntered into his home. "I've done some math. A little over three weeks to go until I win."

"Why don't you just throw in the trench coat now?"

A sassy smile lit her face as she watched him over her shoulder. "Is that the only way you'll defeat me? By default?"

Maybe. "What do you have under the wrapping there?"

She turned around, slowly undoing the ties. Sean's stomach constricted, rooting him into place.

She slipped the coat off her burnished shoulders, revealing the lacy straps of that nightgown. His penis thumped, keeping track of every second he couldn't breathe.

Damn, if she had him beaten at this point, he was in for a long night.

Good.

"I washed the gown," she said, voice low, sinuous as heat floating over a tropical moon. "Who knows where it's been?"

"More." Sean's button-fly strained against his growing arousal.

"Patience." She laughed, presenting her back again, allowing the coat to trail a few inches down. It whispered against the silk, exposing a delicious back. Tapering down to the swoop of her waist and hips.

She walked toward his room, as if sniffing out where it was.

"Get back here," he said.

She ignored him, holding a figurative match to his self-control.

"Is this your sanctuary?" she asked, disappearing into the yawning darkness of the hallway.

She was entering a forbidden place. Privacy. His domain.

"Fiona, you strike me as a woman who requires something much more exotic than a bed. Get out here."

"No," her voice echoed.

Dammit. Stubborn freakin' woman.

Sean adjusted a cock that had hardened to one side of his pants, then went after her. "What's the big deal?" he asked. "It's where I sleep."

He entered the room, muttering a curse when he saw what she'd found.

Fiona was inspecting a pair of underwear. Lacy. Red. Belonging to some woman he'd met a month ago at Bailey's.

"Yours?" she asked.

"Now they are."

She dropped them into the corner again, where he kept all his souvenirs. Call him an aberration, but there were nights he couldn't rest unless he had a reminder in his hand. Unless he had himself in the other.

That was the price of being alone and staying that way.

"So," she said, running a taunting gaze over him, "accoutrements?"

"The safest sex."

Her eyes went darker, then she walked away from the bras, the magazines, the scarves one woman had used to tie him to the bedposts before she left in the morning, never to return.

Fiona stood in front of him, so close he could feel the heat rolling off her skin, permeating him. Then she eased the coat farther off her body, the material caught by her curves, then traveling down toward the floor.

Imagining her in the nightgown had been one thing, but reality was another. Her nipples puckered against the thin material, and the sleekness rippled down every mound, every valley, kissing her skin, laving her with decadence. As he peered lower, he could discern the hair between her legs as it crinkled the silk, tempting him to reach out, to cup her there, to use his thumb to rub her awake.

"I can't figure you out, Mac." The coat finally hit the carpet with a thump.

He felt numb, warm, stimulated. Ready.

She held something in one of her hands.

As he reached out, finally coasting his fingers over her sex, into the silk-covered crevice, he asked, "What do you have there?"

Already slippery. Already his.

Without answering, she nudged one leg against him, spreading, then leaned back her head, bit her lip. After moving with the thrum of his fingers, she wiggled, balanced herself by hooking one set of fingers over his shoulder, clenching until her nails bit into his skin.

Still silent, except for a stray moan here and there, she held up her other hand, presented a tube of lipstick. Using one thumb, she flicked off the cover, bringing it to her other hand to wind it up.

Red. Eve-apple red.

She locked gazes with him as she applied it, the color sliding over her ever-amused lips, leaving a blaze of naughtiness behind. Finished, she pressed them together, then inserted a finger into her mouth, dragging the digit out with deliberate ease.

Sean's fingers left the warmth of her, and he pressed against her hip, throbbing. "Why are you in my room?"

"I'm not allowed?" She covered the lipstick, then carelessly tossed it in the corner, along with his other souvenirs. "Oh, your fingers felt so good, Mac."

She reached down between them, touched herself. Touched him.

He tried to hold it together, even with her palm cupped over his erection, enflaming it. Still, he didn't want to let her in—not here, not inside him. "Like my room, there're places best kept out of reach."

With casual indifference, Fiona traced her hands upward, unbuttoned his top. "Especially under our circumstances."

She shucked off the material, leaving him bare. His ceiling fan whipped air over his sensitized skin while her nails dragged down his chest to rest on his stomach.

When she scratched there, his muscles spasmed, making him grit his teeth.

"There's one thing about you," she said. "You always smell so good. Like…I'm not sure what it is, but it flips my skirt."

As she began undoing his jeans, he held her smooth shoulders, memorizing every move she made. He felt himself getting more turned on with every piece of clothing that hit the ground.

"Maybe it's the perfume of other women," he said.

Cruel. But he wanted to see her eyes. If there was any emotion.

She paused, gaze studied, blank. Then she grinned, bent down as she guided his jeans off. He obligingly stepped out of them.

"I'm happy for you," she said, her face hidden by the fall of her hair.

He glanced away again, not wanting to look at her. Bastard. "Mac?"

She nestled a kiss behind his knee, and he bucked forward with a grunt.

"That didn't pain you, did it now?" she asked, innocent as a frosted slice of virgin snow.

She smoothed her hands over the front of his thighs, her breath moist against his cock as she panted. Her little breaths felt like jabs of fire, scorching him, bringing all the blood thundering to his groin.

"Oh, look at that," she said, low in her throat. "You've got some lipstick behind your knee."

She tickled him there, then tongued the inside of his thigh, and he jerked, the slickness torching him further.

"And there seems to be a strange smudge here." She grazed her bottom teeth over that last kiss, and Sean rocked her closer, needing her so damned much.

Tease. Her hands were on his ass, kneading the twitching muscles, her chin near his ever-expanding hardness. When he glanced downward, the proximity of her red lips made him sweat even more.

She pressed those lips together, then smiled, running her tongue over her teeth. "I've mentioned The Butterfly Flick, haven't I?"

He couldn't say a damned word, wanted only to take her head between his hands and wrap her mouth around his penis, wetting him, suctioning him to a climax.

"Okay, not a talker during foreplay. I can handle that."

"Shut up, Fiona."

"Quiet yourself, Mac. I've got you where I want you."

She rubbed her cheek against his shaft, and he bunched her hair into his fist.

"Back to The Flick." She sighed. "J. prattles on about this little trick. I guess you're supposed to find a real sensitive spot below the base of the penis, wiggle your tongue back and forth and drive a man to the heights."

Dammit, he wanted to scream.

"But I've never tried it before. Where do you think that spot is?"

"I'll show you."

"Mmm." Fiona smoothed the tips of her fingers up the backs of his legs, making the hairs stand on end, making his blood pound and jitter. "I'm feeling kind of shy tonight. I think I'll wait."

"Bitch."

"Bastard."

He laughed, more out of frustration than anything. Out of patience, he led her back to his erection, needing her to alleviate the buildup.

Instead, she stood, shimmying the front of her silk-encased body against his naked one: breasts smoothing over his thighs, his cock, his belly... Then she stood pushing him backward, right into his closet mirror.

It shivered against his back, its cold facade at odds with her moist warmth.

She fastened her lips to his nipple, coating it with slick heat, bringing it to a fevered nub. After she'd sucked it, she leaned her chin on his chest, her nose brushing his jaw.

"Imagine that," she said. "Another lipstick mark for Mac."

He could still feel the ring of her mouth around his nipple, where her lipstick had no doubt branded him. He dug his fingers into her upper arms, ruthless as a swordsman pointing a blade at her throat.

"Is that a sign of possession?"

Her eyes widened. What was that in their depths? Fear? The shadow of a woman who'd gone too far?

She offered a so-what laugh, traced an index finger around his nipple, wiping at the lipstick. She doubled her efforts, trying to erase the mark.

Enough. He captured her mouth with his, devouring her, nipping at the corners, pulling her upper lip into him. Stroking his tongue across her teeth, he plunged farther inside, invading her.

He had her by the elbows, and she tried to pull back, mewling, then fading into him. One of her gown straps slumped onto the side of his hand, and he slipped his fingers beneath it, tugging.

He had her.

But the next instant, he didn't. She pressed against him again, pummeling him against the mirror, the glass quaking in its tracks. He chuckled as the breath left him.

"Stay still," she commanded.

He couldn't. Not anymore. Not with his pulse buffeting his veins. Not with her so near. So far.

Fiona made her way down his torso, leaving a trail of delicate kisses. He could imagine all the lipstick marks, growing fainter with each slick bite, taking ownership of his body. Each kiss palpitated in time to the count of his heartbeat, getting louder, time bombs set to explode.

She reached his penis and, finally, oh, yeah, *finally,* sucked her lips around the tip of it, pulling, taunting. Continuing the torture, she ran her tongue around his head until it was wet with a mixture of his juices and her saliva.

He threaded his fingers through her loose hair, encouraging her. As she took him into her mouth, she swirled her tongue around him, up, down, thoroughly preparing him. Her fingers sought his balls, her knuckles caressing. Seeking farther behind them she caused him to throw back his head until the mirror shuddered again, rattling against his sweat-coated skin, vibrating dangerous heat through his entire body.

Unable to hold back, he came into her, rocketing forward, groaning with the thrusts, the fallout. She held fast, taking him deeper and deeper, nails cutting the backs of his thighs, as he experienced wracking shake after wracking shake.

He couldn't think. Couldn't focus. Could only hold on to her for dear life.

Neither of them moved. Not for a while. They just panted, recovered.

In the relative stillness, she got to her feet. Planting one final kiss on the side of his neck, she gasped against him, finding the throb of his jugular, and singeing the skin with her obvious sense of victory.

"Done," Fiona said, backing away. Watching him with a naughty, hot gaze, she wiped at her mouth.

Sean stretched his arms over his head, keeping a bead on her as she left the room. "Not quite."

"Gimme some food to refuel this fire, and we'll see about that." She turned around, still in her nightgown, still fully armored.

One last sparring tremble seized him from the inside out. One last strain of clenching fulfillment.

He peered at the empty doorway, barely seeing it through his half-closed lids. Barely able to move.

He'd manage the upper hand. Even if it took the rest of the night, he'd get to her.

Chapter Eight

THE SHAKING NEEDED to stop, thought Fiona, as she wandered into the kitchen and headed straight for the refrigerator.

She took a few deep breaths, calming herself, making sure her fingers hadn't turned to butter, before she whipped open the door. A flood of light and coolness claimed her, plastering itself against the stickiness of her skin.

But she still couldn't stop those trembles. The deep belly-jiggering lack of control.

She focused on the food. God, Mac was such a guy. A package of ground beef, way past its due date—so he really *wasn't* a cook. Three six-packs of Corona—better. A mysterious take-out box that she didn't even want to touch. A jar of maraschino cherries with the stems still attached…maybe that meant there was ice cream in the freezer. And a jar of marshmallow cream with the lid half off. She didn't want to venture a guess as to what *that* was all about.

There, see? Now she was calmer. Back to her search.

Fiona wasn't picky when it came to after-sex sustenance. She usually just wanted to get the taste of her partner out of her mouth, to fill up all the untouched places.

She ran her tongue over her lips, tasting salt. *Him.*

"Any specific hankerings?" Mac asked.

Half ignoring him—good game plan, especially since he hadn't put on a stitch of clothing—she left open the fridge and checked the freezer. No ice cream. Drat.

"What do you eat to survive?" she asked.

When he didn't say anything, she turned around to find him shooting a devilish glance at her body.

The sight of him hit her where it counted, all over, including the lacings of her heart. Those long muscled legs, a penis that could only be described as, "Yow," ridged abs, a brawny chest.

And that face. Chiseled from something she couldn't name.

She hardened her resolve, gave a soft, "humph" and turned back to the refrigerator, thankful for the distraction. "Man does not live by copulation alone, you know."

"Says who?"

"Oh, would you just get over here and fix me a marshmallow sandwich or something?"

He ambled across the kitchen floor, gunslinger footsteps thudding on the linoleum.

Gun. Slinging.

Fiona heaved out a trembling breath.

He reached over her, chest to back, the hair of his underarm tickling her shoulder. She stifled a moan of yearning, biting her lip instead.

She'd meant what she'd said about him smelling so good. And not in an artificial designer cologne way, either. Mac had something primal about him—earthy, leathery, like chaps or...

"I could whip up some surprise burgers," he said, touching the package of graying meat.

"Try again." She swallowed as he shifted, his "Yow" nestling between the cheeks of her derriere.

"Beer?"

Was he doing this purposely? Trying to prod her, to slip into her open spaces? His penis had slid downward, inside the backs of her thighs, impeded by the nightgown.

Just for good measure, she wiggled, causing him to start, to nip at her shoulder.

"I guess I should get some drink in me," she said, grabbing two Coronas, moving away.

She heard him take something from the fridge, then shut the door.

"Bottle opener?" she asked.

He accessed a drawer, then handed her the device.

Don't look at him, she thought. *You can still escape without damage tonight.*

If she wanted to.

The beer gasped as she opened one, then the other. The sounds were accompanied by a jar top being screwed off, the metal lid gyrating on the counter.

His voice rode over the noise. "Is the beer what you really want?"

"Sure." She turned around, offered one to him.

He took it, leaning against the counter. He'd already opened the maraschino cherries. Maybe he liked to snack on them? Maybe they gave him a sugar rush?

After she took a step away, creating a space bubble, he chuffed. Took a swig of beer.

Then, he said, "I guess I meant to ask... What do you like to drink? Really like?"

Okay. He was an after-sex talk guy. He didn't seem too keen on the during-sex part.

"Let's see," she said, resting the tip of the bottle against her lips, playing with it. "I adore a nice Moscato Bianco."

"Wine." He took a cherry by its stem, twiddled it between thumb and forefinger. A drop of thick juice fell to the floor.

She paused, glanced up from the splash, then back at him. "Do you have a favorite cocktail?"

"I'm not particular." He took another drink, then set the cherry on the jar's lid. "How about food?"

Fiona crossed her arms over her chest, beer forgotten. "Chocolate. Steak. Potatoes. Why?"

"Just making small talk. Any spices you prefer?"

"Mac." She held herself closer, arming herself. "What's this all about?"

He shrugged. "Ah. Nothing really. We're allowed to talk about this stuff, right?"

Finally, she sipped at her beer, buying time. What was he up to? More unfair techniques to win the bet?

She came up for air, the beverage's cold bitterness quenching her thirst, spinning her head. "I suppose we can chat. But these are weird questions. Even for you."

He took a step toward her, hit a flow of moonlight washing through the window. Faded lipstick kisses decorated his hard body.

They needed to be erased.

But she didn't dare touch him. Instead, she opted for the barred-arm position again.

"Fiona." Soft, low, terrifying in the dark of midnight. "I think you're shyer with your clothes on than off."

"It's all those questions." *Sure, Fi. Sure.* "They're invasive."

He was right in front of her now, all strained power, temptation. What if she could just lean her head against his chest and close her eyes?

What would happen?

She tightened her arms.

"Don't get all worked up," he said, chuckling. "Lakota and I dropped by a perfumery today. Did you know they'll mix a scent that belongs just to you?"

"Sure."

"Hell, I had no idea."

"So you and Lakota were getting in some quality time?" He lifted a rugged eyebrow.

"Strictly a business query," she said, putting him in his place with a grin. "I noticed a definite… change…in Lincoln today."

Suspicion drew his mouth into a line. "Yeah?"

Like she was going to blab Linc's love secrets to Mac, Lakota's keeper. "I think things will improve from here on out. He's not going to mess up anymore."

Mac put down his beer, faced her straight on. "Same with Lakota."

He hooked his index fingers under her nightie straps, lifted, drew them away from her shoulders.

Fiona gulped. "Well. Then we won't need to worry about those two clowns. Will we?"

"That's optimistic."

With lethargic purpose, he positioned her straps just so, then let go. The material fluttered downward, caught by the tips of her breasts. The lace scratched against them, pinpricks of sensual delicacy.

"Mac…"

"You chickening out?" He knuckled over one nipple, and it contracted.

"Never."

"Game on, then." He bent, taking her earlobe into his mouth. Sucking on it, he caused her to clumsily abandon the beer, to abandon all pretenses.

Why not indulge herself a little longer?

He guided her backward, until she hit a stool with the backs of her thighs. At her sharp intake of breath, he lifted her, hefting her on top of it. Pushing up her gown until it gathered around her hips, he pressed on the inside of her thighs until the air throbbed over the naked center of her, leaving her open. Vulnerable.

She anchored herself, bracing the arches of her feet on the most convenient rungs, struggling for balance. He glided his lips to her throat, lightly plucking at her neck veins with his teeth and tongue, traveling down, over her chest, between her breasts.

A strangled mew wrenched from her throat.

She pushed against him, but he urged her farther against the stool, the wall. Through the gown, he licked a nipple, wetting the material, and making her suck in much-needed oxygen between her teeth.

Mac had the upper hand, and he knew it. The thought spurred her into action.

She squirmed away from his mouth, laughing. "What's *your* favorite spice?"

Stalemate.

His breathing rasped against her shoulder, and he backed away, snarling.

Pumped to go.

It looked as if he'd consume her whole if she gave in. His chin was lowered, his hands curved by his sides, his posture stiff, ready to prowl.

Oh, the power. The knowledge of having a man by the short hairs because he wanted her so much.

She almost hated herself for basking in the feeling.

Hated the feeling altogether.

But she couldn't help it. His frustration stoked something inside her. Something she lacked.

His steel-band shoulders rose with every violent breath. "Why the hell do I put myself through this?"

Fiona flexed her torso forward, watching a muscle tic in his jaw. "Because you're an addict?"

Even if he was aroused, she could feel him mentally pulling away. That wouldn't work. She was here to win.

With a slow, tortuous tug, she pulled up her gown, gathering it until she was open to him again.

Posting her foot against the side wall, she got comfortable, skimming her fingers over the inside of her thigh.

"See something you like?" she asked.

He thunked against the counter, watching.

Her fingers sought the folds of her sex. Even at this point, just with the banter, she was hot and sleek for him. Pressing a finger to one side of her clit, she applied pressure, getting off more from the rapt expression on his face than the actual act of touching herself so shamelessly.

She crooked the finger of her other hand at him. "What are you waiting for?"

His only response was to slide the cherry and jar down the counter, nearer. She knew exactly what he had in mind, and she pulsed with the anticipation of it.

He dipped two fingers into the jar, stood over her.

She pushed on her mons, the added weight making her restless. Dammit, she wanted it to be him, rubbing, building her up. *Him.*

Silently, with only the hum of the refrigerator to accompany him, Mac stroked the cool juice over her, fluid strums guiding her hips in time to his patient demands. The syrup felt sticky, heavy.

Then he took the cherry in his other fingers, an outlaw's grin on his lips. Holding it by the stem, he hovered it over her mouth. She went for it, but he jerked it away.

Who was in control now?

Her conscience skipped over itself, repeating the question.

He bent to his knees, placing one of her legs over his shoulder. The back of her knee stuck to his skin.

As he fastened his mouth to her inner thigh, he watched her, nibbling, playing his fingers over her pounding clit. Then, once inside of her, making her ready for bigger and better things.

She thrashed, rocked against his hand, threatening to upset the stool. He held her steady, chuckling.

"Come on," she said, hanging on for dear life.

"What's your favorite music?" asked his muffled voice.

"Mac."

He drew away. "Answer."

She winced. "Um. The Police."

"Ah. A connoisseur of the eighties." He returned to the task at hand. "Good girl."

When his tongue connected, laving away the syrup, Fiona cried out. He circled the most sensitive part of her, sucked until dizziness drew her down.

He took one of her lips between his, let go of it with an insouciant slurp. "Favorite flower."

"You've got to be kidding. Damn—" Was that a sob? "Just…"

He moved an inch backward.

"Wait. Flower." She couldn't think. What were those things called again? "Roses. That's it. Roses."

She could feel his shoulders lift in a shrug. So it'd been a clichéd answer. Big deal.

It was good enough, she supposed, because he was back where he belonged. This time thrusting his tongue inside her, warm, mobile, swirling. Then… something else.

She convulsed, jamming her chin against her shoulder. He'd put the cherry between her folds, was eating it, licking, nibbling, consuming.

Heat flushed over her, poising her on a shuddering breath. He held her hips as she whipped from side to side, agitated.

She cried out, banging her head against the wall, devoured

by a flare of stillness, then a surge of crashing sensation. She grasped at it. Pulsating waves pounding from the inside out, tearing her apart, ripping every shred of emotion and turning it into a physical nerve.

She muffled a cry. Still, his mouth was on her, driving her toward a red wall. Closer, closer, farther, closer…

It shattered as she smashed into it, ramming forward, backward, again and again. Pinpoints of release tingled her skin, moistening it with beaded sweat.

She couldn't catch her breath, couldn't grasp onto anything. Lost, broken…

Oh. There.

Satiated.

She didn't want to open her eyes, didn't want to expose how much she wanted him. Yearned for him.

Breathe. Control.

Finally, she pulled herself together, then chanced a glance. Good thing she'd waited, because he'd been observing her, one hand still between her legs, the other covering her up with the nightgown. He had something in his mouth, and when he took it out, Fiona couldn't help a contented smile from arching over her lips.

He offered the cherry stem to her. It was tied into a knot, just like she used to do in college at the bars, impressing all the boys.

"Done," he said, cocky as ever. Then he went back to his beer, saluting her with the bottle, as if nothing had transpired from point A to point B.

The shakes started up again.

"Done?" she gasped, sliding off the stool. "I don't think so."

LATER THAT NIGHT, after he'd driven into her, spilling himself into a condom time and again, Sean had finally drifted off to sleep. A deep sleep, for the first time in... ever?

He rolled over the TV room carpet onto a blanket, where they'd ended up after a bout with her propped on the kitchen counter, a session in the bed and one in the hallway.

Groggy, he sought her out. Finding her. Drawing her against him because it felt so damned good.

Even though he hadn't bothered to open his eyes, her image was still imprinted on his mind. He didn't have to look to see her. Feeling her bare breasts against his chest was enough.

Content, he must have drifted off again because, when he did officially awaken, it was because the phone was ringing. Sunlight streamed through the windows as he woke up. Something feathered over his face.

He opened his eyes to find Fiona stroking his cheek, watching him.

As the phone screeched, he shifted. She jerked back, creating distance, especially in her dark eyes where he could've sworn something mysterious lingered.

Quick as summer lightning, she turned on the Cruz charm, hiding behind a sexy come-hither expression.

Bitter disappointment filtered his vision, making him glance away. What was his problem? He didn't want a woman gleaming onto him, choking him.

It was time to let her go, wasn't it?

The words "you lose" were busting his teeth, trying to get out. But he couldn't say them. Didn't want to, because if he opened his big mouth, the bet would end. Done. No more sizzling sex. No more pretending that neither of them gave a crap.

And that's what made being with Fiona so much easier.

"The office is calling, sleepyhead," she said. Raising her

arms up, she gave him an agonizing view of her curvy torso, her full breasts.

So she thought she'd gotten away with it. Emotions. But what did he know? Maybe he was wrong, and she'd been waking him up for another go-around.

But what about her eyes? That look?

Sean braced himself for the terror, the urge to flee, but it didn't happen. Instead, he wanted to see the softness again.

Or was this just that after-glow bullshit he'd heard about?

The answering machine picked up the call as they both sat there. Fiona leaned back on her elbows, casual, careless. He rolled over to his stomach, burying his face in his arms.

Damn, he was sore. And it felt great.

"McIntyre," barked Louis Martin's voice. Luckily the boss man had the machine to guard him, or else Sean would have busted the guy against a wall.

"It's Saturday morning," said Fiona, all sing-songy. "Tell me he's not expecting you."

"Where are you?" Louis went silent, probably expecting Sean to pick up.

"I'm there most weekends," Sean said. "I guess he's starting to take me for granted."

Louis made a coughing noise, then hung up without saying anything more.

Both Sean and Fiona said, "Moron," at the same time.

Fiona zapped a finger in Sean's direction. "Jinx!"

"Got me." He rested his head on his forearms, appreciating her skin, every inch of it. Appreciating too much.

Fiona stood, hardly bothered by her undressed state. And no wonder. Though her hips and ass were what could be called "Rubenesque," she didn't have an ounce of fat on her.

"Playtime's over, I suppose," she said.

"Fiona."

Just let it go. Let her go.

She waited expectantly.

Hell, what should he say now? "I've, ah, got to be out of town for a few days. Got to visit a client's celebrity restaurant in New York. Touch base with connections there."

Her expression didn't waver. "Have a fun time. See a Broadway play for me."

"Plays. You like plays."

She hesitated, then shrugged. "Love 'em."

He nodded, not knowing what else to say.

"Well, then." She walked away. "Take a bite out of the Big Apple."

"I'll see you when I get back?" Why'd that have to come out as a question?

Fiona ran a hand along his wall, silent. Then, "I don't know."

"What?" He stood.

Her answer was whiplash smart. "I'm not backing out, you understand. I've got a lot to do this week. I've got to put together an event for Joanie Heflin's Pilates clothes line, and I..."

She trailed off, and Sean cringed for her. She felt the glitch in their arrangement, too, but wasn't about to say anything. Fiona was too much of a competitor.

So why wasn't he reveling in victory right about now? Why wasn't he calling her bluff?

Maybe because she really doesn't feel a damned thing, said all his niggling doubts. The ones that had watched his father fade into nothing.

She'd left the room already, probably going to fetch her nightgown and coat in his room. She'd shed her silk after the kitchen, when they'd stumbled to their next athletic arena.

He followed her, planting his hands on his hips as he reclined against the bedroom wall. She was busy donning her gown, facing away from him.

His image mocked him in the closet mirror. Streaks of last night's sweat blurred the surface, and even now, he could see the hint of red lipstick burning into his skin.

"Wednesday," he said, watching himself say the words. "That's when I'll be in L.A. again."

She was in her coat now, ready to go. Smiling, completely ignoring the bigger issues. "Travel safely, Mac. Don't work too hard."

"Wait." He retrieved her lipstick from the corner, held it out to her. "You're forgetting something."

Morning sunlight glinted off the golden tube, winking, nudging.

Again, with the laugh. "It's another souvenir." She nodded toward his undies-and-bras corner, his shame. "Or maybe you'll need it in New York. You know, for those lonely nights when it's just you and… well…whoever."

Was she wondering if he'd pick up some woman to keep him entertained while he was gone?

He should, just for the hell of it. Just because she didn't own him.

As she pushed the lipstick back at him, she stood on tiptoe. Kissing his nose, she was as flirty as a feline playing with a ball of unspooling yarn.

"I mean it," she said, "have a good time."

And with that, she left, giving him her blessing to stray.

Sad thing was, he knew he wouldn't.

Chapter Nine

DAYS LATER, when Mac popped his head into her office, Fiona almost jumped out of the chair.

"Mac!"

Okay. She needed to tone it down, didn't she? After all, she hadn't missed him *that* much. She'd just watched a lot of TV and gotten caught up on a lot of work. Had gone to sleep at night staring at the ceiling, tracing her fingers over her skin and pretending he was there.

It was always like this at the beginning of an affair, wasn't it? You couldn't stop thinking of the person, couldn't stop the craving for them.

She'd get over it.

His grin drew her out of her chair. He came toward her at the same time. Oh, that scent, that body. Even covered by a classy, black suit, Mac made her feel like they were both unclothed, skin exposed and humming. Awareness vibrated between them, a reminder of the other night.

Lipstick. Cherries.

"You keep things on the straight and narrow while I was gone?" he asked, holding something in his hand.

The hand that had cupped her breasts, explored the center of her and worked her to a moaning peak.

Fiona tried to remain cool. "What're you hiding there?"

He almost seemed embarrassed as his fingers fanned open to reveal a tiny wooden apple with the words "New York" etched into it.

"Oh." She fought the softness, the sap of strength from her body. "You shouldn't have."

But she cradled the apple in her palm anyway. What was he doing buying her another present? If they'd included *his* possessiveness as part of the bet, she'd have whipped the pants right off him by now.

No. Ridiculous. He was merely trying to win that tropical vacation, courtesy of her checkbook. Trying to buy her with sweet gestures and false gifts.

She shouldn't forget it, either.

He shoved his hands into his pants pockets, didn't say anything. Not even an "I missed you, Fiona."

Well, then. There it was. "How'd business go?" she asked.

She wanted to touch him so badly.

"Great. Things are moving right along."

Things. It was no secret that Mac had some catching up to do within the company but, lately, you'd never know it. He was really on his way up, mainly due to Lakota and a couple new acquisitions, including a rising down-home indie actress and a hot Tiger-Beat favorite teen idol. An uncomfortable poke of competitiveness irked her, because she needed to be in the same position.

That's right. She'd caught Louis's telling glances as he walked by her office, checking her progress, keeping her working late into the night.

She ran a thumb over the apple and tucked it into her suit pocket, where she could touch it without him seeing her.

Well, then. Back to business. "So Linc and Lakota have a

Soap Opera Channel special they're filming in the San Diego area this weekend. *'Getaways,'* it's called."

His sharp green eyes cut into her, but she had no idea what he was thinking. "I know. Did Linc invite you down there, too? Just as a thank-you?"

"He did."

"Funny, isn't it?" He sauntered over to a leather chair, claimed it by taking a seat, lengthening his legs. "How their fighting stopped on a dime. How they're getting along so well now."

"Coyness isn't your strong suit." She aimed her own sly glance at him. "You know well and good that they've started seeing each other again."

"Unfortunately, I've been Lakota's confidant." Though his tone was dry, there was a trace of warmth.

When he was done with Fiona, would he move on to the diva?

She chased away the sting of her runaway imagination, told herself she was concerned only for Linc's sake.

"They seem happy," she said. "I hope it stays that way."

"I know, Linc's got a way of getting too intense. Unfortunately, Lakota gave me a rundown of their short but flammable history while I was flying to New York," Mac grunted. "Compelling."

She'd give half her coming paycheck to know what Lakota was telling Mac, but she wasn't about to ask him. Not directly, anyhow. "I thought I'd join them at the bed-and-breakfast this weekend, just for some downtime. You?"

Mac changed position in his chair, edgy. Fiona smiled. So he had the same idea. They'd continue their bet in another location, adding some variety.

"Going down there's not a bad idea," he said.

Excitement zapped through her limbs. Could she wait until the weekend?

The last time she'd seen Mac, she'd drawn away from him. It'd been instinct, a reaction to having him catch her in a vulnerable moment. He'd been sleeping, and she'd been exploring the ridges of his face: his lined forehead, his strong nose and chin. His talented mouth.

God, what had her eyes told him when he'd woken up?

Hopefully nothing, because she'd recovered quickly. Plus, he hadn't called her on it.

She was safe for now. And she wouldn't get caught appreciating him again. It was dangerous. Not worth the heartache.

She returned to her chair behind the giant mahogany desk, a hand-me-down from the last occupant. But she'd adapted well, had made the desk her own after the first day of work.

"I guess I can drive down to San Diego after my event Friday night," she said, picking up a pen, prepared to look like Mac wasn't ruling her every thought. "Grace Paget, my actress turned pop star, is signing CDs and having a mini concert at Spinnaker's Records. Then I'm good to go for the weekend."

Mac casually extracted a Palm Pilot from his jacket, then accessed it. "I'll drive you from there."

He wanted to come to the signing? Wasn't that kind of...well...normal? Something a real boyfriend would do?

He must've seen the doubt written all over her. "Don't get excited. It's a matter of convenience."

"Sure." She relaxed. "And I'm *not* excited. Just—"

Her skin prickled into wary goose bumps. Louis Martin stood in her doorway, backed up by Fiona's assistant, Rosie. The young woman shoved her wire-rims back up her nose and made a here-we-go face.

"Louis," said Mac, obviously not glad to see their boss. "I'm back."

The diminutive man entered, uninvited, and sat in the other chair. Rosie stood, notepad at ready.

"I didn't see your report yet," he said to Mac.

Mac's bullet-path grin split the tension, and Fiona squirmed restlessly in her chair.

"I haven't written any report." Mac turned his attention back to Fiona, and she sent him a wink of solidarity.

Louis's face turned a mottled red. What a Napoleon complex this guy had. "I just checked Karen Carlisle's column online. Fiona, good job of getting Lakota Lang the exposure."

Victory straightened her posture. "Thank you."

"But it's something the *Flamingo Beach* publicist could've done. You need more than Karen Carlisle." Louis leaned forward in his chair. "She's small potatoes, not to mention that the piece was boring. *B-O-R-I-N-G.*"

The air flushed out of her lungs, and she fought the urge to sink back in her chair. She'd been at Stellar for only one week. What did he expect?

Mac chuffed. "Fine job, Martie. Now can you spell ingrate?"

"McIntyre—"

"—Do you know how much effort we've put into Lakota Lang and Lincoln Castle lately? We fished the fat out of the fire with them." Mac stood, clearly irritated. "Fiona's damage control has been right on target."

He was protecting her. *Her.*

"Your soap stars run the risk of getting bland, and you know that's death for publicity," Louis said. "John Q public wants passion, spice."

Fiona couldn't stand it anymore. "Motorcycle crashes, near-death experiences, a stay in rehab? Is that what they want?"

Rosie was furiously taking notes in her corner. But at this, she glanced to Fiona, nodding emphatically. Right-on, sister.

Louis's smile was patronizing, to say the least. She'd seen that sort of gesture her whole life. From her brothers, when she'd first run out to the lawn to play with them. From the Little League fathers, who'd yelled at the coach to take out the girl and give their boys game time. From all her previous bosses, who didn't take her as seriously as they should have.

He continued. "All I'm saying, Fiona, McIntyre, is that you can do better. Capitalize on the conflict between Lang and Castle. It's what keeps the public hooked."

Mac came to stand beside Fiona's desk. "There's nothing to exploit right now, Martie. They're not fighting."

He wasn't mentioning they were back together. Fiona's respect for Mac shot up several degrees. Linc and Lakota didn't need the added pressure of having their personal lives spotlighted right now. Their co-hosting gig this weekend would be enough, with them presenting the image of friendly co-stars.

She sent him a message of thanks with her eyes. Their gazes connected, snapped, sparking with contained fire.

Until they both looked away.

Louis got out of his chair, shook his head. "McIntyre, you used to be a force to be reckoned with. I don't know what the hell took the edge off, but it's gone."

The rest of the sentence hung from the ceiling, a looped rope.

And you could be gone, too.

Their boss left the office, but Rosie stayed, wide-eyed in the corner.

Fiona retained her professional demeanor, even though she wanted to comfort Mac, to tell him that he was great, that she…

That she what?

His mouth was set in a grim line. Fiona just now noticed that his dark blond hair needed a trim, and the realization tugged at her heart.

Rosie stepped out of her corner, her notebook in front of her chest. "Mr. McIntyre?"

"Yeah?" So composed, so beyond her.

"I…" She came closer. "Don't listen to him. We all know you're the best."

Oh, no. Hero worship. Ambitious Rosie was shining with it, almost coming off as a groupie or something.

Mac remained distant. "Thanks."

"And…" Rosie took a deep breath, laughed. "Okay, no more. You get it. I'm gonna go back to work." With one last, lingering, you're-such-a-god glance, she deserted them, flouncing her way into the hall.

Fiona didn't say anything at first. She was too bitter, and not only about Louis's criticism. "That must've lifted your ego."

"Jealous?"

Unbelievable. "Get your mind back in this game. The girl's choosing her allies, and she's picked you." Fiona pressed her lips together, then, unable to help herself, added, "And I'm not jealous, thank you very much."

Put that in your maraschino cherry jar and suck on it.

"I'll check you on that tonight," he said, walking away.

"Don't be so sure about yourself. You're not *my* Apollo."

"You'll come." He lingered by the door, laconic, confident. "Ten o'clock's good for me."

She shooed him away, pretended to be immersed in a random memo. The writing made no sense. Just a bunch of squiggles and numbers.

When she looked up, he was gone.

But that night, they would meet up again, and welcome

each other home with teasing kisses and passionate scenarios. The bet continued, a game that was growing more serious by the day.

Yet Fiona knew that the last inning was approaching.

SPINNAKER'S RECORDS on Sunset Boulevard claimed to stock over 130,000 titles. On Friday night, it was a hip place to hang out, with young customers weighing in at the listening posts, the in-store radio station and coffee shop.

Lincoln was relieved to finally get out on the town with Lakota. Fiona had mentioned that the actress Grace Paget would be giving an acoustic rendering of her first album here tonight, so he and his...he didn't really know what to call Lakota...had agreed to attend.

In baseball caps and sunglasses.

Not that they were big stars, especially at their position on the lower rung of Hollywood nobility. But acting like they were couldn't do any harm.

They stood toward the back of the crowd, brushing against each other, the contact reminding him that they really were together again.

At least as friends.

He had to pinch himself every day. On the set, the status quo remained. Both professionals, both memorizing every line, both blocking out their scenes without even a meaningful glance, both nailing the acting with flair.

But at night... Linc reached out and squeezed Lakota's hand as Grace Paget launched into a love song. At night they "hung out," helping each other memorize up to thirty pages of dialogue per episode. Sometimes they'd vary the routine, going to dinner with their co-stars after they shot their footage.

They were "pals." And it was killing him.

When Grace Paget finished her set and retreated to the signing area, the sizable audience applauded. He scanned the room for Fiona, finding her in the background. She was assessing the crowd, taking up Grace's back.

Typical Fi. Always supportive.

Lakota slipped her arms around his waist, and Linc's arms curved up in surprise.

As natural as you please, she said, "I'm going to buy a copy of the CD. You?"

His hands slowly came down, rested on her upper arms. Wary.

Grace Paget wasn't his thing. Lakota liked pop, he liked jazz, but it was only a minor difference. "Not tonight. I think I'll browse the bins."

Leaning back, she tilted her head. Staring at him, she hooked her fingers in his belt so her nails grazed his belly.

He captured her wrist, halting her. "Kota?"

"Linc." She made puppy-dog eyes at him. "Are you ever going to touch me again? I mean, what's it been, days since we stopped acting like mortal enemies?"

"I wasn't sure what you wanted from me. I thought..."

"You thought what?" She pulled back, but he still held on. "That I wouldn't want you as much as the night we broke up? For Heaven's sake, I've been waiting for you to put the moves on me, boy."

He fingered a strand of red hair that had wiggled out from under her cap, as if hardly believing she was allowing him to touch her. "I didn't want to ruin what we have so far. This...I don't know. Peace. The appreciation of just being together."

"Ah." She laughed. "You are the biggest romantic dope I've ever met."

"I want to wait."

Bling. Where had *that* come from? But as soon as he said it, he knew it was true. He craved the perfect moment with Lakota, to make up for all the ugliness of their past.

She shot him a sidelong glance. "For how long?"

Until you say you love me, he thought.

They were interrupted by Sean McIntyre, who'd quietly come up behind Lakota's shoulder. Lincoln bristled, cupped a palm behind his girlfriend's neck.

Hey. She was his girlfriend again.

"McIntyre," he said, smiling because of the Lakota realization, not because of the interruption.

The other man gave a slight nod of acknowledgment.

Lakota grabbed Linc's possessive hand and enfolded it in her own again. "Sean! Guess what?" She didn't stop for his answer. "I've got an audition next week! I mean, I was going to tell you this weekend, give you all the details, but since you're here... You know."

She was beaming, and Linc couldn't help feeling happy, too. He knew how much Lakota wanted to get out of soaps. Maybe he would again, too. Someday.

Pride made him talk to McIntyre. "She's been asked to read for an action heroine pilot."

"We'll talk about it in Julian. You *are* coming this weekend, right?" asked Lakota. "You and Ms. Cruz can relax. Our soap PR person's taking care of everything."

"We'll be there," said McIntyre.

For a second, the spin doctor's mouth pulled itself out of its stolid line, and Linc's hold on Lakota loosened.

Was Fiona still sleeping with this guy? She was pretty secretive when it came to her affairs, but this one... The pieces weren't fitting where they usually did. McIntyre was a square peg in Fiona's usual pattern. For one, he'd stuck around a lot longer.

Applause filled the store as Grace Paget waved to the audience and sat down to sign her CD and movie posters. McIntyre glanced over his shoulder at the podium, but Linc wasn't sure he was taking in the singer.

That's when he saw Fiona send the guy a saucy grin.

Yup. Still screwing him.

Lakota detached herself from Linc, heading toward the signing line. "I'll meet you in the jazz section," she said, wiggling her fingers in farewell.

"Sure." He couldn't disconnect from her, couldn't pull back his heart, even though the distance was increasing.

"Glad to see you two are still cozy," said McIntyre.

"Don't worry. I'm not going to break your little girl in half."

McIntyre assessed Linc for a moment, probably testing him. Then, "No you won't."

Linc cleared his throat, facing the man head-on. They were the same height, same build, but there was a saw-toothed rustiness to the publicist's attitude that set them apart.

"Same goes for you," he said. "I mean about Fi. That you won't take advantage of her."

"Fiona's a big girl. She's really great at taking care of herself."

"And you, more than likely. I know everything about her. Just about grew up with her." Linc didn't know how much to say. Fi didn't get domestic with her lovers. Still, she might need a bit of protection, here. Linc just felt it.

"Listen." McIntyre put his hands in his pockets, nonchalantly withdrawing from Lincoln's impending attack. "All you have to know is that Fiona won't get hurt. Not by me, anyway."

"What does that mean?"

"She's a romantic death wish." McIntyre glanced away.

"I'm still not getting you." Linc stepped into the other

man's field of vision, all the while knowing exactly what he was talking about.

McIntyre nodded, acknowledging Lincoln's persistence. His caring.

No doubt the PR rep was wondering why Lincoln and Fi had never gotten together themselves. And Linc wasn't about to explain.

"Fiona's made sure that our time together won't go beyond the physical," the spin doctor said. "Has she told you that much?"

Oh, jeez, Fi, not again. Not more games. When would she learn? "What is her grand plan this time?"

"Maybe she should tell you."

"Come on, man," Linc said, "I won't throw a punch at you or anything."

McIntyre held back an obvious laugh, making it painfully clear that he thought a street-smart pugilist could kick the ass of a weight-lifting pretty boy any day.

Lincoln didn't push the issue.

"You asked for it," said the other man. "We've got a bet going."

Why hadn't she told him? "A bet?"

"Fiona thinks she—representative of the female nation— can enjoy a straight-up affair without getting emotional, territorial or possessive."

Linc's shoulders sank. She'd do anything to keep herself lonely, wouldn't she? In college, she'd been popular, always booked for the weekend, always a sparkle in her eye. Never in love. Then she'd met Ted.

He'd sent Fi into a tailspin that hadn't stopped whirring. Since then, she'd pulled out all the commitment-phobic stops in existence. Giving out fake names to the men she was with, inventing lives that weren't her own, breaking off emotional attachments before they had a chance to grow.

But a bet? He had to give it to her. It was an inspired creation.

"Normally," said Lincoln, "I'd ask you to step off. But Fi would kill me."

Before Linc's very eyes, McIntyre seemed to retreat into himself. Was he feeling guilty?

"She's had some real disappointments," added Linc, for good measure.

"Haven't we all." Without elaborating, McIntyre straightened, offered a hand. "See you down in San Diego?"

Had he made his point to the guy? Linc shook hands with him, his grip firm. "You hurt her and, dignity or no, I will go after your ass."

McIntyre grinned without humor. Then he stepped away, a shadow of a man heading toward the door, blending into the night.

Lincoln would have to keep tabs on Fi this weekend. Just in case.

Chapter Ten

EVERYTHING WAS doves-and-loves down at the Soap Channel Getaways shoot outside the small, but unique B&B.

Linc and Lakota, plus their employees, the crew and the soap publicist, were filming on Julian's main street. Located just outside San Diego, the western-flavored town featured homemade crafts boutiques and apple pie. Today had been filled with shots of Linc feeding Lakota caramel treats, with Lakota showing Linc around an abandoned mine, with them both lounging around the quirky B&B. As the humidity wreaked havoc with the stars' makeup, the crew did its best to portray Julian as a romantic escape, with cool-air promises of an autumn bluegrass music and apple festivals.

They would finish filming the special tomorrow, but it didn't affect Fiona since this was the soap PR's gig. She'd spent the day shopping alone, wondering why Mac had done his own thing and become so distant all of a sudden.

He'd been that way last night, too, after the Grace Paget concert and signing. During their two-hour drive to Julian, they hadn't talked much. In fact, she'd been relieved when he'd put on a CD to drown out their silence. Salsa songs, stirring her soul, convincing her that at least they had musical tastes in common.

Besides bedroom tastes.

Was he getting sick of her? Was the inevitable separation beginning? After all, he'd left her alone last night. Not that she'd invited him to her room, but...

She flopped onto her bed, with its horse-patterned comforter and cowboy furnishings. Each room had a different theme—hers was the Wild West. Apple tree branches, budding with the promise of a fall bounty, lingered just outside her window, and she had a whole cabinet full of western movies to keep her occupied.

So why did she feel out of sorts?

With a sigh of impatience, she dug through the VCR collection. *The Magnificent Seven. She Wore a Yellow Ribbon. The Good, the Bad, and the Ugly.*

This room was awful. And for more than just the obvious reasons. It reminded her too much of ranches, proposals, broken dreams.

A knock sounded on her door, and she dropped a movie cassette, heart slamming against her ribs.

She raised a hand to her hair. Still in fine shape. Sniffed her skin. Good old Mango Madness body splash. Not bad for a long day of wandering boutiques.

"Yes?" she asked, airy as could be.

The last voice she expected was the one she heard. "Fiona?"

Lakota?

Getting to her feet, Fiona smoothed down her beige linen sheath and opened the door.

The young star was alone, garbed in shorts and sandals, newly showered with her red hair slicked back from her heart-shaped face. No makeup. No threat of wrinkles.

Fresh as a daisy Fiona would like to yank from the dirt.

"Hi," Lakota said. Her tone was so sweet and guileless that shame slapped Fiona in the face.

She smiled, trying not to wish that Mac was the one standing at her door. "Come on in."

"Thanks." The girl entered, immediately spying the bed and sprinting toward it, hopping on top and bouncing. "Yeehaw! Check this out! You've got a down mattress."

Fiona merely watched, floored. Where had the sophisticate gone? Maybe this wasn't Lakota at all. Maybe one of those perky cowgirl dolls from the crafts store a couple buildings down had come to life, escaped, gravitated toward the washed-out wood and antique-laden hideout that was Fiona's room.

Hey, that scenario was far more likely.

She addressed Lakota, who was now inspecting a creaky lantern hanging near Fiona's bed.

"Mac told me on the drive down that you have a big audition coming up. Good work."

"Thanks. God, I love vintage." Lakota leaned on her elbows, stared up at a stagecoach-wheel light fixture. "Linc should put himself out there, too. He's much bigger than soaps."

"His agent's working on it." Fiona tilted her head, fascinated by this changeling.

"Cool." Lakota settled down, hanging her feet over the edge of the bed. "Sean told me he's in the Caveman Room. Isn't that someone's classic idea of irony? I've got the Paris Room, and Linc's got the Pirate one. Argh."

Fiona raised a brow, nodded and laughed at the same time. "Yes. Funny stuff." Then she gave her guest a quizzical glance. "Well. So you're going from room to room, taking the grand tour again."

Suddenly, the jaded actress appeared. She was hiding under Pippy Lakota's skin, but Fiona could detect her.

Lakota's smile was knowing. "Actually, I've been meaning to ask you something."

Big surprise. "Toss it out there."

"All right. Why didn't you and Linc ever get together? It's been nagging at me."

Direct. She could respect that in another woman.

When Linc and Lakota had dated, Fiona hadn't spent a lot of time with them. She'd been busy putting out fires at her old PR firm—to no avail, it turned out. But the few times they'd all gotten together, Fiona had known Lakota was curious.

Was Mac also? Would Lakota tell him about this conversation?

"Linc never explained?" Fiona asked.

"I never asked him. I don't want the answer sugar-coated, because that's what guys do about the women in their lives. They try to make their girlfriends feel better by lying about female friends."

"Fair enough." Girlfriend, huh? During her last Lincoln heart-to-heart, he'd told her he was waiting for true love before "taking it to the next level" with Lakota again.

Linc. Her sensitive, poet-souled buddy. She'd watch out for him.

Fiona assumed a casual tone. "When we first met in college, Linc was acting in *Waiting for Godot,* and I was taking a stagecraft class, hoping to meet guys. I worked on his production."

Lakota wiggled, obviously wanting to get to the good stuff, the parts she didn't already know. Apparently, Linc had talked about Fiona to *some* extent.

"And…?" Lakota prodded.

"And he was a doll. All the girls wanted Linc, of course." Fiona hadn't made any female friends in stagecraft class; she'd hung out with the boys, as usual. So when the ladies had swarmed Linc, she'd beaten them to the punch. The winner. "I'd kidded around with him during rehearsals, had gone to his campus apartment with a few guys to drink beer and shoot the breeze. But at the closing night party, I got him alone, thinking there'd be a little action involved."

"Good luck," muttered Lakota.

Sexual frustration. Poor girl. "We did kiss, but that's where it ended. It was the most disgusting experience of my life. Not—" Fiona held up a finger as Lakota opened her mouth— "because of bad hygiene, you understand. Linc takes great care of himself."

"Yup."

"But it was like kissing something sexless for me." Fiona shuddered. "I felt it in the pit of my stomach. God, it was very wrong."

"So it was like this invisible force field that kept you from him? Kind of like a magic spell? Because when *I* kiss him—"

Fiona cringed. She really didn't want to hear this. Girl-talk was not her forte. "I suppose you could say we're destined to be something other than…well… lovers. He felt the same way, because when we pulled back from each other, he had the most horrified expression on his face. I laughed out loud, the poor thing, but luckily he joined right in. We got along so well that we never stopped seeing each other. He's my special guy."

She imbued the last phrase with dead-aim significance.

Lakota got it, judging from the cool blue of her eyes. "What about Sean?"

Fiona's attempted laugh fell flat. "Here endeth the lesson. You got what you came for, didn't you?"

"Not entirely."

A tiny bleep of hope flashed across Fiona's radar. "Mac sent you to be a spy?"

"I look out for him, too."

Could this be any more juvenile? "Then tell him I don't pass notes during class."

Lakota frowned, then pouted out her lower lip in an adorable sign of Mac-attack sympathy. "Sean's a great catch, if you ask me."

Was Fiona actually talking about relationships? With another woman, no less? Part of her wanted to dig for more information. Part of her remembered that she had a bet going, and it didn't include giving a crap about Sean and his catch-a-bility.

With all the strength Fiona could muster, she walked to the door, opened it, sparkled a smile at Lakota. "Are you satisfied with how I answered your question?"

Lakota looked Fiona up and down, then slid off the bed, heading toward the hallway. "It explains a lot."

Fiona didn't take the bait. She didn't like to be psychoanalyzed, especially by a girl half a decade younger than she was.

She already knew she wasn't your garden-variety woman. And that was fine by her.

"Just do me a favor?" asked Lakota, stopping on the way to her room.

"The requests never stop."

"Go to dinner with Sean tonight. Do something to put him out of the funk he's in." Lakota dimpled. "The guy's sweet on you, so don't blow it."

Lakota left a shocked Fiona holding the door.

Holding the power to take the next step if she really wanted more.

"I HATE TO SAY IT," Lakota said, a half hour later, "but Fiona's got issues."

She skidded onto Linc's thick comforter, reveling in the way her bare legs and feet sank into the downy softness.

Hopefully, by the time morning rolled around, the cover would be on the floor, the bedsheets tousled by some physical activity.

That is, if Linc was up to it.

He exited the bathroom, a towel cinched around his lean waist. Rivulets of water meandered down his firm chest, his rock abs. Lower, a hint of long beefcake pushed at the terry cloth, making Lakota press her thighs together, quelling the pump of warmth between them.

"She's always marched to her own beat." Unaware of Lakota's erotic state, Linc combed down his wet hair, standing in front of the closet to pick out clothing. "What do you want to eat? There's that café down the street."

Lakota rubbed her legs over each other, liking how it turned her on even more, her words thickening to syrup in her throat. "Let's dine in tonight."

He stopped fussing with his hair, then started again, ignoring the invitation. "They don't have room service."

"Linc. Can't you catch a clue? I want you to jump my bones."

The muscles in his back froze, then he tossed the comb onto a sea chest that doubled as a vanity table. They were in the Pirate Room, with its faux rope gilding, its cannon-and-doubloon decorations. Couldn't he get into the spirit and plunder her?

When he turned around, Lakota could see that his—how should she say it?—"cutlass of love" understood her needs. Now if only it could relay the message right on up to his oxygen-starved brain.

"I realize," he said, "that this is all very romantic. The shiver-me-timbers, the Errol Flynn movies…"

"…The damsel in distress." Lakota started unbuttoning her top. "Or no dress at all."

He covered his eyes with his hand, smiling, turning it into a joke. "I'm cutting myself off. No stimulus, no temptation."

Shoot. Hey, were guys as excited by audio cues as women were? Worth a try. She peered around the room for one of her historical novels. Preferably one with a high horny quotient.

D'oh. She'd left her books in her room. Shrugging, she finished taking off her top, leaving her in bra and shorts. Then she tossed the material away.

Phomp.

"Oh," she said. "That was the sound of a corset hitting the wooden planks."

"Kota…" He blindly waved a hand around, searching for something to talk about. "What were you saying about Fiona? You haven't asked about her since…well, a long time ago."

Lakota rolled her eyes. "I paid her a visit. She told me about your first kiss. Ugh."

"Exactly. Can I look now?"

She brightened, reaching for the clasps on her bra. "Sure."

"I can hear it in your voice. You're still half-naked on my bed. I'm going to have to send you out of here, if you're not good."

There, she'd gotten the bra off. Lace went flying through the air, joining her shirt on the floor.

He heard the plop. No doubt about it, because he flinched when it hit. But he still wouldn't look. She almost had to admire his willpower.

"Do you think Fiona and Sean…?" she asked.

Linc peeked through his fingers. Then his hand dropped to his side.

Lakota preened, cool air from the conditioning unit, along with his suddenly hungry gaze, hardening the tips of her breasts. She loved how he looked at her—as if he'd been on a crash diet and she was a plate of hearty fare.

She scooted back, lying against the pillows, spreading her hair in back of her and allowing her arms to linger overhead. "How long do you think before Sean breaks Fiona's tender heart?"

Linc's throat worked, his Adam's apple bobbing as he struggled to swallow. "It'll be the other way around, believe me."

What was this? She was laid out before him like a feast, and he was just standing there? Was he waiting for something? More encouragement?

She crooked her finger at him, the exclamation mark on her body language. "It's your professional opinion that the two of them aren't going to last?"

Whomp. There it was. His penis stirring under the towel, tapping out Morse code to Lincoln Central.

He couldn't last much longer.

Lakota traced one hand between her breasts—small, but definitely adequate—over her flat stomach, unfastening a button, fingers loitering by her zipper. It buzzed as she opened it, allowing the gape of her shorts to reveal her striped bikini undies.

"I'm right here," she said, dragging out the words.

Clearly torn, Linc rammed a hand through his combed blond hair, ruining the previous effort at taming it. He puckered his mouth, blew out a breath.

At least she was getting to him. "What can I do, Linc? Should I go to Fiona's Cowboy Room and borrow a lasso? Or do you want to go down there yourself? Huh?"

He didn't say anything, just watched her.

"Is that it?" she asked, sitting up, her blood starting to simmer, melting all rational thought. "Maybe you'd like to sleep with your friend instead. Maybe she lied to me and you did put the wood to her all those years ago."

"Don't be unreasonable." He sat on the edge of the mattress, his back to her. "Don't let one more nonexistent 'other woman' ruin this."

Memories pummeled her. Cringing in her childhood bed, allowing "Lara's Theme" from *Dr. Zhivago* to carry her away, to block out the thumping and moaning, as those "boyfriends" had their way with Mom in the family room. Slamming the door to a run-down L.A. apartment and winding up that music box after yet another audition in which an old-goat producer had tried to stick his hand down her top while promising to further her career. Throwing that music box at Lincoln when he'd stayed out too late one night for no logical reason, chasing him away with accusations of "another woman" as the twisted metal scattered over the floor.

Why had she been so afraid of giving herself to him fully? Was it because she knew he'd dump her as soon as he realized what a nobody she was?

On the bed, she shriveled into herself, drawing her knees to her naked chest, resting her chin on them. "I think I'm jealous of Fiona," she said softly.

"Why? There's nothing there." Linc turned around, placed a hand on her head, owning her.

That's right. This was the first step back into their rhythm. He'd claim her, body and soul. The thought made her claw for breath.

But right now, she leaned into his possessive touch, wanting it more than anything else. "She makes it seem so easy. Success. The whole *je ne sais quoi*. I want to be like her. To rule the world."

Linc laughed, petting her. "You're a human whirlwind yourself, you know."

The acknowledgment made her reach out for him, pulling him back to the pillows with her, just to see how much power she did have. "I suppose Sean will take that wind out of her mighty sails."

She could feel Linc's pulse beating through his skin, into her breast, into her own heart.

"You keep saying that," he said. "I'll bet he sinks first. And it'll be ugly, believe me. Fi takes no prisoners."

Lakota caressed his slanted cheekbone. He was so beautiful, with those deep blue eyes, the archer-bow lips. "You've got a bet, buddy. What does the winner get?"

He'd grown still, stiff. He was resisting her even now, with half his athletic body pressed into hers, his towel scratching her upper thighs, crinkling the piece of paper she had in her shorts pocket. "Winner gets a kiss."

Yeesh. "Is that it?"

He seemed crushed, didn't say anything for a moment. Then, "It's everything."

Her stomach pretzeled, going all goofy on her. His romantic streak was dangerous.

She shifted her hips, rubbing against his growing erection and nestling him right between her, where she could gain some amount of satisfaction. She was already slipping and sliding down there.

"I adore you," she whispered, her breath echoing warmth against his ear and back to her own mouth.

He laughed to himself. "I guess that's good enough. For now." Then he relaxed a bit, enveloping her in his arms, lowering his chest to hers.

Her nipples, sensitized to the point of delightful discomfort, combed along his chest. She loved that he had no hair there, was still wet from his shower and slick to the touch.

The sensation caused her to grind her hips upward, into his groin. At the same time, she licked the edges of his ear, huffing air against it. He'd always liked that.

And things hadn't changed. Linc growled, nipping at her jaw, her lips, sweeping her into a dizzying kiss.

As they sipped at each other, prolonging their first sensuous touch in months, Lakota dragged her fingers through his hair, lazily massaged his scalp and neck, moaned into his mouth.

The languid memory of their very first kiss washed through her body: one night on a pier, the salted air tanging his skin, the sweetness of being chosen by the big man on campus, of being accepted.

The surge of that moment revitalized her, causing her to wrap her legs around him and work off his towel with her knees and hands. In response, he soared forward, one hand raking up her spine, the other pressing the back of her head, until their mouths smashed together, devouring.

She came up for air, panting, every pore of skin spinning in circles. "Protection time."

He groaned, resting his mouth against her neck, breathing roughly against her ear.

She worked her hand into her shorts pocket, came out with a form their managers made them sign before having sex with anyone. Standard biz practice. It proved consent, barred anyone from crying foul in the future.

As she leaned toward the night table and a pen, she said, "Tell me you brought the other coverage."

"Do you need it?"

He was asking if she'd slept with anyone since him.

She'd already signed the consent form, so she rested the paper on her chest while he applied the pen to it.

"It'd be safer to use a rubber," she said.

He placed a tender kiss above her top lip. "I haven't been without one since we were together, Kota."

"Please, Linc?"

She held his head to her temple, shut her eyes, nudged even closer. So close she could have crawled into him, blanketed in his warmth.

He made a sound of jagged disappointment, drew away from her, went to his half-unpacked suitcase and withdrew the condom. Unwrapped it.

In the meantime, Lakota pocketed the form, stripped off her shorts and undies, eager to feel him again. "Hurry."

She'd missed true affection, being with someone who cared. And Linc did.

He rested one knee on the bed, fitting the rubber over himself, then crawled the rest of the way to her, framing her face with his hands.

"I'd do anything for you. Dammit, I love you so much."

She hesitated. "Me, too."

Then, fevered, she led him into her, hardly needing any more foreplay.

With his erection prodding her, skidding into her so easily—just as if he'd never left—she believed that she loved him. Had never stopped.

She rocked against him, clinging to his moisture-beaded skin. As he pulsed into her, her muscles embraced him in a welcome-back clench, and he groaned out her name.

Their pace quickened. He braced a hand against the headboard and, faintly, she could hear it pound against the wall with every push of his hips.

The music box of her mind wound up, playing out of control, the tinkling strains of an innocent song racing to catch up with his hammering thrusts.

Mirrors—so many of them—flashed behind her closed eyelids. They blinded her, revolving, spinning until she was lost, confused, grasping for something to hold on to and coming up with nothing but air.

She squeezed her eyes shut, concentrating, moving with him, then...

Open. The room whirred before her, coalescing into crushed-velvet colors, crashing down on her with the reality of Linc, still buffeting her, still seeking.

She helped him, drove him on, sketched her fingers to his corded stomach, his belly button. Linc's most lethal erogenous zone.

She whirled her thumb inside of it, pressing, demanding. "Kota..."

With one final strain, he came, quaking to a climax, crumbling to the bed. To her.

They breathed together, held each other for what seemed like hours. She took advantage of every moment, assuaging her neediness, erasing everything she thought was wrong with her by melding into him.

Finally, when their bodies settled into sticky-salty restfulness, Lakota entangled her limbs with his, creating complicated knots.

Never wanting to be untied.

Chapter Eleven

SEAN DIDN'T KNOW what was what anymore.

Last night's conversation with Lincoln had really thrown him for a loop, so much that he hadn't known what to talk about with Fiona on their endless drive to Julian. Hadn't known what to say to her today, either, so he'd avoided her altogether.

She'd been disappointed in the past.

Why was he feeling badly about that? It had nothing to do with him or their present liaison. In fact, if he had any sense at all, he'd be doing the typical Sean McIntyre escape routine and hightailing it back up to L.A., minus one disturbing woman.

Still, he found himself outside her room that night, a bag of oranges in hand, knocking on her door.

While waiting, he leaned closer to the wood, hearing a few "whoops" and the rumble of wagon-wheel thunder over hard-packed ground.

The Cowboy Room, huh? Sure as hell beat a Caveman Room. The Pirate one had more appeal, quite frankly. Who's idea had it been to...?

The TV chopped to a pause, and he heard her moving around, coming toward the door.

When she opened it, the sight of her dressed in a cute pair of pink shorts with a white top, her dark hair swept into a ponytail, crushed the oxygen from his lungs. A few loose tendrils framed her face, making her dark eyes liquid.

Something shifted in his chest, and he reached up to clutch at the strange tightness, catching himself, recovering.

"Speak of the devil," she said, frowning at the panicked expression that was probably on his face. "I was thinking of running by your room, seeing if you wanted… Are you okay?"

Sean brusquely pushed the bag at her, a decoy. "I bought too many things at the store. Thought you might want some."

Fiona's face lit up, and she took the bag, peeking into it. "Yes! Oranges. God love you. A snack is perfect because I had a big lunch with Linc's handler."

He'd seen Lakota's manager, Carmella Shears, at lunch today, himself, even though he'd been fantasizing about dining off Fiona instead.

They stood there for a moment, all the awkwardness of last night's drive, where she'd watched him with so many doubts in her gaze, coming back to the forefront.

"Well, then," he said, breaking the tension, "I'll leave you alone."

"Mac." She grasped his T-shirt, pulled him toward her. "We've still got a couple weeks left to whip me into an emotional mess."

Damned bet. How could she be so giddy and so aloof at the same time? It was almost as if she'd been encouraged in some way. God knew, last night, their humdrum drive hadn't scored any romantic points.

He remembered the way she'd looked at him that one morning, with her heart beating in her eyes as she stroked his face.

It was pretty close to the way she was watching him now.

Call the bet in, said one part of him.

No, said another. *Forget the bet. Run for your life. Give the both of you a way out. Save some pride. Do it before it's too late.*

"I've been thinking," he said, "that maybe this whole wager has gotten to be more than we bargained for."

Fiona's lips parted and, along with those pink-tinged, cuddly clothes, she seemed in need of comfort.

But she recovered, taking his arm, guiding him into her room, then shutting the door. "Maybe the hallway's not the place for this."

Right. Damned lapse in judgment. "Fiona, come on. Let's forget about it."

She shot him a flirty glance, the wounded girl gone. "What's going on here?"

"Nothing, it's just taking a lot of energy, and Martie is being a real pisser lately. In case you haven't heard, my job's on the line."

A slight shrug. "All of us feel that way."

"But you're still the new guy. You'll get the benefit of the doubt. Me…" He shrugged. "Martie hasn't been shy about letting me know that you could be my replacement."

"Well, isn't that a great excuse for wimping out?" Fiona swayed away from him, set the orange bag on the bed, keeping the mattress between them. "I have to tell you, I've been tempted to back away from the bet, too. Because of work, of course," she stopped, cleared her throat, "but I'm not going to let Louis run my life."

She picked up the television remote control, fiddled with it as she plopped onto the bed, pillows fluffed at her back. On the screen, images of black-and-white mayhem had come to a halt: Dust hovering in the air from a wagon chase. Horses galloping, manes streaming in stiff glory. A cowboy's hat caught flying off his head.

Fiona stared at the frozen moment of action, then at him, grinning. "I'm set on winning this thing."

Deep down, he'd known she'd shove the offer right back in his face. That's what he liked about Fiona, though—her moxie.

He only wished she'd show some disappointment.

Again, something twisted behind his rib cage. Too low for his conscience. Too high for his libido.

What the hell…?

If you win the bet, you win Fiona, too.

The thought reverberated, bouncing around his head. He'd never thought of it that way.

Run, boy, run.

But it didn't happen.

"So." Fiona patted the bed with her hand. "Take a load off."

Bed. Mattress. Fiona.

What was he going to do? Walk away?

Or take a chance, sit on that bed, see where the next day would lead them?

Don't do it, said the little-boy-lost part of him. *Remember Dad?*

That odd fist of…something…thudding behind the protection of his breastplate told him to take a step forward. *Do it, do it, do it…*

"Kick off those boots," said Fiona, acting as if she'd always known he'd stay. "We don't want those Jolly Green Giants dirtying my comforter."

He pulled off a sarcastic shrug, took off the boots, smiling to himself. No one got to him like she did.

When he was settled, she shut off the movie and flipped through the cable channels. They peeled a couple of oranges while watching one of those ubiquitous "inside" entertainment shows.

"Our work rewarded," she said, pointing a slice toward

the screen. She bit into it, and the scent of citrus sprayed the vicinity. "Umm. I sort of feel sorry for the general public."

He watched Fiona eat, enjoying the sight of her moist, sticky lips. "Why's that?"

She swallowed. "Because they have no idea how much of these programs are straight-out lies. It's all image fiddling. Sometimes, just being a part of it, I doubt *I'm* real."

"Sure you are. You're a puppet master. Nobody pulls your strings."

As she drew a knee closer to her, hugging it, Sean wondered if this was what real life felt like. Did normal couples relax in bed, talking about everyday, average things like mortgages and world news and the weather?

Talking about their days at the office?

He pretended they weren't who they were for a second. Him, in his white athletic socks, jeans and T-shirt. Her, in shorts and a ponytail.

Sean relaxed, rested his head on a pillow. Not bad.

Had his dad felt the same, once upon a time?

"Oh," she said, leaning closer, ponytail flopping against his shoulder, "there's Sissy Baker at the Midwest Celebration Awards."

Sissy was one of his new clients, a freckled country actress who'd gone through a painful divorce with Cubby Bryson, a Nashville singer.

"Look at her," said Fiona, sighing. "She brought her sister as a date. She's been doing that a lot lately. Cubby's a creep." She slid a knowing glance at him.

Professional pride took hold of Sean. He'd made certain that Sissy's sister, mother or brother escorted her to every major event, making her come off as the strong, pull-herself-up-by-the-boot-straps victim in the public's eye. It'd been working, too.

"I appreciate your vote of confidence." He ate a slice of orange, and it tasted better than any food he'd ever consumed.

"I wasn't kissing up to you, Mac. I meant it that first day when I said you were good."

He didn't dare glance at her. A woman who respected Sean McIntyre for something more than his skills in bed? Incredible. The realization branded him from the inside.

He was talking before he could stop himself. "You're a different breed, Fi. You know that?"

She drew away from him, her ever-present smile fooling him into thinking she was taking this lightly.

"That's what my daddy always told me," she said.

"What else did your daddy tell you?" His voice had lowered, too, enough so the scrape of an apple tree branch against the windowpane moaned through the room.

"He said I'd grow up to be anything I wanted to be." That filmy sheen of emotion misted her eyes. "Even now I make phone calls back to Iowa—yeah, Corncob, Iowa, if you can believe that—once a week. I talk to my brothers a lot, too. I was lucky to have them growing up. They tried to make up for my mom being gone. We all miss her, even today."

He could tell by the flight-ready angle of her body that they were treading on thin ice, here. Should they be talking about anything beyond superficial factoids? Bantery bonbons?

Sean rested his hands on his belly, showing her he wasn't going anywhere.

This was nuts, but he was doing it.

"I wish my mom never existed for my dad." There. He'd said it. Years and years of built-up bitterness and rage, and he'd been able to utter the sentence without screaming it.

Fiona snuggled onto her side, facing him, her hand on his forearm. Comforting. Real. A warm, firm grip telling him she wasn't going anywhere, either.

At least not right now.

But would she eventually run off into the night, leaving him before he could leave her?

Lincoln's words pounded into his skull. *She's had disappointments in the past.*

Or would Sean stay true to form and end up being the biggest disappointment of them all?

"She just left one day," he said, referring to his mom. "I think only my dad knows why, but he never talked about it. Not to anyone. He's disappeared to the point where you don't know he's in the room anymore."

"Do you think that's what's going to happen to you?" Her fingers plucked gently at his skin.

"No." A remnant of bitterness snapped at him. He chased it away. "I don't know."

There.

Was she going to open up, even a little? He'd feel a lot better about his own loose talk if she did.

"You're not so alone," she said.

He turned his head to catch the empathy on the curve of her plump lips, the inviting velvet-swirl of her gaze. Hesitating, Sean leaned over, hearing the hitch in her breath, then brushed his mouth against hers.

Tenderly, he worshipped the angel-tipped corners of her lips, tasted the sharp sweetness of oranges. He reached one hand out to cup her jaw.

A shower of molten peace swept through him, chasing away the doubts, the fears, blanketing him in a moment of quiet breathlessness.

Unconditional acceptance.

It was their first real kiss. No urgency, no sense of trying to find something lost and unavailable. Just the slow, fluid connection of sipping her into him.

She responded, fingers locked around one of his wrists, her other palm pressed against his chest, welcoming him and pushing him away at the same time.

He wanted her to be pulling at him, beckoning him into a place where she owned the part of his soul that he'd forfeited a few minutes ago.

But when he released her lips, rested his forehead against hers, she reached for his belt buckle.

He intercepted her. "No."

Confusion engulfed her gaze. "I..."

He didn't understand, either. At least not when they weren't kissing or eating orange slices in front of the TV.

She was back to the bet, and he didn't know if he could follow her there.

She got off the bed and crossed her arms in front of her chest. "Maybe you should..."

"...Go?" He got to his elbows.

"Don't you think?" She was back, the old Fiona, chin tilted upward, playful smile in place. "I mean, I didn't tell you, but I've made arrangements to ride back to L.A. tonight with Casey, Linc's handler. We've got some work to do."

"I see."

No he didn't. Had he made a mistake, coming here, pretending they could be normal people?

Wait. Was she shaking?

That's it. Big error. The worst. He had no business toying with her—with himself—like this. Sean McIntyre had his life wired. Why change it now?

He got to his feet, put his boots back on and headed for the door. "So I'll see you in the office Monday."

"You're staying?"

"Why not?"

"Oh. Sure. See you then."

"See you." Sean said.

And he was out the door before he could look over his shoulder at her. Back in his Caveman Room before he could think straight.

He couldn't stop remembering her lips on his, gentle, just as soft with longing as his had been.

That night, he drove home, too. First thing he did was go straight to the corner of his bedroom. To the souvenirs.

Bras. Lacy underwear. *Playboy* centerfolds.

A tube of red lipstick.

He took a garbage bag, tossing away the mementos one by one.

He threw all of them out.

Except for Fiona's mark.

THE BETTER PART of a week had passed, and Fiona hadn't heard from Mac.

Actually, she'd made sure of it. The Pilates fashion show had required most of her attention since it was set to roll this coming weekend. She'd be traveling to New Mexico with her actress client to oversee the event, thus getting her out of the office.

In the meantime, she'd worked on the details from an airplane and a hotel room miles away. Far from L.A., thank God, because an actor who'd had his racy memoir banned by a Bible-belt library had insisted on asserting his First Amendment rights. He'd taken her to Kentucky, where he'd strutted in front of the press with Fiona's guidance. They'd gotten great play in the papers and news.

Success!

Yes, that's what she'd concentrate on. Work, work, work—

—Mac.

That kiss.

The one that had sucked her soul right out of her body.

The feel of it was inescapable.

Now, here she sat on Lakota's twilight-bathed sundeck, having accepted Linc's invitation to enjoy cocktails with them. Fiona ran the rim of her wineglass over her lips, tracing her mouth, cooling the reminder of Mac's tender lip lock.

Tender. Maybe she'd misread the entire night. Mac wasn't that vulnerable. He couldn't have fallen into the trap they'd set for each other.

Really, she thought as she sipped her Riesling, the best thing to do was avoid him.

Avoid her ever-increasing emotions for him.

"You've been quiet since you got here," Linc said.

"Jet lag," she said. "But don't you look smirky."

Linc's goofy grin led to a blush. Right, a blush, from America's soap king, a man women cried over when he made personal appearances. A man who was still surprised that he could cause such hysteria.

"Things are going well," he said.

"With the soap?"

"With everything."

There he went, getting all discreet on her. This happened when he got hot and heavy. Linc didn't actually kiss and tell, didn't go into locker-room graphic detail, but he did talk about his feelings with Fiona. For some reason, he was the only person in the world who thought her qualified to give advice on the subject.

Fiona patted him on the hand. He was holding a half-full water bottle in lieu of alcohol. "I'm happy to see you this way."

"And I hate what's happening to you."

She sat up in her chair. "What do you mean?"

"E-ah." That was his I-shouldn't-have-opened-my-big-mouth sound.

"Spit it out."

"It's…I'm used to seeing you a certain way. Restless would describe it best, I suppose. But right now… What are the words for it?"

"I defy description."

"You'd like to think so. It's McIntyre, I think."

Fiona crossed one leg over the other, bobbed her foot in its sling back heel. "I've got it under control."

"That's what gets to me." A coastal breeze spiked up a tuft of Linc's blond hair. "Ted messed you up, and you've been dealing out revenge ever since."

Ouch. "Ted's history. But, you know, I should've paid a visit to him and Crissy while we were in Julian. His quaint ranch isn't too far away. I could've met their little baby, taken some horseback lessons from the one woman I considered a decent friend. And I was *so* prepared to ride the range, what, with having rested in my Cowboy Room at the B&B."

"I didn't think about that," he said. "Sorry, Fi."

"For what? For Fate's little ha-ha on me? I'm over it." Yes, she was.

Right?

He shot her a glance.

"I am." She drained the rest of her wine.

Lakota shuffled onto the sundeck. Arranging herself on Linc, she snuggled onto his lap and wrapped her arms around his shoulders.

Fiona wasn't sure what to say to her. Why invite guests when the girl had gotten bad news recently? Her audition for the prime-time pilot hadn't panned out. In fact, Linc had confided that the producers had pretty much played the great-another-soap-actress card and dismissed her before she'd gotten a chance to read any lines.

"Hey, Lakota," said Fiona, smiling at her. "How was work today?"

The younger woman sighed into Linc's neck. "Terrible. I didn't have any scenes with Linc."

He stroked his girlfriend's hair, keeping a firm hold on her with his other hand. "She ruled the world today, didn't you? One of her scenes should be used on her Emmy nomination reel."

Lakota raised a brow. "*Daytime* Emmys."

Linc gathered her closer, if that was possible. "Soaps aren't a bad thing." He gave an amiable chuckle. "*I'm* a soap actor."

"The best."

Fiona wished she could cling to someone on bad days, too, but she couldn't imagine being able to. "There'll be a million chances for you to get other shows. You're young."

"Not for much longer." Lakota shrugged at the sad truth, then got out of her chair and returned inside the house.

"Is she okay?" asked Fiona.

"Don't worry," he said, straightening in his chair. "She'll be back in two seconds to tell us her plan for global domination. Quick rebounder."

Fiona tapped her fingers on the chair. Sure enough, Lakota returned, a package in hand.

"I almost forgot," she said, handing it over to Fiona. She went back to Linc, nesting again.

Unable to witness the love-fest anymore, Fiona opened the box. Inside was a bottle of perfume. The design of it was chic, like the angles of a postmodern house. She took out the stopper and sniffed it.

"Mmm." The mysterious heaviness of jasmine with a tease of...what was it?...grapefruit?

She dabbed a drop on her wrist, replaced the stopper,

rubbed skin on skin to spread the scent. "Thank you," she said to the loving couple.

Lakota didn't change position. "It's from Sean."

Fiona froze. Suddenly, the smell overwhelmed her, enveloped her. Stifled her.

A phantom pressure tingled her lips, reminding her of his kiss.

Lakota added, "He went back to the perfumery and had this mixed especially for you."

"Well." Fiona didn't know what else to say. She was imprisoned in her chair, partly from embarrassment—because she just knew what Linc was thinking—partly from an instinctual urge to stay, to accept his gift as if he really did care for her.

Now the young actress was addressing Linc. "Told you Sean would win. You owe me a kiss."

Lincoln shook his head, adapted a couples-only tone of voice—just this side of baby talk. "He can't buy her off. Right, Fi?"

"What are you talking about?"

Linc laughed. "We've got a bet going."

An uninvited blush consumed her. She'd never told him about her wager with Mac. Why? In spite of her bravado, the bet didn't represent the proudest moment in her life, even though she'd convinced herself it was a dandy idea.

Now it was Lakota's turn to act amused. "We've noticed some fireworks between the two of you. And we're just wondering... How do I put this delicately, Linc?"

"There's no way."

Lakota focused on Fiona while resting against Linc's wide chest. "Which master would beat the other one."

Master.

Player.

That's all she was, right? Mac, too. How could she have forgotten? People didn't change because of one kiss. Life didn't work that way. It was too uncompromising, yanking away promises just when you thought you had them in hand.

Though Linc had asked about Mac before, Fiona hadn't known about any bet her friend had made with Lakota. The unexpected wager took Linc one step away from her and one step closer to his girlfriend.

"God, Kota." Linc laughed uncomfortably. "Fi's got a heart, you know."

Act like you don't care, she commanded herself. *It's never bothered you before.*

But she couldn't.

"Maybe I do," she said, voice near a whisper.

"At any rate," said Lakota, caressing Linc's ribs, "my money's still on Sean. I mean, look at that perfume. That's manipulation if I've ever seen it."

Her underdog instincts roused themselves. Jasmine and grapefruit filled her nostrils, yet she fought the takeover of her senses.

So Mac thought he had her where he wanted her? Thought he could kiss her senseless, control her in the end?

Maybe that's all last weekend's kiss had been. Like the vintage nightgown, it was another "gift" to sway her to the losing side.

Ted's voice came to her over the phone again: *Crissy and I are in Vegas. We got married, Fiona.*

Long ago, she'd told herself that she wouldn't be owned again. Beaten down by disappointment.

When she got back from her business trip this weekend, maybe Mac should get a taste of manipulation, too.

She'd mix pleasure and control as carefully as the ingredients of an expensive perfume, creating a dose of superior game playing.

She'd convince herself that he had no hold on her.

Chapter Twelve

THEY DIDN'T SEE each other for the next week and a half.

She was in Santa Fe, then San Francisco, then New York, tending to business.

He was in the office, manufacturing scandals and triumphs in L.A.

It wasn't until the eve of their bet's cutoff, a Saturday night, that they saw each other again. And, even then, it wasn't arranged.

Or so he thought.

Sean followed Lakota out of a rented limo that dropped them off in front of the foliage-encased Malibu mansion of a film producer. As the balmy air licked at his skin, the scent of jasmine reminded him of Fiona.

The perfume.

He'd received a breezy e-mail from her thanking him, and the message had left him isolated.

He wanted to see her again, kiss her. Hold her because, even now, she was running away.

The knowledge weighed heavily, the sort of pressure that had probably kept his father sitting by the window.

Lakota took his arm. "Boy, were we lucky to be invited. I just know tonight's going to change my life."

Loud rock music blasted from a hidden location beyond the mansion as he and Lakota walked to the door. The structure perched on a hilltop, overlooking the beach and acres of vineyard, with cottages dotting the climbing landscape.

"See," said Lakota, "by the time the sun comes up, I'm going to be on the wish list of every mover and shaker here." She gave her tight black dress one last sweep of the palm. "Do I look blockbuster?"

"Always." She'd brought Sean along to the party because she'd convinced him he could hook some more big fish clients here. Besides, he had connections, and Lakota could take advantage of that.

Linc had denied her pleas to come with them, and Sean couldn't blame the guy. These big Hollywood bashes were laced with drugs, alcohol, everything a person didn't need after a rehab stint. Linc had already arranged to meet his agent at El Cholo, the famous Mexican restaurant, anyway.

Not that it dampened Lakota's spirits. As she rang the doorbell, she seemed every inch the budding actress.

It was Sean's job to encourage this transformation into the big time, but it didn't stop his heart from breaking at the sight.

He didn't want to see this business devour Lakota.

"Thank goodness for Fiona," she said as a suited man opened the door. "It might kill me, but I'll have to give her a big old hug of appreciation."

They walked in and were summarily escorted through the fabulous, black-and-white schemed premises.

"Fiona?" asked Sean. "What does she have to do with this?"

Wide-eyed, Lakota ran her hand along the furniture and the antique mirrors. "She's the one who told me to bring you.

This house belongs to Johnny Calloway, the producer who's doing Terry Oatman's comeback movie."

Fiona really *had* been busy, obviously engineering Oatman's return to glory. Impressive.

The silent man led them out of the mansion, past the beach-inspired swimming pool, up a palm-shrouded path toward the music. Of course Johnny Calloway wouldn't tear up his lovely mansion. This was the party house. Sean noticed several other cottages peeking through the greenery.

And then they were inside, a Rolling Stones tune crashing out of a state-of-the-art surround sound system. There were men in suits smoking cigars and other questionable objects, women—starlets and probably hookers—in skimpy dresses giggling and hanging all over the males.

Lakota beamed, and Sean hoped she wasn't feeling at home. He didn't normally attend these things, but when his favorite client—he might as well admit it—had asked, he'd given in.

They wouldn't stay long anyway.

But he did recognize people he'd worked with in the past: powerful corporation owners, directors, celebrities. Wouldn't hurt to network and introduce Lakota to them.

He escorted her around the room for about an hour, all the while wondering if Fiona would show, finding it hard to keep his mind on business.

When he did see her, the room became a much more interesting place.

Decked out in a red dress, its sheer panels floating behind her like the fire of a flamenco dance, Fiona wore her hair down. It fell past her shoulders, a shimmer of waterfall softness. As always, her lips were painted with red.

His red.

Lakota was engaged in an intense conversation with an independent moviemaker, one of those cutting-edge kids who'd applied for about twenty credit cards to finance his first movie.

Lakota saw where his eyes were glued and nudged him. "Go get her," she said over the music.

His first instinct was to act like Fiona didn't matter, but he was beyond that now. Beyond pretending.

He winked at Lakota, making a mental note to keep an eye on her, even though she'd taken command of every introduction he'd initiated. Then, heart in his throat, Sean inserted himself in the circle of men Fiona had gathered just by entering the room.

Even though she had a smile for every guy there, she lingered on him, lowering her chin, watching him with more seductive promise.

"Mac? You know everyone here?"

He didn't give a shit. Instead of answering, he jerked his chin to a deserted corner, hoping she'd follow.

Fiona took her time doing it, too, finally extricating herself from the gossip and accompanying Sean to his chosen location.

"You arranged this," he said, grabbing two glasses of champagne as a waiter passed.

She accepted one. "Thought you could use some help in the office. In Julian, you sounded rather concerned about your place on the nine-to-five totem pole."

Is that all she'd gotten out of their stay in Julian? His concern about work?

What about that kiss?

"Thanks for the professional courtesy," he said, stepping closer, catching the scent of jasmine mingling with the summer humidity. "You're wearing the perfume."

"Why shouldn't I?"

"I don't know. After that memo you sent me…"

"Oh." She laughed, dark eyes gleaming. "I wasn't in the office to thank you."

"So that's why it came off the way it did. Like you have no idea what this has turned into."

Fiona innocently considered him. "Isn't that how it is with us? No tangled emotions to make sex messy?"

The reminder sat like lead in his belly. "You know better by now."

"So, the gift wasn't just another chess move in our competition?" Fiona tweaked his lapel, still teasing him. "You've got no ulterior motives?"

He swallowed, reached out to touch her face. "None."

Her jauntiness disappeared, and she pulled back, lips parted slightly. "Because I feel somewhat claimed."

Rage and panic crashed together in his chest, exploding. His hand dropped to his side. "Stop this, Fi. Stop pretending you haven't felt anything."

"I told you. I'm not that type of girl."

Was there a note of sadness in her tone?

She glanced toward the party, swishing the champagne around in her glass, smiling at the crowd. "I never will be that kind of girl."

A vein in her throat fluttered, and he knew she was lying.

"Tell me you don't want me," he said.

"Sure, I want you. That's been very clear from day one." She sipped, paused. "If you're looking for someone to share in the fantasy you've developed about that SUV you said you'd never want, search out of town."

"Somewhere like Corncob, Iowa?"

That got her. "I'll never be her again."

"Why?"

She hefted out a breath, seemingly exasperated. "Sex is all
I do. Remember? I have one full day to go until I win our
bet, and I can prove I'm not possessive. Or territorial."

"Your eyes have told me something else. Ever since that
first night."

"Can you be sure?"

Silence filled his lungs. No, he couldn't.

Fiona shook her head, giving him a pitying look. Then she
grabbed his hand, tugging him away, out of the party. He
glanced toward Lakota, who was touching her throat and
laughing with yet another guy. Conrad Dohenny, the box-
office hunk of the moment.

She'd do fine.

He followed Fiona as she took him uphill, to another cottage. One with dim lights shining in the window.

"What do you have planned?" he asked, suddenly wary.

"You say that as if you're ready to give up the bet."

Damned wager. He was sorry they'd ever started it.

"Fiona." As she unlocked the door, he held her back, trying to draw her into his arms, to stop this before she ruined
every idiot hope he'd discovered within himself.

"We don't need to do this," he said, searching her face for
any sign of vulnerability.

But there wasn't much light around, and the darkness allowed her to hide.

"Wait here." She slipped inside, came out a moment later.

Silk flitted over his hand, and he retracted it.

His pulse started kicking.

Fiona placed her finger on his lips, quieting any response.
Then she slid the blindfold over his eyes, taking away the
benefit of his sight.

He could only smell her. Hear her.

Touch her.

"Come on," she said, the pull of her voice luring him.

Right into the cottage.

WHAT SHE WAS DOING would cost dearly. But he was getting to her. Taking her over.

Stop pretending you haven't felt anything, he'd said.

Oh, but she had, and it scared her to the point of desperation. She couldn't deal with feelings, with being torn apart by betrayal again.

When Ted had dumped her, she'd told herself, told everyone, that it was no big deal. But once, three months after he and Crissy had gotten married, she'd seen them at a restaurant, and her appetite had disappeared for days.

She'd literally felt broken, her limbs heavy and ready to fall off. Felt like her ribs were cracking under the weight of her mortification.

What was so wrong with her that Ted had married someone else?

And why had he fallen in love with Crissy, who'd somehow wormed her way into Fiona's good graces for a short time?

See, that's why Fiona didn't make girlfriends. Even with females, it all boiled down to a battle—who would win, who would lose.

Most relationships were like that, unless you could find someone exceptional like Linc, who was so nonthreatening and sweet it didn't factor into the equation.

But Mac posed a different problem. Theirs was a contest of wills. Of who could contain the heat and come out on top.

So he'd called her on a tender moment. That didn't mean she wanted him body *and* soul. Did it?

She guided Mac into the cottage, his blindfold allowing her to soften, to stop hiding. As she watched the candlelight swallow him, she melted, losing her proper shape.

His tall body cast a shadow over her, and the trembling started again, deep in her gut, stealing her sense of self.

She let go of him and closed the door, led him to sit in a wide velvet chair. Then she adjusted the blindfold, making certain it was secure. Warped silhouettes danced on the walls from the flames, illuminating the matching ottoman, the canopied bed.

The woman she'd paid to prove her point to Mac.

She was wearing a dress like Fiona's, a garment with much more material than her usual job required. Fiona had met her in a strip bar when one of her "dates" had taken her there, intending to turn her on, she supposed. Oddly enough, she and Brigette—the woman's stage name—had hit it off, had experienced a grand old time with Fiona buying her date lap dance after lap dance from her new acquaintance.

Over time, Fiona had brought more men to the bar, fascinated by how they could lose all strength at the sight of a topless woman.

Feeling sorry for them, too.

So when she found out Terry Oatman's producer was throwing a party, Fiona had invited Brigette, knowing that these crazy get-togethers included all kinds.

Brigette was here to make sure Mac would learn, once and for all, that Fiona wasn't getting emotionally involved.

It needed to be done.

Fiona gestured Brigette forward. The blonde knew to keep her silence. She was wearing Fiona's perfume, as well, just to prove the point.

"You sit right there, Mac," Fiona said, her tone as lazy as a candle's dance. She stroked his temple, allowing herself the freedom of feeling, just this once, while he was blinded. Her head tilted, and she bathed him with a gaze that took in his rumpled hair, strong chin, arms that had held her that night on a bed of pure kisses.

"Is this what you really want?" he asked.

The question tore at her conscience, shredded all the lessons she'd learned up until this moment.

No feeling. No pain.

She moved forward, blocking out the slight injury of his words. "Evidently," she said, scratching her fingertips lightly against his emerging arousal, "this is what you want. And that's what's important."

Before he could answer, she placed her hand over his mouth, her middle finger sinking between his lips, lost in a wet kiss.

Why did he have to be so…so Mac? Regretfully, she took back her hand, nabbed the velvet ties sitting on a nearby table.

"Remember," she said, "it's just sex." With care, she trussed up his hands, running her fingers over his knuckles once she'd secured him.

"I want you to tell me that afterward, Fi." He smiled, almost knocking Fiona over with the power of it. One glance at Brigette told her that Fiona wasn't the only victim. The woman fanned herself like Scarlett O'Hara on a sweltering southern day, then rolled her eyes.

"You know the part where I'm supposed to look in your eyes and find nothing?" He let out a low, gravelly laugh. "You'll see."

But he wouldn't. Not with the blindfold.

Fiona moved away, beckoning Brigette toward him, going to the stereo in order to turn on some lazy music that would drown out the throb of the bigger party downhill.

"Regrets," by the Eurythmics. The tune slithered into the speakers, the pulsating synthesizers contrasting with the chugging beat and the buttery smoothness of Annie Lennox's vocals.

Quietly, so she wouldn't give away her location across the

small room, Fiona spread her hands over her face, blew out the trembling breath she'd been holding.

Brigette gave her a shall-I-go-for-it? glance, and Fiona eked out a nod, muscles fighting the approval.

The stripper started by gyrating to the electronic drums, getting into the groove of her job. Then, she bent to her knees, slid her hands over Mac's lower thighs.

Oh, no. Fiona's eyes automatically shut, but she forced them open again. This wasn't supposed to be bothering her.

Mac had unclasped his hands, spreading them out in front of his chest. His nostrils flared, and Fiona knew he was relying on his remaining senses to connect with her.

Did Brigette's skin react with the perfume the way Fiona's did? Did he want the dancer as much as he said he wanted Fiona?

As the woman sketched her chest up his shins, parting his legs, Mac leaned back his head.

His reaction knifed at her, screwing, bladelike, into her belly.

But his jaw was shut tightly, his fingers still spread as if warding off the sexual advance. Her pulse gave a tiny jump, a spark escaping from a fire.

"I want to see you," he ground out.

Brigette backed off for a minute, seeking Fiona's tacit advice. It was a moment of sweet relief.

Fiona took a step forward without thinking, stopped herself. Was this Mac's way of manipulating the bet again? If she showed weakness here, revealing herself, she'd lose. Everything.

She couldn't give in. Not after she'd promised to never hurt again. Not after the way she'd suffered before.

Fighting the urge to give up, Fiona motioned for Brigette to continue.

The dancer paused, glancing at Fiona with concern. She was losing it, wasn't she?

Go, Fiona motioned, and with one last gaze, Brigette turned around and coasted over Mac's lap, rubbing her workout-tight butt over his thighs, pressing into him, back, nearer his groin.

Fiona paced toward them, fidgeting with her hands. Brigette winked at her; she'd been instructed on how far to go. They weren't friends, but the woman was a professional, knowing her tip would be higher if she obeyed instructions.

As Brigette gyrated, Mac strained, cursed, rested his forehead and hands against the dancer's spine. And Fiona knew the exact moment he realized the body wasn't hers.

He straightened, and his mouth went as tight as barbed wire. "Go, Fiona," he said, strangled.

His anger almost brought her to her knees, slumped with relief. Thank God the dance was over.

He didn't want the other woman, did he?

So when was the buzz of power and victory going to screech through her? Shouldn't it have happened by now?

It only took her three strides to cross the room. Gathering herself, Fiona daintily helped Brigette off Mac's lap. The other woman stood to the side, waiting.

"Territorial?" Fiona asked with a hint of trembling flirtatiousness, untying his wrists.

She coaxed the blindfold from his gaze, tried to smile at him. "Possessive?"

His pupils contracted, adjusting to the dim light, closing in on themselves until she thought he'd leave her altogether.

He sat rigidly, almost threatening in his growing rage. "What's this about?"

"Isn't it obvious?"

Fiona stood next to Brigette. The blonde rested a hand on

Fiona's shoulder, then ran the inside of her calf over the outside of Mac's leg.

She'd wanted to see how he'd react to the invitation, no matter how remote the possibility of it happening.

Red began to creep up Mac's throat, his face. The color marked him.

Fiona lifted an eyebrow, fighting for composure. *He didn't want the other woman.*

Adrenaline, cold and insistent, built in her. *Run.*

Mac shook his head, glared at the carpet. Then, to Brigette, he said, "Will you excuse us?"

"You sure?" she asked, doing her job very thoroughly.

With subtle precision, Fiona lightly pushed Brigette toward the door.

"All right, all right," the woman said. "Tough crowd."

Fiona wouldn't look at him. Wouldn't sink into the disappointment in his eyes.

She was *this* close to winning. Wasn't that what she wanted?

Fiona went to where her purse lay in the corner, and she paid Brigette, who efficiently left them alone as Fiona turned off the stereo.

Keeping her back to Mac, she glued herself together. Returning to her old flippant self.

When she turned around, Mac was on his feet. If she'd expected that gunslinger stance, she was in for a rude awakening. In lieu of an intimidating glare, he wore disappointment.

It was worse than taking a bullet.

"You're a piece of work," he said, voice dry. "You really aren't going to change."

For years she'd trained herself to survive. To avoid caring. And, see, she'd let him down. But better to have the inevitable goodbye now rather than later, when it would hurt even more.

"I never promised more than a good time," she said. "I don't turn into a quivering puddle of emotion just because of a bottle of perfume."

"Or a kiss," he said.

The music from the big party knocked around the room, and a sob worked its way through her chest, decimating everything in its path. Still, Fiona held on, controlling the damage. After all, that's what someone in her line of work did best.

Finally, he spoke, his words as heavy as rocks being pushed up a mountain.

"I'm sorry for you, Fi. I'm sorry for the both of us."

He watched her, the area around his eyes bruised, even though the rest of his tough skin didn't show it.

Then he walked out the door. She started to go after him, but couldn't manage more than a step.

"Sean?" she said, voice caught in her throat.

But he was gone.

Hadn't she known all along that, in the end, he'd walk away from her?

Because she always managed to make sure of it.

Chapter Thirteen

WHEN LINCOLN PHONED Lakota, telling her he had great news, he didn't expect to find her celebrating with the summer's biggest action star at The Cool Cat Lounge.

He didn't expect to find Conrad Dohenny's arm around her while they leaned against the glowing blue bar in the midnight-dark room. Didn't expect the flare of crimson jealousy that shrouded his gaze as he watched them: Conrad with his grunge-glamour, shoulder-length brown hair, his lanky frame pressing nearer and nearer to Lincoln's girlfriend.

Knocked for a loop, he could only stand among the throng of pretty people and watch, stunned.

He wanted to wring the guy's neck, no matter where Dohenny ranked on the Young Hollywood power lists.

Linc took out his cell phone, dialed Lakota's number. Obviously a little tipsy, she glanced around, tossed up her hands in goofy realization, then accessed the call.

"H'lo," she yelled over the lounge noise.

A cigarette girl swayed by him in time to the Rat Pack-era music, winking. Even though she was your basic L.A. beauty, her gesture didn't affect Linc. "Kota, what're you up to?"

Laughter. Linc could see Dohenny trying to get the phone away from her.

His confidence slipped. He'd trusted her, not only day to day when they did their scenes together, but with his heart. Had he been wrong to do that?

She used her arm to keep Dohenny at a distance, and Linc's spirits lifted.

"I told ya," she said, slurring slightly, "I lef' the party with some new friends and came to The Cool Cat. Where're you? 'S noisy."

She glanced around, as if he might be there, but Linc didn't bother to hide. No matter. She didn't spot him since she was now focused on Dohenny playing with her hair.

Don't fly off the handle, he thought, all his rehab training rushing back to calm him. *Center yourself.*

"I'm coming to take you home," he said, then flipped the phone closed with more force than was necessary.

She stared at her cell phone for a moment, then tucked it away into the little black purse that matched her little black dress.

How could you have a relationship with someone if you had to keep an eye on them all the time? She said she loved him, and he believed her. But what should he be thinking now?

Out of the corner of his gaze, he saw a guy wearing a rumpled button-down shirt, jeans and an assassin's focused intensity inching toward the bar.

Linc bristled. Smelled like paparazzi. Worse than the stench of booze, a bane which made him sick enough to dull the craving.

He was headed toward Dohenny, a favorite tabloid magnet because of his "bad boy" image. And now the movie star was whispering in Lakota's ear. She was listening, leaning against him, the worse for wear after a drink or two. Linc knew how Lakota got when she'd had too much alcohol.

Careless. Just as he used to get.

When Dohenny bent to bite at Lakota's neck, Linc shook his head, managed his temper. Okay. That was it. He hadn't wanted to embarrass his girlfriend, hadn't wanted her to know he'd been spying like the world's biggest loser from across the room. But what choice did he have now?

He made his way toward them, but not before Lakota pushed at Dohenny. He didn't take the hint, cupping her head in his hands, darting his tongue in her mouth.

Jeez. Why'd he have to go and do that?

A flash went off and, at first, Linc thought it was his impulsive fist whipping out to smack Dohenny. But that wasn't it. Both Dohenny and Lakota were glancing toward the photographer and the mini-camera he was holding.

There was a shouted curse, a general stir among the hip, young crowd. Varying levels of celebrities shifted, avoiding the scandal or running to it, as one of the men in the star's entourage grabbed the assailant by the collar.

"How the hell did you get in here?"

The photographer swatted at the bodyguard. "You have no right to touch me like this!"

The beefy men took the skirmish outside, securing the camera in the process. And that's when Linc stepped in.

Dohenny had resumed his pawing of Lakota and, as she swatted his busy hands away, she glanced up. Saw him.

"Lincoln!" She swayed, smiled brightly, genuinely excited to see him. "Conrad, this is my boyfriend I was talkin' about."

The star seemed unconcerned, his long-lashed blue eyes unfocused. "Oh."

"Linc, Conrad's gonna get me a part in his next movie. Sweet, huh?"

Usually, Linc didn't make a big deal out of his height or build, but he used both to full advantage as he hovered over the smaller star. "I'm sure he will, Kota."

Dohenny looked away from Linc. The jerk had been lying to her. He'd probably been expecting to notch another mark in his bedpost tonight.

Without blowing his top, Linc gently took Lakota's elbow. "Let's go now."

He led her away, but Lakota hesitated. "This is a professional," she mangled the word slightly, "opportunity!"

"He's not serious." Linc persuaded her to follow him again, getting as far as the lit candles fluttering inside the blue glass cups near the lounge's entrance. Security cameras and bouncers lingered nearby, as well, keeping the club exclusive. Heck, Linc wouldn't have even gotten in if he didn't know the bouncer.

She skidded to a stop, glassed-in flames playing with the red highlights in her hair. "I was working my connections, ya know."

"You can make it without sleeping around."

Her speech slowed, sobered. "How do you know?" Those pale eyes grew huge, the sheen of tears covering them.

"Because I've still got a little faith in you." He held her face in his hands, unable to stop a smile from stretching across his mouth. "Even a schlep like me can make it on something resembling talent."

She glanced sidelong at him, grabbing onto his arms for balance.

He couldn't hold his news inside anymore. "My agent told me that Roger Reiking's daughter is a big fan of mine. She showed him *Flamingo Beach,* and he requested that I audition for a role in a romantic comedy he's putting together. A featured role."

Lakota just stared at him, as if assimilating the words. Wasn't she happy about this?

"He's probably only making his daughter happy," he said,

miffed by her reaction. "What's wrong? It's *the* Roger Rei-king. You know, Oscar-winning director?"

She blinked. "I'm happy for you." Then she laughed, combed her fingers through her already disheveled hair, hugged him. "It's just so surprising, is all. I'm ecstatic for you."

He remembered her failed audition for the TV show, re-membered how much she wanted stardom and he just wanted to be lucky enough to earn a living acting—in any capacity. "I'm sorry."

"Don't you apologize." She disengaged from him, wiped away a tear, made a dorky sad/happy face. "Look, I'm so joy-ful, I'm crying for you."

God. He could feel it already—the tension, the inferiority of her staying in the soaps while he took bigger chances.

"I won't leave you. I'm probably not even going to get it, so…"

"You won't leave me behind?" For a second, hope bright-ened her smile, but then it crumbled. "You're meant for big things. I'm not." She started tearing up in earnest. "I'm gonna hold you back."

"You won't. Aw, come on, stop crying." He smoothed her hair.

"The thing is," she said, backing away from him, "I'm en-vious of you. Truly. I don't know if I can stand it."

Would she have been able to say that to him all those months ago? Or, instead, would one of them have sabotaged the relationship, avoiding the real issue?

Competition.

"We'll work this out," said Linc, reaching out a hand for her to take it.

She looked longingly at his outstretched fingers. Linc felt his throat close up.

By this time, Conrad Dohenny had gotten tired of the bar

and weaseled up behind Lakota. He set his hands on her shoulders, and Linc's chin lifted in response.

"There you are," said the box-office champ.

Lakota didn't move, just watched Linc as if he was going to drop her high and dry.

"Man," he said to Conrad, smiling amicably, "you really don't get the hint."

"Who are you anyway?" asked the movie star, puffing his chest. "You're nothing. So shut the hell up."

Dohenny pulled at Lakota's dress, stretching it.

"Hey," she said, drunken slur returning with a vengeance. "This is a DKNY original. Do ya mind?"

"Do you?" The star raised his eyebrows, and the candles spotlighted just how bloodshot his gaze was.

Booze. Jeez. "Listen," said Linc, "she told you to leave her alone."

Conrad stepped around Lakota, and she stumbled backward against a wall. A candle chinked against the wall, the flame wavering.

The star's entourage had gathered in back of him, as if Linc was going to start something and they'd end it.

"Hey." Linc held up his hands, palms out. "Let's just call it a night."

The bantam rooster pushed Linc, barely nudging him.

Great. Why did everyone assume that, just because he had muscles, he was eager to fight?

Linc held his ground. "Now, that's not necessary."

Conrad turned to his cronies, laughing. Then, without warning, he lowered his head and rammed into Linc's chest, throwing the bigger man into the wall.

Glass crashed, and Lakota screamed.

It didn't take long for Linc to make Conrad back off. All he had to do was get him in an armlock, then push him toward the entourage, but they swelled over Linc, jamming him against the wall again.

He didn't even see the fire as it slurped along the curtain.

Minutes later, the bouncers broke up the fight and helped Linc put out the flames by spraying the area with extinguishers, but not before the entryway had been damaged. And certainly not before the skirmish had been caught on the security camera.

As Linc and Lakota stood by, Dohenny's handlers calmed the star down. Too bad the soap actors hadn't traveled with their own personal assistants or handlers tonight. They could've used the company, also.

But Linc did the next best thing. He got out his cell phone and dialed the number of the one person he trusted most in life.

She answered on the second ring.

"Fi," he said. "I think I'm in trouble again."

FOR SEAN, Lakota's own dead-of-night call hadn't bothered him. He'd been sitting in his TV room, staring at screen static for the past... Hell, he hadn't known how long it'd been since the station had gone off the air.

All he'd known was that he couldn't move from his chair. Not after tonight, when Fiona had made it painfully clear that there would never be more than physical intimacy between them.

But he'd been a fool to hope otherwise. She was right. She'd never promised him anything, so why had he expected it?

Because of what was in her eyes.

It seemed so simple, didn't it?

Now, hours later as the sun rose through the window of his office, Sean tried to get his mind back on work yet again, because this was urgent. No time for messing around, agonizing over something he couldn't have.

He needed his job to save him. It had always provided an identity when everything else faded or crashed down around him. It had always been there for him, even during the downhill ride of the past few years.

Only now, when he had nothing else, did he realize how much his profession should've meant to him.

His assistant, Carly, rushed into the office, her hair in a still-wet-from-the-shower ponytail. He'd gotten the poor girl out of bed, enlisting her help in the mess Lakota had helped to create.

"I've got them," she said, holding up a manila envelope like it was the Olympic torch.

"You miracle worker," said Sean, in full business mode. Here it went: the pressure, the image voodoo.

"I have to tell you," said the girl, handing over the materials, "your phone calls to the right people helped. I only hope copies weren't made."

Sean opened the envelope, slipped out the contents. One videotape. One packet of negatives and pictures, recently developed at an all-night photo shop. Dohenny's people had sold them for a hefty price, claiming that one more kiss with a pretty girl wouldn't do the actor any harm or any good, either way.

"You can bet someone has insurance with the video," he said. "I talked to The Cool Cat Lounge, as well as Conrad Dohenny's publicist. They're all happy to keep this under wraps, especially since our big box-office star looks like an asshole on the tape."

"But he's so cute," said Carly.

He held up a warning finger. "Don't ever date anyone in the biz."

When she grinned, Sean knew his advice was useless. He sifted through the pictures, coming upon the one where Conrad was sticking his tongue down Lakota's throat. This could come in handy.

"Thanks, Carly," he said. "I owe you big time."

The assistant nodded and left the office.

Sean flapped the picture against the desk. Had Fiona managed to get a hold of anything? How was she doing on her end?

Hell, why worry. She didn't want anything to do with him, so why should he be concerned about helping her out?

The picture caught his attention again. Lakota looked like she wasn't fighting Dohenny, even though she'd said she hadn't meant for things to go this far. Connecting her with a superstar would do wonders for her career. She could ride the story's coattails to something bigger.

If he could manage to spin the story into something more than it was, he could build her up.

Sure, Linc would look like a cuckold, and that would put the clamps on Fiona to spin it the other way. Bottom line: this picture could hurt them both.

So should he use it for Lakota's advantage?

He paused only for a second, then picked up the phone.

MAC HAD ASKED her to meet him in the office's conference room, but that hadn't stopped Louis Martin from butting in on them.

She'd managed to get a copy of the tape—an inferior one, she thought, watching the original that Mac had procured—but that was all she'd secured.

However, it was all she needed, unless more copies of the tape existed.

The three of them watched the events unfold on a television screen. Fiona struggled to keep her mind on the analysis, having been successful at treating Mac as a business associate so far.

Personal concerns had no place right now.

Last night's Cool Cat fiasco played out before them: Linc and Lakota's melancholy exchange, Dohenny's attack, the fire.

By the time the show ended, their boss had already jumped out of his chair. "This is the best thing that could've happened."

Fiona thought about Linc's woeful phone call, his crushed heart. Lakota's ambition and jealousy. "How does a fire translate into 'good'?"

Louis rubbed his hands together, eyes focused on the ceiling. "Don't be so softhearted, Cruz. Mr. Dohenny's going to pay for the fire damage. It was smart of you to suggest assault charges as leverage since the tape clearly shows who's at fault."

Fiona clutched the arms of her chair. "This tape makes Linc look like a bar brawler."

She caught Mac stroking his stubble at the other end of the table, and her skin heated.

Louis gestured toward the TV. "This is your chance to give Lincoln Castle a personality. You can get a lot of mileage out of an alpha-male type. Women swoon for that stuff."

The boss turned to Mac, seeking agreement, but without even looking, Fiona knew Mac wouldn't acknowledge Louis.

"Anyway," he continued, "you guys can really play it up. If the tape just happens to get leaked to the press, you can spin it as Lincoln Castle defending his lady love from a rapacious brat *and* a fire. Lakota will bask in a lot of press, too, if you get it right. This is a publicist's paradise."

Memories assaulted her: Her last job, a golden opportunity, a massive blowout resulting in her shame.

Nothing was foolproof.

Louis shuffled toward the door. "We'll see your true colors, my worker bees."

Mac's chair moaned as he leaned back his head, apparently trying his best to ignore Louis. The slight worked, because their boss's face flamed.

"Don't assume that arrogance, McIntyre. Straight up, your job is on the line. In fact," he darted a glance at Fiona, "let's just say there's going to be a few less jobs at the end of the month. Layoffs, unfortunately. And there'll probably be room for only one of you."

Fiona shot up in her chair, driven by fear. "Is that some kind of threat?"

"It's reality." Louis opened the door. "I'd say 'May the best man win,' but Cruz hasn't proven that she's got any balls yet. And that's a disappointment."

On that note, he left. Left Fiona feeling sapped, mortified. Before getting fired from her last job, no one would've talked to her with such derision. Back then, she'd been flying high, only to crash and burn in the next minute. Without warning.

She chanced a look at Mac. He was staring at the table, jaw gritted so tightly she thought his head would smash into pieces. But it seemed as if something had imploded inside him already.

"If you're anything like me," he said, tone riding a blade of anger, "you're ready to shove this table down Martie's throat."

Could they talk to each other without all their personal anguish coming to the surface? Could they keep their love lives out of the office, as promised?

"I'd like nothing better than to feed him some desk." Fiona watched him, almost wishing he'd make eye contact, even if she didn't deserve it. "He's been Big Brothering me since day one."

"Why does it matter?" asked Mac, finally looking up. "What happened at your last firm?"

As soon as their gazes locked, Fiona was a goner, lost in his eyes, the wounded loneliness, the wary caution.

Maybe, just this once, she could offer a part of herself to him. If it was a consolation prize, then so be it, but at least it was something she could give him without losing her entire sense of self.

"I dropped the ball," she said, smiling to ease the burden.

"You?"

"Yeah." She swallowed, coating her scratchy throat. "Me. I represented Candy-O."

"Wow. Big-time punk actress," said Mac, duly impressed. His admiration fortified her, even temporarily.

"Even after what I did, yes, she is. I thought I'd reached the heights of my career by getting Zap Soda to sign her for a series of commercials."

This was sounding more familiar to Sean. As he recalled, Zap Soda and Candy-O had suffered some kind of hush-hush falling-out. "Let me guess. Things blew up in your face."

"Did they ever. It was revealed that Zap's factories were dumping toxic materials into bays, that they were responsible for a lot of wildlife disasters."

"And Candy-O, being the big environmentalist..."

"...freaked out. How could I have made such a misjudgment?" she said. "I'd almost ruined her career by aligning her with evil."

"She's not a forgiving woman, I hear. The toughest businesswoman out there."

"It's the truth."

Sean hadn't thought it possible, but Fiona had drawn into

herself, fading into the cushions of her chair, losing her zest. His father, all over again. If he could have, he would've gone to her, offered her the comfort of his arms.

But he knew how that would turn out. "You could've spun her out of the situation."

"That's what I said. But, instead, she decided to take the error personally, to drum me out of my job." She smiled, probably to cover the embarrassment. "Luckily she kept the debacle under public wraps, so she does have some pity in her soul."

Did she feel the same way about her career as he used to? Did a part of her die every time failure reared its head?

If he knew Fiona, the answer was yes.

Without preamble, she stood, came toward him. Sean's heartbeat went into overdrive as she came closer, then sat in the next seat. He could smell her fresh hair, her skin.

Remnants of his perfume.

"We can't work as a team from across the room like that."

The revelation of her failure had worn her down, replacing his vibrant Fiona with a crinkled copy. It didn't sit well with Sean. He ached to build her up again.

But she wouldn't accept his affection. And he couldn't accept seeing her so sad.

He reached into the envelope, slid the picture of Lakota and Conrad Dohenny down the table in front of her.

"The reason for the Cool Cat scuffle," he said.

She took a good gander at it. "Oh, poor Linc. Does Lakota know you have this?"

"No. It could do wonderful things for her career."

"That's right." Fiona caught his gaze, eyes dark, deep with emotion. "And it would kill Linc to have this plastered all over the papers."

He couldn't do this anymore. Playing with people's lives.

Taking orders from a power-monger like Louis. Sitting this close to Fiona and not being able to do anything about it.

She was still wearing her corporate demeanor, but as he watched her, she changed. Softened under his gaze. Her eyes begged for him to stay in this meaningless, empty groove where they could talk around the core matter.

"I can't sit here pretending like I'm not chipping away every time you look at me, Fiona," he whispered.

"Please, don't." Her voice weakened, pleaded.

He leaned his elbows on the table, trying to get her to glance his way, just one more time. "Why are you so damned stubborn? This could be easy, if you'd…"

His words trailed off as a sheet of hair fell forward, covering her face.

"I don't want to deal with this." She laid a finger on Lakota's picture, indicating heartache. Deception.

"Or this," she added.

She pointed to her heart.

He sucked in a breath, tucked her hair behind an ear. A tear slipped down her face and, with a resigned movement, she snuffed it away with an index finger.

This wasn't what he wanted, seeing her fall apart. It reminded him of coming home to see his dad flake away day by day.

Lakota's picture caught his gaze. Damn games. He'd grown to hate his job, just as much as he hated himself most times.

Truthfully, until Fiona had shown up, he'd despised coming into the office. Despised the fact that he didn't have the strength to leave the predictable routine of his job—his echoing life—behind.

He indicated the photo while getting to his feet. "There's a price to pay for every decision. If that picture leaks to the press, she becomes a tabloid star. Linc looks like a fool. If it's kept in the vault with the negatives..." He left it up to her imagination.

"And what about the security video?" She was peeking up at him, her position inferior to his. For once she wasn't making sure he knew how tough she was.

Impulsively, he moved closer, but Fiona didn't flinch. His heart swelled, making him whole. With slow care, he stroked her hair. She relaxed into his hand, and an eternal moment passed, creating a bubble where nothing else could touch them.

Carly shouted, "Bye, Sean," as she passed in the hallway. The interruption jerked his hand, and Fiona leaned away.

"What do you want to do with the video?" he asked, unable to let go, even if the connection only consisted of his eyes caressing her.

She stared at the table, miles from the old, brusque, it's-all-about-a-good-time Fiona. Sean held his breath.

"I'd just as soon cover that video with a hill of dirt," she said. "The whole episode doesn't sit well with Linc. Or with Lakota, I'll guess."

"Then you've got your answer." He ran his hand over her jaw. One final touch. "Screw Louis and his ambition."

She met his gaze. "Screw our jobs, too, I suppose. He won't be happy."

Who cared about the job part. Or Louis. Living life under the thumb of a creep like Martin wasn't the way to go. It'd taken Fiona to shake Sean up, to awaken him.

He leaned against the table, relieved now that everything seemed so clear.

There was no way he'd stay at Stellar, not after Louis's threat. Not if it'd cost Fiona more than he was willing to pay.

Everything seemed so much simpler now.

Why couldn't she see that, too?

"Don't worry," he said. "We'll take a few hours to find a way to get Linc and Lakota on top."

And then he'd be done, leaving Fiona in peace. Finding some for himself, also.

She smiled at him, a glint of respect underlying all the other emotions he saw in her eyes.

He hoped she wasn't looking too closely, discovering that deep inside, he'd already left the building.

Left *her* because there was no other choice if he wanted to stay in one piece.

Chapter Fourteen

WHEN LAKOTA ARRIVED at Fiona's World War II-era high-rise apartment across from The Grove shopping center, Linc answered the door.

He was dressed in lounge gear: surf shorts, a Rob Machado T-shirt, his sandy hair sticking up as if he'd been tearing at it.

No greeting. Just a cautious, sweeping glance. They hadn't seen each other since The Cool Cat, and he'd spent the night at his place, shutting her out.

And she knew why. Because of his movie audition and what she'd said to him about being jealous. About keeping him behind in his career.

Linc retreated into the apartment while the aroma of Lobster Bisque filled the air. Fiona's voice accompanied the scent. "Hey, Lakota."

"Hi." She took a look around before going to the cooking alcove. The spin doctor didn't really have much furniture on hand. It was almost like she hadn't bothered to move all the way in. Boxes were stowed under a rickety metal dining table. A futon, beanbag and lawn chair were the only places to sit.

The sight made Lakota a little sad for Fiona, but she wasn't sure exactly why.

When she saw the kitchen, she was struck by the same pity.

No oven warmers to add a homey touch, not even a toaster or blender.

Fiona was holding a pair of prongs over a pot of boiling water, steam lending her cheeks a pink-tinged warmth. And she needed it, because the rest of her was downright maudlin, her black hair tied at the nape of her neck, her shorts and top basic and ordinary.

Where had her flair gone?

"You a cook?" Lakota asked to break the ice.

In response, Fiona leaned over, opened the freezer. Packages of single-portion frozen gourmet dinners slumped over each other.

Again, a twinge of sympathy attacked Lakota.

But who was she to feel sorry for someone else? She'd spent a sleepless night, calling Linc's number, not calling it, bothering Sean instead.

Fiona removed a packet of goopy beige matter from the hot water. "You already caught up with Sean?"

"I did." Not that she was happy about her publicist quitting his job today, but he'd told her to stick with Fiona. He sounded so confident in his associate's abilities that Lakota decided that giving her a chance wouldn't be a bad thing.

"Then you're up to speed," said Fiona. "Why don't you take a seat? I'll be out there to talk turkey in a sec."

Maybe that's why the PR rep looked so glum, because she had to handle both Linc and Lakota now. But Lakota was surprised Fiona didn't seem more stressed out by the prospect. Didn't she realize Sean had left all of them behind?

Not that Lakota understood his motivations, she thought, as she wandered to where Linc had plopped onto the futon. Her ex-publicist didn't want to talk about his reasons for quitting; he'd just wanted to reassure her that she'd be well taken care of with Fiona.

Should she sit next to Linc, pretending she hadn't let her ambition get the best of her last night?

Lakota lowered herself to the beanbag, offering a smile to him. "How are you?"

Fiona banged around in the kitchen, bowls clattering together, spoons chirping, providing a background for Linc's frown.

"I miss you," he said.

"Linc." Why'd he have to be so sincere? So open? "How can you say that after what I did?"

"You didn't mean it."

Didn't she? Last night, Conrad Dohenny had seemed like her ticket out of soaps. This morning, she knew she'd been persuaded by champagne, knew that the box-office giant had been full of hot air.

And that Linc was the real thing. "I thought I'd done some maturing after we broke up, you know. But the old Lakota, the one who threw things and had temper tantrums, came back full force last night. She was just more subtle about it."

He held out his arm, and she came to him, resting her head on his shoulder. Ah, there. This was where she was meant to be.

"Maybe I'm just a sucker," he said, "but I love you too much to let you go. It took me one bout with insomnia to think it over, and the bed felt awful empty without you in it."

She wrapped her arms around him, sighed, holding him tightly. He enveloped her in his strong arms, and she knew she'd never been so safe in all her life.

He'd never leave her behind.

"That's what I want to see," said Fiona, balancing bowls of soup and setting them on a scratched glass coffee table with an unrolled Sunday *L.A. Times* lying on the surface.

She collapsed in the lawn chair, shoulders curled forward instead of thrown back. "I called you both over for a serious talk. Today's a slow news day, so that's why you haven't seen The Cool Cat video on the air."

"I hope we don't," said Linc, his voice vibrating through Lakota's body.

She held him closer, wondering if Fiona would bring up that Conrad Dohenny kiss picture. It had cost her a pretty penny to buy the thing, but during his last call, Sean said Fiona had possession of it now.

True to the rumor, the publicist produced the photo from under the newspaper, holding it out to Linc and Lakota. The bisque went untouched as they peered at Conrad and his invasive tongue.

After a moment, Linc tossed it away. Lakota watched it arc through the air and jet to a graceful landing on the shag carpet.

Fiona ignored Linc's cavalier gesture. "Lakota, do you want the tape released?"

Though the memory of Linc defending her somewhat appealed, she didn't want to come off as a helpless weakling who stood in corners while men rescued her. That didn't mesh with the action heroine prime-time plans. "No."

"How about the picture?"

Linc's arms stiffened, and she knew it was because he was reliving Conrad's tongue in her mouth. She wished she could forget his stale-alcohol taste, the wet, sloppy, drunken celebrity spit.

When Lakota didn't say anything, Fiona continued. "PR wise, it would give you exposure. But is it the kind of reputation you want?"

Conrad's New Whore! She could see the headlines, could imagine the interviews on the tabloid TV shows, could almost digest the offers: *Playboy, Penthouse,* maybe a cheesy reality television hostessing job.

And Linc. What would the publicity do to him? It would make him seem stomped-on, cast-off.

For Lakota, the picture lost its colors right before her eyes.

"There's a lot more to you than kissing Conrad," said Fiona. "And I'm not really sounding as ambitious as a real PR rep, am I?" She laughed, but without mirth.

"Thank you," said Lakota. "But I'd rather keep a little dignity. What I have of it."

Linc blew out a breath. "Thank God."

"I'm never letting you down again," said Lakota, pressing her cheek against a chest made for her.

"Excellent." Fiona clapped her hands together, minus the enthusiasm.

Where had the tiger gone?

"So," the publicist continued, "Sean and I talked about several ways to market the two of you. Fairy-tale couple. Linc and his own photographs, showing the deep, sensitive artist he is. If that Roger Reiking movie happens, we'll need to step up the pub."

"It'll happen," said Lakota, sending a worshipful gaze up at him.

He kissed her forehead, smiled against her skin. "And Lakota?"

"We could explore avenues for her love of vintage items." Fiona poked at her bisque with a spoon. "A show on the Travel Network, for instance, where she can spotlight different antique malls across the country. Or maybe you could mix that with adventurous trips, to project that image, I mean. Sean couldn't make it here tonight, but we'll brainstorm with him later. We just wanted to ask you both about the picture and video before we acted."

What was she talking about? "Fiona, I don't think Sean's going to want anything to do with this."

The other woman gave Lakota a confused glance. "He'd better."

"Why? He quit so he doesn't have to deal with other people's baggage anymore. At least, that's what he told me an hour ago."

Fiona just sat there with her mouth open. Linc, however, spoke for her.

"Kota, you must've misunderstood him."

"No, he was clear."

Fiona darted up from her lawn chair, started pacing. "I can't believe this," she said to no one in particular. "I knew he was pissed at Louis, but... What exactly did he say?"

So he *hadn't* told Fiona. Weird. "Um, maybe you two had better talk. Don't you think?"

Linc nodded sagely. "Fi, when you told me you and McIntyre were almost finished...personally... Does this have anything to do with that?"

"I don't know." She stopped fidgeting, and some of the liveliness flushed back into her cheeks. "He can't do this. Not when he's so damned good."

"I guess I owe you a kiss for that bet," said Lakota to Linc. "She chased my publicist away from his work, she's such a heartbreaker."

Linc leaned his mouth toward her ear. "Later."

Oh, yeah, there'd be a "later." She'd make sure "later" made up for all her shortcomings.

Louder, Linc said, "Call him, Fi."

"Oh." Her eyes widened, and her hands flew in front of her chest, barring the suggestion. "He won't want to talk with me."

Linc whipped out his cell phone. "Kota, what's his number?"

She flashed out her own device, pressed speed dial, handed it to Fiona.

"No," the woman said. Boy, did she look horrified.

"It's ringing," said Lakota.

Fiona frowned, fluttered her hands—yeah, *fluttered*—and finally grabbed the phone, retreating down the hallway. A door closed, and Lakota cuddled up to Linc again.

"It's time for me to pay up," she said, voice sultry and very Rita Wilde-ish.

"I think the bet's a draw," he said, adjusting her so her mouth was near his, her heart pulsing against his chest. "They're both losers until they work this out."

"We're not. I'm going to take you higher than the clouds, and never let you down."

Linc laughed, rubbed his lips against hers. His words were soft kisses, hinting, promising. "Wasn't that from Script 1024? Rita and Colt Rettinger's first kiss?"

Lakota felt herself blushing. "So sue me if I'm a little tongue-tied. I can't think when you're around."

"Then don't think."

His mouth met hers, warm, inviting, all-encompassing. Her senses whirled with the musky scent of his skin, the soap he used every morning, the scratch and burn of emerging whiskers, the sound of them tasting each other.

Minutes must have passed, all of them filled with nothing but dizziness and contentment, a nap on a sandy beach under the sun with waves singing her to sleep. The next thing she knew, Fiona was back in the room, setting Lakota's phone next to the uneaten soup. The woman couldn't keep the longing from her eyes, her posture.

Lakota and Linc still touched each other, smiling at Fiona.

"I guess you've proven me wrong," said the PR woman.

"Finally?" asked Linc, fondness carrying his voice.

"Finally." She'd dropped her facade and, in its place, stood a revealed woman, stripped of protection. "You two show me that maybe things can work."

She closed her eyes, then opened them, exposing a place so vulnerable, even Lakota gasped.

"He's coming over," said Fiona, a quiver in her tone. "To my place."

WHEN FIONA had gotten the news about Scan quitting, she finally understood the definition of loneliness. Of hurt.

After their time in the office today, she'd expected to see him tomorrow, and the day after that. But she wouldn't anymore. The realization left her flailing for an emotional handle. She hadn't wanted to admit it, but she was in love with the guy.

In love.

Oh, God. What if he turned out to be another Ted? What if he used her up and tossed her away after he'd gotten tired of her? How would she cope?

Could she?

The strange thing was, it'd actually wound her more to never see Sean again, wouldn't it? Yet maybe being with him was worth all the pain, all the numbness of being rejected.

What if...?

Fiona almost didn't dare wonder, but couldn't stop herself.

What if Sean really did love her, too?

As she waited for him to knock at 11:00 p.m. on the Sunday night before the bet expired, Fiona tried not to bite her lip in a fit of nerves. She'd ruin the makeup she'd put on because she wanted to impress him. She'd even taken a yellow dress out from the back of her closet, something she hadn't worn since... Well, since she'd believed in soap-bubble dreams.

When she'd last been in love.

Yup, this was actually her. Fiona Cruz. Totally out of control.

Totally on the line.

When the knock came, it startled her, even if she'd been expecting it. She walked to the door, and every barefooted step seemed like a tour through a dream—surreal, unmanageable.

She opened the door to find Sean, worse for the wear, his white shirt uneven because he'd lined up the buttons incorrectly and slipped them through the wrong holes. His darkblond hair kicked up in places, stubborn as the man himself, his green eyes sharp and broken as discarded glass littering a gutted-out street. Even his outlaw-careless smile had lost its edge.

She'd never been so damned glad to see anyone.

"You quit, did you?" she asked, holding on to the door frame for support. They hadn't talked about this over the phone. It'd been hard enough to invite him over.

Because Fiona *never* allowed men in.

He was busy scanning her, the hunger in his gaze almost scratching at her. "I didn't want to distract you with my drama. I... Is that what this is about?"

Definitely not.

She flew at him, taking a fistful of shirt in hand, pulling him toward her until they were kissing, almost swallowing each other up in their desperate good-to-see-you-again.

His hands were planted in her hair, angling her head, positioning her so his mouth could devour. Her arms hooked upward, clinging, fingers abrading his hunched-over back.

They swayed together, stealing each other's air, pressing, urging, seeking.

Fiona's heart was near to bursting with happiness, the culmination of all that wanting and waiting.

As they back-stepped into her apartment, he kicked the door closed, then slowed down the pace, sliding a thumb under her chin, petting her neck, stretching the kiss into one long marathon of moaning desire.

Fiona hadn't kissed like this since she was a teenager, exploring, half-afraid of what might come next. That same innocence captured her now, and a laugh bubbled in her chest because she was so thankful for the return of it.

Oh, it was good to relax, to be held up by his strong arms, to know he wouldn't let her fall just because her knees were turning to orange marmalade. There was no need to wrestle him, to let her body tell him that she had just as much power—if not more—than he did.

No, this was different, like nothing she'd ever felt before. Lazy, sweeping pulses of the lips, a sipping sweetness that allowed her time to open her eyes half-way, to spy on him through her lashes, to stroke along with every slow glide of his mouth, to sample the mint of the gum he'd probably been chewing before knocking on her door.

Cocky bastard.

He'd maneuvered her through the living room, past the skeletons of her furniture and her old life, toward the bedroom. She let him guide her farther, willing to go wherever he'd take her.

"You never gave me an explanation—" she gasped as he tenderly kissed her earlobe "—Sean."

He paused, long enough for her to hear their blood echoing in each other's veins. "Sean. I like the way it sounds when you say it."

They stopped in a slant of moonlight coming through her window; it reclined on her bed, the centerpiece of yet another room she needed to lend some life to.

"Why did you leave today and not even tell me?" she asked, smoothing her knuckles over a cheekbone. This time, she didn't have to pretend she wasn't feeling anything.

He smiled, and Fiona framed his face with her hands. A work of imperfect art.

"I realized," he said, "that I was sticking around for the wrong reasons. Life is too short to spend it pleasing people like Louis, living the lives of others when I didn't have one myself. And I left because you wanted the job more than I did."

"Oh, Sean."

Should she say it? The L-word? He'd just admitted that he'd made a sacrifice because of her. The words built up in a ball of anxiety yet, still, Fiona hesitated.

He stepped forward, and the moonlight highlighted her lipstick on his cheek.

Marked territory. Hers.

This time, she left the brand alone.

"I love you," she said.

She'd never been so vulnerable in all her life.

A pent-up breath shuddered out of her, as she added, "I love you so much that it might be the end of me."

She laughed at the exaggeration, knowing it was true, anyway.

"Stop that." He traced a finger under her jawline, drawing her gaze to his.

Every splinter of color in his green eyes revealed a different path into the future. A future with him.

"I love you, too, Fiona. I have for a while."

Thank God. "I'm scared." There, she'd finally said *that*, too. Her shoulders relaxed, the weight lifted off of them. "I'm so afraid of what might happen, because…"

"What?" he asked gently.

She smiled, tilting her head at him to control the weariness. But then, tired of holding it in, she let it go with a tiny, sad laugh. "I was engaged once."

He squeezed her bare shoulder, stopping the imminent flow of tears. "A disappointment from the past."

"Right." Now he was using his fingertips to lull her, dragging them over her collarbone. She moved with drowsy, sexy caresses. So much better, so much... "He fell in love with my best friend, and they went on to have a baby, a nice house, a cozy marriage. I couldn't have given that to him, you know? I've lived with that knowledge for years, proving myself right, I guess."

His fingers eased behind her neck, kneading the tightened muscles, causing jagged bolts of warmth to steal through her.

"It's so much easier to disappoint yourself rather than having someone else do it for you," she said.

"You don't ever need to worry about that again."

He stole his fingers under one of her dress straps. His touch heated onto the patch of skin that had so recently been covered. It made her suck in a gust of air.

She recovered, shrugging so that the strap tumbled down one shoulder. "We did things a little backward, didn't we? First comes sex, then comes love... I'm not sure what comes after that."

"Marriage?" The word came out thick, heavy.

"It won't be like it was with your dad," she said, taking his hands and tugging him toward the bed. She wanted him so badly she was about to combust.

"I'm willing to take that leap of faith," he said. "As long as I've got you jumping with me."

She turned around, tacitly asking him to undo her dress. He did, the zipper groaning down in its descent, the night air shivering her skin as the folds of material parted, opened.

As she stepped out of the clothing, Sean took off his shirt, his pants.

No underwear for him though.

He moved toward her, hitched his thumbs over the elastic of her comfy briefs. Tugging, he let the air breathe over her, then pulled them all the way off.

She braced herself on one of his shoulders—something she'd be free to do from now on if she needed it—while she stepped out of the undies.

Then, in a slow journey, he ran his hands over her body, memorizing the shape of her arms, her plump breasts, her rib cage, the swerve of her waist, her belly. She saw herself through his eyes: a woman's woman, with extra curves here and there, with voluptuous promises to offer the right man.

She saw everything now.

And, as he looked into her eyes, she knew he saw, too.

A glance at the clock by her bed revealed that it was 11:59. One minute before the bet was supposed to end.

Oddly enough, she didn't really mind losing this time.

Fiona kissed her prize again, flowing into him, taking him back with her until they could crawl onto the bed. Her body fit perfectly beneath his, ready to be orchestrated, played by his hands. His mouth.

He teased her breasts to hard peaks with his fingers, licking her nipple, blowing on it until she thought she'd cry out from the sharp sensation. Drowning in pleasure, she skimmed her toes over his calf, between his legs, up, up, until she reached his inner thighs, then down.

Nice, this leisurely exploration of each other. She took her time learning every thatch of fine hair on his chest, sifting through it with her distended nipples until the wisp of skin on skin made her wiggle her hips, slipping over his rigid penis with the slickness of her growing excitement.

She'd grown swollen with wanting him, blood pounding between her legs, making her ache, stiffen, search him out.

He used his fingers to work her further along, his thumb circling her clit, awakening a rhythm in her hips that corresponded to every stroke. When he nestled two fingers inside her, slipping in and out with fluid thrusts, she grabbed at his arms, needing to be anchored before she took off.

He pushed her until she thought she would shatter. But she held on, moaning, louder, louder, until she hung halfway off the bed, her hair brushing the carpet, her torso arched, her sex rocking against his hand.

"Fiona," he growled, as if she was getting away.

With one tug of his arms, she was back on the bed, beads of sweat dripping down her skin as she sat upright. She positioned herself against the pillows, one leg still off the bed.

While she panted, he left her for a second.

"Get back here," she said, laughing, ecstatic. So giddy and full of electricity. "I'm not done with you."

He prowled back to her, a predator. "One last layer of protection, Fi, and you're mine."

Rubber. She felt it covering his hard-on as he coasted along her inner thigh, as she spread herself open for him and thrust her hips up to take him inside.

They strained together, sweat mingling, muscles laboring. With smooth strokes, he pounded into her, and she gyrated her hips, wanting more. Getting more.

The cadence of their lovemaking increased, with him ramming forward. She accepted every drive, every bolt of collecting heat that was gathering in her core, flaming upward, tearing through her belly, her limbs.

Everywhere.

He consumed her, covering her, lending her breath as he kissed her to climax. Lightning, swift as the bite of a night creature, flashed into her body, her brain, illuminating her from the inside out.

Ripping her apart. Zinging her back together again.

Washing her in perspiration as a fall of soft contentment pattered her back to reality. One final rumble of thunder roared through her body as she bucked against him.

He hadn't spent himself yet, and she reached between his legs from the back, finding a place she knew would give him release.

Laboring, groaning, releasing, he shuddered from the same storm, collapsing against her.

This time, when it was over, they lingered, holding each other.

That lipstick was still on his cheek. "You've got something," she said, flicking a finger over the mark.

At first, he didn't seem to get it. Then a smile beamed over his face.

"It's there to stay," he said. "Branded."

She snuggled into him and, for the first time since...well, never...she fell asleep in a man's arms, in her own bed.

Dreaming of paradise.

Epilogue

ON A WHITE-SAND BEACH in St. Vincent, pristine mosquito netting rode a tropical breeze. The material was attached to a gazebo, the pale structure contrasting with the gem-blue of the sea and the lush vegetation.

Everything was more vivid out here, Sean thought as he tipped back an ice-flaked bottle of beer. More alive.

Just as he'd been these past two months.

The netting parted, letting in the sun. The light flashed off the band of gold on his finger, the ring winking at him.

He tossed away the magazine he'd been reading. *People,* complete with an article about Lincoln Castle, and how he'd become a hero by saving a drowning child while the actor was on location in Europe for that romantic comedy.

Linc's new publicist was good. He had to hand that to her. She'd also gotten Lakota good exposure for a valuable painting she'd discovered in one of those vintage stores.

A silhouette blocked the sun, shading him. A figure as voluptuous as the local fruit he'd been eating lately.

She moved forward. Fiona. His wife.

The sun filtered over her, and he saw that she balanced a fruit platter in her hands. Bananas, coconuts, oranges and...

He laughed. A spray of maraschino cherries.

"*People* magazine, huh?" She sat next to him, plucked a cherry from the selection of snacks. "My former assistant has really been good for Linc."

"Rosie's been good for Lakota, also." As she ran the cherry over his bare chest, his nipples tightened. Tease.

"Where Linc goes, so does Lakota. You talked to her last. Isn't she due back on the soap next week?"

Lakota was working on that travel show Fiona had suggested before she quit Stellar. Still going to auditions, still hanging in there.

"Let's talk about something else," he said. "Namely..." he pulled her into his arms, hugging her until she nuzzled against his neck "...not talking."

"Okay," Fiona mouthed, sighing into her cozy spot.

He enjoyed the feel of her, would for the rest of his life. Even if they were interrupting their jaunt around the Caribbean—on both their tabs, even if he had technically won the bet—they'd always be on a holiday. Next week, they'd be returning to the States to meet his family, her family, to see Linc and Lakota, who were a lot like family.

After that they could go wherever they pleased, until their comfortable savings ran out. Then...? They'd talked about opening a bar on the sands of some island maybe, living real lives and not existing through others.

"Sorry to break the silence..." she said, sketching her fingers over his legs, higher...

"No you're not."

She laughed. "...but I brought reading material, too."

She produced a book from the folds of her sarong. *The Sensuous Woman.*

"Think I can practice The Butterfly Flick?" she asked, all playfulness.

The Flick. They hadn't gotten around to actually doing it

until things had been worked out between them, once and for all.

It'd been worth the wait.

"Anything for literacy," he said, sinking down in his lounge chair as Fiona undid the drawstring on his pants. "Anything to keep you happy."

And as that wolfish howl returned and screamed through his veins once again, he knew it cried for only one person.

Fiona. And it always would.

He'd bet on it.

Blaze™

Red-Hot Reads—
look out for more sizzling stories!

Buy any **Harlequin® Blaze**™ novel
and receive

$1.00 OFF

Available wherever Harlequin books are sold.

5 65373 00076 2   (8100) 0 11177